Vows

SAY I DO

REBECCA WINTERS
JENNIE ADAMS
MARION LENNOX

WEDDING *Vows*

SAY I DO

REBECCA WINTERS
JENNIE ADAMS
MARION LENNOX

Published in Great Britain 2015
by Mills & Boon, an imprint of Harlequin (UK) Limited,
Eton House, 18-24 Paradise Road, Richmond, Surrey, TW9 1SR

ISBN: 978-0-263-25376-4

011-0615

Harlequin (UK) Limited's policy is to use papers that are natural, renewable and recyclable products and made from wood grown in sustainable forests.The logging and manufacturing processes conform to the legal environmental regulations of the country of origin.

Printed and bound in Spain
by CPI, Barcelona

MATRIMONY WITH HIS MAJESTY

REBECCA WINTERS

Rebecca Winters lives in Salt Lake City, Utah. With canyons and high alpine meadows full of wildflowers, she never runs out of places to explore. They, plus her favourite vacation spots in Europe, often end up as backgrounds for her romance novels, because writing is her passion, along with her family and church.

Rebecca loves to hear from readers. If you wish to e-mail her, please visit her website at: cleanromances.com.

CHAPTER ONE

"SINCE the last two major college riots, we have to take what happened today seriously, Alex. I'm urging you to move yourself and your loved ones to one of your residences in the mountains away from the public where you're not so vulnerable."

"We've been over this ground before, Leo. I refuse to let fear rule our lives."

"Then at least consider permanently closing off public access to the castle and estate. There are too many radical student elements out there wanting to bring down the monarchy. They never stop thinking up new and ingenious ways to wreak havoc for the sheer hell of it."

"I agree there have always been those fringe elements in society, but I'd rather employ more security than shut myself off from the people."

In Alex's six years as king of the Romanche-speaking Valleder Canton in Switzerland, Leo had kept everyone safe, freeing Alex to attempt to do the job his father had done so superbly over a thirty-year period as sovereign.

He eyed Leo, the forty-year-old widower who'd been Interpol's top agent before becoming Alex's head of state security. They'd grown to be close friends.

"Tell me what happened."

"An extremely attractive American woman came through on the 10:00 a.m. tour of the castle. After it was over she told the guide she had business with you and asked that she be given an audience on a private matter. When told you didn't meet with the public she said, 'Not even if I have something of value to return to him?'

"Naturally the guide called for security. They brought her by police car to the downtown office. During my interrogation she said she had a ring of yours and knew you would want it back."

"A ring?"

Alex shook his head. "Where do these crazies come from? The only ring I have is the one my father gave me prior to his death six years ago. You're looking at it."

Leo folded his arms. "It's obvious the woman intentionally created a scene to see what would happen, and of course she got her wish.

"She was searched and her passport seized. When I asked to see the ring, she said she hadn't brought it with her because it was too valuable. But she had photos of it in the purse we confiscated."

A sound of incredulity escaped Alex's lips.

"This woman knew she would be detained and questioned. I'm positive she wanted to see how our security system works at the castle. Since the last demonstrators' attempt to storm the north gate, it isn't out of the realm of possibility they're hatching another plan to get the whole canton's attention and stir up trouble. Frankly I don't like it. Especially with your wedding only three weeks away."

"I don't like it, either," Alex admitted in a grim tone. If any of those incidents had hurt one of his family, he'd never forgive himself for not taking greater precautions. Thankfully Leo had been on top of things.

"What do you know about her?"

"She's a resident of Aurora, Colorado, named Darrell Collier."

Colorado?

Alex had been there, but he'd also been to several of the states in the U.S., even lived for a short period in Arizona.

"The woman is traveling alone under a newly issued American passport. She's never applied for one before. Her nonstop flight to Zurich originated in Denver, Colorado, yesterday morning.

"When she deplaned, the douanier asked her the reason for her visit. She said she was taking a short vacation. She rented a car and drove here last night where she stayed at the Hotel Otter. This morning she showed up for the tour.

"I checked her employment. She works for Gold Jet Airlines in the States making reservations. There's no police record on her, no outstanding warrants for her arrest in the U.S.

"I suppose she could be someone with a mental condition who stopped taking her medication. But my gut is telling me she's very much in her right mind and working for some anti-royal group trying to discover the castle's vulnerabilities.

"How many tourists traveling alone go straight from the plane to one castle for a short visit? It just doesn't add up. So far she's been calm and cooperative. She's one cool customer."

"In other words she's willing to sacrifice herself for information," Alex muttered.

The other man cast him a shrewd regard. "She hasn't committed a crime and knew we had to release her. She's been escorted back to the airport in Zurich. I've already alerted the American authorities. Once her flight leaves for the States, they'll keep tabs on her. It's the best we can do about her for now. My main concern is you and your family."

That was twice in few minutes he'd talked about Alex's family. Leo had more than a passing interest in Alex's cousin-in-law Evelyn who lived on the estate and had lost her husband. Nothing would please him more than to see the two of them get together. But since Evelyn was a royal, Leo would never dare to presume.

"Greater measures need to be taken to protect all of you," Leo emphasized again.

Alex decided to help things along. "Let's double the security on the whole estate. It wouldn't hurt if you went along with Evelyn the next time she goes riding or shopping. Warn her and the boys to be extra careful. Coming from you personally, she'll take it better than from me."

"I'll be happy to do that," he answered in a calm voice, but Alex saw the flare of excitement in his eyes. "This is a start in the right direction. I'll take care of it immediately."

As he stood up, he put an eight by ten envelope on the desk in front of Alex. "These are enlarged copies of the colored photos of the ring which could have been purchased in any of the canton's souvenir shops. There's an inscription on the band in Romanche, but the sentiment doesn't send up any red flags. My men are tracking down the regional jeweler as we speak.

"Like I said, she came to the castle with a definite agenda."

After he left the room, Alex reached for the envelope whose contents served as a reminder of his official engagement to Isabella. It wouldn't be long before he was a married man. He hadn't been able to put it off any longer. If it had been up to Isabella, they'd have said their vows several years earlier.

His alliance with the princess of San Ravino, Italy, would cement certain lucrative business relationships Alex's father had instigated with the king of San Ravino when Alex had been in his mid-teens.

On his father's death bed he'd said, "A king needs a wife, Alex, and your mother needs a grandchild. Isabella is an intelligent, beautiful woman and will give you children you can be proud of."

Admittedly Isabella with her black hair turned heads. Nine years younger than Alex, she would be biddable and make the perfect consort. Alex agreed the princess had qualities he admired. There'd be no surprises. Everyone was excited for the wedding. Everyone except him…

With a jerking motion he upended the envelope. Out spilled four photos of a man's gold ring taken at different angles.

As Leo had said, the colorful enamel work showing the Valleder coat of arms appeared on pins, rings, virtually any piece of jewelry a tourist could take home as a reminder of their trip to the heart of the Swiss Alps.

The last photograph revealed the inscription on the inner band in the Puter dialect. Alex looked closer.

More than a cousin.

He closed his eyes tightly in pain.

This was the ring his deceased cousin, Chaz, had given him on his sixteenth birthday—the same ring he'd somehow parted with during a certain vacation to Colorado when he and Chaz had turned twenty. On that trip his cousin had urged him to forget he was a royal and simply live it up like they were two ordinary guys.

Alex sprang from his swivel chair, hardly able to comprehend that the young woman he'd given it to under fuzzy circumstances could be the woman who'd come to the castle trying to arrange a meeting with him.

These photos were the proof that something of significance had happened on that trip. He didn't like what he was thinking, especially when his recollection of those events was a blur. This had to be an extortion tactic.

With no time to lose he pressed the programmed digit on his cell phone. It was his private line to Leo.

"Yes, Alex?"

"You've more than earned your pay today, my friend."

"What do you mean? What's going on?"

Alex wished he knew. "It's my ring, Leo. One I parted with a long time ago, but the memory is hazy." Since that experience he'd done everything in his power to be a good king, including agreeing to marry the princess his parents favored. No hint of scandal had touched his life until now, less than a month before his wedding…

"When exactly?" the other man fired.

"Thirteen years ago while I was on a trip, Chaz and I spent a wild night drinking with some girls. Things got out of control. I'd forgotten until I saw the photos."

Leo let out a low whistle. "That doesn't sound like you."

"Don't be fooled. I have a few skeletons lying around."

His friend made a strange sound in his throat. "This one might have come back to bite you, if you follow my meaning."

"I know exactly what you mean."

Depending on this woman's agenda, she could hurt him and the people he loved in ways he refused to let happen.

There was a palpable silence, then Leo asked, "How can I help? I've done everything to keep this suppressed, but you never know."

"Tell me about it," he muttered. "I'm going on a private fishing expedition, Leo. Alert your most trusted men to board my jet within the hour. The second this woman's flight leaves the ground, I want to be notified."

"Consider it done." After another silence, "Alex—"

"I know what you're going to say, Leo. But I'm afraid the time for damage control was years ago."

By the time Darrell Collier's jet landed at the Denver airport, she'd cried all the tears she was going to cry. Her final, foolhardy attempt to unite her adopted son with his phantom father had completely failed. To her deep-felt sorrow, Phillip would never know the name or the whereabouts of the man who'd impregnated Darrell's sister before disappearing from her life.

Deprived of the father he'd never known, Phillip was entering his teens with a giant chip on his shoulder.

Darrell loved him with her whole heart and soul, but his anger at fate had made him so difficult to handle these days, she realized she needed to get professional help for him.

Things were building to a crisis state. She felt more helpless now than when Melissa had died after giving birth twelve years ago, leaving Darrell to raise her sweet little dark-blond boy alone.

It had been the two of them against the world.

After her final effort to make contact with his father, it was still the two of them forging ahead alone. That was the way it would always be.

She could only hope that in time he would let the anger go and embrace his life. He had everything to live for, but right now he couldn't see beyond the unfairness of an existence without a dad. Emotionally he reminded her of Melissa, who'd also felt deprived because of a car accident that had robbed them of their parents.

Her pain had turned her into a willful and tempestuous teen their grandmother couldn't handle. It appeared history would be repeating itself unless Darrell took an active stance to help Phillip before it was too late.

Having a plan was better than no plan, she told herself as she took the train to get her luggage. After retrieving it, she left the terminal and headed for the parking lot, anxious to get home. She'd been gone three days and missed him horribly. She couldn't wait to pick him up.

Eventually she reached her compact car. As she was putting

her suitcase in the trunk, two men suddenly appeared out of nowhere dressed in shirt sleeves and Jamaica shorts.

"Ms. Collier?"

Though it was midafternoon and there were other people around, she suddenly felt nervous. "Yes?"

They flashed her their photo ID cards.

FBI?

"If you'll come with us, we'll take you to a place where you can meet with the king of Valleder in private."

Darrell was convinced she was hallucinating. After the balmy temperatures in Switzerland, this long walk in the sweltering one hundred degree July heat must have gotten to her.

"The king is *here?* In *Denver?*"

"Yes, ma'am. He's made it possible for you to discuss a certain private matter with him."

The other federal agent handed her the envelope containing the photos she'd left with the police in the capital city of Bris.

So he *had* recognized the ring.

After giving up all hope, she was incredulous this was happening now. In a daze she slowly shut the trunk lid.

"The king is waiting. We'll bring you back to your car later."

The next few minutes passed in a blur as she was helped into the back seat of an unmarked car. One of the agents sat next to her. The other sat in front next to the driver. At a glance she realized there were several unmarked cars with agents forming a cortege.

The driver left the airport and took the E470, a toll road that eventually led to the Centennial Airport where the private jets landed. They wound around to a gleaming white jet with the Valleder royal coat of arms on the side.

She saw the stairs being lowered. Security people were everywhere.

One of them greeted her after she'd gotten out of the car. Another stood at the bottom of the stairs.

"His Majesty is just inside. Go ahead."

Feeling she was in some sort of trance, Darrell climbed the steps, wondering if she'd wake up before she reached the opening.

"Oh—" she cried softly when a well honed male who stood six foot three stepped out from the interior.

He was a stranger, yet because of certain physical traits that reminded her of Phillip, he looked familiar, too.

A relentless afternoon sun gilded the natural highlights of his wavy dark-blond hair.

The Internet pictures of the king of Valleder could never do justice to his rugged masculine appeal, let alone capture the intensity of his unique hazel eyes.

His gaze traveled over her classic features that hadn't seen makeup in twelve hours. It lingered on her puffy, tear-swollen eyes the color of drenched pansies. With her shoulder-length ash-blond hair needing a shampoo, and her aqua blouse and skirt looking less than fresh, she'd never felt a bigger mess.

The realization that she was standing before the king she'd risked a great deal to meet was so surreal, she couldn't think clearly.

He had her at a distinct disadvantage. As his gaze swept over her feminine attributes, heat rose through her body from her curling toes to the crown of her head.

Compelled by a force stronger than her will, her gaze took in his white sport shirt covering a well-defined chest. He wore tan chinos that molded his rock-hard legs, hinting at powerful thighs.

Looking at him made her realize that one day her tall, lanky son would resemble his attractive father in quite a few ways.

"Ms. Collier, I presume?"

Still in disbelief that he'd flown all this way, she was too tongue-tied to think with any coherence. She cleared her throat. "Yes. I know you're the king, but I—I don't know what to call you," she stammered in embarrassment.

"I realize the situation is foreign to you. Under the circumstances just call me Alex. It appears we have something important to discuss. Please come in." He spoke impeccable English with virtually no trace of accent.

Once over the threshold, she entered a world where only the privileged conducted business thousands of miles above the earth. Besides everything else, the air-conditioning was heavenly.

He led her to a room with a grouping of furniture much like an elegant den. The second she sat down on one of the couches, a steward appeared with a tray of drinks. She chose cola, then sat on the edge of the luxurious white upholstery unable to relax. Again she had the feeling she was existing in another state of consciousness.

He took a chair opposite her, the picture of urbane sophistication while he drank coffee.

"Why don't we start by you telling me how you came by that ring."

He'd come straight to the point, not appearing worried about the history behind it.

Her heart pounded so hard she was certain he could hear it in the confines of the room.

"My sister entrusted it to me."

He put the coffee cup on a side table and leaned forward. "What's her name?"

How strange to be talking about her sister, the woman he'd enamored to the point she would have done anything for him, and did.

"Melissa Collier. Does that mean anything to you?"

He eyed her with an enigmatic expression. "I'm sorry to say it doesn't."

His response came as no surprise to Darrell. After thirteen years, how many men in his position remembered the names of the girls they'd been with for a one-night stand? Particularly a rebellious yet vulnerable teen like Melissa. She'd probably made up a fake name so she wouldn't get into trouble with the management where she worked.

He rubbed his lower lip with his thumb, mesmerizing Darrell. "Why didn't she come to Bris?"

Darrell drew in a shaky breath. "Because she died twelve years ago."

Lines darkened his striking features. "I'm sorry," he whispered, sounding surprisingly sincere.

"So am I." Her voice faltered.

"How did she die?"

There's your opening, Darrell.

Yet oddly enough she found herself unable to go on. No matter how long she'd prayed for this moment for Phillip's sake, what the king was about to hear was going to change his life. She found she couldn't do this to him. The shock would be too enormous to any man, let alone a king— What had she been thinking?

"It doesn't really matter. All I know is, she wanted you to have the ring back because she knew it was valuable."

"The ring has gotten my attention. Now I want to know what's behind it."

Darrell felt ill. "I—I made a mistake coming to Switzerland. Haven't you ever made one?" she cried in panic. "Let me just get the ring for you and then you can go home and we'll forget this ever happened. Please—"

"I'm afraid I can't do that."

Tears ran down her face. "I don't want to hurt you. I don't want *anyone* to be hurt—"

She had to get out of there, but before she reached the doorway, he said, "The best way to hurt me is to make a scene in front of my staff. Why don't you sit down and answer my question about your sister."

Realizing he wouldn't go away until he knew the truth, Darrell wiped her eyes and finally did his bidding.

"Two days after she gave birth to an eight-pound boy, a brain aneurism took her life."

A pulsating silence filled the cabin.

His body didn't move, but she saw a flicker in the depths of his eyes, turning them the green of a stormy ocean.

"Do you have pictures of them on you?"

She'd thought he'd deny it was his son, or at least question her outrageous suggestion that he might have been the father.

He did neither. Instead he'd responded in a forthright manner that astounded her.

"I have a packet in my wallet. The photo of Melissa is her junior year high school picture. The rest are pictures of my son taken on every birthday in case I ever found his father and he wanted to see them."

One dark brow lifted. "Your son?"

"Yes. I adopted him."

"You never married?"

"No."

Her hands trembled as she opened her purse and pulled the packet from her wallet.

He got up and reached for it.

She held her breath while he stood there with his legs slightly apart, studying each photograph with an intensity that held her spellbound.

The likeness of his son to him couldn't be disputed.

"What day was he born?"

"February 27. He'll be thirteen on his next birthday."

He examined the pictures for a long time. "What did you name him?" His voice revealed a husky quality that indicated he was deeply moved. Another surprise.

"When Melissa had an ultrasound and found out she was going to have a boy, she named him after you."

His gaze shot to hers. "I have several names."

Darrell's mouth had gone dry. "I know. I saw the long list on the Internet. You told her you were Phil from New York. So Melissa called him Phillip."

A haunted expression crossed over his features, making the thirty-three-year-old monarch appear older than he was.

"Now that I see her picture, I do remember visiting a dude ranch in Colorado Springs in June thirteen years ago. A college girl a little shorter than you with hair several shades darker than yours worked there."

"Yes. That was Melissa. She was a room maid for the summer. Except that she wasn't in college. She was only seventeen, and had another year of high school ahead of her."

His lips thinned.

"Don't worry," Darrell murmured. "I'm sure she lied about her age. She looked older and couldn't grow up fast enough. She said you'd both been drinking and got into a sleeping bag under the stars. That's when you parted with the ring.

"Knowing Melissa, she probably begged you to let her put it on. Especially after you told her you were really a prince.

"I thought the whole story was bogus. But two weeks ago when I consulted a heraldry expert who identified your family's coat of arms, I had to take it seriously.

"The Internet articles and pictures of you helped me with the rest. Not only was one of your names Phillip, I read that you were the prince of Bris before your coronation six years ago. Suddenly everything fell into place. But like all fairy tales, her glorious interlude with you came to a bitter end.

"When she reported for work the next day, you'd already disappeared without a trace. All she had of you was the ring. Before she died, she begged me to find you. After the funeral, I hid it away."

His jaw hardened. Darrell could feel the tension emanating from him.

"How you must despise me." His deep voice throbbed with self-abnegation. "Under the circumstances, why didn't you tell the police what you've just told me? It was the perfect opportunity to expose me."

Though she didn't want to feel any compassion for him, there was something innately honorable about him owning up to his past behavior without offering excuses.

She hadn't expected it of him. She hadn't expected to have a positive feeling anywhere in her body for this man who'd made her sister pregnant, indirectly bringing on her early death.

Darrell rubbed her eyes with her palms.

"The last thing on my mind was creating a scandal for you. What happened between you and Melissa has happened to millions of couples since time immemorial. The difference is, not every child turns out to be the son of a king.

"Phillip wants his father more than you can imagine. Lately he's been angry over the fact that you're out in the cosmos someplace, unaware he's alive. He's wishing with all his heart and soul that he had a dad like his friends. He's become quite inconsolable.

"But now that I've found you, I realize it was a mistake. I had no right to disrupt your life even if my son is suffering. He wouldn't be the only child in the world to grow up without a father.

"The problem is, after raising him from birth I love him

too much. The saying about a mother rushing into a burning building to save her child is truer than even *I* knew until now."

She lifted her head and stared up at him with glistening eyes. "In this life there are some things that happen which are better left alone. This is one of them."

"How can you say that?" he asked in a low voice. "I'm responsible for her pregnancy. I wish I'd known of Phillip's existence from the beginning."

"It would only have complicated your life. While I was checking out of the Hotel Otter, I overheard the desk clerk telling a tourist that there's going to be a royal wedding at the end of July. I heard him say you were marrying a princess named Isabella.

"Learning you've been betrothed for several years, that news made me glad I hadn't been able to talk to you. Please be assured neither you nor your intended bride will ever see or hear from me again."

Alex moved as if to speak but Darrell rushed on, not giving him the chance to interrupt her. "If you'll wait before flying back to Bris, I'll drive home and ask one of the agents to bring the ring to you."

She jumped to her feet, "Forgive me for forcing you to fly all this way. I'm so sorry—" she whispered before rushing out of the cabin and down the stairs of the jet.

"Please take me to my car, then follow me home. I have something of the king's you need to return to him before he leaves the airport."

The agent looked surprised, but he helped her in the car and instructed the man at the wheel to go back to the main airport's parking lot.

A half hour later Darrell was still trembling as she pulled into the driveway of her small, two-bedroom condo. The agent's car pulled in behind her.

She dashed in the house and hurried up the stairs to her closet. The ring was inside a little velvet pouch she kept in the pocket of an ancient winter coat she'd never thrown out.

Within seconds she'd run back outside and handed it to him through the car window. He nodded to her before they drove off, taking all incriminating evidence with them. Only then did she realize the king still had the pictures of Melissa and Phillip.

That was all right. Whatever he did with them, it didn't matter. She had duplicates.

So…it was over. Phillip's father would remain Phil from New York. End of story.

The pilot buzzed Alex. "Your Majesty? We're ready for takeoff at anytime."

Alex's hand closed around the ring the agent had brought to him moments ago. "Thank you. I'll get back to you in a minute."

He'd laid out Darrell Collier's photos on the desk in front of him. As he studied each one, his father's voice seemed to call out from the grave. "Always remember that one day you'll be King."

One wild night thirteen years ago he'd rebelled against the rules governing his royal life with *this* the result.

He actually had a son from his own body named Phillip.

Alex was a father!

Dear Lord—how could he just fly back to Switzerland as if nothing had happened, his secret safely hidden forever?

Maybe an ambitious king with no soul, or an unscrupulous man with no moral conscience, was capable of it. Ms. Collier had made a promise he would never hear from her again, that Phillip would never learn his father's identity. Alex believed her.

But he knew himself too well. There was no way he could turn his back on his own flesh and blood no matter how the reality would impact his personal or political life. The knowledge that he had a son living in Denver, Colorado, would eat him alive.

Phillip hadn't asked to be born.

He was the innocent product of an irresponsible twenty-year-old and an underage teen! By some miracle Darrell Collier had been there to mother Phillip and do the job Alex should have been doing all along.

Twelve years without a father.

Alex couldn't imagine it, not when his own father had been such a dominant force in his life.

Without hesitation he buzzed his pilot. "I'm not leaving Denver yet. Stand by. I'll get back to you as soon as I know my plans."

He then rang the agent who'd brought him the ring. "Get everyone ready. I have a visit to make to Ms. Collier's home."

After a strange silence, "Yes, Your Majesty."

CHAPTER TWO

DARRELL got in her car and drove over to the Holbrooks's to pick up Phillip. En route she phoned to tell him she was on her way.

It was ten to six in the evening when she pulled up in front and honked. Phillip was waiting for her, and came out the door with his sleeping and duffel bags.

Hugs from him had been on short ration over the last year, but he actually gave her one after getting in the car. It melted her heart.

She'd been away three days, the longest separation they'd ever had. Over the years the two of them had enjoyed her airline perks. They'd gone on many vacations to fun places around the U.S. and Hawaii. But the trip to Bris had been for her eyes only, which meant Phillip had to stay with his best friend. Many weekends she'd let Ryan sleep over at her condo while his parents were out of town.

"How did it go while I was away?"

"Okay."

"Tell me about the swim meet."

"I didn't place."

Then he didn't try hard enough because he usually took more firsts than the other guys on the team!

"Oh well, There's always next time."

"How come you didn't take me to Chicago with you?"

She drew in a deep breath. "I couldn't. It was an exhausting business trip. But I have an idea. After we get back to the condo and I freshen up, how would you like to go somewhere for dinner? You name the place."

"Why do we have to go out? Can't we just stay home?"

To her disappointment, he was more truculent than usual. She reached out to squeeze his arm. "Sure we can. I'll fix us some tacos and we'll just hang out."

When he didn't respond she said, "I don't know if I told you Danice was transferred to Washington D.C. She's invited us to spend the Fourth of July with her. That's the day after tomorrow. We'll watch the fireworks from a boat on the Potomac. It'll be fabulous. What do you say?"

"I'd rather not go."

Darrell moaned inwardly. "How come?"

"Danice treats me like a little kid. I hate it."

Danice was her good friend, but right now Phillip didn't care how he sounded. She started to feel panicky. His depression was definitely worse.

"Here we are," she said unnecessarily as she pulled into the garage of their condo. "Take your clothes into the laundry room and we'll get a wash started."

"Mrs. Holbrook already did mine."

"That was nice of her."

When Darrell reached for her suitcase and saw the Zurich tag on the handle, she tore it off and stuffed it in her purse before entering the hallway.

She was convinced he was suffering more than usual because he'd just come from Ryan's, whose father was known as Mr. Dad.

Phillip only had a mom. Life was unfair.

It *was* unfair.

Darrell no longer had a sibling. With her grandmother already passed away, Darrell had been virtually alone when she'd taken on the role of mother to raise Phillip.

Over the years she'd dated off and on. She'd even come close to marrying her boss earlier this year. But he was too soft on Phillip who needed a strong hand. Darrell had feared her son would always be in the driver's seat after they married, so she'd stopped seeing him except in connection with her work.

Since then she hadn't dated anyone.

"Phillip?" she called to him. "I'll be upstairs changing, then I'll come down and fix us a meal."

"Okay."

The condo felt like an oven. On the way up to the bathroom she turned on the air-conditioning to cool off the house.

Once beneath the spray, she quickly lathered her hair, then used the blow dryer until the strands swished soft and silky against her shoulders.

Afraid to keep him waiting too long, she applied a fresh coat of coral frost lipstick, then slipped on white shorts and a sleeveless navy top. Dispensing with shoes she hurried downstairs. He needed to talk.

She knew the drill. They would discuss all sorts of things, but inevitably he'd bring the conversation around to the father he was growing to hate for not being there for him.

It was so sad he'd reached the age where he understood about a man sowing his wild oats without compunction, and one had taken root in the Rocky Mountains.

Heartsick for Phillip who was acting out with increased frequency, she walked in the family room off the kitchen to find him. He was playing a video game. In her opinion they were a curse. No communication could go on with his hands on the controls, and his eyes glued to the screen. Luckily he enjoyed sports, which kept him busy a lot of the time now that it was summer.

"Want to grate the cheese and cut up the tomatoes?"

Without saying anything he got up and followed her to the fridge. Athletically inclined, he looked good in his old cutoffs and T-shirt. One day he would look…fantastic, just like his father, whose arresting features and physique eclipsed those of any man she'd ever known.

She could still picture him standing in the doorway of the jet, staring at her with those hauntingly beautiful green-gray eyes. They seemed to follow her into the kitchen where she fried the tortillas and ground beef. Then she and Phillip sat down to eat.

She was glad to see his dark mood hadn't affected his appetite. She waited until he'd finished off his third taco before venturing into uncharted waters.

"Sweetheart?" she began. "I love you more than you'll ever know, and it hurts me that you're so unhappy. There's an old adage that says something like, 'Give me the wisdom to accept the things I can't change, and help me to change the things I need to do something about.' It's a good rule to live by.

"No matter how much you want things to be different, your father didn't stay in Colorado, so he didn't know you were born. That's the painful fact of the matter.

"Now the ball is in your court. You can either make up your mind it's not going to ruin your life, or you can grow up an angry man so fixated on your own hurt, you'll never live up to your full potential.

"I know I'm just your dumb mom, but between us, we're all we've got. I promised your mother I'd love you and take care of you forever. So I think the time has come for you to go to a counselor you can talk to. Someone impartial who will listen to whatever you feel like saying and won't judge you."

"No way—" He flung himself out of the chair. His blue-gray eyes glittered with unshed tears. "I'm not crazy!"

"Of course not, but you *are* in pain and a counselor might be able to help you where I can't."

His expression stiffened. "I won't go to a shrink and you can't make me!"

The next thing she knew, the front door slammed.

Darrell sat there in shock. Just before he'd bolted, he'd looked and sounded exactly like Melissa.

With her heart aching, she ran over to the sink to look out the window. He was already halfway down the street on his dirt bike. He'd never exploded like this before. She had to go after him. Grabbing her purse, she hurried into the garage and backed the car out.

She doubted he had a destination in mind. All she could do was drive in the direction he'd gone. But after ten minutes of searching the neighborhood for him, she realized he intended to stay lost for a while.

Defeated, she drove back to the condo and made a call to a couple of his friends. Eventually she found out from Steve's stepmom he'd gone swimming. They'd probably be back in an hour.

Relief swept through Darrell. Hopefully he would come home a little less angry and they'd be able to start over.

While she cleaned up the kitchen, she heard the doorbell ring.

He must have come back to get his swimming suit and had forgotten his key.

She hurried to unlock the door.

"Phillip sweetheart?" she cried as she flung it open, prepared to give him a hug whether he wanted one or not.

But instead of a belligerent twelve-year-old boy standing

there on the porch, a solidly built male filled the aperture. A man she'd presumed was already in the air on his way back to Switzerland.

Beyond his broad shoulder she glimpsed a bulletproof limo with smoked glass parked in front. She didn't doubt for a second his security people had surrounded the complex where she lived, providing heavy protection for him.

"Hello again, Darrell Collier. In case you've forgotten, my name is Alex." His deep male voice resonated to her insides.

Speechless and feeling light-headed, she held on to the door for support. "I—I'm sorry, Alex." She stumbled over her words. "But I never expected to see you again."

He studied her upturned features for a moment. "You made that abundantly clear when you flew out of my cabin a little while ago."

Her heart thundered in her chest. "Didn't you get the ring?"

His eyes glinted with a mysterious light. "It's in my pocket."

"Then I don't understand. If you're here to give me hush money or some such thing, I wouldn't take it. I swear before God I could never do that to you or anyone else."

He said nothing.

She shook her head, causing her hair to swirl a silvery-gold. "You shouldn't have come," she said in a shaky voice. "Phillip will be home soon and see the limo. If he finds you here, he'll ask questions and it won't take him long to notice certain…similarities."

Her unexpected visitor straightened to his full, intimidating height. "Then I guess I'll have to take that chance because you and I still have things to discuss. May I come in?"

She couldn't sustain his penetrating glance and averted her eyes. "I—I don't think that's a good idea."

"I happen to disagree with you," he came back with a

strong hint of authority in his voice. "If you prefer, we can sit in the limo."

"No—" she blurted. With her bare legs showing and no shoes on her feet, the thought of being confined with him sounded far too intimate.

"Are you going to make a grown king beg? It's a position I don't recall having been in before."

Everything he said and did was getting under her skin, confusing and exciting her when she shouldn't be having any feelings at all!

She moistened her lips nervously. "I didn't mean to be rude. Please— Come in."

"Since you put it so nicely, I think I will."

His male mouth twitched, revealing a charm that was lethal. No wonder Melissa had fallen for him. Of course he'd only been twenty or so at the time, but it wouldn't have made any difference. Some men were just endowed at an early age with a raw, virile charisma few women could resist.

When Melissa had talked about lying in his arms beneath the stars, Darrell had absorbed the revelation on an intellectual level. To see her sister's lover in the flesh was like coming too close to a solar flare that scorched the body and filled her with a strange envy.

Melissa may have only been a teenager, but she'd known rapture with this exciting man who ruled a kingdom. She'd carried his son to term. Those joys were something Darrell had yet to experience for herself, if she ever did.

Her front door opened into the small living room with its traditional decor. His presence dwarfed the interior.

"Make yourself comfortable. I'll be right back."

She felt his appraising gaze on her legs as she darted up the stairs. By the time she returned wearing a pair of pleated white sailor pants and leather sandals, she felt a little more presentable.

Darrell found him studying some framed family pictures. He appeared deep in thought.

When he heard her enter, he put down the picture of Phillip and turned in her direction. His eyes roved over her trembling figure, silently acknowledging the change in her attire.

"By the way you answered the door just now, I take it you haven't seen Phillip since you arrived back."

She smoothed her damp palms against her hips, a gesture he also noted. "Actually I have. But while we were eating dinner, I said something that upset him. He flew out the door and went off on his bike. I was hoping he'd decided to come back."

He frowned. "You seemed unduly anxious. Does he often blow up like that?'

Already he was sounding like a concerned parent. She hardly knew what to make of this remarkably handsome stranger from another continent.

"I said something that frightened him."

"What was that?" her guest persisted.

"The three days away from him let me see how depressed he has become. I told him I was going to take him to a counselor to help him deal with his issues of abandonment. He yelled that he wasn't crazy before he charged out of here like a torpedo."

She rubbed her arms with her hands. "On the flight home from Switzerland, I made up my mind I wasn't going to wait any longer to get help for him. I knew he would fight me on this, but I'm committed. In all honesty, I should have taken him to a doctor long before now. He's showing the same pattern Melissa did."

He moved closer, his gaze intent on her face. "Tell me about your family."

"My parents met at Denver University. Mother would have been a teacher. Dad was studying to become a geologist. Melissa had barely turned two when they were killed in a car accident and my grandmother Alice took on the responsibility of raising us.

"She was a wonderful person. We both adored her, but Melissa had a harder time of it. She yearned for our parents even though she didn't remember them. As she got older, she felt more and more sorry for herself. In time she grew petulant like Phillip and became too much of a handful for Grandma whose health began to fail.

"When Melissa had an opportunity to work at the dude ranch through a close friend's family, she didn't hesitate. She knew a lot of famous VIPs vacationed there. She'd made up her mind she was going to meet an important man who would take her away and give her the kind of life that would make up for her deprivation."

His eyes studied her intently. "What about you? A teenager burdened with sorrow and a new baby to raise. How did you do it all?"

"Grandma's house was paid for. I took a night job I could do at home for the airlines making reservations. Eventually I was able to start taking college classes and graduated in communications.

"The company gave me a promotion, so I sold the house and bought this condo, which is closer to my work. Everything seemed fine, but it wasn't fine to Phillip."

Darrell's eyes filled with liquid. "It's a tragic irony Melissa met *you,* a *real* prince. There's a lesson to be learned here in getting what you wish for..." Her voice trailed.

He trapped her gaze. "I can't do anything about your sister now, but it's not too late for Phillip."

Her thoughts reeled. "It is where *you're* concerned," she said in a dull voice.

She heard his sharp intake of breath. "He's my son. It's high time we got to know each other."

"You don't really mean that. You couldn't—" she cried. "It will change your whole life."

"That's what children do when they come into the world. He's a precious gift."

"But you're a king! This is going to complicate your life in ways I can't even begin to imagine, starting with salacious reports from the press."

"What else is new. I'm a man first, Darrell. When I fathered Phillip, I wasn't yet a king. I've already missed the first twelve years of his life. As my mother keeps telling me, a grandmother needs grandchildren. After she gets over the shock, she's going to be thrilled."

Darrell was afraid to believe him. But when she looked deeper into his eyes, she knew instinctively he believed what he was saying.

She swallowed hard. "You haven't even met him yet. He's very complex."

"You mean he's damned difficult most of the time, but sweet as honey at unexpected moments?"

"That's exactly how he is," her voice shook.

He put his hands on his hips in a wholly male stance. "He's a Valleder all right. Our genes don't lie. After we meet, he might never grow to like me, but we share the same blood. That makes us family, sight unseen."

Darrell hugged her arms to her waist. "What about your marriage? Phillip's existence is going to come as a huge shock to the woman you've chosen. It isn't fair to her."

His eyes held a faraway look. "The news that I have a son is going to turn the entire canton on its ear. However I'm not particularly concerned about anyone but Phillip. You've had the whole responsibility of him all this time. Now it's my turn."

She bit her lower lip. "It'll transform him to know he has a father he can talk to on the phone sometimes."

His expression sobered. “I hope so, but first we have to get over the biggest hurdle. He has viewed me as a deadbeat dad for a lot of years. I have a feeling this is going to take some time.”

He checked his watch. “It’s starting to get dark. Where do you think he could be?”

“I called some of his friends. They went swimming at the condo pool.”

“Why don’t we drive over in your car and find him. I’ll tell him I’m an old friend of his mother’s and we’ll go from there.”

Her heart raced too fast. “I don’t know, Alex. Maybe you’d better think about this for a while longer. Once the water spills over the dam…”

A shadow crossed his face. “Isn’t this why you came to Bris?”

“Yes. But when I found out you’re going to be married soon, I was glad I’d been prevented from meeting you.

“My grandmother died when Phillip was nine months old. She urged me to adopt him. She also told me not to go looking for you unless I was prepared to deal with the consequences. Until Phillip became so difficult, I’d made up my mind to follow her advice.

His eyes narrowed on her face. “I don’t know of another woman whose love for a child she didn’t give birth to would cause her to put everything on the line to make him happy.

“For you to sacrifice your own life for him tells me all I need to know about your character. My son has been more fortunate than he’ll ever know,” his voice grated. “I owe you a debt of gratitude I’ll never be able to repay for what you’ve done, Darrell.”

“It’s been no sacrifice—he was the most adorable baby on this earth. I fell in love with him on sight. He’s my life!”

“To know I have a son makes me feel the same way,” he asserted in a solemn tone. “So why don’t you make that phone call. After seeing his pictures, I’m eager to lay eyes on him in person.”

She felt that eagerness. It wasn't an emotion he could feign. Nervous excitement welled up inside her. "All right. The phone's in the other room."

He followed her to the family room. As she picked up the wall phone receiver in the kitchen and started to press the digits, they both heard the front door open.

"Mom? What's that black limo doing outside our house? Doug saw it on his way over to the pool and told me."

Her anxious glance darted to Alex before she hung up the phone. In the next instant Phillip appeared in the family room. His hair was still damp from his swim. It looked darker when it was wet.

Melissa had been a beautiful girl with a ton of boyfriends. Darrell had always thought her son was the best looking boy out of all his friends. He seemed older than most of the seventh-graders and was growing more attractive all the time. Talk about the acorn falling close to the mighty oak—

But Darrell received an unexpected jolt when Phillip took one glance at Alex and went pale with fright. She recognized that look. What on earth?

His gaze switched to Darrell. "Is this that counselor you were talking about?"

Aghast, she said, "No, sweetheart. No— This man—" She struggled. "This man—"

"What your mother is trying to say is that I'm Phil."

With those words, Darrell felt a strange charge in the atmosphere followed by a stillness that fell over Phillip.

He studied Alex for such a long time, Darrell wondered if he'd slipped into some kind of catatonic state.

"You're my dad," he finally muttered because he could see part of himself in the imposing stranger whose candor took Darrell's breath.

"I'm sorry it has taken us so long to meet."

Phillip's body started to tremble in reaction. His eyes filled. "I hate you."

"Phillip—" Darrel was horrified.

"I don't blame you," Alex responded with a calm she could only envy.

"I'd hate me, too, if I were in your shoes. But there's something you need to know. My father's brother was in a serious boating accident while I was on vacation in Colorado Springs thirteen years ago with my cousin Chaz. The doctors weren't sure he was going to live.

"When we got the news, we flew straight home. Fortunately he pulled through. I would have come back to Colorado later, but my father had other plans for me. By the time I tried to reach your mother by phone, it was fall and she didn't work at the dude ranch anymore. For security reasons no one would give me any information about her. I'm afraid time and circumstances separated us through no fault of our own."

During Alex's explanation, Phillip's hands kept forming fists. Suddenly he dashed out of the room. Darrell heard him run up the stairs and slam his bedroom door.

She shook her head. "I can't believe he said that to you."

"After knowing what he's been thinking all these years, *I* can. In fact I would have been surprised if he'd said anything else."

"He's changed so much from the darling, funny boy who used to play jokes and tease."

She almost choked on her tears. "I—I'd better go up to him."

"Let's let him work this through on his own. He's just sustained an enormous shock and will come around when he's ready."

Alex had a lot more confidence in the situation than she did. Maybe it took a man's perspective in a crisis like this. Except that Alex wasn't just any man.

Darrell eyed him covertly. Though he hid it well, she knew

Phillip couldn't be the only one shaken. Alex had just come face-to-face with a son he didn't know he had until a few hours ago.

Her heart warmed to him because he'd given his son certain information to make him feel better about the circumstances surrounding his conception.

She'd seen Phillip's eyes flare in surprise at the unexpected explanation. It remained to be seen if he would accept what his father had told him.

At the crucial moment Alex had known exactly what to say to disarm him. It was the master stroke of a man who put out fires every day in his role as king.

She was still unable to credit that he was willing to risk the fallout from the public scandal this would create in order to be united with his son.

Even if he tried to keep the news quiet, it would come out. His sterling reputation as the ruler of the canton would be tainted.

The woman he was betrothed to would suffer anguish.

He talked about his mother being thrilled with the news once she heard she was already a grandmother. But that wasn't the way it was likely to work. His mother would not be thrilled or anything close to it!

Darrell was frightened for him.

Her anxiety must have shown on her face and in her body language because he said, "Relax, Darrell. I know what I'm doing. While we wait for him to reappear, how about feeding a starving man."

He wanted food at a time like this? But then she remembered that Phillip could always eat in a crisis. It was one telling example of the ties that bound this father to this son.

"I have tacos left over from dinner. I'll warm them up for you."

"Sounds delicious. What can I do to help?"

"There's instant coffee in that cupboard."

"I'll make it," he offered. "It's something I'm good at."

The man was good at so many things, Darrell was in danger of losing her perspective altogether.

They worked in harmony, then sat down at the table like two ordinary people. But there was nothing ordinary about this situation or him!

Terrified of what was going on upstairs, she sipped her coffee without tasting it.

Alex on the other hand seemed to devour the six tacos with relish. After drinking several cups of the steaming brew, he made a sound of satisfaction.

"The Valleder Canton is renowned for its excellent cuisine, but I have to tell you they don't serve anything this good."

The secret to not falling apart right now was to keep making small talk.

"Yes, they do. I had a fondue bourguignonne dinner to die for at the Hotel Otter. But I must admit authentic Mexican food is hard to come by outside the western part of the U.S."

When her cell phone rang, she jumped up from the table and hurried over to the counter to get it out of her purse. She checked the caller ID. It was Danice who no doubt was trying to make final plans for the Fourth.

Darrell couldn't talk right now. Later on tonight she'd return her call.

Alex took the dishes over to the sink. "If you want privacy to talk to the man you're involved with, I'll be happy to go in the living room,"

"I'm not involved with anyone right now, but thank you anyway."

He studied her briefly. "Being a good parent is a full-time job."

"For Phillip to say what he did to you doesn't make me sound like a good parent or anything close. I've never seen him that rude to anyone in my life."

She was about to ask Alex how he knew about the trials of

a parent when he said, “My cousin-in-law, Evelyn, is raising two boys on her own. They run her off her feet.”

The comment about something from his personal life made her hungry to hear more. “What happened to her husband?”

A bleak look entered his eyes. “Chaz was flying his light plane when he ran into bad weather over the Alps and crashed.”

“Oh how awful,” Darrell whispered, strangely moved by everything he said or did.

“It was one of the worst moments of my life,” he confessed.

She could hear the pain in his voice. “How old are his children?”

“Nine and ten.”

“Such vulnerable ages. My heart goes out to them and their mother.”

In the midst of the silence they heard Phillip say, “What are their names?”

They both turned in his direction.

Alex had been right to leave him be. His curiosity over his father had won out. No telling how long he’d been listening on the other side of the doorway. Darrell didn’t dare breathe while her son’s whole attention was focused on his fascinating father.

Alex glanced at him while he finished rinsing off the plates. “Jules and Vito.”

“One of the guys in my French class is named Jules. We all had to pick a name.”

Alex folded the dish towel. “What did you choose?”

“Philippe.”

“That’s your grandfather’s name.”

“I thought that was *your* name.”

“It’s one of them. But my mother and closest friends call me Alex so there’s no confusion.”

Phillip took another step closer. “Is he still alive?”

"No. He died six years ago. But your grandmother is very much alive. Her name is Katerina."

"If you could never find my mother, how do you know about me?"

"Because I went searching for your father," Darrell declared.

Phillip looked at her in disbelief. "But I thought you didn't know anything about him."

"I didn't. But he gave your mom a very unique ring. I'd forgotten about it until a few weeks ago."

That was a lie of course. The ring had haunted her for years, but it would still be in her old coat pocket if Phillip had let go of his pain.

"I decided to have it traced…and found your father."

"When?" Phillip demanded.

"Yesterday."

His astounded gaze switched back to his father. "You live in Chicago? I thought you were from New York."

Darrell shook her head. "No, sweetheart. I never went to Chicago or New York."

"I don't get it."

"Maybe this will help." Alex pulled the ring from his pocket and handed it to Phillip who took it and began examining it with interest.

"This looks like a knight's shield."

"That's exactly what it is," Alex asserted. "My cousin, Chaz, gave it to me when I turned sixteen. He had it engraved. It says, 'More than a cousin.' The shield represents the coat of arms of our family."

Finally Phillip raised his head. "Where do you live?"

"Switzerland."

Surprise and wonder broke out on Phillip's face. "That's where they speak four different languages. I learned about that in my French class. Which one do you speak?"

"All of them," Alex answered.

"Even that funny one called Romanish or something?"

Alex smiled broadly, causing Darrell's heart to flip over. "Especially that one."

"How come?"

"Because my home is in Bris, the heart of the Romanche-speaking Canton. It might interest you to know there are five forms of Romanche, a language dating back to Roman times."

"Do you speak those, too?"

"Yes."

It was too much for anyone to absorb, especially a young American teen who'd just been united with the father he'd always wanted to meet.

"When I had to leave Colorado, I gave that ring to your mother to remember me by. It's a family heirloom. Now it's yours, Phillip. No one else in the world is entitled to wear it unless they're a Valleder."

"A Valleder?"

"Yes. If your mother and I had married, your legal name would be Phillip Collier Valleder. If you've got some tape, I'll fix it so you can wear it now."

"There's some in the drawer." Phillip opened it and handed the dispenser to Alex. In a minute the ring slid on his finger and stayed put.

Her son's eyes squinted up at him. Darrell could hear his mind working. "What's your legal name?"

"Alexandre Rainier Juliani Phillip Vittorio Valleder."

"Whoa."

A deep laugh escaped Alex's throat. It was so contagious Phillip smiled. Darrell hadn't seen one like it in years…

But when the laughter died down, Phillip grew sober again. "Do you have a wife and kids?"

Alex's eyes were hooded as he said, "You're my only child."

"But at the end of this month he's getting married to a woman named Isabella," Darrell informed her son to make certain he understood the situation in no uncertain terms.

After reflection Phillip said quietly, "Did you love my mom?"

CHAPTER THREE

THE question had been thrown out like a live wire.

Alex put his hands on Phillip's shoulders. "We only knew each other for a few days. Not long enough to find out our deepest feelings. But we were obviously attracted enough to spend all our free time together. I wish I'd known about you."

Darrell felt his thick-toned voice resonate to her bones.

"Whether you believe me or not, I'm thrilled to discover I have a son. This is the most exciting moment of my life. I couldn't get here fast enough. I love you, Philippe." The admission came out as naturally as the French version of Phillip's name.

After a throbbing silence Phillip whispered, "I'm sorry for what I said to you earlier. I…love you, too."

In the next breath both of them were hugging. They held on to each other for a long time.

The moment was so profoundly tender, Darrell pressed a hand against the strange pain in her chest.

"What would you like to do about our situation?" Alex asked once he'd finally let his son go.

Phillip stared up at him with a new light shining from his eyes. "Will you come and visit me sometimes?"

"Of course."

"Can I come and visit you sometimes?"

"Whenever you want. It's up to your mother."

Phillip flicked her a glance she couldn't decipher. Then he looked at Alex again. "How long are you going to stay in Denver?"

"I have to fly back to Switzerland tonight." While Darrell's heart plummeted for Phillip's sake, Alex unexpectedly said, "How would you like to come with me and see where I live? That invitation includes your mother. You're welcome to stay with me for as long as you want."

"Mom—"

Phillip was ready to burst with joy.

Darrell knew what he was asking, but everything was happening way too fast.

"I'm afraid you can't go right now, sweetheart. For one thing you don't have a passport."

Alex eyed her with a direct stare. "That's no problem. Trust me."

Of course it wasn't a problem. He was the king. He could let anyone in his kingdom he wanted. It appeared he wanted his son.

"What's the other thing?" Alex challenged her.

He knew exactly why she was holding back! The news about Phillip would be like a hundred megaton bomb exploding in his country.

How could he just get off his private jet with a son in tow no one had ever seen or heard of? Surely he would want to prepare his family first. His fiancée most of all…

Darrell tried to put herself in the other woman's place. The shock of learning the king she was going to marry came complete with a twelve-year-old son would destroy her dreams of starting out marriage in the hope of raising a family of her own.

"Phillip? Remember that Danice asked us to spend the Fourth with her?"

"But I told you I don't want to go."

Alex flicked her a penetrating glance. "You have other plans made?"

She averted her eyes. "Not yet. That call in the kitchen was Danice phoning to finalize everything." She could feel both of them looking at her, yet neither said a word. Already father and son were in lockstep.

The onus was on Darrell. If she said no to Phillip, he wouldn't understand. Not when she'd gone all the way to Switzerland to find his father.

Now that she'd achieved her goal, a whole new range of problems loomed over the horizon. She was starting to get scared and Alex knew it.

"Tell you what, Phillip. I'll go out to the limo so you and your mother can talk in private." He was reading her mind. "Come outside when you're ready and let me know what you've decided."

"Thank you, Alex," she murmured.

"But, Mom—"

In a few swift strides his father left the house. Phillip turned to her ready to do battle.

"Before you say anything to me, young man, I want to ask you a question." He blinked. "What else did your French teacher tell you about the Romanche-speaking canton?"

He blinked again and shrugged his shoulders. "I don't remember."

"It's ruled by a king."

"That's cool."

"Cool doesn't begin to cover it. Your father has a very important job which is different from the jobs of any of your friends' dads."

"What is it?"

"Did your teacher happen to mention the name of that particular canton?"

"No."

She drew in a deep breath. "It's the Valleder Canton."

He cocked his head. "That's Dad's last name."

"That's right. Your dad…is the king of Valleder."

Phillip let out a bark of laughter. "No, he's not."

That had been Darrell's reaction when she'd first read the information on the Internet.

"Your father's waiting for us. We better hurry and get packed."

She started up the stairs. He was close on her heels.

"Mom—come on. You're joking, right?"

She kept on going.

"Mom?"

She pulled his suitcase out of the hall closet before hurrying into his room and opening drawers.

"Some dads drive buses, others are engineers, lots of them run businesses…and a select few on the planet rule over their own country. I thought I'd let you know that before you run outside and tell him we're going with him.

"Once we reach the airport, I don't want you to be surprised when you hear his staff and security people call him 'Your Majesty.'"

Five minutes after Alex climbed in the limousine, Phillip came flying down the walkway toward him. The resemblance between them shouted his paternity. Alex suffered pain to realize he'd already lost twelve years with him. Only now could he appreciate Chaz's joy when Vito was born.

"I can't describe the feeling, Alex. You'll have to have a child of your own to understand what it's like!"

At last Alex knew exactly what it was like. He had his own

wonderful child. Incredible. Phillip was his son! Realizing he was a father filled his world with possibilities he'd never considered before.

Phillip opened the door. "We're coming with you! Mom said to give us about twenty more minutes."

The excitement those words engendered caused Alex to shove every other concern to the back of his mind. "Take all the time you need."

Phillip scrutinized him for a moment. "Mom told me something else, but I didn't believe her."

His son expressed himself exactly like young Jules. That was because they both had Valleder blood flowing through their veins.

"I didn't believe it, either, when my father who was dying said, 'Alex? Promise me you'll look after your mother and be a good king.'"

There was another full minute of silence before a hint of devilry entered Phillip's eyes. "Did it freak you out to be a king at first?"

Just then Phillip sounded so much like Chaz, Alex was dumbfounded. When they'd buried Chaz, Alex never expected to see traces of his cousin come to life in Alex's own son.

"Don't tell this to anybody, but it still freaks me out."

"You have to worry about terrorism and stuff, huh."

For a twelve-year-old, Phillip understood too much.

"It's part of my job, but certainly not all."

Phillip studied him. "Mom told me you're getting married to a princess." After a slight hesitation, "I wish my real mom hadn't died."

With that comment Alex was beginning to understand the burning issue Darrell had been forced to deal with over the years where Phillip was concerned. Having a son who had been deprived of his birth parents and suffered over it couldn't have been easy for Darrell who'd devoted her life to raising him.

His brows knit together. "I'm sorry, too, but look at it this way. You've been lucky enough to have *two* real moms, Phillip. Your second mother loves you so much, she came looking for me and wouldn't stop until she found me." In fact she'd taken a dangerous risk. The analogy of the mother and the burning building was no joke.

"Think how happy her efforts have made you and me. She didn't have to do anything at all. In fact another kind of mother might not have spent her time and hard-earned money to make your wish come true."

Hoping Phillip would think long and hard on that he added, "Why don't you go inside and see if she needs any help. After her long flights to Switzerland and back, she must be exhausted."

She'd put her son's welfare before anything else. What an amazing woman she was…

Phillip appeared more subdued before he nodded and hurried back to the condo.

The moment he disappeared inside, Alex pulled out his cell phone to alert his pilot, then tell his security staff he was ready to leave with Ms. Collier and her son.

Once that was taken care of, he phoned Carl. If there'd been anything urgent from his private secretary's end, Alex would have heard from him by now.

"I'll be home in the morning, Carl. Do me a favor and tell the staff to get the Saxony apartment ready by the time I arrive back in Bris."

"I'll see to it at once, Your Majesty. I understand Princess Isabella has a preference for daffodils. Shall I arrange for some?"

Alex's hand gripped his cell phone tighter. "You've misunderstood me, Carl. I'll be bringing my twelve-year-old son and his mother with me. Fill the drawing room with white roses, and make certain there are plenty of snack foods and fruit drinks on hand for Phillip."

"Phillip?" Carl whispered in an unsteady voice.

Alex couldn't help but smile. He'd always wondered if the secretary who'd worked for Alex's father and was loyal to him could be shaken by anything.

Now he knew he'd given the sixty-year-old man a minor coronary. This was only the beginning, but no force could stop him now. Phillip needed his father. Alex found he didn't like the idea of any other man taking over that role no matter the consequences of his actions.

"Until I tell my mother, I know I can count on your discretion, Carl."

"Of course, Your Majesty."

After the click, Alex made his last phone call for the night.

"Leo? Sorry to waken you, but I thought you'd like to know the crisis has been averted."

"So she doesn't pose a threat?"

"No," he lied.

"Thank God."

"As it turns out, she's the mother of my son, but thirteen years ago she was a girl who has changed a great deal since then."

"Sorry, Alex. We must have a bad connection and I heard you wrong. Say that again."

The connection was perfect.

"Darrell Collier has been raising my son for the last twelve years. I'm afraid I parted with that ring one starry night in the Colorado mountains where she was working for the summer. But as I told you, the memory is vague due to too much alcohol on both our parts.

"When Uncle Vittorio had a bad accident while I was on vacation with Chaz, we had to fly home. Since I traveled incognito, Ms. Collier didn't know who I was or where to reach me. So we never saw each other again. For Phillip's sake she's been trying to find me."

He heard the other man make a strange sound in his throat. "You call this a crisis averted?" Leo blurted in genuine alarm. "After hearing news of this magnitude, how in the hell are you even functioning?"

"I admit I was in shock until Phillip came running in Darrell's house. He's a living miracle, Leo. I'm bringing him and his mother home with me tonight."

"What?"

"I'm his father. He's never given up hope of being united with me."

"Obviously Ms. Collier never got over you, either, or she'd be married by now."

Alex let the remark go. For the moment it was too complicated to explain about Melissa, let alone Darrell's sacrifice. For several reasons no one could know the truth yet. Darrell was Phillip's legal mother. For the time being that was as much as Alex wanted anyone to know.

First and foremost, he needed Darrell with them in order to establish a bond with his son.

"It's only natural he wants to see where I live and spend time with me. We need to get acquainted, but I can't do that in Denver while I have so many commitments back in Bris right now."

"Alex—you're not thinking like a king whose marriage is three weeks away. You haven't thought through the myriad ramifications."

That was all Alex *had* been doing. But no matter what he had to face, it took a back seat to the joy he'd felt when Phillip let go of his pain and hugged him. An inexplicable sense of their belonging together had assailed him. At that moment his gratitude to Darrell knew no limits.

"Who else knows about this besides me?"

"Carl. But he's the soul of discretion."

"How much does Phillip look like you?"

"The second you meet him, you'll know he's mine."

By the silence, Alex could tell Leo was still trying to absorb the earthshaking news. Finally he said, "I'll make certain bodyguards are assigned to them."

"Thanks, Leo."

"Alex—I'm not speaking as your security advisor now, but as your friend. Take my advice and don't bring them to Bris until after your wedding. Then it can be handled privately. Give this more time or the press will tear you to pieces."

Not just the press, Alex muttered inwardly. His uncle Vittorio, the second most powerful man in the kingdom, would be outraged and poison the cabinet against Alex, forcing him to step down. Fortunately he was still in Greece on a cruise with Alex's Aunt Renate.

As for Alex's mother, she would go into shock. But he had faith she would recover. He had a plan how he would handle Isabella's parents. Which brought him around to thoughts of Isabella and her reaction. This news would crush her in ways he didn't want to entertain. There was no way around the fact that Alex was about to do an unthinkable thing to her…

But the truly unthinkable thing would be to turn his back on his son. Already Phillip had a stranglehold on his heart that took precedence over every other consideration.

He lowered his head. "If I don't follow through, Phillip will take it as a rejection, Leo. I can't risk it. He's too emotionally vulnerable."

After twelve years Alex had to act immediately or he could never hope to have a close relationship with his newfound son.

"Isabella's going to find out!"

"I intend to tell her the truth before she hears it from another source."

"That's a terrifying thought, Alex."

Leo was wrong. The only terrifying thought was that Phillip had been alive all these years and Alex hadn't known about it. He closed his eyes for a moment, thankful that Darrell's love for Phillip had driven her to unite him and Alex.

"I want him with me forever. I love him, Leo."

"Understood," his friend whispered at last. "But you *are* the king. My first instinct is to want to protect you. Hell, Alex, I'm sorry to have come at you like this. I have no right."

"No man had a better friend. That gives you the right. If this had happened to you, I'd be voicing the same concerns."

"What in the name of heaven are you going to do?"

From the limo window Alex could see the lights go out in the upstairs portion of the condo. His security people had started to close in.

"The only thing I can do. Take it a step at a time." Alex had never been a father before. He needed time for the wonder of it to sink in. There were plans to make. "We'll talk when I land."

After ringing off, Alex levered himself from the back of the limo in order to help Darrell, who'd just locked her front door. He was glad to see that Phillip was carrying both their bags. Two security men offered to assist him but Phillip held on to them all the way to the limo.

Alex's first little parental talk with his son had produced results. His heart swelled with fatherly pride. Too many emotions were welling inside of him from all directions.

As Darrell walked toward Alex, the glow from the street lamps highlighted the silvery-gold sheen of her hair.

Unable to keep from studying the contours of her lovely face and figure, he felt the same quickening in his blood as before when she'd first walked up the steps of the jet. To his chagrin it was much stronger now.

The fact that he'd never had this kind of reaction to Isabella caused him to groan because he knew he was in trouble. Worse, there wasn't a damn thing he wanted to do about it. What in heaven's name was happening to him?

Darrell discovered there were two bedrooms aboard the plane. For the flight to Switzerland Alex had installed them in the one normally reserved for his mother. When Phillip joked about the queen-size bed being named after his grandmother, laughter pealed out of Alex.

Though he indulged his son and seemed to find him a never ending source of entertainment, Darrell was concerned Phillip's sometimes cheeky nature was too over the top.

He hadn't inherited that behavioral trait from Melissa, so Darrell had assumed he must be more like his father. But Alex wasn't anything like Phillip in that regard, which made Darrell wonder where exactly the imp in Phillip had come from.

After he'd changed into sweats and climbed under the covers he looked up at Darrell. "Dad's awesome."

The hero-worship in her son's eyes was clear for anyone to see. For the last hour Phillip had fired one outrageous question after another at his father until they were all worn out from laughing.

"I agree."

"My friends are going to freak when they find out he's the king of Valleder."

"You're right about that. Just remember that for now it's our secret, and we're simply your father's guests. The woman he's going to marry doesn't know about you yet. After he's told her, then you can claim him."

"You don't think she's going to like me, huh."

Darrell struggled for the right words. "I doubt your father would choose a woman who wouldn't like you, but she's going to need time to get used to the idea that she has to share him with you." All of three little weeks in fact.

"Why? Steve's stepmom likes *him*."

"I'm sure in time Isabella will come to love you, sweetheart. But she's a princess who's been planning to marry your father for a long time. She doesn't know he has a son. It's going to be a shock to her."

The whole thing was a shock to Darrell who couldn't get Alex's image out of her mind. What was wrong with her to be thinking intimate thoughts about a betrothed king who'd once slept with her sister? None of it made sense!

Phillip frowned. "Do you think Dad wishes you'd never found him?"

"No," she said without hesitation. "Otherwise you wouldn't be on his royal jet right now."

He sighed. "Dad said he's glad I'm learning French. He keeps calling me Phillip."

"Of course. One of these years he'll have you speaking Italian and German and Romanche, too."

"He's super intelligent. No matter what you ask him, he knows all about it."

She nodded. "From the day he was born, he was tutored by experts to be king one day. He has to be on top of everything."

Being a father to a child he hadn't known about would have thrown any other man, let alone a king. Yet he'd let nothing stand in the way. Darrell had a foreboding there was going to be a huge price Alex would have to pay. It terrified her.

"Someday I'm going to be as smart as he is."

"You're his son, so I wouldn't be surprised. But you'll have to start taking your homework more seriously."

"I know."

She turned out the light. "I'm going to say good-night to him, then I'll be back."

"Okay."

Her fear for the whole situation caused her to leave the cabin for the den where the three of them had been talking earlier. Alex was just coming out.

They would have collided but for his quick reflexes that sent his hands to her shoulders to steady her.

She let out a small cry of surprise.

"That was close," he murmured without relinquishing his hold on her.

"Yes." She exhaled the word, afraid to look at him. Even though the jet was full of his staff, in the dimly lit passageway it felt like the two of them were far removed from the rest of his entourage.

His male warmth enhanced the tang of the soap he used, overwhelming her with telltale sensations and yearnings.

A long time ago Melissa had experienced these same feelings. With the help of alcohol she'd acted on them and he'd been willing. To Darrell's shame, she couldn't seem to control her attraction to the man who'd given Melissa a son.

If he'd been a normal man who'd married her sister, Alex would be her brother-in-law. Instead he was engaged to be married to another royal. Darrell needed to keep that fact foremost in her mind. He was off-limits to her and always would be.

Guilt drove her to back away from him, forcing his hands to let go of her.

"I know it's late," she said in a breathless voice, "but now that Phillip's in bed, there's something we have to talk about."

"If you're referring to our son, he seemed fine to me earlier."

"I agree. I'm afraid I'm the one who's nervous. My relationship with Phillip is changing. When I think of the life we've had in Denver all these years. Now everything's different."

Her head fell back as she looked up at him through eyes that had turned a deeper shade of violet. "I keep wondering what I've gotten us into. I—I'm scared."

His lips tightened, giving him a forbidding aura that made her tremble.

"What are you really saying, Darrell? You want me to instruct my pilot to turn the jet around?"

"No—Yes—" she cried, covering her face with her hands, "This is going to ruin your life—" The words came out muffled.

To her surprise he removed her hands. Still holding them clasped in his he said, "Look at me."

She was afraid to, but his compelling demand had her lifting her chin. His gaze probed hers.

"The fact of Phillip's existence trumps all royal oaths and pledges. There's no question this is going to change things. But I'll make you this promise. I'll do everything in my power to shield Phillip from any unnecessary hurt."

Darrell could hardly swallow. Once again she eased herself away from his touch.

"Melissa begged me to look for you because she believed in you. Now that I've found you, I believe in you. I know you'll do everything in your power to make Phillip feel secure in your love. But I'm not naïve.

"Though I may not have been born to royalty, I've read enough history over the years to know the normal challenges of living take on a life of their own within a royal household.

"I have to admit I'm afraid for all of us. For you! Your wedding day should be one of happiness and joy. If the monarchy suffers, then I'm going to feel responsible. So I'm begging you to rethink what you're doing. It's still not too late to go back to Denver and give this a little more time."

He stared at her through shuttered eyes. "It was too late the moment I saw the pictures of the ring. I'm the one who set things in motion thirteen years ago. Therefore that absolves you of all responsibility. As I told you earlier, I can never repay you for restoring my son to me. Perhaps he'll be the only son I ever have, the only child…

"Since no man can know what the future holds, we'll think only the best thoughts."

The best thoughts? her heart cried hysterically.

"Just so you know what to expect ahead of time, a helicopter will be waiting at the airport in Zurich to fly you to the castle. You'll be taken to one of the apartments on the second floor, which has been prepared for you and Phillip.

"Anything you need, whether it's food or fresh towels, all you have to do is pick up the phone and press line two. Rudy will see to your requests and arrange a morning city tour for you. It will give Phillip a feel for the place.

"To reach me, press line one and my private secretary Carl will get word to me. I plan to join you at the pool by midafternoon for a swim and an early dinner."

"Where will you be until then so I can tell Phillip?"

She watched his broad chest rise and fall. "San Ravino."

"Is that where the princess lives?"

"Yes. By noon tomorrow she'll have heard the truth from me in person."

"Oh, Alex—" she cried softly, forgetting she wasn't going to look at him. "Isn't there anything I can say to get you to reconsider acting too hastily?"

"No."

Darrell moaned because a chiseled mask slipped over his striking features. She could feel it lock into place like the suits of battle armor on display in his castle's ancient war room.

"The matter's settled, Ms. Collier."

In an instant he'd put an impenetrable barrier between them, one that froze her out with devastating force.

For a few minutes she'd forgotten he was a king and had pled with the man. But she wouldn't be making that mistake again. "Good night, Your Majesty."

Darrell hurried down the corridor to the bedroom. Almost crazy from lack of sleep and the incredible circumstances of their lives, she got ready for bed in the dark, then slid under the covers, taking care not to disturb Phillip. Before long oblivion took over.

Toward morning her troubled dreams had changed into a nightmare. At one point she came awake in a cold sweat with the very real premonition that the fairy tale Melissa had envisioned would not end in the traditional manner.

In Darrell's dream she was hidden in the crowd of spectators lining the streets on Alex's wedding day. The disillusioned citizens of his kingdom were booing the broken king and his twelve-year-old American offshoot sitting in the carriage between him and his grieving queen.

Quickly, before Phillip woke up and asked her why her face was wet, she rushed into the bathroom to shower. When she emerged a few minutes later, he was awake. The room steward had already delivered their breakfast trays, but Phillip's was still untouched.

"How come you're not eating?" she asked as she pulled a hydrangea blue two-piece suit from her luggage.

"I'm not hungry."

That had to be a first for him.

"In that case, you'd better shower."

"Okay." He rolled out of bed. "I can't wait to see Dad."

"I'm sure he feels the same way, but he's a busy man, so you're going to have to be patient."

"I know."

No. Phillip didn't know. He didn't have a clue, and patience was not his strong suit.

Alex had been inspired to suggest a tour of the city. The key to handling Phillip's nervous energy was to keep him busy, something his father seemed to understand instinctively.

For herself Darrell was glad they would be kept so occupied she wouldn't have a lot of time to imagine what was happening in San Ravino.

She shuddered to think of the princess who was probably eating breakfast right now with no idea that in a few hours her whole world was going to be shattered.

CHAPTER FOUR

"WHOA, Mom!" Phillip's hungry eyes had just taken in the setting of the medieval castle at Bris, bordered in back by Lake Bris. Darrell's heart echoed his words as the helicopter set them down on a helipad amidst the private, velvety green grounds east of the massive stone structure.

Accompanied by bodyguards who'd taken pains to explain everything they were seeing during their flight from Zurich, it truly was like being in a fantastic dream. From this height she could see other parts hidden from the public to the west that included a palace, a stable, tennis courts and a swimming pool.

On Darrell's first visit to the castle the other day, she'd had to stand in line with other tourists at the front entrance, and saw but a small portion of the magnificent royal estate. Only from the air could you appreciate its vast size and splendor originating from the Middle Ages when the earliest Valleder kings built the city's stronghold to keep the enemy at bay.

From the ticket window she'd followed the guide straight down to the vaulted, lonely dungeons every tourist came to see. But the tour had passed in a blur because her mind had been focused on meeting Phillip's father. Such wasn't the case with her son this morning. All Darrell had to do was look at his face to realize he couldn't wait to go exploring in those dark, dank places. This was his legacy after all.

For her the real wonder of the castle lay in the rooms upstairs where the public was never allowed to go. Rudy, the man named who'd been on Alex's staff for years and spoke excellent English, met them at the base of the grand staircase. He took over and gave them a cursory tour on the way to their room.

Both she and Phillip marveled at the grand knights' halls, the secret twisting passages between lavish bedchambers, the Gothic windows with glorious views, a large, frescoed chapel. There was so much to see, it would take weeks!

"The Grand Kitchen," Rudy explained, "still has its original wooden ceiling and four massive oak pillars which were installed in 1270." He showed them the Plessur Bedchamber containing the original bird and ribbon decorations dating from the 1580s. When he escorted them to the expansive Hall of Arms covered with escutcheons of the Valleder bailiffs, Phillip went into ecstasy and didn't want to leave. But Rudy reminded him, "There's much more to see."

He was right. The King's Chamber with its original thirteenth-century wall paintings showed rustic scenes of animals in a meadow with St. George slaying a beast on the chimneypiece. Not far from that room they entered the magnificent Great Hall of the Prince of Bris with its original octagonal table and tapestries.

Finally Rudy escorted them to the Saxony apartment where they would be staying. It was two bedrooms really, both with enormous canopied beds and fireplaces, and joined by a set of carved doors. "This is awesome!" Phillip exclaimed. Rudy laughed, obviously finding her son amusing. But Darrell was so overcome by the room's beauty, she stood in place, speechless.

There were slender black marble pillars and shimmering checkered wall decorations. Her neck hurt from viewing the coffered ceilings, which dated from the fourteenth century. She was charmed by the two recessed windows with window seats overlooking the lake. Above the arches of each window was a fabulous cloverleaf design. The same set of windows graced the smaller, adjoining room. Exquisite.

"Hey, Mom— Come here! Your room has a balcony!"

Rudy had opened a pair of doors that went from the inlaid-wood floor to the vaulted ceiling. The inserts told a Biblical story in gorgeous stained glass. Beyond them lay the shimmering waters of Lake Bris.

The sculptured stone balcony could have been made for Romeo and Juliet. It hung out over the water, taking her breath. So did the view of the mountains rising from the other side of the lake.

"His Majesty asked me to take you on a tour of the city. I'll come by for you in twenty minutes. In the meantime, make yourselves at home. Your bags have been brought up."

Once Rudy had gone, Phillip let out a whoop of excitement and began exploring his room. He soon discovered a mini-fridge had been installed. It was filled with drinks and treats. "Dad's the best! I wish he hadn't had to leave."

"You know why he did."

"Yeah… I can't wait to see him!"

Darrell felt the same way. Alex's presence had an electric effect on her, but she kept those thoughts to herself.

Later in the day she lay in the sun on one of the pool loungers. She'd put on a pair of denim shorts and a white halter top. When a shadow fell across her, she thought Phillip had come back outside after going to their apartment for a snack. Following the sightseeing visit of Bris he'd grown tired of waiting for his father, and had rediscovered his appetite.

But when she opened her eyes, she had to look up a long way before she encountered a pair of eyes that were intensely alive and had taken on the green of the immaculate lawn. They'd been studying the lines and curves of her body without her realizing it. A tiny gasp escaped her throat.

The excitement of seeing Alex made her pulse race until she remembered his meeting with Isabella, which had to be one of the worst moments of their lives. Yet Darrell couldn't tell by his demeanor how he'd been affected. He was like the proverbial rock you could cling to no matter the fury of the storm.

She noted inconsequentially he was wearing a silky Ceylon-blue shirt with beige trousers. In danger of staring at the hard male lines of his unforgettable face, she got up from the lounger dragging the towel in front of her. Though her outfit was perfectly modest, the way his gaze traveled over her body and slender legs caused her to feel exposed.

Before she could gather her wits he said, "Forgive me for arriving late, but it couldn't be helped. Where's our son?"

Anyone hearing him would assume she and Alex were man and wife. Thank goodness no one was around except his security people who'd positioned themselves at a discreet distance.

"He got hungry and went back to the apartment."

"How do you like your accommodations?"

The question threw her because he was avoiding the subject of Isabella. It made Darrell want to cry out in exasperation. But as she'd learned to her chagrin last night, he couldn't be moved by begging or pleading.

"Surely you already know the answer to that. I've never been in a more beautiful set of rooms in my life. The balcony overlooking the lake makes me feel like I'm living in a medieval tapestry. Undoubtedly the chatelaine of the castle, one of your female progenitors, stood in that very spot watching for her knight to return from battle.

"Before I came outside I must have spent at least an hour examining the stories in the stained glass."

His eyes gleamed with satisfaction. "What does Phillip think of things so far?"

"He just keeps walking around examining everything and saying 'whoa' every few seconds. Unfortunately he's already told me how cool it would be to attach a rope from the balcony and lower himself into the blue depths, which must be hundreds of feet below."

A mysterious light entered Alex's eyes. "I know someone who once did that very thing and got into a lot of trouble for it. Great minds think alike."

Forgetting that he could be implacable, she cried, "Alex—please don't keep me in suspense any longer. I have to know what happened today!"

He held her imploring gaze. "The princess came back to Bris with me."

Darrell could scarcely credit what he'd just told her. "She's here? At the castle?"

"Yes. She wants to meet Phillip. I think it would be best if she met him before being introduced to you."

Her hands crushed the toweling. Darrell couldn't be jealous of the woman he was about to marry. She just couldn't be! "Of course."

She knew it was for the best, but it hurt because she could already feel Phillip slipping away from her. It surprised her how possessive of him she was. But then her maternal instincts had never been tested to this degree before.

He was Alex's son, too. She'd better get used to sharing him. Yet the thought of the two of them enjoying each other's company in the presence of Isabella left Darrell feeling oddly bereft.

"I've arranged for the three of us to dine informally within the hour. I'll walk you back to the apartment to get him."

If Darrell were prone to fainting spells, she'd be sprawled across the pool tiles by now.

For Isabella to be willing to meet Phillip meant she was so madly in love with Alex, she'd put up with anything to become his wife, even if she was dying inside. Under the circumstances of their approaching wedding, that was the best news possible for Alex.

"She must be a wonderful person."

He nodded. "She's remarkable."

Of course he would never tell Darrell about the pain and the tears that had gone on behind closed doors before his fiancée had made the decision to face this crisis head-on. Already Isabella was showing a queenly composure Alex could only marvel at.

"I hope Phillip makes a good impression." Her voice trembled. "Naturally you and I both love him, but you know how unpredictable he can be at times."

"It's one of his most endearing qualities," Alex stated matter-of-factly. "Isabella will find him intriguing."

Spoken like a proud father who accepted his son without qualification.

It thrilled Darrell that Alex loved him so much. However it would take time for Isabella to develop a relationship with him. The thought of Phillip having a stepmother brought a sharp pain to her heart, one she needed to squelch in a hurry.

By tacit agreement they started walking toward the entrance leading to the Saxony apartment. As the castle loomed before her, the old adage about a man's home being his castle brought a faint smile to one corner of her mouth.

"What are you thinking about?" He noticed everything. When Darrell told him, he chuckled.

"I'm still having trouble believing all this is real," she confessed with a sigh. "To think that several days ago I was in line with other tourists outside the castle, trying to imagine your world. Little did I know what lay in store once you recognized the ring," her voice throbbed.

"Your arrival shook my world, too, Darrell. I'll never be the same again. You do realize you've raised a surprisingly unspoiled child."

"I don't know about that, but he *is* an original thinker. When he realizes Isabella is younger than his friends' mothers, he'll like that a lot." She needed to keep her thoughts centered on the princess. "Does she have siblings?"

"Yes. A brother two years her senior."

"Then she's been broken in"

A half smile creased the corner of his male mouth. "Most definitely."

"Knowing that will please Phillip. He'll want to meet him. You know. Get the inside scoop on what it's like to live with a princess."

The low laughter she loved rolled out of Alex. "I can see you've never had a dull moment with him."

She sent him an unguarded smile. "Dull is the one adjective that will never apply to Phillip."

He opened the door for her. "I envy you all those years with him."

By the depth of his tone, she knew he meant it. "If you want to know a secret, I don't think he'll ever forgive me for not looking for you sooner."

His eyes darkened with emotion. "Thank God you found a way to get my attention. You were incredibly courageous and resourceful. If my father were alive, he would tell you you're one of those rare female warriors upon whom future generations depend to raise up worthy sons."

Darrell half scoffed. She wondered if any woman had ever received such an unusual compliment.

Deep in thought she moved past him, but her shoulder accidentally brushed against his chest. Little sparks of fire crackled through her nervous system. She hurried up the stairs ahead of him so he wouldn't see how shallow her breathing had become.

Even though it had only been for one night, Alex had been her sister's lover. Her awareness of that fact intensified her guilt in ways she didn't want to explore right now.

It was a good thing she wouldn't be going to dinner with the three of them. The more she was around Alex, the harder it would be to keep her attraction to him a secret, especially from Isabella, who was about to become his wife.

A woman in love sensed when another woman was interested in her man.

Of course the princess had no worry in that regard. Alex was pledged to her. Their future marriage had been decreed and settled years earlier. Darrell was an idiot to go on entertaining forbidden thoughts about him.

"Phillip?" she called out after entering the apartment. "Your father's back!"

When he didn't answer, she hurried through the door to the adjoining room where he planned to sleep. "He's not here!" She turned to Alex. "I don't know where he'd be."

Something close to a grin broke out on his rugged features. "Considering it's our son, we both know the possibilities are endless. But you don't need to worry. He's been assigned a bodyguard. I'll call him."

While he pulled out his cell phone, Darrell went over to the armoire where one of the maids had hung Phillip's clothes. She picked out the navy blazer and khaki's he wore to church. Even if Alex said the dinner would be informal, she wanted Phillip to be on his best behavior in front of Isabella.

After reaching for his white shirt and striped tie, she took everything over to the bed.

Alex spoke in Romanche, preventing her from understanding him. She had to wait until he'd hung up.

"Where did he go?"

"After touring the dungeon, he went to Carl's office. They're having an off-the-record chat about what it's like to work for me."

"Oh, no— Does Carl know Phill—"

"Yes," Alex broke in, reading her mind with ease.

"Everyone must know by now. You two look too much alike to deceive anyone."

One of his expressive brows quirked. "The family resemblance is strong. As you said earlier, the water has spilled over the dam. There's no putting it back."

She moaned. "You put on a brave front, but I know deep down you have to be apprehensive about everyone's reaction."

"You're wrong, Darrell. My biggest concern is that when the novelty wears off, Phillip won't like it here, and he'll want to go home."

She couldn't believe he'd just said that.

"Alex—he has already bonded with you. It's uncanny how well you get along and understand him."

"It's because I see certain traits of my cousin Chaz in him. He'll never be a conformist."

"You're right, but that won't prevent him from wanting to spend as much time with you as possible."

Lines marred his features. "You just hit on the problem."

"I—I don't understand," her voice caught.

"I may be his father, but I'm also the king. The two don't necessarily mesh."

Her anxious gaze swerved to his. "Weren't you and your father close?"

"If you mean did we love and respect each other, then yes. But it was never the kind of relationship you're envisioning.

Father was the king. He belonged to every man. I was a typical selfish child who wanted him to myself.

"Phillip's been deprived of his father all these years. Now that we've found each other I'm afraid he's going to feel cheated in a brand-new way. I would understand if he didn't want to hang around waiting to spend time with me. That's what is haunting me."

Put like that Darrell was haunted too. Not just for Phillip who *had* been hanging around all day waiting, but for Alex.

He'd just revealed something of his inner struggle as a child. He'd said it with a hunger that bespoke needs as strong in their own right as his son's. She would never have guessed…

"But he knows you came to get him the second you found out you had a son. You didn't let your kingly duties stand in the way. You're one man in a million to have claimed him in front of everyone. He feels loved."

"I pray to God that's true," he murmured.

"It is, and it's all he ever wanted. Just try to get rid of him now and see what happens," she teased to cover her emotions.

His expression grew solemn. "Where did you come from, Darrell Collier?"

The pounding of her heart almost suffocated her. "That's the question I've been asking about you since we met aboard your jet. The chance of your world and Melissa's colliding is so remote as to be almost impossible, yet it happened."

If she kept the vision of him and her sister wrapped up in his sleeping bag, she might just make it through this painful experience without revealing her inner turmoil.

His chest rose and fell visibly. "I have to be honest and tell you the memory of that night is so vague that without the photos proving the existence of the ring, I wouldn't have recalled it."

"So what you told Phillip wasn't completely true."

He rubbed his bottom lip with his thumb. "If you mean that I spent as much time as possible with your sister, then no. Nor did I try to get in touch with her again. There was only the one night, but Phillip didn't need to know that."

Darrell hugged that piece of information to her heart. "I agree."

"Chaz and a girl who worked at the ranch fixed me up with your sister. We went to a local bar and began drinking. One thing led to another.

"I'm not proud of my behavior, Darrell. Obviously I'd decided to do a little rebelling against my gilded cage. But the next day as I nursed a hangover all the way back to Switzerland, I vowed never to put myself or another woman in that position again. You have every right to hate me for what I did."

"Of course I don't hate you. That rebellion produced a wonderful boy. He's my life!" her voice shook.

In fact knowing Melissa was simply a girl who happened to be there at the right time and place verified Darrell's opinion that all the feeling had been on her sister's part. Otherwise Alex would have come back to Colorado to take up where he'd left off.

The knowledge that Melissa wasn't the great love of his life gave Darrell a lot to think about. To be betrothed to a princess who was only thirteen at the time meant Isabella hadn't started out as his great love, either. But that obviously changed when she grew into the woman he adored.

Alex made an odd noise in his throat, jerking her torturous thoughts back to the present. "Phillip has become my life."

Darrell felt the truth of his declaration to the marrow of her bones. "He already feels the same about you, Alex."

"Mom?"

Phillip's voice broke the odd tension between them.

"I'm in your bedroom, sweetheart!"

"I heard Dad was back." He came running into the room. "Dad—"

Alex moved to meet him halfway and they hugged.

"Are you free now so we can do something?"

"Not exactly. I brought Isabella with me." Phillip's face fell. "She's waiting to be introduced."

"Is she upset?"

"I think it's more a case of her fearing you won't like her."

"Sure I do. She's going to be your wife."

Phillip had never sounded more mature. He couldn't have said anything guaranteed to please his father more. The fact that Phillip meant it made all the difference.

"Are you hungry, son?" Alex asked in a thick-toned voice.

"Kind of."

"That's good because we're going to meet Isabella in the small dining room downstairs for dinner in a few minutes."

"I've laid out your clothes on the bed," Darrell informed him.

"Okay. I'll hurry."

Alex followed her out of the bedroom into her room. "I've arranged for your dinner to be sent up here."

She turned to face him. "Thank you."

"Darrell—I hope you understand why I didn't include you this evening."

She bit her lip, hoping she hadn't let her disappointment show.

"You don't have to explain. I'm glad I don't have to be there. Phillip will be much more at ease if he's not constantly wondering what I'm thinking. He's his own person and will make his own judgments. I'm sure Isabella will be more comfortable, too. This wouldn't be easy for any woman."

He studied her for a minute. "Thank you for being so unselfish."

Oh, Alex. If you only knew the truth.

"You don't need to thank me. I—I know how important this first meeting is," she stammered. "I'll look forward to getting to know her another time. In fact speaking of time, I'm going to have to get back to my job in Denver pretty soon. So why don't you and Isabella decide what would be best where Phillip is concerned and let me know tomorrow.

"This summer he's enrolled in swimming, tennis and baseball. He'll tell you none of that matters, but I wanted you to know that he has plenty to do if he flies back home with me right away."

Her tongue was starting to run away with her, but she couldn't help it. "The important thing here is that you and Isabella work things out so your wedding goes smoothly. I'll do whatever I can to help."

"I'm ready," Phillip announced, preventing her from hearing Alex's response.

His gaze seemed reluctant to leave hers before he leveled his attention on his son. "I like that blazer."

"Thanks. Will you help me with my tie? I hate them."

"So do I," Alex muttered.

Normally that job was Darrell's domain, but he had a father now, one who performed the task with obvious pleasure.

Darrell winked at Phillip. "You're a sight fit for a king,"

Phillip screwed up his face. "That was corny, Mom."

"I know, but I couldn't help it."

Alex's broad shoulders shook in silent laughter. Their eyes met in shared amusement before he guided Phillip toward the door.

"I hope everything goes well," she called to them.

Phillip hung back. "Aren't you coming?"

"Not this time. I've got a phone call to make so I'll still have a job when I get back to Denver."

"You're not going to lose your job, Mom. Jack told me the

other day he's hoping you'll change your mind and marry him. You've got it made."

"Who's Jack?" Alex asked. By this time they'd crossed over the threshold.

"Mom's boss," came the answer before the door closed.

The click set off a symbolic echo in her heart.

Up to now she'd been focused on Isabella and how hard it was going to be for the princess to have to share Alex with his son.

But watching them walk out of the room just now made Darrell realize she, too, was going to go through a serious adjustment letting Phillip go with his dad.

Darrell had to admit it pained her to be left behind this evening. She was so used to being the center of Phillip's universe, she was actually jealous of Alex's power over him.

Her son's eagerness to go off with his father whether she went with them or not came shouldn't have come as a shock. It was clear they were both anxious to make up for lost time.

That's what she wanted for them! But this was only the beginning. Soon Alex was going to be Isabella's husband… Just imagining it produced excruciating pain of a different kind.

Before Darrell broke down in tears, she showered and changed into a nightgown and robe to have dinner. Once she'd eaten, she realized that too many flying hours had made her desperately tired. Bed called to her.

After brushing her teeth, she doused the lights and turned in, hoping she wouldn't have more disturbing dreams.

Sometime later she thought she heard a noise.

"Phillip?" she called softly in the darkness, too groggy to turn on a light.

"No," came that deep, vibrant male voice.

CHAPTER FIVE

"ALEX—" Suddenly Darrell was wide-awake and sat up. "W-what time is it?"

"Midnight. I'm sorry to have disturbed you. Phillip and I needed to talk. He's asleep now."

She smoothed the hair away from her face. He stood a few feet away from the bed. Anyone looking in right now would be scandalized to see the king in her bedroom. But everything about their situation was unique. Her heart was beating far too fast to be good for her.

"Tell me what happened—"

She heard him exhale. "Our son was such a perfect gentleman, I hardly recognized him."

Since Darrell understood exactly what he meant by that, she didn't misconstrue his words. "He loves you so much, he obviously didn't dare do anything you could fault."

"Isabella wasn't exactly herself, either, though she tried."

"So all in all the evening turned into a disaster," Darrell finished for him.

"That's one way of putting it." But he said it with a chuckle, which in turn caused her to do the same.

"I know it isn't a laughing matter," she said when she'd sobered. "Do you think they liked each other?"

"I think they will once the shock wears off. It's one thing to have intellectual knowledge of each other, and quite another to sit across a table from each other face-to-face for the first time. Everything became real tonight."

Darrell could second that!

She sat up a little straighter. "I'm sure you're thankful this initial meeting is over. Tomorrow it will be easier."

"She's leaving first thing in the morning."

Uh-oh. "Is Phillip upset you're going back to San Ravino with her? If he is, I'll have a talk with him."

"Thank you, but that won't be necessary. She wants to speak to her parents alone, and will send for me when the time is right."

Alarmed, Darrell said, "They don't know yet?"

"She thought it would be better to meet Phillip first."

Darrell put her hands to her face. "It's going to be horrible, isn't it."

"That remains to be seen."

"I feel terrible for her, Alex."

"So do I. Her parents are very decent people. But even decent people have their limits."

Tears trickled out of her eyes. "Do you think Phillip has any idea how important tonight was?"

"Yes." His voice grated. "That's why we talked so long. I heard all about Steve and his divorced parents. We discussed what it was like for his friend to live in two different households with two moms. Our son is much more prepared to deal with this situation than I'd given him credit for."

"He's devoted a lot of thought to it. Too much," Darrell murmured.

"Our son is terrific, but you already know that."

"I do." She wiped the moisture off her cheeks. "We just have to hope Isabella and her parents will be able to work through their pain. Is there any way of putting off the wedding another week or two? Just to give them a little more time to get used to the idea?"

"We talked about that possibility, among others."

"What others?"

"Her parents will probably be able to deal with it as long as Phillip is never allowed to succeed me as king."

"King—" she blurted incredulously. "Phillip?"

Until Alex had brought up the subject just now, the thought had never entered her head. "Did you assure her Phillip is the last person in the world who would want that job one day, let alone be qualified?"

The silence lengthened before he said, "Who knows what's in store for our son." Alex sounded so serious, she started to get nervous.

"I can tell you right now it won't be that!" she cried.

He shifted his weight. "Did I mention his asking me if he was a prince now?"

She made a protesting sound in her throat. "He was just kidding around, Alex. You know how he is. Isabella has nothing to fear from him. When you two have children, they'll be royals from birth. I hope you explained that to him. After I get him alone I'll explain to him."

"Let's not worry about that right now. How would you like to go horseback riding after breakfast in the morning?"

He'd changed the subject too fast.

"I'm sure Phillip will love it."

"Surely you realize I'm including you in the invitation," he said in a voice that brooked no argument.

"Isabella wouldn't approve of it no matter how hard she's trying to be brave about this, so—"

"Be ready at nine," he cut in on her abruptly. "Sleep well."

Within seconds he'd disappeared from the suite.

Shivering with apprehension because the situation was

growing more complicated by the minute, she burrowed under the covers. Five minutes later she was still wide-awake.

Not only their conversation but his presence had given her a serious case of insomnia. The time for gut-wrenching honesty had come.

She hadn't wanted him to leave just now…

Frightened by her feelings for him, which were intensifying beyond her control, she pounded her pillow in an effort to get more comfortable so sleep would come. This insanity had to stop.

One way to cure it would be to leave Switzerland immediately. But how could she do that when nothing had been resolved regarding visitation arrangements?

Just saying the word "visitation" made her cringe.

The thought of leaving her son for any length of time was unbearable.

Yet he'd feel the same way when he had to leave his father.

She wept into her pillow.

What had she done?

Alex had just seen a sober Isabella off at the helipad when his mother phoned, asking him to come by her apartment.

He grimaced. The castle grapevine was alive and doing well.

"Is it true?" she questioned the moment he entered the day room of her suite.

This morning his mother wore a casual dress in a melon tone that suited her light brunette hair. She appeared ready for her daily walk with the two dogs she'd raised from puppies. Since his father's death, they'd brought her a lot of comfort.

He studied her for a long moment. One day soon he intended to tell her the whole truth. But for now the preservation of their family's happiness necessitated his holding back certain information.

"That depends on what you've heard." He kissed her cheek. "If I could have told you sooner, I would have, but Isabella deserved to hear the news before anyone else. She's on her way back to San Ravino as we speak."

Her dark gray eyes looked at him in anguish. "Then it *is* true."

"That I have a twelve-year-old son named Phillip?" He met her gaze head-on. "Yes."

She sank down on the couch, rubbing the dogs' heads absently. "How long have you known?"

"Three days ago Leo came to me with a story about a woman and a ring."

She moaned. "I could expect this from almost anyone else in the world, but not my only son." Her voice shook. "To do this to Isabella..."

Her eyes filled with tears. "How did this happen, Alex? You know what I mean."

He moved toward her. Though he'd braced himself for this inevitable confrontation, it was still difficult to see his mother in pain.

"Chaz and I went to a bar with a couple of girls while we were on vacation in the States. We all drank too much. I only spent one night with her before Chaz and I got word that Uncle Vittorio was in that accident and we had to fly home.

"I don't honestly remember giving her the ring Chaz gave me. When we flew out of Colorado Springs, I knew I wouldn't be back. Nine months later she gave birth to my son, but she had no way of contacting me because she didn't know who I was.

"Phillip has grown up wanting to know his father, so in desperation she used the ring to try to find me."

His mother's expression twisted in agony. "Well, she certainly did that, didn't she."

The dogs moaned at the harsh tone in her voice.

"Every day since your father died, I've asked why he was

taken from us so prematurely. Now I can see it was to spare him this grief." She took a shallow breath. "You've always been so wise, Alex. Whatever possessed you to fly them here, and allow them to stay at the castle?"

"Because he's my son and deserves the very best, despite my irresponsible behavior. He needs love. Isabella understands this and realizes why I refuse to keep him hidden like some bastard child. She knows everything. She had dinner with him last night. We're going to work this out."

Visibly shaken, she got to her feet. "You think for one minute Ernesto and Tatia are going to stand for this?"

His brows furrowed. "Isabella's parents don't have a choice any more than I did."

Her gaze bore into his. "Oh, yes, you did. You could have kept this private, and dealt with him and his mother behind the scene." Leo had suggested the same thing.

"I could have." He folded his arms. "But when you meet Phillip, you'll understand why I didn't."

She shook her head in bewilderment. "Bringing your former lover into our home is political suicide, and so cruel to Isabella I can't imagine what you're thinking."

Though he tried to control it, his temper flared. "Darrell Collier is Phillip's mother, the only parent he's ever known. Would you have me tear him apart from her because of the way it will look to everyone else?"

"You didn't need to bring them here," she reiterated. "It was a grave mistake on your part."

"He's my son, Mother. He needs me, and I…need him."

She shook her head. "I can't believe this has happened."

"I had trouble believing it myself until I met him. He's wonderful. You're going to love him."

His mother looked away. She was trembling.

He moved closer. "The second Darrell came to the castle

asking for an audience with me, Leo did everything he could to keep it quiet, but the rumors began flying anyway. You know as well as I do the best way to handle a situation of this magnitude is to expose it immediately."

"With what results?" Her voice throbbed.

"I don't have the answer to that yet. In this scenario no one set out to hurt anyone, least of all Phillip, who's an innocent. But I *do* know this much. I already love him and want him with me always."

"At the cost of the monarchy?" Her voice rang out. "He can never be your legitimate heir."

Alex struggled to tamp down his anger. "For the sake of argument, why not?"

She let out a cry of alarm. "Because no child of a commoner can inherit the title. It's the law and you know it."

"Laws can be changed."

"Then you'd be the first Valleder king in over a thousand years to do away with it."

"You have to admit it's archaic."

Their eyes held while she digested his blunt honesty. "But you wouldn't change it."

He took a fortifying breath. "No, Mother. I wouldn't."

Until he saw that steely look enter her eyes, he thought his answer had satisfied her. She stared at him like she'd never seen him before.

"This isn't as much about your son as the woman who gave birth to him. Something tells me you never got over her. Why else would you give her a ring that could be traced? It explains your irrational decision to put her in the Saxony apartment. No wonder you've kept putting off your marriage to Isabella."

"Stop, Mother. You're wrong you know."

She shook her head. "No, I'm not. The maid told me she's

blond and enchantingly beautiful in that special American way. She wears no wedding ring.

"How shrewd of her to come forward weeks before your wedding and present you with the fruit of your passion, knowing the twelve-year-old son of her body would blind you to your royal duty."

"Mother— There are things you don't know."

"I'm not blind, deaf and dumb, Alex." Her voice trembled. "I know you're not in love with Isabella and never have been. But I thought—I hoped that with marriage and children, love would come the way it did with your father and me."

"I'm hoping for that, too," he declared. At least he'd always held that hope, but Darrell's sudden advent into his life had knocked him sideways. The more he was around her, the more he wanted to be around her all the time. If the truth be known, he *wanted* her. It was a fact he could no longer deny.

She shook her head. "What you've done is make it almost impossible for that to happen now. Not with that woman back in your life!"

His mother was right. No one knew that better than Alex.

"Ms. Collier has no shame, no decency. To think you lost your heart to such a person pains me as much as your father's death."

Alex ground his teeth. "Before you jump to any more erroneous conclusions, I'm going to ask a favor of you. This is important." He checked his watch.

"I'm due to take Phillip riding right now. During your walk with the dogs, why don't you pass by the stables in say three hours. That way your first meeting with him will be informal and spontaneous, putting him at ease. Later on in the day you and I will have another private talk."

Her expression remained wooden. "Are you asking as the king, or as my son?"

"Both. I swear on father's grave that if you'll do this,

certain things will become clear and help you get through this without completely despising me."

At the mention of his father, she lowered her head. That was the way he left her as he slipped out of the apartment. At their next meeting he would tell her about Melissa. By that time she would have come face-to-face with her grandson.

Knowing his mother as he did, her heart would soften. She'd want Phillip to stay in Bris and become an intrinsic part of the family. Once that happened, she wouldn't be able to dismiss Phillip's second mother so easily…

A steep hill rose beyond the lake bordering the back of the royal estate. It led to vineyards and ultimately the forested slopes of the mountains overlooking the magnificent Rhine Valley.

By the time the three of them dismounted to rest and take in the view, euphoria had overtaken Darrell.

During the climb, Alex had put Phillip to work checking the riverbank for signs of dead fish, which he explained was a problem in the lower Ungadine called Whirling disease. His minister of fisheries was working with some biologists to eradicate it.

Phillip thought the term "whirling" was too funny, but he took his father's suggestion seriously. Already Alex was making his son feel important. He managed him without dictating. Phillip had never been more pleasant or well behaved.

While she wandered around stretching her legs, Alex tied up the horses. She hadn't ridden one in years. At the end of the day she would be sore, but the glorious ride had been worth it.

Phillip didn't seem to have the same problem, lucky boy.

"Dad? Have you ever climbed up to that ridge?"

"Many times."

"With my grandpa?"

"No. He was always too busy."

"How come he was so mean?"

"Not mean, Phillip. It's just that when he pledged to serve the people of our country, he meant it. You have to understand he represented the House of Valleder. It has reigned over this canton for centuries.

"The castle here in Bris has been our ancestral home since the Middle Ages. Father never forgot his duty for a minute."

Darrell could hear her son's mind taking it all in.

"How long was he king?"

"Thirty years before he died of a heart attack."

"I bet you miss him a lot."

"The whole family does."

Following his father's soulful remark Phillip eyed him with a distinct glint.

"What do you bet I can climb to the top of that ridge and back in half an hour."

"I used to make that trip in twenty minutes," Alex said with a deadpan expression.

Phillip let out a whoop. "You're on!" He high-fived his dad before taking off. Pretty soon he'd disappeared in the pines.

Alex put a booted foot on the log, turning to Darrell with one of those white smiles that melted her insides.

He looked happy.

In jeans and a navy pullover, he was jaw-dropping gorgeous.

There wasn't another man to equal him.

This must have been the way Melissa felt when she'd gone to that bar with him years ago. No woman would be able to resist an invitation to join him in his sleeping bag. Darrell took back everything she'd ever said to her sister about not having shown more sense.

"I'm sure it isn't really possible to imagine your life if you weren't raised to be a king, but I'm curious to know what you think you might have done with your life if you'd been born as say…Alex Smith."

He leaned on his knee with one arm. "That's easy to answer. I would have worked in counterespionage developing various codes no enemy could crack."

"How fascinating! I remember the story of the Wind Talkers who were Navajo military men used during the war. No one could break their code."

"Exactly. We speak a lot of languages here in Switzerland, and each one has its different dialects depending on the region or valley. The Romanche dialects are complex and fascinating to me, as is the Navajo language you were referring to."

"Phillip has a lot to learn."

"Hopefully he'll want to. Our language will be lost if we don't endeavor to keep it unified and used. When I wasn't busy with some regimen or other, I began making my own dictionary of Romanche words and idioms, incorporating the dialects.

"On mountain hikes I always carry a notebook with me in case I meet a fellow countryman who could give me a new word here or there to add to my collection."

"You're a very brilliant man. Phillip's in awe of you."

"My father was the brilliant one," he informed her. "He was first to introduce a program at the university in Bris to get as much information as we can from the old people still living within the canton. Once they're gone, any knowledge they have will die with them. I'd hate to see Romanche go by the wayside."

"Thank goodness for a sovereign like you who cares enough to preserve your heritage," she said emotionally.

He moved closer to her. "The main reason I spent time in Arizona was to visit some Navajo reservations and see how they preserve their dialects and gather information. But I must admit the idea of being a secret agent has headed the top of my list for a profession."

His eyes narrowed on her face. "What about you? If there'd been no Phillip, what would you have done?"

"That's an easy question to answer, too. My grandmother never did have very good health. I probably would have tried to get into medical school somewhere. Maybe become an internist. But like you, I had other responsibilities that pretty well grounded me to one place and one priority."

"I'm assuming you're the one who chose to stay home with your grandmother while your sister went to work at the dude ranch."

"Yes, but in all fairness to Melissa, she waited on my grandmother, too. Though I worried about her, I was glad she could get away to do something she thought would be fun. Her best friend's uncle had horses, so she went riding a lot. The dude ranch was the perfect place for her, and it paid a good salary."

But Melissa had ended up taking on more than she could handle when she'd met Alex.

Darrell wouldn't have been able to forget him, either. Her desire for him had already become so acute, it was a full-grown pain only he could assuage. Yet to even entertain thoughts of him was taboo.

A relationship with the king of Valleder wasn't possible, not on any level. Melissa's brief interlude with him had been one of those fantastic accidents in life that had defied the odds.

To stand around alone with him any longer pretending she didn't have feelings for him wasn't only ridiculous, it was unbearable. Finally she made the decision to separate herself from him. There was only one way to do it.

After loosening the reins around the tree trunk, she climbed back on the surefooted mare Alex had chosen for her.

In a few swift strides he closed in on her. "What do you think you're doing?"

"I'm going to see if I can beat you and Phillip back to the stable."

His features tautened visibly. "Why?"

Don't ask me that question.

"Our son loves competition. For once I'd like to be the one to give him a run for his money."

"Surely not at the expense of a broken neck."

She frowned. "Am I such a lame rider?"

"Anyone can have an accident. While you're my guest, I prefer to keep you safe."

So saying he reached for her, pulling her off the horse before she was ready.

The momentum brought their bodies together. Helplessly she slid down his powerful physique until her feet touched the ground.

The incredible sensation caused a gasp to escape her lips. Their eyes met by accident. His blazed a hot green.

"Alex—" she whispered mindlessly, caught in a sensuous thrall where the world seemed far removed from them at this moment.

An answering moan came from his throat before his mouth closed over hers with a kind of refined savagery she would never have suspected.

She kept telling herself this couldn't be happening. Not possibly.

Like a drowning person going under for the third time, her life flashed before her. She thought of all the reasons why this was wrong—out of the question…

He was going to be a married man within a few weeks.

But the rightness of being in his arms, the feeling that they were two halves of a whole transcended every moral objection. Fused to him like this, everything changed.

She didn't need his hand at her waist crushing her to him

because she molded herself to him of her own free will, wanting to merge with him.

His other hand cradled the back of her head, the better for their mouths to savor the intoxicating elixir while they slowly began to devour each other. Their mutual hunger wasn't some vain imagination. It was a kind of craving she'd never known in her life, like a force beyond herself that wanted, needed everything this man had to give.

Every kiss he gave her went deeper and longer, driving her wild with desire. The increasing urgency of his demand set off an explosion of need inside her.

Feverish with longings her arms slid around his waist and she found herself melded to every hard line and sinew. All she kept praying was don't stop this ecstasy, don't ever stop.

Her legs grew heavy. Her palms throbbed with pains brought on by too much pleasure. His mouth was driving her mad with the things he was doing to her.

"I'm back!" shouted a voice in the distance.

Both of them groaned before she cried, "What if he's seen us?" In panic Darrell tore her lips from his and jerked away from those strong arms holding her possessively.

The motion made her dizzy. He steadied her swaying motion.

"Are you all right?" he whispered.

"Y-yes. You go to him."

Alex's recovery was much faster than hers. He moved toward Phillip, giving her a chance to gain her equilibrium behind the protection of the tree. By the time they'd joined her, Darrell was astride her horse ready to go back.

She was still so shaken by what had transpired, she struggled to pretend nothing was wrong. "Did you make it in ten minutes?" she forced herself to ask Phillip.

"No, but I will next time."

"Eleven and a half minutes isn't bad for your first time."

Alex tousled Phillip's hair. "Now we'd better go. I've discovered I'm hungry for lunch."

Heat enveloped her.

"Me, too," Phillip declared.

After they'd climbed on their horses, she trailed them down the mountain. Phillip did most of the talking. He couldn't fathom that Bris was a four-thousand-year-old city built by the Romans. It was a good thing he was so eager to learn from his father. It prevented him from noticing how quiet she'd become.

Little did her son know her emotions were in utter chaos.

A line had been crossed today.

She didn't have the power to turn back time to prevent the experience from happening. However she could make certain there would never be a repeat.

There was no excuse for losing her head. Until he'd admitted that he hadn't been emotionally involved with Melissa, she would have assumed he'd lost his because she reminded him of her sister. Though the two of them had different coloring, physically they resembled each other in many ways.

Darrell could have understood him getting caught off guard in a small detour down memory lane, but according to him he couldn't even remember that night with Melissa clearly. So what was the explanation?

Certainly it was a mistake! One of those heart-stopping, forbidden mistakes of unmatchable rapture she would remember for the rest of her life.

Deep in agonizing thought she scarcely remembered the ride back to the stable. Once she'd walked outside the barn, she caught sight of a cute, dark blond boy running toward Alex. He was calling out something to him in Romanche.

"Speak English, Jules."

The boy reminded her of Phillip when he'd been a few years younger. They all bore that distinguishing Valleder stamp.

Alex put his hand on the boy's shoulder. "Where's Vito?"

"Around the front with Aunt Katerina."

He guided him closer. "Jules? I'd like you to meet a relative from Colorado in the United States. I hope you'll all become good friends."

Jules looked up at Alex in surprise. "I didn't know we had relatives in America."

"You have *one*. His name is Phillip. He's my son."

The boy's light blue eyes rounded in disbelief. "No, he's not—"

For Darrell it was déjà vu because Phillip had sounded exactly like that when she'd told him his father was the king. The two boys had so much in common it was uncanny.

"Freaky, huh," Phillip spoke up.

Alex smiled at his son. "Jules doesn't know what freaky means."

"Crazy."

Jules was understandably bewildered. "How old are you?"

"Almost thirteen."

Going on a hundred, Darrell muttered inwardly. Alex flashed her an amused glance as if he'd just thought the same thing. Her heart lurched every time he looked at her.

"Isabella's not your mother," Jules declared.

"No," Darrell interjected, trying to ignore Alex. "*I* am. My name is Darrell Collier. I'm very pleased to meet you, Jules." She put out her hand, which he shook politely. But it was clear he was puzzled.

Who wouldn't be? The poor boy didn't know Melissa had given birth to Phillip. But this was hardly the time and place for Darrell or Alex to get into the specifics.

Unfortunately it left the impression that Darrell and Alex had been lovers. One day soon the truth would come out. In the meantime she had to withstand Jules's curiosity.

He finally switched his gaze back to Alex. "Then how come you're going to marry Isabella?"

Darrell had anticipated his question and was ready for it. "Because she's a royal princess and they love each other very much."

"Isabella's really cool," Phillip piped up.

Jules glanced back at his new relative in fascination. "What does cool mean?"

"She's a fox."

Well, well, well. If her son said it, it meant Isabella was a true beauty.

Of course she would be, but the knowledge acted like a dagger plunged in Darrell's heart.

"A fox?" Jules questioned.

Alex burst into laughter.

Jules looked so worn-out trying to figure everything out, Darrell took pity on him.

"What Phillip's trying to say is that Isabella is a lovely person."

Those light blue eyes studied her, then Phillip. "Do you want to come and see Great-Aunt Katerina's dogs?"

"Sure. What kind are they?"

Jules looked to Alex for the answer.

"In English they're called golden retrievers. Stick with my son, Jules, and your English vocabulary is going to skyrocket."

"Go on with him," Darrell urged Phillip. "I'm going back for a soak in the tub."

He grinned. "You didn't do half bad on that horse, Mom."

"Thanks a lot, *Roy*."

Her allusion to Roy Rogers, the famous cowboy, would be lost on Jules, but Alex and Phillip laughed.

"Come on, Dad."

She felt Alex's gaze compelling her to look at him, but that was all over. She didn't dare allow herself another second alone with him. She didn't want a postmortem of what had happened up on the mountain. Until Alex and Isabella sorted things out in the next couple of days, she intended to stay sequestered in the apartment away from everyone.

Turning on her heel, she took a path through the trees that would lead back to the castle without her having to see Alex's mother.

One day they would have to meet, but not right now. Not while the feel and taste of her son's hands and mouth had rocked Darrell's world.

CHAPTER SIX

ALEX left Phillip and the boys in his mother's apartment. She'd invited all of them to lunch. Knowing they'd be occupied several hours at least, he slipped out to take the inevitable phone call from Isabella.

Her parents expected him for dinner. That gave him three hours to talk to Darrell before the helicopter took off.

He had an idea she'd barricaded herself in the suite. The passion they'd shared had not only scared the daylights out of her, but it had changed him into someone he didn't know anymore.

He took the stairs down to the second floor and walked through the hallway until he reached her door. Before he knocked, he pulled out his cell phone to call her.

There was no answer, however he hadn't expected her to pick up.

He knew instinctively she was hiding from him. Maybe she would answer the door if he knocked, thinking it was the maid. But there was no response—no sound to indicate she was inside.

In his gut he knew she'd made up her mind not to open it, not even for the king.

But the *man* could gain access to her without anyone knowing about it—the man Alex had been repressing since that wild night years ago—the man who seemed to have been reborn since discovering he had a son…

The only way to do this meant going through the music room on the first floor located directly below the Saxony apartment. The rope Chaz had attached from the balcony to reach both floors still hung outside the window.

Driven by a need he could no longer control, Alex went downstairs and stole inside the room past the grand piano. He opened the window to test the rope's strength, figuring it would still hold him. If it didn't, he'd fall in the lake. It had happened many times before without incident.

After getting out on the ledge, he grasped the thick cord and started climbing hand over hand.

It wasn't as easy as it used to be. The years had taken a toll on his athletic prowess. If Chaz saw him now, he'd laugh his head off.

One more burst of energy and he would be home free.

"Darrell Collier?" he called out to her. "I'm coming up to you so be warned!"

In the next instant he heard an answering scream. Luckily the thick castle walls would have muted her cry.

"I hope you're presentable because I'm almost there. We have to talk."

He threw his arm over the balcony wall and hoisted himself so only his head and shoulders were visible.

She stood there clutching the lapels of her robe to her throat. "Are you out of your mind, Alex?"

He could read several emotions coming from those violet eyes, but the dominant one was fear for his safety.

"That all depends on your definition," he drawled.

She stamped her foot impatiently. "You're going to fall!"

"It wouldn't be the first time."

"Be serious," she begged. Her face had gone pale.

"I've never been more serious in my life. I have to fly to Italy in a little while, so I won't be able to see you or Phillip until tomorrow."

Her appealing body was trembling. "You could have phoned me with that information."

"I tried. When that didn't work I knocked on your door."

She bit her lip. "I—I was asleep."

"Here at the window you mean?"

Suddenly her color came flooding back into her cheeks. "This isn't funny, Alex. You could plunge to your death. Please come inside," she implored him.

"You're sure? I wouldn't want you accusing me of taking advantage of you."

"Yes, I'm sure!" she practically shouted at him.

"Since you asked me so nicely, I think I will."

Another lunge brought him within a foot of her. She backed away like a frightened fawn in the forest.

She had every right to be nervous of him. At the moment he was feeling invincible. But it was the wrong decade, the wrong country, the wrong woman.

"I'm not going to apologize for kissing you today. I thoroughly enjoyed it. You're a beautiful woman. It was one of those incredible summer mornings, and I couldn't resist.

"That's no excuse, but it's the best explanation I can offer. As long as I'm engaged to Isabella, I swear it won't happen again. That's what I came to say. I want you to be able to trust me. If we don't have that, we don't have anything."

"I agree." Her voice caught. "What happened was both our faults. Of course I trust you. I think the situation with Phillip threw us, but no longer."

Phillip had nothing to do with the chemistry between them, Alex reasoned to himself. But he decided to let her remark pass because he had tangible proof she desired him, too. She could deny it all she wanted, but the fact remained they were both on fire for each other with no help in sight.

"You sound totally recovered."

"I am," she assured him. After pausing for breath she asked, "Where's Phillip now?"

"With mother and the boys. Though she's not ready to admit it yet, she's having the time of her life getting to know her grandson. The boys are in shock. The reality of Phillip has already shaken Vito out of his morose state. As for Jules, he's just plain delighted with his upstart cousin from across the Atlantic."

Her mouth curved upward, bewitching him. "Upstart is right."

"Darrell—" he said before she could say anything else. "I know how hard the situation is on you. I don't expect you to remain in this limbo forever. Just give me until tomorrow. After being with Isabella, I'll know a lot more."

She nodded. "It's all right. I checked with Jack. He told me to use this time for my vacation."

Alex's hands curled into fists. No doubt *Jack* was counting the hours until she flew back. What a fool her boss was to let her out of his sight.

"Is there anything I can do for you before I leave? Anything at all?"

She shook her gilt-blond head without looking at him. "I feel like I'm living in a dream. How could I possibly want anything more?"

How indeed.

"I'll be in touch with you in the morning and we'll go from there. Do me a favor and answer the phone so I don't have to risk my life a second time in order to have a conversation with you?"

She lifted anxious eyes to him. "I'm sorry. I promise to answer it."

Before he proved that he couldn't keep a promise to her five minutes, let alone a lifetime, he slipped back over the side of the balcony.

"Alex—"

She sounded terrified for him, but he kept on going, not daring to let her cries stop him or heaven help them both.

When he'd swung himself back inside the music room and had locked the window, he phoned the palace security guard out in the hall. "There's a rope hanging from the balcony of the Saxony apartment to the outside of the music room. It's a security risk and needs to be removed ASAP."

"I thought you didn't want it cut down."

"I've changed my mind." I don't trust myself anymore.

"Yes, Your Majesty."

"Mom?"

"Hi, sweetheart!"

"Jules and Vito are with me."

Glad she was showered and dressed in a blouse and skirt, she hurried into the drawing room of their apartment. The ten-year-old Vito looked like the rest of them. With so many similarities, they could all be brothers. It really was remarkable.

"You're Vito. I'm so happy to meet you."

"Hello, Ms. Collier."

"Call her Darrell," Phillip told him.

While they shook hands his darker blue eyes studied her with interest. "Jules and I have to go to the dentist. We're going shopping, too. Can Phillip come with us? Mother says it's okay. We'll walk him back after dinner."

She looked at Phillip. "Would you like to go?"

"Since Dad's not here, sure."

"Then it's fine with me." She looked at the boys. "Tell your mother thank you."

"I will," Vito replied, sounding too grown up for his age.

As they started to leave she heard Jules say, "You're lucky. Nobody ever gets to stay in this apartment."

"Why not?"

"We don't know. Mother says it's a secret," Jules explained.

"Why don't you just ask Dad?"

Vito shook his head. "Mother said it wasn't our business."

"Then I'll ask him when he gets back from Italy."

Darrell thought she heard the word "cool" come from Jules before the outer door closed.

She walked around the room, stopping to smell the gorgeous white roses that gave off a heavenly perfume.

Not even Isabella had slept in here?

Whatever the reason, Alex had taken Phillip to his heart, breaking rules only a king could do if he wanted to.

He'd risked causing what could be an insurmountable problem in his coming marriage to the princess in order to claim him and make up for the last twelve years.

A man like that didn't come along very often in life. Isabella could have no conception of how lucky she was.

Before Darrell fell apart over her feelings for Alex, she phoned Rudy and asked him to have a car waiting for her. There was a famous art gallery in the center of the main shopping district she wanted to visit. Anything to get her mind off of Alex, who would be spending tonight with Isabella. The images of the two of them entwined together while he convinced her their marriage would work made Darrell writhe in pain.

She grabbed her purse and flew out of the apartment. If her bodyguard thought she was having some kind of nervous breakdown, he'd be right!

Alex had just finished shaving when his cell phone rang. He checked the caller ID and clicked on. "Mother?"

"I'm on my way to your apartment. You can't leave for San Ravino until we've talked." The line went dead.

He rushed to get dressed. By the time he'd shrugged into his suit jacket, she was at the door. The dogs preceded her into his living room. After shutting the door he leaned against it, waiting…

"Oh, Alex—he's so much like you when you were that age, I can hardly believe it!" There were tears in her voice as well as her eyes.

Gratified by her response, he drew in a deep breath and walked toward her. "I see you and father in him, too. And Chaz…"

She nodded. "Yes. He has a way of expressing himself like your cousin. He and the boys could be brothers."

"So now you know why I had to bring him with me."

"*I* understand it," she whispered, "but your uncle won't."

He tautened. "We can thank God Uncle Vittorio and Aunt Renate are away on a trip. I agree he would go into a black rage knowing what happened on that vacation in Colorado years ago.

"Perhaps now you understand why it was imperative I announced paternity before their return from the cruise."

His mother stared at him while streams of unspoken thoughts passed between them. "Yes," she eventually agreed in an unsteady voice. Her wet eyes gazed at him for a long time. "But you might have done it to the peril of the monarchy."

Lines darkened his face. "I love Phillip."

She let out a weary sigh. "How could you not? But you can't expect Isabella to take him to her heart."

He grasped her hands. "She's making a gallant effort."

His mother shuddered. "I can't imagine how she's going to get past this, Alex. It's not just the reality of Phillip. You brought his mother with you. How painful for Isabella to have to live with the fact that you were intimate with the woman staying under our roof."

He let go of her hands to rub his chin where he'd nicked himself with the razor. "It's asking a lot of Isabella, but so far she's handling it. I'll find out how well when I see her tonight." After checking his watch he said, "I have to go."

"Wait—"

His gaze swung back to hers. "What is it?"

"Since Ms. Collier is Phillip's mother and has worked her way into the castle, how do you know she won't make trouble for you and Isabella?"

Alex had been waiting for that salvo. "If that had been her intention, she would have surfaced years ago instead of this week. Even then she couldn't go through with telling me I had a son. I had to fly to Colorado in order to pry it out of her.

"At that point she still begged me not to act on the knowledge. When I brought her and Phillip back with me, she asked me again to turn the plane around because she knew what would happen if I didn't.

"Darrell is still suffering over it. If you knew her as I already do, she's frightened of hurting Isabella, so you don't have to worry about her causing problems."

"Listen to you defend her!" Her voice shook. "She's gotten to you the way she did once before. You were obviously so taken with her, you gave her the ring your cousin had made specially for you. Now that she's found you, she has decided to enamor you all over again."

Darrell didn't have to try. Whatever had driven them into each other's arms today, it hadn't been planned, not on either of their parts. His heart almost failed him remembering the lushness of her avid mouth opening to the pressure of his.

"By claiming Phillip so readily, you've allowed her to

believe anything's possible!" his mother exclaimed. "The more I hear about this woman, the more I don't trust her."

He moved to the door, then looked back at her. "If I didn't know something you still don't know, I wouldn't trust her, either."

"What more could there be?"

It was time for the whole truth.

"Phillip's birth mother was named *Melissa* Collier."

That caught his mother's attention in a hurry.

"She died of an aneurism after giving birth to Phillip. Her sister, Darrell, adopted him. The only reason Darrell came looking for me was to help her unhappy son and honor her sister's dying wish that he get to know his father.

"In point of fact, Darrell had no prior knowledge of my existence until two weeks ago when she had the ring traced and saw a picture of me on the Internet. She noticed the strong resemblance to Phillip and jumped to the only conclusion she could.

"Therefore you're going to have to reassess your thinking about her. She has no designs on the man who impregnated her sister." In fact she had every reason to despise him, which made what happened up in the mountains even more remarkable.

If ever anyone looked shell-shocked, it was his mother. "This is unbelievable."

"But true. And you have to admit Darrell's done an amazing job of raising her sister's son."

His mother made a cry like she'd been mortally wounded. "I'll grant you he's a fine boy, but what you've just told me alarms me even more."

"Why?"

"Because I can tell this woman means something to you. I can *feel* it!"

She wasn't his mother for nothing.

"I admit I admire her." He wished that was all he felt for her. "Darrell was only in her teens when Melissa died. Since then she has sacrificed her life for Phillip. She could have put him up for adoption instead of adopting him herself. She's made the perfect home for him. He's bright, talented."

A frantic look crossed over his mother's face. "Does Isabella know he was adopted? Does she realize Ms. Collier isn't his real mother?"

His lips thinned. "Not yet. If she agrees to marry me, I'll tell her the truth on our honeymoon. Hopefully the news that Darrell and I were never involved will relieve her fears.

"But for now, no one but you and Phillip know the truth. I don't want Phillip hurt by this.

"Make no mistake—" His body went rigid. "Darrell's his real mother. It was her eyes he first saw when he came into the world."

The most fabulous eyes Alex had ever seen. Like the rare violet hue of the morning sky silhouetting the peaks of the Alps.

"You know what I meant—"

He opened the door. "I don't have time for this now, Mother. Isabella and her parents are waiting for me."

The whirr of the helicopter's rotors sounded overhead. Phillip and the boys ran into Darrell's room to look at it from the balcony.

"Dad's back! We're going to go meet him.'

"Wait, Phillip—" Darrell cautioned.

"Why?"

"Because he always has important things to do first."

"That's what mother says," Jules muttered. Vito nodded. They adored Alex, but they also revered him as king. Phillip had a different problem. To him Alex was his father. Period.

"He said he'd phone you when he could, sweetheart."

"But it's already afternoon."

Darrell was painfully aware he was long overdue. He and Isabella must have managed to work things out, otherwise he would probably have come home a lot sooner.

In order to pass the time without falling apart, she'd talked Phillip into taking a walk on the extensive grounds with her. Then they'd gone swimming with the boys.

The four of them would still be having fun if clouds hadn't started to gather. At the first sign of lightning she'd insisted they go indoors. A storm was almost upon them. Darrell was thankful the helicopter had landed before Alex got caught in the downpour.

She shivered when she remembered his cousin's plane had gone down in bad weather, leaving his sons fatherless.

They were so darling, Darrell couldn't help but love them. She could tell Phillip liked them, too. It was a heady experience to be looked up to by the younger princes who were already enriching his life.

Alex had been worried about Phillip not wanting to hang around waiting to spend time with him. But his fears were groundless. You couldn't separate Phillip from his father now or ever.

"I'll get it," Phillip called out the second the phone rang.

Darrell's heart raced so hard it was a good thing he picked up instead of her. Since he'd climbed up her balcony, the less she had to interact with Alex the better.

Their conversation didn't last long. Phillip hung up and turned to her with an excited look on his face.

"Dad wants us to meet him at his office. He says he's got something special planned and you have to come, too, Mom, because we're going to have dinner with Aunt Evelyn after."

Aunt Evelyn…

Darrell hadn't even met the boys' mother yet, but Phillip was already calling her aunt.

"Hurrah!" Jules cried enthusiastically.

Under the circumstances Darrell couldn't refuse. It was a good thing she'd put on her pleated tan pants and fitted purple top. Not too dressy, not too casual for her first meeting with his cousin-in-law.

The boys knew their way around the castle blindfolded. She followed them down the exquisitely sculpted marble staircase to the first floor. They took a right through the magnificent vaulted corridors lined with paintings and tapestries leading to the king's official workplace.

"See the flag?" Vito spoke up.

"Yes."

"If the Valleder flag is posted, then you know Uncle Alex is in the city and his ministers can have access to him."

"That's very interesting. Thank you for telling me."

"You're welcome."

The boy knew everything and took it all so seriously, Darrell decided he had the makings of a king.

Then she glimpsed the real king. At the first sight of Alex in a black turtleneck and jeans standing in the huge double doorway, her pulse skittered off the charts.

The boys huddled around him while he gave their dark blond heads a gentle roughing.

Yesterday she'd felt those strong hands in her hair and knew how it felt. She almost passed out reliving the sensation until she remembered he'd spent the night with Isabella.

Judging by his laid-back demeanor, he'd won Isabella over and there was going to be a wedding. Then she would always have the right to his affection.

Darrell couldn't bear it.

"Mom?" Phillip shook her arm, jerking her from a place

she'd promised herself never to go again. Her gaze happened to collide with a penetrating pair of eyes that were more gray than green at the moment.

"When a storm rages, there's a knight whose ghost walks around the castle below the waterline. Chaz and I only saw the back of him one time. I thought we'd all go down and search for him now."

The boys laughed nervously. Phillip smiled, but his heels moved up and down, indicating his adrenaline had kicked in.

"Think you're up to it?"

Alex had issued her a direct challenge she couldn't refuse. In truth she didn't want to. Who else besides Alex would think up something this entertaining for a bunch of adventurous boys on a dark, dreary afternoon inside a castle of all things?

"I wouldn't miss snooping around this place for anything in the world."

Another smile of satisfaction curved his lips. "Then let's go."

With a heavy-duty flashlight in hand, Alex strode down the hall forcing everyone to run after him.

"Admit you're a little freaked, Mom."

She was, but not for the reason her son was suggesting.

Alex led them down another hall and through a heavy wooden door to the ancient part of the castle. A circular stone staircase over a thousand years old seemed to go down, down forever. The only light came from the slit windows spaced every so often. Rain beat against the panes.

Without the flashlight they would have been entombed in total darkness once they reached the bottom.

Alex flashed the beam around the vast cavern with its labyrinths and pillars. Water dripped from the dank walls where moss was growing. Above them she could hear the waves on the lake crashing against the castle walls. It caused her to shiver.

"Whoa—" Phillip whispered. Vito stood manfully by himself, but Jules stuck close to his uncle.

"Stay with me everybody," Alex warned them. They advanced a few feet.

"What are those chains for?" Jules asked.

Darrell could see them lying on the stone floor at the base of one of the pillars.

"When it's good weather, the knight is the castle's prisoner."

"No, he's not, Dad—"

"Shh. I think I can hear him," Alex whispered. He handed Phillip the flashlight. "Go ahead with the boys. See what you can find."

"Come on you guys. Dad's only teasing us."

Strange how the darkness made Alex stand out to Darrell as if it were full daylight. She could feel the warmth from his body though they weren't touching. She knew he was smiling.

"I take it you and your cousin used to come down here to play."

"All the time."

"Did your parents know?"

"Not if we could help it. Security wasn't as tight back then, so we got away with a lot."

"Your son appears to be fearless. You couldn't have planned anything more thrilling than this. He's going to want to bring his friends down here when they come to visit."

The second the words left her mouth, she realized her mistake. "I shouldn't have said that. I apologize."

"For what?" The air sizzled with tension.

"For assuming that everything's normal when I know it's anything but. I—I've been thinking about you and Isabella. The only way your marriage can work is for us to set up a visitation schedule that will make her happy.

"Phillip knows exactly what's at stake here. He might not

like it, but now that he feels your love he'll be able to plan his life around the times when he can see you. It'll work. Maybe next time he can bring his friend Ryan."

She heard the changed tenor of his breathing. "Of course his friends will always be welcome, but I want him around more than two or three times a year, Darrell. I want you to move to Bris."

Her heart slammed into her ribs. "You couldn't mean permanently."

"Is that so hard to understand? It would solve a lot of problems."

For you and our son, Alex. Not for me or the princess or the monarchy.

"I couldn't do that. My life's in Denver. Yours is with Isabella and the family you're going to raise. After your wedding is over and things have settled down for you, Phillip can fly here to see you. As long as he can talk to you on the phone between trips, it'll be fine."

Sucking in her breath she added, "It's awfully chilly down here. I think I'll wait for all of you upstairs."

Relying on her instincts to guide her, she turned back toward the staircase, needing to get away from him before she found herself considering his wishes.

To her dismay she stumbled into the bottom step. But the cry she emitted came from the feel of Alex's hands on her hips. At the first touch she longed for him to turn her in his arms and kiss her as if they had the right to lose themselves in each other.

But he belonged to someone else and she needed to get far away and stay there.

"Did you hurt yourself?" He'd asked the question out of concern, but the way his hands slid up her arms before relinquishing her body told her he hadn't forgotten yesterday's incident. The one she hadn't been able to dismiss from her memory no matter how hard she tried.

"No—I'm all right, thank you."

Frightened by her weakness for him, she began the long circular climb, knowing he couldn't come after her while the boys were still down there.

By the time she reached the top, to her surprise the rest of them weren't far behind her. They filed into the lighted hallway.

"Mom? I didn't think you'd get scared down there."

"I didn't, either." Her voice shook.

But being alone with Alex for any reason was too dangerous now. A few minutes ago she'd been willing to crush him in her arms and be swept away again by the passion that had flared between them on the mountain.

She addressed Jules. "Did you see the ghost?"

"No, but we heard something."

"It was a rat," Vito informed him. Darrell cringed.

"Maybe next time," Alex muttered, taking the flashlight from Phillip. "It looks like the worst of the storm has passed over. Let's hurry home to your mom. I bet she's fixed her homemade Wiener schnitzel for us."

The last thing Darrell felt like doing was meeting the boys' mother. She was too shaken up by what had happened in the dark.

To have lost control yesterday was one thing. To almost lose control again today was something else. She hadn't imagined Alex's low moan once his hands had molded to her body. Desire had engulfed both of them.

Maybe it was because he represented forbidden fruit that she trembled even thinking about him.

Possibly the fact that she was forbidden fruit produced a similar response in him.

This close to the wedding you'd have thought just the opposite would be true.

Maybe this was Alex's own sort of private bachelor party—

a kind of midnight-hour urge to let go before he became a married man.

That explanation made the most sense to Darrell.

It was kind of like his princely lapse with Melissa years ago. Only her sister hadn't had the sense to run from the fire.

Apparently the Collier women were pushovers, but Darrell was putting an end to it right now.

CHAPTER SEVEN

"Do you know going down those steps made me a little dizzy?" Darrell said loud enough for everyone to hear. "I need to rest for a while. Will you please tell Evelyn how sorry I am? We'll meet another time."

"It made me kind of dizzy, too," Jules piped up. Bless his heart.

Alex herded them along the hallway. "Go ahead with the boys, Phillip. I'll see your mom to the apartment, then I'll come."

No!

"Actually, Alex, I'd like Phillip to come with me."

Maybe it was the tone in her voice. Whatever the explanation, for once Alex didn't insist and her son didn't fight her.

"Sure, Mom. You don't look very good."

"If I feel better later, we'll walk over."

The boys acted disappointed. She didn't dare glance at Alex.

Shifting around she headed toward the center staircase.

It seemed to take forever until she could hurry up the steps and down the hall to their apartment. Phillip followed her inside and shut the door.

She went on through to her bedroom. After slipping off her sandals, she lay down on the bed, curling up on her side.

Phillip sat next to her. "You don't like Dad, huh."

She threw her arm over her eyes. What he'd just said was better than hearing "You're in love with him, huh." But neither version was satisfactory.

"What makes you say that, sweetheart?"

"You never want to be around him. I know it's because he hurt my real mother. But he didn't *try* to hurt her."

Darrell was his real mother, but she knew what he meant.

"I don't dislike him, Phillip. I've come to realize he's a wonderful man."

"Then how come you're mean to him?"

She raised her head to look at him. "Mean?"

"Yeah. He does all these neat things and you always want to stay in here."

Good heavens.

"That's so the two of you can have time together alone."

"But he wants you to do everything with us."

"He said that?"

"No. But I can tell. Remember at the house when he said he didn't blame me for hating him?"

"Yes?"

"Well I think he thinks you still hate him."

Phillip had it all wrong, but she couldn't tell him the truth.

Another troubled sigh came out of him. "Even if you don't like him, can't you try to be nicer?"

If only Phillip knew the truth. Thank goodness he didn't! "Of course, sweetheart."

"Thanks." After a minute he asked, "Mom?"

"Yes?"

"I wish he wasn't getting married. I wish—"

"I know what you wish," she interrupted him. "You wish your real mother were still alive so the three of you could be a family."

But even if Melissa were alive, nothing would be different. Alex would still be marrying Isabella. Phillip's fantasy wasn't written in the stars.

She sat up. "Do you know what I think?"

"What?"

"We need to go home tomorrow and let him get married." I need to get as far away from him as possible. "After his honeymoon I'm sure he'll want you to come and stay with him until school starts."

"But you won't be here."

"No. My home is in Denver, but you have two homes now."

"I don't want two homes. Steve hates it."

"You never told me that before," she said and slid to the edge of the bed. "No matter what, you've finally been united with your father. Just remember that last week you didn't even know him or know where he lived."

"I know."

She could hear the tears in his voice.

"Do you like it here, Phillip?"

"I *love* it. Do you?"

If ever she heard a searching question, that was it. "Who wouldn't love Switzerland. It's out of this world."

"Dad's so fun. I don't want to leave, but I don't want you to go." Moisture bathed his cheeks. He burrowed his head in her shoulder.

"I have to go home, sweetheart."

He sniffed. "Then I guess I'll go with you. Isabella won't want me around for all their wedding stuff."

Such a gut-wrenching dilemma for a twelve-year-old. It thrilled her he loved Darrell that much, but her heart ached for him.

"Tell you what. I'm not feeling as nauseous as before. Let's spend the rest of today with your father."

"Honest?"

"Yes."

Because Phillip had made a decision, she could get through a few more hours in Alex's company knowing other people would be around.

"When he comes back with us to say good-night, then you can tell him we're flying home the minute we can make reservations."

"Okay."

"Think of all the fun stuff you have to tell your friends. You can show them the pictures you've taken. They'll love all the souvenirs you bought them the other day with the boys. Especially all that Swiss chocolate!"

"Yeah."

With the matter settled for the time being, they both freshened up before leaving the castle. Phillip knew the way to the pale yellow palace located on the west end of the grounds. It lay nestled amidst a grove of giant trees like a hidden jewel.

"Hey, Mom—don't you think this place looks like that house in *Sound of Music*?" They'd just entered the courtyard where water had pooled here and there because of the storm.

"A little, but this is much grander."

"Vito said their grandparents live here with them."

"How lucky the boys are to have Evelyn's parents around now that their father is gone."

"Not *her* parents, Mom. They live in Bavaria. I'm talking about dad's aunt and uncle, but they're away on a trip right now. Jules says his Grandpa Vittorio is mean."

"Is that description yours or his?"

"His. He says Vito's afraid of him."

That didn't sound good.

Phillip knocked on the door, breaking her train of thought. Soon a maid answered followed by the boys.

Once inside the elegant foyer flanked by various rooms,

Darrell marveled over the twin staircases on either side rising like a swan's neck to the second floor.

The beauty and symmetry of the architecture was stunning.

"I've always loved this palace." Alex's deep voice came from somewhere behind her.

She swung around and discovered him standing next to a very pretty brunette woman. She appeared to be in her early thirties.

"Evelyn and Darrell? It's time you two met."

"Hello," Darrell said first and extended her hand. "Thank you for inviting us to your home. I've been anxious to meet you. Your boys are charming."

Evelyn flashed her a friendly smile. "So is Phillip. I don't believe this family has ever had so much excitement."

"I'm sure you haven't," Darrell said.

Thankfully the other woman didn't sound judgmental, which was more than Darrell could have hoped for.

"Come in and sit down."

The room they entered was surprisingly comfortable and modern in its decor. Darrell found the nearest chair. Alex remained standing while Evelyn took a place on one of the couches opposite her.

"We're expecting Aunt Katerina any minute. I was so wishing you would recover enough to make it."

Alex's mother was coming, too? Darrell had hoped to avoid meeting her this trip, but maybe it was better to get it over with. After all, she was Phillip's grandmother.

"I'm feeling better, thank you. It will be an honor to meet her."

Evelyn cocked her head. "I can't believe Alex talked you into going down under the castle. Charles could never get me near it."

"I'm afraid Phillip wouldn't have let me live it down if I hadn't joined in."

"Jules was very impressed with you. It was the boys' first time ghost hunting. He told me I had to go next time."

Alex chuckled. "If you two will excuse me, I believe mother has arrived."

After he left the room Evelyn confided, "Another Valleder in the family has already transformed my boys' lives. What's amazing is how much they look alike. All three could be brothers."

Darrell nodded. "That's what I was thinking earlier. If I didn't know better, I would have thought they were all Alex's children."

"Vito reminds me of Alex's father, very serious and steady. Jules on the other hand has a happy-go-lucky temperament, more like my husband's."

Darrell's glance darted to a credenza against the wall. "Is that a picture of your husband?"

"Yes, that's Charles."

"I'm so sorry about his accident."

"So am I…" Her voice trailed.

"May I look at it?"

"Of course." She got up and handed it to Darrell. "It's a family portrait of the four of us taken a few months before his plane crashed."

"I don't know how you lived through it," Darrell murmured, fighting tears.

"I'm afraid I'll never get over losing him."

As Darrell studied it, she was astonished to discover that Alex's cousin looked enough like him to be his brother. In fact the more she looked at the picture, the more she noticed striking similarities between the boys' father and Phillip. If he was as wonderful as Alex, she couldn't imagine how Evelyn was functioning.

"Darrell?"

At the sound of Alex's voice she glanced over at the entry, almost dropping the picture.

"I'd like you to meet my mother, Katerina Valleder."

The lovely brown-haired woman possessed all the style and grace of a former queen. At a glance Darrell could see she'd bequeathed her good looks to her son who was devastatingly attractive in a formal, dark blue suit. The pristine white shirt and specially monogrammed tie with the Valleder crest proclaimed him the royal head of their centuries-old dynasty.

She got up from the chair. "How do you do, Mrs. Valleder." They both shook hands. Darrell knew that wasn't the way his mother was normally addressed. No doubt people said "Your Highness." Yet Alex had made it easy for Darrell.

He made everything easy. She trembled to realize she'd never be able to banish his image from her mind, or heart.

His mother's gray eyes studying Darrell so intently reminded her of the man who haunted her dreams. "It's a pleasure to meet the mother of my grandson."

"Thank you. He has yearned for a grandmother since he was old enough to ask why he didn't have one like his friends."

Alex took that moment to tell his mother what Phillip had said on the jet about the queen-size bed. The older woman actually laughed and Evelyn joined in. When it subsided she said, "I see you're holding a picture of Evelyn's family."

"Yes. We were just remarking on the dominance of the Valleder genes."

Katerina nodded. "After spending a few hours with the boys, I've decided Phillip is a composite of all the men in our family."

Emotion welled up in Darrell to realize her son came from a great heritage. Whatever their true feelings, these women *were* great to be kind and gracious to her and Phillip. Their impeccable breeding could be a model for others.

Melissa had gravitated to Alex, instinctively recognizing

without knowing that he was a man hewn from clay reserved for those with a special destiny.

"I wish you could have seen the boys' eyes once we started down that spooky staircase with Alex today. They're all so cute—"

"Aren't they?" Evelyn's eyes had grown moist.

Darrell handed the picture back to her. She set it on the table, then smiled.

"Now that everyone's here, shall we go in to dinner? It's ready."

Alex escorted his mother across the foyer to the charming dining room. Jules took over and helped her to her seat at one end of the table. Vito assisted his mother to the chair next to her.

Not to be outdone, Phillip—a quick study—came around and guided Darrell to her place opposite Evelyn. It was a first for him. Judging by the mirthful glance Alex flashed Darrell, he knew it, too.

Enjoying the moment too much, she averted her eyes while he sat down at the head of the candlelit table. It was resplendent with royal Valleder china and silverware placed on the cutwork lace linen.

He patted the chair on his right side for Phillip to join him. Once he was seated, Alex looked at his nephews. They weren't really his nephews, but as he'd told her and Phillip, he felt like their uncle. "Who wants to say grace?"

Darrell fought not to laugh at the dismay on their faces.

"Maybe Phillip would like to say it," his mother suggested.

"Sure, Grandma."

He folded his arms, closed his eyes and gave the usual prayer Darrell had taught him to say over the food.

After a collective "amen," Alex thanked him, then two of the staff began serving dinner.

Darrell was so proud of Phillip right then she could have burst. Though he was like an unpolished diamond and always would be, he had his shining moments and this had been one of them.

She saw the tender look Alex gave his son. It dissolved Darrell's bones.

No sooner had they started to eat than his cell phone rang. She noticed him glance at the caller ID, then get up from the table. "Excuse me for a moment."

The moment turned into twenty minutes. By the time he came back in the dining room, they were finishing their strudel dessert.

"I'm sorry, but something important has come up and I have to leave."

"Are you going to San Ravino to see Isabella?" Phillip asked the question no one else dared.

"Yes."

"When will you be back?"

"Tomorrow."

A crestfallen look crossed over Phillip's face, one everyone could see.

"Thank you for dinner, Evelyn."

"It was my pleasure."

Darrell knew everyone at the table was thinking how outspoken Phillip had been. It was something they would have to get used to because he'd been born with that trait. She couldn't look at Alex right then.

"I'll take Darrell and Phillip home when I go," Katerina spoke up.

"Thank you, Mother. I'll see you tomorrow, Phillip."

"Sure, Dad."

Alex flashed Darrell a hooded glance she couldn't decipher before he departed. It left her shaken. Did he kiss Isabella with the same passion he'd kissed her? Was he counting the minutes until they were together? Darrell couldn't take much more of this.

Ten minutes after he'd left the palace she heard the helicopter taking off. Phillip's expression mirrored her spirits, which had plummeted to a new low.

"Good afternoon, gentlemen."

Alex looked around the oval conference table in his office where his executive staff and ministers were assembled. Leo exchanged a private nod with him.

"I can only recall two times since I became king that I've had to call for an emergency session. Both times were due to the threat of a student uprising. This time the situation is different.

"I just flew back from San Ravino. After a great deal of soul searching over the past few days, Isabella and I have decided to call off our wedding."

The silence that filled the room was deafening.

"I've prepared a statement for the press, which I've given to Carl. Regardless of what you might hear, the princess and I parted on amicable terms."

More silence, the kind produced by shock reverberated throughout his office.

"As all of you have heard by now, very recently I discovered I have a twelve-year-old son who was born and raised in Colorado in the United States without my knowledge.

"The king could have ignored the revelation, but the man could not. Phillip Collier is my flesh and blood. I love him and have claimed him.

"Because of this action I'm fully aware that public sentiment will go against me. If I think it's for the good of the country, I'll step down."

At this point many heads had lowered, but not Leo's. The other man's eyes remained suspiciously bright.

"I recall a conversation I once had with father. He told me he didn't have any friends. His comment hurt me. When I asked him why, he said, 'That's the definition of a king.'

"I didn't understand what he meant, but I do now. No matter what decision you make as sovereign, you're going to hurt someone.

"By recognizing my son, I dare say I don't have a friend left, starting with the great men I've let down assembled in this historic conference room.

"But when I met Phillip for the first time and he said, 'You're my dad,' something went through me I can't describe. All I know is, I wanted to be all the things I could see in his eyes."

He cleared his throat. "Thank you for coming, gentlemen. That's everything."

On his way to his inner office to phone Darrell, Carl intercepted him. "Your Majesty? While you were in conference, Ms. Collier phoned to say that in case you were wondering, she and your son have gone into town to do some shopping for a few hours."

Disappointed they weren't immediately available, he thanked Carl before ringing Rudy. "How long ago did Ms. Collier leave the castle?"

"The car just pulled away."

"Alert the guard at the outer gate to prevent them from leaving the grounds."

Without conscious thought Alex left his office via a private staircase. Summoning his driver, he climbed in the back of his limo and told him to head for the north gate. He didn't expel a breath until he saw the limo between the security men's cars stopped at the gate.

Alex jumped out of the car before it had pulled to a stop.

* * *

"Hey, Mom? There's Dad!"

Darrell's hands clutched the armrests. What a fool she was to think she and Phillip could slip away from him, even for a few hours. At this point she was afraid to spend any more time with him.

When he suddenly climbed in the limo and sat across from her next to Phillip, the blood pounded in her ears.

His gaze narrowed on her face. "I got your message, but you can't go shopping yet or you'll spoil my surprise."

The car started to move, but instead of going to the castle, it appeared to be headed toward another part of the grounds.

Darrell's body trembled. She couldn't take another one of his surprises, let alone handle being in his presence a second longer.

"Will I like it?" Phillip teased.

"It's guaranteed."

"Where are we going?"

"You'll find out."

Eventually the limo pulled up to one end of the stable.

Phillip darted her an excited glance. Darrell had an idea Alex was going to give him his own horse. The boys each had a pony.

Alex turned to his son. "Go inside that door. It leads to the vet's office. He's waiting for you."

"The vet?"

"Yes. I'll be along in a minute."

On a new burst of energy, Phillip climbed out of the limo and sprinted inside.

"Alex—I'm glad we're alone because there's something important I have to tell you, and—"

"Isabella has called off the wedding," he broke in on her. "Permanently."

"Oh, no—"

The stabbing pain of guilt drove Darrell from the car. She headed blindly for the castle, running faster than she'd ever run in her life. But she couldn't outrun the limo. It drove alongside her until she slowed down and Alex urged her to climb back in.

Embarrassed to have caused a scene, she did his bidding. He didn't say anything until they'd arrived at the castle and he'd escorted her to the apartment she and Phillip had barely vacated. Once he'd opened the door for her, he followed her inside.

She whirled around, wet-faced. "Let me talk to Isabella in person. I can fix this."

He shook his handsome head. "This can't be fixed."

"Of course it can! She's in pain and frightened. Any woman would be. I don't care if she was raised a princess. She's never been married, and she wants it to work! I need to reassure her she has nothing to fear from Phillip."

He studied her through veiled eyes. "It's not Phillip she's worried about."

"Then what?" She kept wiping her eyes.

"I'm afraid it is I she doesn't trust."

"Of course she does. Otherwise she would have broken her betrothal to you long ago. Please let me try to appeal to her. I'll be happy to fly there right now if she wants."

"That would be like pouring acid on an open wound."

"Why?" she cried out aghast.

He rubbed the back of his neck. "You really need me to spell it out?"

"Yes!"

His gaze played over her features. "She says I'm different since coming back from Denver. She senses something she's never felt before."

"That's because you just found out you're a father. Of course you're different. Your entire world has been turned upside down."

"True, but this is something apart from Phillip."

She feared what was coming but she faced him without averting her eyes. "What exactly?"

"Contrary to what you overheard the desk clerk tell that tourist the day you were checking out of the Hotel Otter, Isabella and I were never a love match. But both of us were willing to fulfill our royal duty in the hope that love would grow."

She swallowed hard. "Didn't you ever sleep together?"

"No."

"Because of rules?"

"No."

"Didn't she ever want to?"

"Yes."

Darrell reeled from his blunt honesty. His admission brought her indescribable joy, but she could never let him know that.

"When I told her I had a son, it changed how Isabella feels about me."

"But that was thirteen years ago when you were only what? Twenty? Did you tell her Melissa died so she doesn't need to feel threatened?"

He didn't answer right away.

Her eyes widened. "She still thinks *I'm* that woman doesn't she!" Darrell's body started to shake. "How could you do that to her? To me?" She thumped her chest.

"I need to tell you a story first."

"I don't want to hear it!" she raged while he stood there as calm as a summer morning.

"You'll want to hear this one. The whole good of the monarchy hangs in the balance."

Put like that in such a solemn tone, he'd left her little choice but to listen.

"Let's go out to the balcony."

She didn't want to go anywhere with him, but he left her alone in the drawing room, expecting her to come to him. She could either comply with his wishes or string this out until she had a heart attack.

Defeated, she chose the former and found him staring out over the placid water that had formed whitecaps in yesterday's storm.

He must have sensed her presence. "I wish you could have met my cousin, Chaz. It's the name I made up for him because he didn't like the name Charles."

Darrell blinked in surprise.

"We were the same age. He could be a hellion. That's what made him so fascinating to me. Growing up I suppose you could say he was my alter ego.

"When I was old enough to read, my father put a little sign at the top of my bathroom mirror. It said, "One day you'll be king. Remember."

A moan escaped her throat.

He turned to her. "I agree it was a terrible thing to do to a child. Uncle Vittorio was no different. If anything happened to father or me, the line of succession would go to him and eventually Chaz.

"At times he could be cruel, even abusive. He was a man who believed in corporal punishment to curb any rebellion in his son. When Chaz started drinking too much, I understood. He came to me when things got bad with my uncle. I often covered for him. That's why he gave me that ring."

Darrell's stomach lurched remembering what Phillip had said about the boys' grandfather being mean. How awful they had to live in such close proximity to him.

"My uncle was very ambitious, and still is. He would do most anything to be king, and has resented the fact that Chaz died instead of me."

"That's horrible," she whispered.

"In order to honor my promise to Father to marry Isabella,

I'd hoped she could get past this and agree to go ahead with the wedding while believing you are his birth mother."

"I still don't understand why you haven't told her the truth."

He eyed her balefully. "Because up to now it's been less complicated this way. The truth wouldn't change the fact that I fathered a son with a woman from my past. That's what has hurt Isabella.

"However once my uncle learns of Phillip's existence and discovers you didn't give birth to him, he'll enjoy humiliating you and the memory of your sister. It could bring up a lot of unnecessary pain which could end up hurting Phillip. As it is, I fully expect my uncle to rally the cabinet to repudiate me and my bastard son, forcing me to step down so he can be king."

The air got trapped in her lungs. "Your own uncle would do that?"

Lines of strain bracketed his mouth. His expression haunted her. He unexpectedly moved toward her and cupped her face in his hands. "The new millenium hasn't changed the nature of some men," his voice grated.

"Does your mother know the wedding is off?"

"Yes."

"Does she know about Melissa?"

"Yes."

"I'm glad you told her the truth, but she must be devastated!"

"I'm not going to pretend she's happy about my broken engagement, but one look at Phillip caused her to accept him as her grandson. That in itself is an indication of where her true heart lies."

She bit her lip. "There's absolutely no chance of Isabella changing her mind?"

"None. If there were no Phillip, we would have gone through with the wedding and done our best to make a good life together. But Phillip's existence has changed destiny. Now Isabella will have a chance to find the kind of love she's seen with some of her friends' marriages."

Darrell's eyes played over his face. "And what about you?"

"Does it matter? After what I've told you, you have every right to loathe me. As my father once told me, a king has no friends because every decision he makes offends someone."

Darrell didn't want to hear about all the damage his father and uncle had done to him. "Let's leave my feelings out of it," she blurted. "What's going to happen when the country hears you're not getting married?"

"I guess I'm going to find out. It'll be on the five o'clock evening news."

"Already?" The thought of Alex being forced to abdicate tortured her.

"I've just come from a cabinet meeting where I explained the situation and gave a statement to the press. If there's a groundswell of resentment against me, I'll step down."

"What exactly did you tell them?"

When she heard everything she felt ill.

"This is all because of *me*." She buried her face in her hands. "My trip to Bris has ruined your life."

"It gained me a son, Darrell," his voice shook. "No man could receive greater news."

Her head flew back. "But you're no ordinary man—" The tears streamed down her cheeks. "You're a king who might have to give up everything."

His eyes blazed with green fire. "*You* gave up everything for Phillip. Do you regret it?"

"Of course not!" she cried.

"Then we understand each other," he said on a note of finality.

While she stood there shivering, his cell phone rang. He answered it and spoke in Romanche for a few minutes. When he clicked off he said, "Something's come up. I have to get back to my office. Tell Phillip I'll phone him as soon as I'm free."

She watched his hard-muscled body leave her bedroom. The second she heard the outer door close, she flung herself on the bed and sobbed. Fifteen minutes later she was still agonizing over the reason for his broken engagement when she heard her animated son calling to her.

Jerked back to the present, she rolled off the bed and stood up, smoothing the hair out of her eyes. "I'm in my room, sweetheart. What is it?"

"You won't believe it. Dad got me a dog! It's a St. Bernard from that monastery in the Alps I told him I saw on television. It's the kind I always wanted. He's beautiful."

As her son came running into the bedroom, he was crying for happiness. A St. Bernard was his dream dog, but the condo didn't allow pets, not even miniatures.

"I'm going to train him how to save me and bring me drinks in a keg."

Darrell was in too much emotional turmoil to respond.

"He's almost all white and he's an older puppy because the monks weren't going to sell him, but they did it for Dad. I told him we wouldn't be back until after the wedding, so he's going to take care of him. But I wish we never had to go… Can I keep him, Mom?"

He wanted her permission.

"Mom?" he asked tentatively. "You've been crying, huh. Did you tell Dad to send the dog back? Is that why you didn't come inside the vet's office?"

"No, sweetheart. Of course you can keep him."

"Then what's wrong? Did you two have a fight? Where is he?"

"He's in his office working."

After calling off a royal wedding the entire country had

been looking forward to, he was probably trying to put out a dozen fires at once.

"Can I phone him?"

"After the great amount of trouble your father has gone to, I know he'd appreciate a call from his son thanking him for the dog."

"I love you, Mom." Almost knocking the wind out of her with his hug, he reached for the phone.

CHAPTER EIGHT

"YOUR MAJESTY? Your son is on line two."

"Thank you, Carl." He shoved his paperwork aside and turned on the speaker. "Phillip?"

"Dad— Thanks for the dog. I love him more than anything! Mom says I can keep him. You're the best! I love you."

Alex realized that Darrell was going to leave it up to him to tell Phillip about the wedding being called off. Nothing could have pleased him more.

He got up from the chair. "I love you, too, and I think this calls for a celebration. Why don't you and your mother come to my apartment in an hour and we'll have an early dinner together."

"I can't wait!"

The lump was still lodged in his throat. "Neither can I. See you soon."

The second Phillip hung up, Alex called the kitchen to arrange for dinner to be sent up, then he left the office for his suite.

He showered and dressed in a sport shirt and slacks, unable to remember the last time he'd been this excited about anything.

Heaven forgive him but he hadn't given Isabella a thought since he'd kissed her a final goodbye.

If ever he needed proof that a marriage between them

would have been dead wrong, the euphoria he was feeling right now was it.

He'd instructed his staff to set the table on the terrace off the sunroom. It overlooked the ancient part of the city with its cobblestoned streets and Romanesque churches. Phillip would enjoy looking through the binoculars.

As he went to the bedroom to get them, his cell phone rang. He checked the caller ID and clicked on.

"Mother?"

"Whatever you're doing, I have to talk to you now."

He gripped the phone tighter. "What is it?"

"I just had a phone call from Carl. Your uncle heard the news through a palace source. He and Renate have cut short their trip. They're on their way home."

Alex wasn't surprised. "If he thinks he can put me and Isabella back together again, I have news for him."

"That's not his agenda, Alex. It never has been," his mother confessed.

His brows knit together. "What are you talking about?"

"When your cousin died, and you still didn't seem eager to marry Isabella, it was Vittorio's intention to talk you into marrying Evelyn."

Evelyn?

Alex was dumbstruck.

"Finding out you and Isabella are not getting married is the reason he'll be arriving before morning. Carl let me know Vittorio has been secretly calling cabinet members to form a coalition forcing you to marry Evelyn for the good of the monarchy. He expects you to send Darrell and your son packing."

Over the years Alex had tried to control his anger against his uncle for the way he'd treated Chaz. But by trying to pull off a coup like this to get closer to the crown, he'd started a war. One Alex vowed his uncle wouldn't win.

"He's out of his mind. It'll never happen."

"I'm afraid his jealousy of your father has driven him beyond rationality."

"Dad?" a voice called out. "We're here!"

"Mother? I'm sorry but I have to go. Thank you for telling me this. I'll be in touch later." He clicked off.

"Come out on the terrace."

In a few seconds his son ran in to thank him again. Alex leveled his gaze on Darrell.

The white sundress against her golden skin was as stunning as her hair. The last rays of sun picked out the individual strands of gold and silver. Combined with eyes of amethyst, he couldn't look anywhere else.

"I'm going to call him Brutus."

With that declaration Alex was forced to pay attention to his son.

"It's the perfect Roman name."

"This is a fantastic view of the city," Darrell murmured. "It's like being in the helicopter."

"Try these." As Alex handed her the binoculars he'd brought out, her flowery fragrance swept him away.

He noticed her hands weren't quite steady as she lifted them to her eyes.

"How incredible. You have to see this, Phillip." Ignoring Alex, she handed him the glasses.

"Whoa—You can see everything!"

"From the time I was old enough to wander around by myself I always loved this view. So did Chaz. He would bring over his telescope and we would spy on people. When my father caught us, we were permanently banned from this apartment."

Phillip laughed. "I bet you got in a lot of trouble."

Darrell didn't want to think about what form it had taken for Chaz.

“Hey, Dad, what’s the secret about the apartment Mom and I are staying in? Jules and Vito said nobody ever gets to stay in there.”

Phillip wasn’t the only one who was curious. Darrell had been dying to know.

“That’s because down through the centuries it’s been reserved as the bridal chamber after a royal wedding.”

Darrell tamped down her moan.

“The rest of the time it remains vacant.”

“You mean it’s never been used since Aunt Evelyn and Uncle Charles got married?”

“That’s right. At least not officially. Unofficially Chaz and I sneaked in there and slept in our bedrolls many times. We got a huge kick out of knowing that no one else in the castle knew what we were doing.”

“That’s so cool. If I could live anywhere in the castle, that’s the place I’d choose.”

“I figured as much, so I decided to let you stay in it.”

“Are you and Isabella going to use it? You know, after you get married?”

A band constricted Darrell’s lungs while she waited for Alex’s answer.

“No.”

“How come?”

He put an arm around Phillip’s shoulders, guiding him to the table. “Because Isabella and I decided to call off the wedding.”

Phillip’s head jerked around. His face had closed up. “Because of me, huh.”

“No.”

“You don’t have to lie, Dad. Isabella hates me. That’s why she broke up with you.”

“Hate’s a strong word. I’m afraid she can’t get over the fact that I met your mother first.”

"You couldn't help that!"

"You're right. We agreed Isabella needs to be the first and only woman in her future husband's life."

"Do you feel awful?"

"I would if I didn't know that deep down she'll be a lot happier with someone else."

"Aren't you going to miss her?"

"Not in the way you mean. I wasn't in love with her. We didn't ever date the way your mom has done with Jack. It's not the same thing."

"Does this mean you have to find another princess to marry?"

"Actually I don't have to do anything."

When that news sank in, Phillip's smile returned. "That's because you're the king."

Alex's mouth curved into an irresistible smile. "For once that makes me really happy." He looked at Darrell with an almost triumphant gleam as he said it. She glanced away for self-preservation and found a place at the table.

They all sat down to eat.

"Hey, Mom—we don't have to go home now. Can Brutus sleep in my room? I promise to do all the work."

Darrell had just unfolded her napkin. "Why don't we talk about that later."

"I think now is a good time," Alex inserted. "Whenever I have a problem to solve, I call my cabinet together and each one of them presents their point of view. Why don't you go first? Tell your mother and me what you think would be best for your happiness."

Phillip put down his empty milk glass and stared soberly at his father. The white moustache added to the poignancy of the moment. "I wish Mom and I could live here with you all the time."

Alex nodded. “That idea makes me the happiest, too. What about you, Darrell?”

He hadn’t helped the situation with that kind of input. Her emotions were too churned up to think or eat.

“I have a life and a job in Denver, but you can stay with your father for the rest of the summer. We’ll e-mail each other every day. It’ll work.”

“You could get another job here.”

“I’m sure I could, but our situation isn’t like anyone else’s. Your father is a world figure who leads a public life, so he has to live above reproach.”

“What does that mean?”

She sucked in her breath. “It means no one would respect him if his son’s mother were to live here, too. People can be cruel about things they don’t understand. A king who doesn’t have the respect of his people is no king at all.

“When I say I can’t live here I mean not in this castle, this town or this country. It would never look right.”

Phillip fought tears. An uncomfortable silence ensued. Finally he said, “I don’t feel like eating.”

Darrell could relate.

“Can I go say good-night to Brutus?”

“All right, but don’t be too long.”

He stood up eyeing them both. “I wish…oh forget it,” he muttered and ran out of the apartment.

“If you can’t guess what he wanted to say, I can,” Alex drawled.

By now Darrell was a trembling mass of feelings. “This is an absurd conversation. Phillip knows you have to marry royalty.”

“You’re wrong. I told him I didn’t have to do anything because it’s true. I can conduct my personal life as I wish. If I want to marry you, I can,” he added.

"How many of the kings before you have married a nonroyal?"

"None. They've gotten around it by having mistresses, but that's not my style. There's no law against a so-called mixed marriage, only against our children inheriting the throne."

Our children?

"How about it, Darrell? Would you like to take me on as your husband?"

She pasted a superficial smile on her face. "I've decided you have a lot more of Chaz in you than I originally thought."

"We weren't cousins for nothing. Since my first attempt to get married for the good of the monarchy has failed, and you've rejected Jack's proposal, why don't we enter into an arranged marriage for the noblest of reasons. *Our* son.

"For one thing it will solve the 'beyond reproach' problem. For another, my mother will be relieved I'm no longer a good for nothing bachelor. Best of all, our son will be elated."

Darrell jumped up from the table. "Don't say any more. This isn't a joke."

His gaze trapped hers. "I do know the difference. In this case I think Phillip's idea is brilliant even if he didn't come right out and say the words."

Suddenly Alex was on his feet, an imposing figure. "Darrell Collier? Will you marry me and come live at my castle with me and our son until death do us part and beyond?"

Her heart was thundering in her chest. "This is preposterous!" She was shaking so hard she had to hold on to the back of the chair. They faced each other across the table. As long as it was there between them, she felt a little more protected.

"Phillip confided that you don't like me very much because I hurt your sister. I can understand that. It's something I'm going to have to work on if you'll give me the chance."

Darrell moaned. That day in the mountains when they'd

kissed each other like two desperate lovers made a mockery of Phillip's remark.

"I know you don't hate me," he continued in that deep cadence. "At least not for what I did to your sister. So I'm assuming you've allowed Phillip to go on thinking something that isn't true for another reason altogether."

Her proud chin lifted. "Then please allow me to keep my reason to myself."

"Of course. But that doesn't have to stop us from getting married to give Phillip the family he's always yearned for. If the ceremony is performed soon, it will make the most sense.

"Everyone will realize ours was a real love match, the kind that produced a son long before we took our vows. Isabella will be vindicated in her feelings. It will help her to recover faster knowing I married for love."

Darrell wished he'd stop talking. She couldn't take any more.

"In view of our feelings for each other, people might tend to forgive me for unintentionally hurting Isabella. They understand a true romance when one comes along. A wedding between a royal and a commoner who already have a son could set the seal on the future of the country, bringing us into the twenty-first century."

"Or turn everyone against you—" Her voice trembled.

"In case things get worse, I'll step down."

She tried to swallow, but couldn't. "You don't mean that."

He folded his arms. "Try me and see. Chaz and I used to talk about it all the time. Confronted with a choice, which I didn't have before Phillip came into my life, I'd rather be his full-time father in Denver."

She shook her head, causing her hair to swish against her burning cheek. "What kind of a king are you?"

"Certainly not the one my father envisioned."

"You know what I meant, Alex. Don't patronize me over something this crucial."

"You think that's what I'm doing?" he fired back. "Your sense of duty makes you more fit to be a king's consort than any of the royal princesses I know.

"As I told you before, father would be proud of you. Maybe appealing to your noblest instinct is the way to win you around."

"It's not a case of winning me around. I couldn't marry you under *any* circumstances."

"If I moved to Denver, marriage wouldn't be necessary. I'll buy me a mountain cabin with horses above Colorado Springs. Phillip can travel between our two homes, just like Steve does."

She lowered her head. "There's no use talking to you."

"I'm sorry you feel that way. You're free to leave my apartment at any time. But before you go, I have one more thing to tell you."

Her heart was bumping like an off-balance washing machine.

"I don't want to hear it. Every time you say something like that, I realize I'm in a little deeper, making it impossible to extricate myself."

His satisfied smile twisted her insides. "Then I guess you have some real soul searching to do."

Her nails bit into the skin of her palms. "Your mother wouldn't let you step down."

"Aside from the fact that my decision is law, I cut the apron strings when I was Phillip's age. I follow my conscience." His gaze impaled her. "Just as you followed yours when you came to the castle requesting an audience with me. Contrary to common belief, it isn't only mothers who run into a burning building."

When she saw the determination in his eyes, she knew this was no game. He was in deadly earnest.

It shook her so violently she had trouble catching her breath.

"You can't abdicate. This is your life. There are too many people depending on you. You can't do it. I won't let you do it."

"Good. Then we'll say our vows tonight in the chapel."

She broke into frightened laughter because he always meant what he said. Her eyes searched his. "Why tonight?"

"That was the one thing I still had to tell you. The news about Isabella and me has reached my uncle's ears. My source tells me he's coming back from his trip and will be here before morning. He's the prince of Plessur, the second most powerful man in the country next to the king.

"As I told you, he's always wanted the crown for himself and wants to force me to marry Evelyn in order to get closer to it. If he gets enough members of my cabinet behind him, things could get ugly."

Darrell's hand had gone to her throat. "What's wrong with him?"

"He's totally irrational right now, but if I pull a checkmate strategy tonight, my marriage to you will be a fait accompli. To try to undo it might prove more embarrassing to him than to me."

Darrell was aghast. "This is like something out of a Machiavellian drama."

His eyes had formed slits. "Welcome to my world."

"You're not joking. That's what is so frightening about this."

"I would never lie to you, particularly about something this vital. If we've said our vows by the time he arrives, it will make his position much more difficult."

Another shiver attacked her body.

"The sooner I make an honest woman of you, the faster the nine-day wonder will be over. Depending on how many friends I have at the highest government level, everything should get back to normal."

A cry escaped her lips. "When it comes to you, there's no such thing as normal."

What he'd just told her had sent her into shock.

"I'm a normal man, Darrell. In case you were wondering, I want you in my bed."

His stark frankness knocked the foundations out from under her.

"I plan to be your husband in every sense of the word. Don't tell me you'll marry me if you can't be a wife to me. Being around Phillip makes me hungry for another child."

"What if I can't?" her voice squeaked.

"Have children, you mean?"

"No. I meant, what if I can't marry you?"

A remote expression crossed over his rugged features. "In that case I'll move to Colorado Springs and make a new life for myself."

"You could marry another princess!"

"For you to say that means I never knew the real you."

She tossed her head. "I'm not sure who the real me is anymore. I only know that you'd be giving up the great heritage you were born to. Who would rule if you didn't?"

"Depending on public sentiment, my mother would act as regent until Vito comes of age at eighteen."

She groaned because there was no satisfactory solution.

He moved closer. "Having met Phillip, I've discovered fatherhood is more important than anything else. In time I hope to find a woman who wants me as much as I want her. Someone Phillip will like."

There wasn't a woman in existence who wouldn't want him. She needed to get away from him to think. While they'd been talking it had grown dark.

"I—I'd better go check on him."

She started walking through the sunroom to the outer door of his suite. He stayed where he was.

"I'll be by in a half hour to hear your answer."

After she closed the door, he pulled out his cell phone and called his mother.

"This isn't the king calling. This is your son begging for your help. I need you to phone the archbishop and ask him to come to the castle immediately. He'll do it for you."

His mother gasped. "You're going to marry Darrell."

He swallowed hard. "If she'll have me."

Now came the waiting. He needed his mother on his side. One minute turned into two.

"I'll call him now and tell him to meet us in the chapel."

His eyes misted over. "I've always loved you, but in case you didn't know it, this is your finest hour."

"I love and believe in you, Alex."

"Then I'm a lucky man."

"I'll gather those people closest to you."

"Bless you."

He clicked off. After clearing his throat he phoned Leo. His friend picked up on the second ring.

"Alex?"

"Are you in the city?"

"Yes. What can I do for you?"

"I think I'm getting married in a little while."

Leo let out a low whistle.

"It's the only way to do my duty and keep my son with me."

"I have to tell you you're the most courageous man I've ever known."

"Insanity runs in the family, Leo, but I'll be damned if I'll let Uncle Vittorio have any say in things. Would you believe he wants me to marry Evelyn? Of course it's never going to happen, and you and I both know why."

Though they'd never discussed it, Alex knew how Leo felt about her. He had a hunch Evelyn was starting to take an uncommon interest in his chief security man. Alex intended to keep helping that relationship along, but he had to work out his own destiny first.

In a few minutes he'd brought Leo up-to-speed about what was going on.

"I want you to place extra guards at all entrances to the castle ASAP. No one except the archbishop is to be let in."

"Understood."

"Should Uncle Vittorio decide to pay me a nocturnal visit, check with me first before allowing him in. By that time I should be a married man. I'll send Darrell and Phillip to the cabin in the Upper Ungadine by helicopter. Since the slide it's impossible to get to it without one. We'll have our privacy there.

"Vittorio will assume I'm enjoying the privileges of the bridal chamber in the Saxony apartment. It wouldn't surprise me if he barges right in. If he does, I'll be waiting for him."

"That could be dangerous."

"It's been coming on for a lifetime." Alex's voice grated. "As soon as I hang up with you, I'll dictate a press release for Carl to give the paper in the morning."

"Getting the people on your side this quickly could work, Alex. Everyone in the conference room was deeply affected by what you said."

"First I have to convince Darrell."

"If she's fighting you, then she's even more courageous than you are. I think you've met your match."

Alex knew he had…

"I've only got a few more minutes on my side to make a miracle happen."

"I'll take care of everything."

"I know you will. I owe you, Leo." Alex knew exactly how to render payment.

"It's an honor to serve you, Alex. We'll stay in contact."

Alex hung up, then started unbuttoning his shirt as he strode toward the wardrobe in his bedroom.

He opened the door and pulled out his ceremonial outfit that had been cleaned and prepared for his wedding to Isabella.

His gut was telling him he needed to pull out all the stops if he had any hope of getting Darrell to go along with his plans.

CHAPTER NINE

THE Valleder Canton is reeling tonight with the news that King Alexandre Phillip and Princess Isabella of San Ravino, Italy, have called off their wedding permanently.

In a speech made before his cabinet earlier today, the king stated that after a period of deep soul searching, they decided to break their engagement. He insisted their parting was amicable, and hopes the public will give the princess her privacy at this sensitive time.

Those sources closest to the king blame the breakup on the beautiful blond American woman he became involved with thirteen years ago. They have a twelve-year-old son together named Phillip.

Last week his mother, Darrell Collier, from Denver, Colorado, was seen at the castle taking a tour. Since then Phillip has been seen in Bris in the company of Princess Evelyn and young Princes Vito and Jules.

Certain sources have revealed that the king has always been in love with his son's mother, which is why he waited so long before making final wedding arrangements.

We have yet to hear from Princess Isabella's spokesperson, but there is speculation that public sentiment is building against the king who up until now has enjoyed unprecedented support, even subduing those protesters who want the monarchy abolished.

The news that he's been privately carrying on a torrid liaison with a commoner might just bring about an end to his six-year reign. There's speculation that Prince Vittorio of Plessur could ascend the throne but he hasn't been available for comment, nor has the Queen Mother, Katerina. This news has already impacted the stock market and several sensitive trade negotiations wi—

Unable to stand listening to anymore, Darrell shut off the TV and flew out to the balcony. Sick to her very soul, she stared down at the dark swirling water below.

Night lent a brooding element to the castle. In former times Alex's ancestors had counted on their forbidding fortress to intimidate their enemies from without its thick walls. Today Alex faced an enemy from within. But it had all started because she'd come looking for her son's father.

By finding Alex, she'd set off a chain of events that had put the monarchy in jeopardy just as she'd feared.

She couldn't undo the damage now, but she and Phillip could fly back to Denver and stay indoors. If they were out of reach of the press for a time, Alex could concentrate on what he had to do to secure his position without worrying about them.

His question was still ringing in her ears. *How about it, Darrell? Would you like to take me on as your husband?*

Surely he hadn't really meant it. It couldn't possibly work no matter how much he wanted Phillip with him. She had to get out of there.

"Mom?"

Her son came running in the apartment. "You should see Brutus. He's the cutest dog ever!"

Darrell left the balcony and hurried into the bedroom to

meet him. "I'm glad you're back, sweetheart, because we're leaving for Denver as soon as we can get packed."

On cue his face crumpled. "How come?"

"I'll tell you about it once we're on the royal jet."

"But I don't want to leave Dad."

"We have to." She grabbed her suitcase and started throwing things inside. "It's all over the news that the monarchy is in trouble. Every minute you and I are here, it causes more trouble for him. Please do as I say and get your things together."

"But, Mom—"

She rushed past him to find his suitcase and start gathering up his belongings. It didn't take her long. He followed her around in a daze.

When she'd finished, she phoned Rudy and told him to have the helicopter waiting out on the pad.

"Come on, Phillip. It's time to go." Carrying both cases, she started for the drawing room.

"Not so fast. I need an answer to my proposal first."

In the next instant Alex appeared in the doorway blocking her exit. His dark blond male virility dazzled her as did all six foot three of him. Her hands let go of the suitcases, which fell to the floor.

He'd dressed in the same splendid white ceremonial clothes he'd worn at his coronation. The royal-blue band stretching from the gold epaulet on his right shoulder and across his chest to the other side of his waist proclaimed him the king.

Again she realized the Internet picture couldn't possibly capture his spectacular living presence as monarch of the realm.

For once Phillip was absolutely speechless.

Alex flashed his son a smile that brought a lump to her throat. "I've asked your mother to marry me so we can be a family, Phillip. The archbishop is waiting in the chapel downstairs to perform the ceremony. But I think I've scared her."

Phillip turned to her with wounded eyes. "You really hate Dad, don't you."

"No, sweetheart—" she cried out. "That's not why I wanted to leave."

"Your mother thinks she can put me and Isabella back together if she returns to Denver, but that isn't possible. Isabella doesn't want to marry a man who already has a son he loves. I don't blame her."

"Neither do I," Phillip murmured. He stared at Darrell for a long moment. "If you're afraid my real mom will hate you for marrying Dad, you don't need to be. All this time I bet she's been hoping *you'd* find him and marry him."

Oh, Phillip.

Tears trickled down Darrell's cheeks. "Excuse us for a minute, Alex." She ushered him into his bedroom and shut the door.

His face gleamed with moisture. "I wish you would marry him, but I know you don't love him."

"Sweetheart, we've barely known each other a week!"

"I loved him the night he came to the condo."

"Because you knew he was your father."

"Yeah. But he's so awesome I bet you'd learn to love him if you'd give him a chance. Grandma told me she and Grandpa didn't like each other very much when they first got married. Then he got bucked off his horse because he wasn't a good rider. He got a broken leg so she had to take care of him. She said that's when they fell in love."

Darrell could hardly believe Katerina had confided that to Phillip.

"I can't see that happening to your father," she quipped to hide her tumult.

"Neither can I, but you know what I mean."

"I know what you mean."

"I love him so much. He's the best father in the whole world."

"Better than Ryan's dad?"

"Dad's not like anybody else. He's—"

"A super hero?" she found the words for him.

Phillip's moist eyes blazed with light. "Better! He's like somebody too good to be true, but he isn't. I mean he's alive and he's real and—"

"And you love him with all your heart."

"Yeah." He wiped his eyes.

She sucked in her breath. "If we become a family, it's possible Alex will have to step down from the throne."

"Why?"

Darrell explained what she'd seen on the TV. "That's why I wanted us to leave, to give Alex a chance to fight for his right to remain king without worrying about us."

"But he doesn't want us to go."

Her son spoke the truth. Becoming a father had transformed Alex. Though he'd proved to be the dutiful son, she realized there was a part of him that had longed to be a free spirit like his cousin.

She remembered what Alex's own father had put on his bathroom mirror. Darrell shuddered at the thought of being raised by such a stern, autocratic parent.

Her chest heaving, she looked all around. To agree to marry Alex meant all this would be her home from now on. It was a world so foreign to her, she still couldn't comprehend it.

If she said no to his proposal, he would still embrace fatherhood. He loved Phillip enough to give up the kingdom. But he would leave a heartbroken mother and family behind, not to mention a whole country who needed his unique strength and leadership.

If she said yes, it meant staying to fight for what was rightfully his. Knowing the history between Chaz and his father, she couldn't doubt Alex's conviction that his uncle was a frightening adversary.

Would it really come to a coup?

No one had the answers yet.

Only a few weeks ago she'd consulted a heraldry expert. If he'd told her that the king of Valleder would ask her to marry him within the month, she'd have laughed hysterically all the way home.

Jack had wanted to marry her. When she'd turned him down, she'd believed it was because Phillip manipulated him too easily. But that was just an excuse to put him off. The truth was, Jack had never set her on fire.

Only one man had ever managed to do that. Those thrilling moments in Alex's arms had taught her the true meaning of passion. She realized she could never marry a man unless he could affect her in the same way.

While they'd been fused together by the most overwhelming chemistry, she'd lost all awareness of her surroundings.

Alex said he wanted another child.

He'd said he wanted it with *her*.

Trembling with trepidation and excitement, she looked at Phillip. Her son eyed her with an earnestness and pleading that was her undoing. Taking a sharp breath she said, "Do you want to tell your father I'll marry him?"

Phillip gave a resounding whoop before running through to the other room. When Darrell caught up to him, he was already in his father's arms. The bear hug they gave each other was all the more touching because of his elegant attire.

"Phillip?" she reminded him from a short distance off, attempting to tamp down her secret joy. "You'd better hurry and get into the same outfit you wore to dinner with Isabella."

"I'll help you," Alex murmured. They went back in his bedroom. Within two minutes he was dressed. He lifted his head. "Dad? Since Mom has decided to marry you, you don't need to worry she hates you anymore."

As Alex performed his fatherly duty tying his tie, his eyes sought hers. She couldn't read their enigmatic expression. "This is it then." His voice sounded thick with emotion.

She didn't know if her heart could withstand the knowledge that she was about to become his wife.

"Yes. I-if you two will excuse me, I'll change."

Alex shook his head. "You're perfect as you are." His eyes made a slow sweep of her face and body. Warmth spread through her system, reminding her that he wanted a wife in the Biblical sense. "In that white dress you look like a royal bride. I thought as much when you came to dinner earlier."

The simple cap sleeves and full skirt were hardly the attire for the bride of a king, but there was no help for it now.

He patted Phillip's shoulders. "Shall we go?"

"I've never been to a wedding," Phillip said as they filed out of the apartment. "Do I have to do anything?"

"You're my best man so you'll stand on my other side while your mother and I exchange vows."

"That's all?"

"No. There's one more thing."

"What is it?"

Alex paused midstride. "When the archbishop tells me to give your mother the ring, you'll hand this to me." Alex reached in the right pocket of his trousers and pulled out a jeweled ring.

Phillip examined it. "Hey, Mom—this is heavier than the ring Dad gave me. It could weigh you down."

Alex chuckled. "Better put it in your blazer pocket until time. It's seven hundred years old."

"Seven hundred?"

From a long distance off Darrell could see Alex's mother standing at the doors of the chapel in a ceremonial white dress and tiara.

When she smiled, Darrell wanted to cry because it looked so sincere.

Out of love for her son and the good of the monarchy she was willing to help carry off this charade. Whatever her true feelings, her behavior would lead anyone to think she was happy about this unorthodox alliance so soon after Alex's broken engagement.

In a surprise move she draped a white lace mantilla over Darrell's hair. It fell to her waist. Borrowed or new, it made Darrell feel bridal and more prepared to enter the church.

His mother kissed her forehead, then Phillip's cheek. Lastly she kissed her son on both cheeks before walking inside. The three of them followed her into the large, dimly lit interior. But for the frescoes, the medieval atmosphere gave Darrell the impression she'd been sent back in time.

"Are you sure there's only one ghost haunting this castle?" she whispered unsteadily.

Alex slid his hand beneath her veil and rested it on her waist to guide her up the center aisle. "Stay close to me. I won't let any harm come to you."

His touch sent little shivers of delight through her nervous system.

Sixty or so men and women obviously loyal to Alex had assembled, but her attention was focused on the archbishop in colorful vestments. He was a wiry man who stood waiting before the ornate shrine.

At their approach, he made the sign of the cross in front of Alex. "Your Majesty."

"Thank you for coming at this late hour, Your Grace," Alex said in English.

"Please meet my son, Phillip, and his mother, Darrell Collier."

The seventyish-looking man gave a slight nod to the two of them, but his eyes settled on Darrell.

"In entering into this union, you have a responsibility like no other. I will pray to God you are equal to it."

Darrell's mouth had gone dry. "Thank you, Your Grace. God has already been plagued by my prayers."

He studied her for another minute, pondering the veracity of her words. Suddenly he nodded as if in satisfaction.

Alex's hand gave her waist a reassuring squeeze.

The archbishop told Phillip to stand on the other side of his father. Afterward he summoned Alex's mother to stand next to Darrell.

"Let us pray."

Darrell bowed her head. From that point on they were treated to a ceremony in Romanche. She understood none of it, but it didn't matter and knew it didn't bother Phillip. When the ceremony was over, his parents would be married.

"Darrell Collier?" the archbishop unexpectedly said in English again. "Do you pledge your life and devotion to God and your liege unto death and beyond?"

"Yes," she said in a quiet voice.

"Alexandre? Do you pledge your life and devotion to God, country and your chosen bride unto death and beyond?"

"Yes," he proclaimed in a deep voice that reverberated in the vaulted interior.

"Take your bride's hand and bestow the ring."

Darrell felt him turn to Phillip before reaching for her hand. He slid the ring on her finger.

"You are now husband and wife in the sight of God. May He bless your union. May He guard you against all evil. In the name of the Father, the Son and the Holy Ghost, Amen."

"Amen," the congregation repeated.

"God save the king," the archbishop declared in a strong voice.

"God save the king," everyone said more forcefully.

Darrell didn't know the protocol at the wedding of a king, but evidently it wasn't that different when it came to the traditional kiss.

Alex pulled her close. "I've been waiting for this since that day on the mountain," he whispered.

She only had a brief glimpse of lambent hazel eyes before he covered her mouth in a kiss that let everyone know they'd done this before, that this was no arranged marriage.

But with an audience watching them, she couldn't respond with the same abandon as before.

What Alex didn't know was that the knowledge that she'd be alone with her new husband in a little while had caused a secret fire to burn hotter and brighter inside her.

Aware that everyone's attention was on them, she eased away as best she could, only to be confronted by the archbishop whose raisin dark eyes were smiling at her.

They wouldn't do that if he didn't approve of their marriage a little bit, would they? After all, he was supposed to have performed Alex's marriage to Isabella in the city's main cathedral.

"Welcome to our family, my dear," Alex's mother spoke behind her.

She swung around. "Thank you, Your Highness."

"Call me Katerina."

Her eyes stung. "I'd love to."

She grasped Darrell's hands. "You've transformed my son. I've never seen him like this before."

"Phillip has been transformed, too."

The older woman kept staring at her. "Whatever force is in play, I want you to know I'm on your side."

"You'll never know how much that means to me."

"When Alex is ready to share you, come and see me."

"I promise." Without conscious thought she hugged Alex's mother and received a hug back.

"Mom?"

Darrell let go of Katerina and turned to her son. He was grinning. In a quiet voice he said, "I guess you like Dad more than you thought, huh."

"I guess I do."

"Darrell?" Alex called to her. "I'm afraid we're in a hurry, but everyone wants to meet you before we leave. We have some papers to sign as well."

"Of course. I'm coming."

He put a familiar hand at the back of her waist and ushered her through to the anteroom off the chapel where she put her signature next to Alex's on their royal wedding certificate. When they'd finished business, Evelyn and the boys were first in line to congratulate them.

"It was the most touching ceremony I've ever seen. I wish my husband had been here to see how happy you've made Alex. I'm so glad he married you instead of Isabella," she said sotto voce.

There was a sweetness in Evelyn. Her words seemed to have come straight from her heart. It was another sign that Darrell had done the right thing.

"Thank you, Evelyn. I'm so glad to have a friend. Phillip loves you already."

Evelyn smiled through the tears. "Our boys are going to be inseparable from here on out."

"I know."

Darrell reached down to touch their cheeks.

Jules stared up at her. "Can we call you Aunt Darrell?"

"I want you to!"

"Darrell?" Alex grasped her hand. "I'd like you to meet my minister of communications."

For the next while she accepted the warm congratulations from people who were clearly behind Alex and wished them both well. It provided her a small glimpse into his world and what he would expect of her. No bride had ever married royalty more unprepared.

To her relief he finally told her they were leaving. He drew her through a door that led down a private passageway.

"Where's Phillip?"

"Mother's taken charge of him. He'll meet us at the helicopter."

They weren't spending the night in the Saxony apartment? He'd opened it up for her and Phillip to stay there, yet it seemed he had no intention of honoring tradition by spending his wedding night there. Probably because she was a commoner. But somehow it hurt.

"Where are we going?" she asked, hoping her voice sounded level.

"It's a surprise. You and Phillip will fly there first. I'll follow."

A honeymoon à trois.

Why would she expect anything else? Alex enjoyed kissing her enough to marry her in order to keep Phillip an integral part of his life and hopefully have a child of his own.

But he wasn't in love with her!

One day the passion on his part would fade. If she kept that truth uppermost in her mind, their arranged marriage could work. As long as he never knew her deepest feelings.

When they came to another door he moved her against the wall. Keeping her there with his body, he lifted her chin with his hand. "Don't be alarmed if I don't join you until morning."

She started to panic. "Are you in danger?"

His brows furrowed. "Not in the way you mean. Leo, my head of security, just informed me Uncle Vittorio will be arriving by car in the next hour. I need to be here, but I don't want you or our son anywhere around. This king intends to honor his vow to be your devoted servant."

She knew his devotion would never be in question because that was the way he was made.

He lowered his head and pressed a long, hard kiss to her mouth. To convince her or himself?

When he raised up, she held herself rigid so he wouldn't notice how out of breath she was.

Without saying anything he opened the door that led to the outside of the castle. A limousine was waiting.

He helped her into the back seat. "Stay safe for me."

Another brush of his lips against hers and the car sped off in the darkness toward the helipad.

She pulled the mantilla off her hair so she could see out of the window better, but he'd disappeared. It wasn't until that moment she realized if anything happened to him—anything at all—she wouldn't be able to bear it.

Her heart gave a great lurch. Impossible as it might be after only one week, she knew she was painfully in love with him.

As her hand gripped the lace material, she became aware of the ring he'd given her. It was old, encrusted with jewels and too big for her.

She would need to examine the family heirloom in the light before she gave it back to him to keep with the crown jewels. This was a ceremonial ring only meant to be worn on an occasion like this.

Darrell was a Valleder now. She couldn't help but wonder what would have happened if she'd been the one working at that dude ranch rather than Melissa. Would he have fallen for Darrell because he couldn't help himself?

Could she have won Alex on her own power? Enough that he would have broken his betrothal to Isabella in order to marry Darrell?

Those were questions for which she had no answers.

To be loved for yourself and no other reason would bring the greatest happiness.

To Darrell's sorrow, she would never know that kind of joy because for one thing, Alex had married her to keep Phillip with him. For another, it was Isabella who'd broken the engagement, not the other way around. Those were two facts Darrell would always have to live with.

Maybe it was possible Alex would come to love her as Phillip had suggested, but she was selfish enough to wish he'd loved her at first sight.

Since Darrell had never believed, in fairy tales like Melissa, why couldn't she be happy over what reality had presented her?

All of a sudden the door to the limousine opened, surprising her. "Where's Dad?"

"Hi, sweetheart. He had a few things to do and will join us in a little while."

"Where are we going?"

"He didn't tell me, but since it's your father we're talking about, I'm sure we'll love it."

"I wish he was here," he grumbled as they climbed into the helicopter. She echoed his feelings.

The pilot flashed them a broad smile. "Congratulations on your marriage, Your Highness."

"Thank you, but you don't need to call me that. I'm no royal princess. Darrell and Phillip will do just fine."

"Darrell it is. Alex has asked me to give you a moonlight tour of the Ungadine Valley on our way, so strap yourselves in."

"Cool!"

Once the rotors were whirring, they rose from the ground so fast

Darrell almost lost her stomach.

She looked below at the receding castle, experiencing a deep ache in her heart. Alex was down there waiting to face his uncle.

"Look, Mom. That's the ridge where we went horseback riding."

Phillip's enthusiasm would have to make up for both of them.

The Swiss Alps were one of the most beautiful sights on earth, yet she wouldn't be able to enjoy anything until she saw Alex again and knew all was well.

"Hey—what happened over there?" he asked the pilot.

"There was a forest fire followed by a rainstorm. It caused a huge mud slide."

"Was anybody hurt?"

"Fortunately not. This region is off limits to the public."

"How come?"

"Because this is your father's favorite mountain retreat."

"Where?"

"We're coming up on it in a minute. One of his staff is already there with your bags and will see to your needs."

Another pain stabbed Darrell. So this was what it was like to go on a royal honeymoon. No privacy from the retinue of people ready to serve their king.

Before long the helicopter set down in a clearing next to a tiny log cabin that looked like it had been there for years. A male staff member came out the door to greet them and show them inside.

The clean interior was sparsely furnished, providing just the basics. A log wall with a fireplace separated one little bedroom and bathroom from the kitchen cum living room area. Upstairs was a loft reached by split log steps. Phillip whooped with excitement, declaring that's where he would sleep.

After a meal of ham and cheese rolls served with salad and fruit, Phillip was ready to crash and went up to bed. Darrell changed into jeans and a T-shirt, then went upstairs with Phillip to wait for Alex.

Before going to bed, she opened the window to let in the night air. The temperature at the top of the world was much cooler than in the valley. But nothing could bring down the fever brought on by a longing to know her new husband's possession, even if only one of them was in love.

When she started to chill, she climbed under the covers next to Phillip and waited.

One hour turned into another. The night was endless. If she slept, she couldn't remember. It wasn't until morning she heard the long awaited sound of the helicopter. Was it getting ready to take off, or had it just landed?

She rolled over and sat up. Maybe Alex was here!

Phillip was still asleep. With her heart thudding, she threw off the covers to get out of bed and slammed into a powerful male body just entering the loft. Alex's arms went around her to steady her like they'd done on the jet.

He'd changed out of his royal attire and was wearing a burgundy polo shirt and khakis. But when she looked up at his face she saw a different man from the one who'd told her to keep herself safe for him.

Lines of tension defined his arresting features. His eyes had gone dark and looked so haunted, she knew something dreadful had occurred.

By now Phillip was awake. "What's wrong, Dad?"

She put a hand on his arm. "Tell us."

A pulse throbbed at the side of his mouth. "My uncle has suffered a minor heart attack."

"Oh, Alex—I can't believe it came to this. How serious is it?"

"Provided there are no complications, he should recover just fine. They'll probably send him home from the hospital tomorrow, but I'm afraid we'll have to go back to Bris. Everyone's at the hospital."

"Of course."

"I'll be dressed in a sec, Dad."

Darrell nodded. "I'll go downstairs and pack up my things."

He gripped her upper arms in front of Phillip. "I'd hoped to spend a week up here. Just the three of us without another soul or worry to disturb us. We'll come back here in a couple of days."

"That'll be great, Dad. I always wished we had a cabin!" Phillip called over his shoulder before leaving the loft with his suitcase.

Alex drew in a fortifying breath. "Of all the outcomes, this wasn't the one I'd anticipated."

"Don't you think I know that? Alex— Since this is life threatening, maybe Phillip and I should fly back to Denver for a while. You know. Just to stay out of the way while he's recuperating."

The second the words left her lips his expression turned black. His hands slid to her wrists. He looked pointedly at her hands devoid of jewelry.

"My ring kept slipping, so I removed it and put it in my purse for safe keeping," she explained in a rush.

His grimace deepened.

"We took sacred vows last night. Perhaps you didn't understand how binding they are, but it's too late for regrets. You're not going anywhere. We're husband and wife now, and that's the way it's going to stay."

He set her aside and left the loft ahead of her.

"Alex—" she called down to him, anxious to explain, but he didn't pause. She didn't dare shout at him in front of Phillip and his staff. That was the problem with going on a honeymoon that included more than two people!

She hadn't meant to upset him. He'd taken it all wrong because he didn't understand how guilty she felt about everything. His uncle was in the hospital because of her.

If she'd never come to Bris…

But she couldn't keep harking back to that. She *had* come, and it *had* turned the Canton on its ear exactly the way he'd prophesied.

They were in this together now. Alex expected her to hold up her end of the bargain.

She could hear her grandmother talking about Melissa's pregnancy. "Don't go on about it, Darrell. Spilt milk can't be put back in the bottle. We've got no choice but to help her and love her. That's all there is to it."

How Darrell had loved her pragmatic grandmother who'd sacrificed her whole life for them. About now Darrell needed to call on her grandmother's wisdom and try to live up to her example.

Knowing Alex was anxious to leave, she hurried below. If they were returning to the castle she needed to wear something dressier than casual clothes. The maid who'd packed her bag had included a print skirt and blouse. They would have to do. Once at the apartment she would shower and change into a suit to wear to the hospital.

"I've never even met your uncle. Do you think he'll die?" Phillip asked Alex on their flight back to the castle.

"Not if he follows doctor's orders. He needs peace and quiet. How would you like it if the boys slept in the Saxony apartment with you for a couple of nights?"

"That would be the best! I'll tell them to bring their sleeping bags and we'll camp out on the balcony."

"Sounds like a plan. I'll suggest they bring the telescope. You'll be able to see all kinds of animal life on the slopes beyond the lake."

"Is that okay with you, Mom?"

"Your mother will be sleeping in my apartment from now on. I've already had her things moved."

What Alex had just said was perfectly logical, yet Darrell

could scarcely breathe because he'd sounded possessive just now. It sent a little thrill through her body.

"You can move in there, too, Phillip. I have an extra bedroom."

Her hand clutched her purse tighter. Of course he wanted Phillip close to them.

"Or, you and Brutus can have the Saxony apartment to yourself."

Phillip's eyes rounded while Darrell's head lowered to hide her surprise.

"You mean the whole thing?"

"If you want. It would be a shame to lock it up again until somebody else in the family gets married."

"Like Vito or Jules, huh."

"Or you."

"But I'm not a prince."

"You're my son. That's all that matters."

CHAPTER TEN

DARRELL had never loved Alex more than at this moment.

When they arrived at the castle she hurried up to his apartment while he and Phillip went to get the boys.

She hadn't been in the suite long when her cell phone rang again. Jack had been calling her, but this time it was Danice. She picked up and said hello.

"Darrell? I can't believe what I've heard on the news in the last twenty-four hours. First it was announced that the king of Valleder broke his engagement to Princess Isabella. Then it was announced he had a twelve-year-old son and married his former lover who just happened to be *you*.

"I know you met a guy when you flew to Switzerland on vacation last week. I also know he asked you and Phillip to spend the Fourth with him. But you didn't tell me he was the king! He's the hunkiest male I've ever seen in my life.

"Jack called me a few minutes ago. He's positive it's a mistake, or else there are two Darrell Colliers. He's been trying to reach you. I've never heard him so upset and I've worked for him for a lot of years. Is it true? Did you really marry him this fast?"

Darrell bit her lip. "Yes, but don't believe all the gossip you've heard."

"Of course not. The media lies about everything. I know you adopted your sister's baby. What's the real truth?"

Darrell gripped her phone tighter. Danice didn't know anything about Darrell's reasons for going to Switzerland in the first place. "One day I'll tell you everything. It's very complicated. Suffice it to say neither Alex nor the princess were in love."

"Obviously not, otherwise he wouldn't have been a goner the second he met you. However for *you* to do something so out of character means he must really be something."

Her eyes closed. "He is," she said in a tremulous voice. "Listen Danice—I can't talk now. Alex will be coming any minute. Would you do me a favor and tell Jack I'll call him tomorrow? I need to turn in my resignation. I'll call you right after."

"I can't wait to meet your lord and master in person."

"He isn't like that."

"You sound different. Happy. If anyone deserves it, you do."

"People don't deserve things."

"They do when they're as selfless as you've been. Does Phillip like him?"

Tears threatened. "He adores him."

"Then the king must really be amazing because it took Jack a good year before Phillip gave him the time of day."

"I know."

There was a reason for that. It was called being father and son.

"I can tell you can't wait to be with your husband. Do you call him Your Highness when you're alone?" she teased.

Darrell chuckled. "No,"

"All right. I guess I'll have to wait to hear all the exciting details. You'd better call me."

"I promise."

After they hung up, Darrell started to empty her suitcase.

She'd been in Alex's apartment before, but Phillip had led her out to the sunroom. She'd only glimpsed the other parts of the suite, which was really a home within the castle.

Unlike the Saxony apartment, which had been left virtually untouched since the Middle Ages, Alex had modernized the rooms in his suite for day-to-day living. Still elegant enough for a king, it had all the amenities of modern-day living.

She found the spacious bathroom and showered before dressing in her blue suit. When she entered the bedroom she discovered Alex had come in. "I'm ready," she announced.

His eyes traveled over her, eventually fastening on the ring she was wearing again. "You look lovely. Where are we going?"

She blinked. "I thought you wanted me to go with you while you visited your uncle."

"You misunderstood me then. I have to be in residence at the castle in case I'm needed, but I have no intention of seeing him for quite some time.

"I asked Evelyn to keep an eye on the boys until they go to sleep so you and I could spend a little quiet time together."

His face had a gaunt look, yet for all that he was more attractive to her than ever.

"How long has it been since you had a good sleep?"

He pursed his lips. "Since the night before you came to the castle in the hope of talking to me."

She lowered her head. "I know what you mean. We're both sleep deprived."

"Phillip pointed out I have a *king*-size bed just waiting for us," he quipped. His dark mood seemed to have vanished. "If it's all right, I'd like to lie down and hold my wife for a few hours."

The blood pounded in her ears. "Aren't you hungry?"

"I had breakfast before I flew to the cabin for you. Do you want something from the kitchen?"

"No, thank you."

"Then while I change, why don't you put on something comfortable."

He disappeared into the bathroom, leaving her trembling like a leaf in the breeze.

Once she heard the door close, she was galvanized into action. By the time he emerged in a white toweling robe, she'd done his bidding and was wearing her light yellow fleece robe. One look at him left her weak.

He seemed to be waiting for something. She didn't understand when he reached for a coin. He'd left change lying next to an urn of at least three dozen red roses placed on his dresser.

"Heads or tails? It's your call."

"For what?"

"Who gets into bed first." After tossing the coin, he raised his eyes to her. "It came up tails."

"Alex—" She laughed nervously. "Don't be ridiculous."

"What did you choose?" he persisted.

"Neither one," came her meek response.

"That's what I thought."

Before she could countenance it, he picked her up in his arms and started carrying her through the suite to the outer door, not missing a breath.

"What are you doing?" Her lips accidentally brushed his hard jaw, turning her body molten. She felt the tremor that shook his powerful body before he opened the door and went out in the hall where a security guard was standing nearby.

"Alex—" She was so embarrassed she hid her face in his neck.

"I never understood the ritual of carrying the bride over the threshold, but I do now. It solves a big problem when she's terrified of her own husband."

He took her inside again and shut the door. When they reached the bed he followed her down with his body.

Darrell looked into his eyes but they were shuttered. "You know I'm not frightened of you. But I can't get my mind off your uncle. Did he have the attack before you even talked to him?"

"No. During our confrontation he ordered me to divorce you and marry Evelyn. When I refused to discuss it, he became ill."

Her eyes filled. "I'm so sorry, Alex."

"He'll be all right. In the meantime, I want to forget everything and concentrate on my wife. I need you to hold me right now. Would that be too much to ask? I'm tired of plotting and planning and trying to make everything work."

He said it with a half smile but she knew deep down he meant every word of it.

Recognizing how truly exhausted he had to be, she turned on her side and nestled in his arms with her face resting in the hollow of his shoulder.

He let out a long, drawn-out sigh, like Atlas letting go of the cares of the world. "This is heaven…." His voice trailed. He wrapped one powerful leg around both of hers, locking her in place against him. She felt him bury his face in her swath of silky gold hair.

Within a minute she could tell he was asleep.

She lay there for a good half hour while her mind tried to absorb what her body was feeling.

Every girl had times growing up when she wondered who her husband would be, how she would know he was the one.

If it hadn't been for Melissa…

With the greatest care Darrell eased away enough that she could feast her eyes on his face without him being aware of it. He had fantastic bone structure. She loved the way his hair was cut just short enough that it was still wavy.

His strong nose and chin made him aggressively male. But of all his features besides his beautiful eyes, it was his mouth she loved. Wide and sensuous, it could go fierce or tender depending on his mood.

That mouth had swept her into a vortex of desire days ago. She craved to be caught up in it again. But she would have to be patient. It was a virtue she needed to work on. For the present he required a lot of sleep without interruption.

Now that she'd been lying down for a while, she noticed the room had grown cooler because of the air-conditioning.

Inch by inch she stole out of his arms, intent on finding him another quilt. Since she didn't want to make noise opening cupboards, she went into the other bedroom and pulled one off the bed.

When she returned to their bedroom she found his long, fit body in the same position she'd left him. He was that tired.

Holding her breath, she covered him, still unable to believe she had the right to be with him and take care of him forever.

Not far from the bed there was a couch with a throw facing the fireplace. She tiptoed over to it and lay down, pulling the material up to her shoulders. There was too much temptation lying next to her husband.

Since her first flight to Switzerland, she felt as if she'd been wandering in a strange and marvelous dream. Maybe now they could both get the sleep they needed so badly. When he woke up, she wouldn't be far from him. Then maybe their marriage could really begin…

Something wasn't right. Alex had been breathing in the faint scent of Darrell's fragrance still lingering on his robe, but when he felt blindly for her, his hand didn't come in contact with warm, firm flesh covered by her modest robe.

Alarmed, his eyes opened to a room cloaked in darkness. He jackknifed into a sitting position and checked his watch. It was ten after ten. He'd slept close to ten hours!

Where had Darrell gone? Was it possible she'd acted on what she'd suggested at the cabin and had taken Phillip back to Denver?

It would be just like her to think she could fix the situation by staying out of sight.

Maybe he was getting ahead of himself and she was either in the bathroom or down in the Saxony apartment. Forcing himself not to panic he called to her.

When no answer came he was filled with dread and flung off the quilt she must have thrown over him while he slept. How long ago had that happened?

"Darrell—"

"I'm over here on the couch."

He had to stop to catch his breath. "What are you doing so far away from me?"

"I woke up a while ago and knew you needed your sleep, so I did some phoning in the other room, then came back in here to rest until you awakened.

"I was afraid you were sleeping too long and something was wrong. I—I'm so glad you're up at last."

So was he…but it was for a completely different reason.

"Are you all right, Alex? Please tell me the truth. I know you have serious issues with your uncle, but he's still family and you wouldn't be human if you weren't upset."

Alex got out of bed with the intention of joining his wife on the couch when he heard a pounding on the other side of their bedroom door.

"Dad? Mom?"

At the sound of their son's anxious voice Alex moaned, unable to believe Phillip's timing.

The need to make love to his wife was causing him physical pain. But it appeared Darrell wasn't suffering from the same problem. She switched on the light. "I'll see what he wants," she said before padding over to the door in her robe and bare feet.

Alex decided something was seriously wrong. Otherwise he knew Phillip wouldn't have disturbed them before morning. While he pulled on some boxers and retied his robe, he heard muffled voices. It sounded like Vito and Jules were out there, too.

When he opened the door to the drawing room, Jules ran over to him sobbing. "I'm so sorry, Uncle Alex. I didn't mean to drop him."

"Drop who?"

"Brutus," Vito said with tears rolling down his cheeks.

Alex's glance flew to Darrell, who was on the house phone. Phillip was standing next to her sobbing his heart out, too.

He got down on his haunches, putting his hands on Jules's shoulders. "Take a deep breath and tell me what happened."

"W-we were on the balcony and I was holding Brutus, but he kept wiggling around and all of a sudden he fell over the wall."

"Did it just happen?"

"Yes."

After another quick glance at Darrell whose pained eyes looked to him for help, he ran out of the apartment and down the stairs past his security people to the Saxony apartment. He could hear everyone running after him. The fastest way to the water was over the balcony.

Removing his robe he did a cannonball into the lake. He heard Darrell's scream just before he hit the water.

The puppy wouldn't have fallen more than a few yards from the exterior wall. Depending on its instinct to survive, it could still be paddling around, but who knew how long its strength would hold out.

It was a warm summer night. The lake was like a sheet of glass, making it easier to spot anything in the water.

"Do you see him, Dad?"

Alex kept swimming back and forth, drawing closer each time to the castle wall. Suddenly he saw something brushed up against the mossy stone.

A sleek little head and a paw trying desperately to catch hold.

With one strong lunge Alex reached the puppy whose exhausted body slumped against his shoulder. By now one of the castle patrol boats was headed toward him. Thanks to Darrell's quick thinking in calling them the puppy might have a chance to live.

They flashed a searchlight over the water. He gave a shout and waved a free hand. Quickly they came alongside and took the puppy from him before he hoisted himself into the craft.

"After you hand me a towel, call my driver to pick me up at the marina, then phone the vet and tell him I'm coming to the stable with Brutus."

Alex put the dog in the middle of the towel and began drying him as best he could. It had to survive, not so much for Phillip's sake, but for Jules's. The boy was overly sensitive like Chaz. If Brutus died, he'd never forgive himself.

If Leo were here he would say "What a hell of a night."

All Alex knew was that his heart couldn't take any more shocks.

Was it asking too much to live long enough to make love to his legally wedded bride? Only time would tell if she came to his bed willingly, but at this rate he was never going to find out!

The boat reached the marina in record time. "Here, Your Majesty." One of the men tossed him a yellow slicker to put on.

"Thank you for your help. Do me one more favor and call my wife? Tell her to meet me at the vet's office."

After that everything happened fast. Before long five people were huddled around the vet, who was examining the dog.

Alex stared at his wife who was draped in a blanket she'd

pulled from one of the beds to cover her robe. She was trying to comfort Jules, whose shoulders shook with silent tears.

"It wasn't your fault, darling. If I'd been holding him out there, the same thing could have happened. Puppies are like jelly. You can't get a good hold on them,"

Her comment made him laugh. A miracle.

The vet finally raised his head. "This little fellow has lived up to his breed's reputation. He's going to be fine by morning."

Darrell squeezed Jules. "You see? Thanks to your uncle, everything's all right." Her voice shook.

"Dad always makes *everything* all right."

When Darrell looked over at Alex, her eyes were glowing like purple fire. He couldn't get her back to the castle fast enough.

"Okay, everybody. There's been enough excitement for one night. You heard the doctor. Brutus will be back to himself after breakfast. No more holding him on the balcony. You can take him for walks, preferably on solid ground," he teased. "Let's go home and get some sleep."

"Could I stay with him tonight, Dad? I don't want him to be lonely."

The vet gave Alex a nod.

"It's up to your mother."

"Can we stay, too?" the boys asked her.

"There's no place for you to sleep."

"We don't care."

"I've got some blankets around here," the vet offered.

Alex decided it was a brilliant idea. "It's fine with me. I'll send a car for you in the morning and we'll have breakfast together."

"Hurrah!"

Darrell hurried out to the limousine ahead of Alex. When he caught up to her she said, "I think I should stay with the boys so the vet can get some sleep. As for you, a hot shower is in order." She stared at him with accusing eyes.

"That spectacular stunt you pulled off the balcony was even scarier than the one the other day. The news of this will probably make tomorrow's headlines. But please don't do it again or you'll put me in an early grave."

The fear in her voice pleased him no end. "Well, we can't have that when we haven't even gotten to the good part yet."

"There'll never be a good part if you're dead!"

On that note she clutched the blanket around her shoulders and hurried back inside the vet's office. Maybe it was a trick of light but he thought she looked paler than before. At least she still wanted him alive.

Much to the amusement of his security people, Alex returned to his apartment in the slicker and his big bare feet, hardly the attire for a king supposedly enjoying his honeymoon.

Once he'd showered and changed, he'd go back to get her, and this time there'd be nothing to stop him.

But as soon as he was ready to return to the stable, his cell phone rang. At three in the morning it could only mean trouble unless it was Darrell needing to talk.

He checked the caller ID. "Leo?"

"I heard what happened. Are you all right?"

"That depends. Darrell's not in love with me, but she married me to stay close to her son. I convinced her that Isabella deserved to find true love with someone else.

"Now I'm going to let you in on another secret no one knows about except Darrell and mother. The reason Uncle Vittorio had a heart attack was because I refused his demand that I divorce Darrell and marry Evelyn."

"Evelyn—"

"My uncle's an emotionally sick man, Leo. But I have a plan that could thwart him once and for all. It involves you."

"How?" His friend's voice sounded unsteady.

"When Uncle Vittorio comes home from the hospital in the

next eight to ten hours, he needs peace and quiet. So, I'm sending Evelyn and the boys with you to my cabin in the Upper Ungadine. It's been cleaned and stocked with provisions. Seven days ought to give you and Evelyn time to sort out your feelings, which I know have been growing over the last year. There's no man I'd rather see marry Evelyn than you."

His friend grunted. "Her parents would never approve of a nonroyal marrying their daughter."

"Times are changing. I've already set a new precedent. Uncle Vittorio will hardly be in a position to disapprove of the head of security for a new son-in-law. His silence on the subject will carry weight with her folks who want her to be happy.

"So do whatever needs doing to clear your desk, then report to the helipad by nine in the morning. I'll have Evelyn and the boys there. She'll think it's a security measure. In the meantime, no one will know where the four of you have gone."

"But, Alex—what if Evelyn doesn't want to go?"

His brows furrowed. "Then isn't it time you found out how she really feels about you, my friend?"

"Hell yes, but I have to admit I'm terrified."

"Now you have some comprehension of what I've been going through with Darrell."

"You've at least got the wedding ring on her finger."

"You mean the relic that keeps falling off? I'm afraid that's the story of our marriage so far. We haven't even had the honeymoon yet."

"Whose fault is that?"

"Like you, I'm terrified to find out."

"Give it time, Alex. It's only been a week since you met."

"I didn't need a week."

"That's what it was like for me the first time I met Evelyn. But at that point she was a happily married woman."

"That was then. You still have a whole future ahead of you. I'll be damned if I'm going to let Uncle Vittorio ruin it for either of us."

After hanging up, he summoned his driver to take him to the stable. It was past time to get his wife to himself.

Evelyn put a hand on Darrell's arm. "Could we talk for a minute before you go back to the castle?"

"Of course. It's almost morning anyway."

Darrell followed Evelyn down the stairs of the palace where they'd just put the three boys to bed. The second Evelyn had been told about the accident, she'd come to the stable insisting everyone go home to bed for what was left of the night. The puppy had gone to sleep, so there was no point staying there on the floor in the vet's office.

Evelyn ushered her in the sitting room off the foyer. The minute she closed the doors she said, "When I told you at the wedding that I was glad you'd married Alex, I really meant it. He's terribly in love with you you know."

Darrell wiped her eyes. "He couldn't be. He was just glad to have a legitimate excuse to get out of his marriage to Isabella."

"It's true he didn't love her, but he would never, ever have turned around and married you this fast if his heart weren't involved. Charles suffered over the fact that Alex would never know true happiness.

"When Alex brought you home, I saw something in his eyes that's never been there before. Trust me on this."

Darrell made a protesting sound. "It's because of Phillip. He loves him."

"That's obvious. But I'm talking about you. Even Katerina has noticed the incredible change in him. We had a talk earlier tonight. She told me my father-in-law was hoping for a marriage between me and Alex, but it would never happen under any circumstances.

"Vittorio has forgotten it takes two people in love to make a marriage work. I've met someone here I care about, too. I didn't think it was possible after Charles, but it has happened. The problem is, I'm afraid he'll never do anything about it because he's a nonroyal."

"Who is it?"

"Leo."

"He's a very attractive man," Darrell murmured. "Is there anything Alex or I could do to help things along? They're best friends."

"No. If Leo can't reach out to me the way Alex has done to you, then his love isn't strong enough. Darrell—if your feelings for Alex are as deep as I believe they are, don't hold back now. You have no idea how fearful Alex is underneath."

"What do you mean?"

"By marrying you he's done something that in ways has isolated him."

"I still don't understand."

"He's always known what he had to do to be a king in a royal marriage. But to be the husband to a woman like you is unknown territory. He and Charles used to talk about what it would be like to fall in love with a commoner.

"Even if their hearts were involved, they both agreed it could end up in disaster. No matter how strong Alex is, I know there's a part of him fearful you won't be able to handle court life and one day you'll leave him and go back to Colorado. He's very vulnerable right now."

Evelyn's observations reminded Darrell of something Alex had said last week about Phillip wanting to go home once the novelty had worn off.

But Alex was wrong then, and he was wrong now!

Excited to prove it to him, Darrell jumped up from the couch. “Thank you for the talk, Evelyn. You’ve helped me more than you will ever know. I need to get back to the castle. Would you do me a favor and find out where Alex is right now?”

“Of course.” She picked up the phone and made an inquiry before hanging up.

“He’s on his way to the vet’s office.”

“That’s perfect. It gives me enough time for my plan to work. I need some information. Will you help me?”

Evelyn’s eyes lit up. “Anything you want.”

In a few minutes Evelyn’s driver took her back to the castle. On the drive home Darrell’s mind was bombarded with thoughts that hadn’t made sense before, but suddenly everything was clear.

The Saxony apartment had been Chaz’s favorite spot to get away from authority. But that little mountain cabin had been Alex’s private getaway.

Their choices were very telling, especially after he’d told her he would live in a cabin in Colorado if he stepped down from the throne.

After the talk with Evelyn, Darrell was beginning to realize how much Alex had been forced to hide his real self in order to be king. Only by an accident of birth had royal duties been thrust upon him. Chaz had understood that weighty responsibility and had run from it. No doubt he’d tried to get Alex to run from it, too.

Maybe the best way to be a good wife to Alex was to find ways to make him feel like he wasn’t the king when they were together. Phillip had already done that by just being himself.

Darrell was having a more difficult time of it. Twice Alex had told her his father would have approved of her. It wasn’t a compliment. Not at all.

Alex could have had a princess for a wife, but in the end

he hadn't wanted one and had claimed Darrell, the farthest thing from princess material in existence.

Earlier Alex had told her he was tired of plotting and planning in order to make everything work. But *she* wasn't!

CHAPTER ELEVEN

AFTER visiting the vet's office without finding his wife, Alex had gone to the palace where Evelyn lived convinced Darrell had decided to spend the night there with the boys so she wouldn't have to face him. But she wasn't there, either.

If she wasn't ready to sleep with him, then he'd give her all the time she needed.

She'd almost married Jack so Alex had assumed she'd been to bed with him. But what if she hadn't? What if she hadn't been intimate with any man? Was it possible?

It was time to find out.

Alex returned to the castle and strode down the hall to his apartment. But he was stopped dead when he saw a note in English taped to the outer door.

Have left for the Zurich airport. In compliance with Your Majesty's wishes, I made arrangements with your pilot aboard the royal jet. Darrell.

He felt as if he'd been kicked in the gut. If she was trying to save him from himself, it was too late now.

Reaching for his cell phone, he called his pilot. "Is my wife on board yet?"

"Yes, Your Majesty. She just arrived."

"Don't you dare take off."

"She said she had your permission."

"She lied. Have you forgotten you take your orders from me?"

"No, of course not. I apologize for assuming it was all right."

"I'll be there within a half hour. Don't let her off that plane. That's a command."

"Yes, Your Majesty."

In a fury, Alex hung up and told his helicopter pilot to get ready. Five minutes later he climbed inside and gave him his instructions.

"Did you fly my wife to Zurich earlier?"

"No. You told me to wait for my orders from Leo."

That meant she'd left the palace by car and had chartered a helicopter in town, no doubt with Evelyn's help. In the process she'd sworn her bodyguard to secrecy. She could charm anyone, even his most trusted security men.

He knew she wouldn't have planned to go back to Denver if she hadn't already discussed it with Phillip. But their son was still asleep. And he didn't want to wake Evelyn again.

He gritted his teeth the whole distance to the airport. The way things were going, it was a miracle his jet was still resting there on the tarmac.

Alex jumped out of the helicopter and raced up the steps of the plane three at a time only to be stopped by another note taped to the door.

No kings allowed inside by order of the management.

What was going on in that intriguing mind of hers?

He could bang on the door, but he wasn't about to give all his security people the satisfaction of seeing him reduced to begging his wife to open up. It had been bad enough when he'd gone to her condo and she'd forced him to remain standing on her porch for what had seemed like hours.

Once again he pulled out his phone and called his pilot so he'd put Alex through to her.

She answered on the fourth ring. The wait had raised his blood pressure. At this rate *he* was due for a hospital visit.

"Alex? The captain said it was you on the line. Where are you?" She pretended to sound exhausted.

He didn't buy it for a minute, but he controlled himself enough to say, "Outside the door of the jet."

"I'm sorry to hear that. Good night."

Click.

She'd hung up on him!

Close to being in a rage he yanked on the door, expecting it to be locked. Instead it opened, causing him to almost fall from the impact of his shoulder against it.

Muttering a curse unfit for anyone's ears he headed down the passageway for his den, but she wasn't in there. The place was like a tomb.

He charged toward his mother's bedroom. It was empty.

"Darrell?"

"Do you have to make so much noise? You sound like a bull in a china shop. I'm trying to sleep."

His jaw almost cracked in response. She was in *his* bedroom. He moved to the doorway out of breath. "I want to know what you meant by your note?"

"Which one? The first note was to let you know where I went so you wouldn't worry." His eyes closed tightly. "I'm sorry if you haven't figured out the second one yet."

He folded his arms to tamp down his adrenaline rush. "I thought we had an understanding," his voice rasped.

"You mean about staying married? Of course we do, but the castle is like a hospital. You can't ever get any sleep with family, pets, staff and security men coming in and out at all hours of the night. So I thought I'd fly here and hoped the *man,* not the king, would come after me.

"As you reminded me earlier, we haven't even gotten to the good part yet. If anyone tries to find us, we'll just tell the pilot to take off."

He swallowed hard before turning on the light.

She was sitting up in the bed wearing an orange and blue pajama top that said Denver Broncos. "Good morning, my darling husband. That's what I should have said on the phone just now. It's already getting lighter in the sky so I shut the curtains."

She'd put her gleaming hair in a ponytail. There was something different when she looked at him with those violet eyes and smiled. He felt their brilliance like the blinding light after emerging from a deep black cave.

Throwing back the covers, she held out her arms. "Come here," she begged in an aching voice.

Out went the light. Like a drowning man who'd suddenly discovered sand beneath his feet and could make it to shore, he reached for her.

"Darrell—" he cried against her lips. "My love—"

"Ah, that's what I've been desperate to hear," she whispered, helping him out of his clothes. "Anything else can wait until much later."

"Did I please Your Majesty?"

After hours of lovemaking they'd both slept, but she'd awakened first and couldn't resist embracing him.

A deep groan escaped his throat, delighting her.

"Does that mean you want to be pleased again, or are you starving for food?"

"Both," he murmured against her throat, sending a thrill

through her body that set her trembling all over again. "But the food can wait. *I* can't."

"Neither can I—"

Another hour of rapture turned Darrell into a wanton. "I didn't know it could be like this—" She half lay on top of him, breathless and feverish for more.

"It isn't like this for anyone else. Thank heaven you're my wife." He kissed her with voracious hunger. "I may have to rule my kingdom from this bed."

"You won't hear any complaints from me, but everyone else who loves you might raise objections. By the way, I forgot to ask you when you first charged in here. How's Brutus?"

He chuckled into her silky hair. "Much better than I was."

"That's what I thought. You know what your problem is? You try to be too many things to too many people. You do it better than anyone I've ever known or heard of, king or no king. But now that you're my husband, I'd like you to turn all that off at the end of the day and come home to me like any other normal man."

"You can ask me that after what we've just shared?" His mouth closed over hers once more.

"You know what I mean," she said in a euphoric daze.

"Spell it out for me, darling."

"All right." She kissed his raspy jaw, loving the differences between them. "The castle is like something from a fairy tale. There aren't words to describe the fabulous world you were born into. Yet there's a part of me that also wants a home of our own."

"Done!" he cried into her hair.

"With a yard where you mow the grass and I weed the garden."

"Done!"

"And when the sink plugs up, you have to get out a wrench to fix it."

"Done!"

"Where it's not too far away so that when you leave for work every morning, you can get there in your helicopter in a big hurry."

"Done!"

"Now I know you can't really do any of that, but maybe we—"

She stopped talking. Her eyes widened as she looked at him. "What did you just say?"

"I said I love you. I said I'll grant you all those wishes. One of my homes in the next valley over would be perfect for the family we're going to raise. I knew I wanted to live there with you the moment I saw you from the doorway of the jet. I knew it when this feminine blond beauty came walking up the steps to me.

"The sun illuminated your eyes. Beyond their exquisite violet color, I saw pain, worry, sorrow, fear, incredulity—so many things that told me your true character before I even knew the exact reason for your visit to Bris. It didn't matter that you were a complete stranger to me. At that moment love hit me like a thunderclap."

"It did me, too," she confessed.

"Most people will tell you it isn't possible. They say you have to live with someone for years and years before you can call it love.

"I disagree. Love can and does happen with a mind and power all its own. By the time you left the plane to get me the ring, I'd become a different man.

"It would have been easy enough to leave things alone because I hadn't met Phillip yet. I knew he had a wonderful life with you. I could have flown away and never looked back, rationalizing that you would marry one day and supply him with a stepfather.

"But I didn't do that because I couldn't. You were there in Denver with our son. I had to see you again to find out if I'd truly lost my heart. When you gave me a hard time before letting me in your house, I determined to make you mine whether you came screaming or not."

"Oh, Alex—" She pulled his head down and began suffocating him with kisses. "While I was warming up those tacos, I had this dream that we were married and I was taking care of my wonderful husband at the end of a busy day.

"You have no idea how much I long to cook and clean for you, fold your socks in your drawers. You're everyone else's king, but you're my very heart.

"I want to have your baby. When I realized you were the man who'd made Melissa pregnant, I was horribly jealous of her, which made my guilt so much worse.

"I'm sure there'll be duties I have to perform as the king's wife, but I want to do the little personal things behind the scenes for you that no one else knows about. I also want to go to school and learn Romanche so I can be a real asset to you.

"Do you think it's possible we could combine two totally different lives and be happy?"

His sensuous smile melted her bones. "I'll let you know after we get down to the good part again."

Her heart filled her eyes. "I thought you were hungry."

"I am. For you."

"It was already better than good the first time you kissed me," she cried softly. "I was transparent that day on the mountain. I wanted you in every way a woman could ever want a man. I didn't want you to be the king. I didn't want you to belong to anyone but me."

He sobered, staring at her intently. "Chaz and I used to talk about what it would be like to find the right woman and marry her. By some miracle we both got our wish. Now I find I'm greedy and want one more miracle."

Darrell traced the line of his male mouth with her fingers. "Maybe it's already happened. I hope it has. I can't wait to feel your baby kicking inside me."

Alex drew his wife into his arms while he digested her words.

As he rocked her warm, curvaceous body against him she said, "My only concern is that your uncle will still try to turn public opinion against you for marrying me. So I think for the time being Phillip and I should go back to Colorado."

"We're married, Darrell." He crushed her against him. "Do you think I'd let you out of my sight for one second now?"

"Just until the doctor says your uncle is better. Phillip will understand. It *is* doable, darling."

He rolled her over so she was lying beneath him. "You made a vow to me before God. Did it mean nothing to you?"

Tears filled her eyes. "It meant everything. I just want to do the right thing for you. You're so wonderful, words can't express how I feel."

"Then the right thing for you to do is to go on loving me, just like this, no matter what happens."

"Is that a command?" she teased.

He struggled for breath. "No. I want you at my side, in my bed, because you want to be, and for no other reason."

"Done!"

EPILOGUE

Two months later Alex entered the conference room at the castle, nodding to Leo before looking around at his assembled cabinet. Today Alex's Uncle Vittorio had joined them.

"Gentlemen? Thank you all for coming on such short notice. I have several announcements to make.

"First of all, Uncle Vittorio has finally been given a clean bill of health, for which we're all grateful."

The room filled with applause.

"He, along with Aunt Renate, will be hosting an official engagement party for their daughter-in-law Princess Evelyn to our esteemed friend and colleague, Leo."

Thanks to Phillip who visited Jules's and Vito's grandfather on his own and had a long conversation with him, Alex's uncle had been won around by him. That had turned the tide, another miracle Alex hadn't been expecting.

"All of you will be receiving invitations. I'll leave it up to Leo to announce the date of their marriage. Needless to say, the young princes are ecstatic their stepfather-to-be was once a counter-espionage agent."

Everyone laughed, even his uncle. They all broke into enthusiastic applause, the kind that had to have lifted a weight from Leo's heart. Now for the risky part.

"Lastly, my wife and I have just learned we're expecting our second child."

The silence that followed was as palpable as the applause had been.

"Darrell would have been here with me, but she's too nauseated, so I left her at the house. You've had two months to form a consensus about me remaining king or stepping down. I'm prepared to hear what you have to say."

To his shock, his uncle Vittorio stood up. He stared at Alex for a long time. "My brother said you would make a good king." The older man who was looking trimmer because of his new diet, cleared his throat. "My brother was wrong."

Alex was waiting for the rest…

"I have it on good authority from Phillip that you are a *great* king. To quote him, 'You're the smartest man he knows. You love people, children, animals and most of all, his mom.'

"With such praise as that, may I voice my opinion first. God save the king."

While Alex stood there stunned, everyone repeated it and got to their feet clapping.

Suddenly the door opened and a wan-looking Darrell stepped inside. But her morning sickness only managed to give her an ethereal blond beauty that caused every head to turn.

How had she handled the helicopter ride? Alex's heart almost failed him. He'd wanted her here so badly. With her holding him up, he could face anything.

"May I add one more voice? God bless my beloved husband."

INVITATION TO THE PRINCE'S PALACE

JENNIE ADAMS

For Kara

Australian author **Jennie Adams** grew up in a rambling farmhouse surrounded by books and by people who loved reading them. She decided at a young age to be a writer, but it took many years and a lot of scenic detours before she sat down to pen her first romance novel. Jennie has worked in a number of careers and voluntary positions, including transcription typist and pre-school assistant. She is the proud mother of three fabulous adult children and makes her home in a small inland city in New South Wales. In her leisure time Jennie loves long, rambling walks, discovering new music, starting knitting projects that she rarely finishes, chatting with friends, trips to the movies and new dining experiences.

Jennie loves to hear from her readers and can be contacted via her website at www.jennieadams.net.

CHAPTER ONE

'YOU'RE here. I expected to have to wait longer.' Melanie Watson tried not to sound too desperately relieved to see the cab driver, but she *was* relieved. She'd been saving money to try to start a new life away from her aunt, uncle and cousin. She still didn't have enough, but tonight she'd experienced very clearly just how soul-destroying it truly could be to live among people who postured rather than accepted, who used rather than loved.

The family's gloves had come off and Mel had made the choice to leave now whether she was quite financially ready, or not.

Mel had waited until her cousin had disappeared into her suite of rooms, and until her aunt and uncle had fallen into bed. She'd cleaned up every speck of the kitchen because she never left a job half done, and then she'd ordered a cab, left a note in her room, packed her life into suitcases and carried it to the kerb.

Mel tried to focus her gaze on a suburb painted in shades of silvery dawn. The sun would rise fully soon. The wispy chill would lift. Clarity and the new day would come and things would look better. If she could only stay awake and alert for that long.

She really felt quite odd right now, off kilter with an unpleasant buzzing in her head. She didn't exactly feel she might be about to faint, but…she didn't feel right, that was for sure.

'It's a nice time for a drive. It'll be really quiet and peaceful.' That sounded hopeful, didn't it? At least a little bit positive and not overly blurry?

With the kind of anonymity born of speaking to a total stranger, Mel confided, 'I'm a bit under the weather. I had an allergic reaction earlier and I didn't get to take anything for it until just now. The medication is having a lot stronger impact on me than I thought it would.'

She'd got the treatment from her cousin's stash while Nicolette had seen off the last of the wealthy guests. Maybe Mel shouldn't have helped herself that way, but she'd been desperate.

Mel drew a breath and tried for a chirpy tone that emerged with an edge of exhaustion. 'But I'm ready to leave. Melbourne airport here we come.'

'I arrived earlier than anticipated so I'm grateful that you are ready.'

She thought he might have murmured, 'Grateful and somewhat surprised' before he went on.

'And I'm pleased to hear your enthusiasm despite the problem of allergies. Might I ask what caused them?' The taxi driver's brows lifted as though he didn't quite know what to make of her.

Fair enough. *Mel* didn't know what to make of herself

right now. She'd fulfilled her obligations, had pulled off all the beautiful desserts and other food for the dinner party despite harassment from her relatives and cleaned up afterwards when the party had finally ended.

Now she really needed her wits about her to leave, and they weren't co-operating. Instead, they wanted to fall asleep standing up. Like a tram commuter after a big day's work, or a girl who'd taken a maximum dose allergy pill on top of a night of no sleep and wheezing and swallowing back sneezes and getting a puffy face and puffy eyes.

'My cousin bought a new perfume. She sprayed it near me and off I went. Apparently I'm allergic to gardenias.' Mel dug for the remnants of her sense of humour. She knew it was still in there somewhere! 'Just don't give me any big bunches of those and I'm sure we'll be fine.'

'I will see to that. And you are right. It is a good time for a drive. The Melbourne cityscape is charming, even in pre-dawn light.' His words seemed so serious, and his gaze focused on her eyes, then on the spot where the dimple had come and gone in her cheek as she made her small joke. Would the dimple have offset her red nose and puffy face? Somehow Mel doubted it.

Mel focused on him, too. It was difficult not to because the man was top-to-toe gorgeous. Tall, a little over six feet to her five feet four and beautifully lean. Mel blinked to try to clear her drowsy vision.

He'd spoken in that lovely accent, too. French? No, but something European, Mel thought, to go with his tanned skin and black hair and the almost regal way he carried himself. He had lovely shoulders, just broad enough that a woman could run her hands over them to appreciate their beauty, or lay her head to rest there and know she could feel secure.

He wore an understated, expensive-looking suit. That was a bit unusual for a cab service, wasn't it? And his eyes—they weren't hazel or brown but a glorious deep blue.

'I just want to curl up.' Maybe that explained her reaction to him because his broad shoulders looked more appealing by the moment.

'Perhaps we'd better get your luggage loaded first, Nicol—' The rest of the word was drowned by the double beep of a car's unlocking device. He reached for the first two suitcases.

She must have given her full name of Nicole Melanie Watson when she booked the taxi. Since going to live with her aunt and uncle at age eight, Mel had only been known by her middle name. It felt strange to hear the first one again. Strange and a little shivery, because, even hearing only part of the word, his accent and the beautiful cadence of his voice made it sound special.

Oh, Mel. For goodness' sake.

'It's a pretty set of luggage. I like the floral design.' Was *Mel* making sense? She'd rescued the luggage when her cousin Nicolette had wanted to throw it out, but of course this man didn't need to hear that. And *she* didn't need to be quite so aware of him, either!

'You wouldn't lose the luggage easily. The design is quite distinctive.' He cast her a sideways glance. 'You are quite decided about this?'

'I'm decided.' Had he had people try to scam him out of fares? Mel would never do that. She knew what it was like to try to live on a tight budget. Her aunt and uncle might be well off, but they'd never seen the need to do more than meet the basic costs of taking her in. Once she reached working age, they'd expected her to return their investment by providing cheap kitchen labour. For the sake of her emotional health, Mel had to consider any debt paid now. 'I won't change my mind.'

She glanced to where he'd parked and saw, rather than a taxicab, an unmarked car. The cab agency had said there was a shortage of cabs but she hadn't realised someone might come for her in their private car in their off-duty time. Wouldn't that be against company policy?

And the car was a really posh one, all sleek dark lines and perfectly polished. That didn't seem right for a cab driver, did it? How would he afford it? Mel frowned.

'Did you come straight from a formal dinner or something?' It must have been a really late night.

The words slipped out before she could censor them. The thought that followed worried her a little, but he'd have had sleep wouldn't he? He looked rested.

You'll be perfectly safe with him, Mel. It won't be like—

She cut the thought off. That was a whole other cause of pain for Mel, and she didn't want to let it in. The night had been tough enough.

'Most dinners I attend are formal unless I have a night with my brothers.' Rikardo spoke decisively and yet…his guest didn't look as he'd expected. She didn't…

seem as he'd expected. Her openness and almost a sense of naivety…must be because she wasn't feeling well.

He tucked the odd thoughts away, and tucked his passenger into the front seat beside his. 'You may rest, if you wish. Perhaps by the time we arrive at the airport your allergy medication will have done its job and you'll be back to normal.'

'I doubt that. I feel as though I've been felled by elephant medicine.' She yawned again. 'Excuse me. I can't seem to stop.'

He'd collected a drowsy and puffy version of Sleeping Beauty. That was what Prince Rikardo Eduard Ettonbierre thought as the airport formalities ended and he carried Nicolette Watson onto the royal private jet and lowered her into a seat.

She'd slept most of the way to the airport and right through the boarding process. The medication had indeed got the better of her, but she was still very definitely…a sleeping beauty.

Despite the puffy face she seemed to have held her age well since the days when she'd been part of his university crowd during his time in Australia. She'd been two years behind him, but he'd known even then that Nicolette wanted to climb to the heights of social success.

Though their paths had not crossed since those days, Nicolette had made it a point to send Christmas cards, mark his birthday, invite him as her personal guest to various events, and in other ways to keep her name in front of him. Rik had felt awkward about that pursuit.

He didn't really know what to say now, to explain his lack of response to all those overtures.

Perhaps it was better to leave that alone and focus on what they were about to achieve. He'd carefully considered several women for this task. In the end he'd chosen to ask Nicolette. He'd known there would be no chance he would fall for her romantically, and because of her ambitious nature he'd been confident she would agree to the plan. She'd been the sensible choice.

Rik had been right about Nicolette. When he'd contacted her, she'd jumped at this opportunity to elevate her social status. And rather than someone closer by, who might continue to brush constantly through his social circles once this was all over, when their agreement ended, Rik could return Nicolette to Australia.

'You should have allowed me to carry her, Your Highness.' One of his bodyguards murmured the words not quite in chastisement, but in something close to it. 'Even driving a car by yourself to get her— You haven't given us sufficient information about this journey to allow us to properly provide for your safety.'

'There is nothing further to be revealed just at the moment, Fitz.' Rik would deal with the eruption of public and royal interest in due course but there was no need for that just yet. 'And you know I like to get behind the wheel any time I can. Besides, I let you follow in a second car and park less than a block away. Try not to worry.' Rik offered a slight smile. 'As for carrying her, wasn't it more important for you to have your hands free in case of an emergency?'

The man grimaced before he conceded. 'You are correct, Prince Rikardo.'

'I *am* correct occasionally.' Rik grinned and settled into his seat beside Nicolette.

Was he mad to enter into this kind of arrangement to outwit his father, the king? Rik had enjoyed his combination of hard work and fancy-free social life for the past ten years. As third in line to the throne, he'd seen no reason to change that state of affairs any time soon, if at all. But now…

There were deeper reasons than that for your reluctance. Your parents' marriage...

His bodyguard moved away, and Rik pushed that thought away, too. He wasn't crazy. He was taking action. On these thoughts Rik turned his attention to the sleeping woman. Her hair fell in a soft honey-blonde curtain. Though her face still showed the ravages of her allergy problem, her features were appealing.

Long thick brown eyelashes covered eyes that he knew were a warm brown colour. She had soft pink lips, a slim straight nose and pretty rounded cheeks. She looked younger in the flesh than in the photo she'd emailed, than Rik had thought she would look now…

She sighed and Rik had an unexpected urge to gently kiss her. It was a strange reaction to what was, in the end, a business arrangement with a woman he'd never have chosen to know more than peripherally if not for this. A response perhaps brought on because she seemed vulnerable right now. When she woke from this sleep she would be once again nothing but the ladder-climbing socialite he'd approached, and this momentary consciousness would be gone.

The pilot commenced take-off. Rik's guest stirred, fought for a moment to wake. Her hand rose to her cheek.

'You may sleep, Nicolette. Soon enough we will take the next step.' He said it in his native Braston tongue, and frowned again as the low words emerged. He rarely spoke in anything but French or English, unless to one of the older villagers or palace staff.

Nicolette turned her head into the seat. Her lashes stopped fluttering and she sighed. She'd cut her hair too, since the emailed photo she'd sent him. The shoulder-length cut went well with the flattering feminine skirt and silk top she wore with a short cardigan tied in a knot at her waist. The clothing would be nowhere near warm enough for their arrival in Braston, but that would be taken care of.

Rik made his chair comfortable, did the same for his sleeping guest, and took his rest while he could find it. When Nicolette sighed again in her sleep and her head came to rest on his shoulder, Rik shifted to make sure she was comfortable, inhaled the soft scent of a light, citrus perfume, and put down the feeling of contentment to knowing he was soon to take a step to get his country's economy back on its feet, and outwit his father, King Georgio, at the same time. Put like that, why wouldn't Rik feel content?

'You had an uneventful flight, I hope, Your Highness?'

'Not too much longer and we'll be able to disembark, Prince Rikardo.'

Mel woke to voices, snippets of conversation in English and another language and the low, lovely tones of her taxi driver responding regally while something soft and light and beautifully warm was draped around her shoulders.

'What—?' Heart pounding, she sat up abruptly.

This wasn't a commercial flight.

There were no rows of passengers, just some very well-dressed attendants who all seemed to make her taxi driver the centre of attention in a revering kind of way.

Mel's allergy was gone. The effects of the medication had worn off. That was good, but it also meant she couldn't be hallucinating right now.

She had vague memories of sleeping…on an accommodating shoulder.

Yet she didn't remember even boarding a flight!

This plane was luxurious. It had landed somewhere. Outside it was dark rather than the sunshiny day she'd looked forward to in Melbourne, and Mel could feel freezing air coming in through the aperture where another attendant waited for a set of steps to be wheeled to the edge of the plane.

She should be feeling Sydney summer air.

Memory of that expensive-looking car rose. Had she been kidnapped? Tension coiled in her tummy. If anything was wrong, she'd left a note saying she was moving to Sydney. Her relatives might be angry to lose their underpaid cook, but she doubted that they would go looking for her. Not at the expense of their time or resources.

Breathe, Melanie. Pull yourself together and think about this.

The driver had asked her if she was 'sure about this'. As though they already had an arrangement? That would make it unlikely that she'd been kidnapped.

But they *didn't* have an arrangement!

Mel turned her head sharply, and looked straight into the stunning gaze of the man who'd placed her in that car.

She'd thought, earlier, that he was attractive. Now Mel realised he was also a man of presence and charisma. All those around him seemed to almost feel as though…they were his servants?

Words filtered through to Mel again. French words and, among those words, 'Prince Rikardo'.

They were addressing her driver as a prince?

That was easy, then, Mel thought a little hysterically. She'd fallen down a rabbit hole into some kind of alternative world. Any moment now she would sprout sparkling red shoes. *That's two different fairy tales, Mel. Actually it's a fairy tale and a classic movie.* Oh, as though that mattered! Yet in this moment, this particular rabbit hole felt all too real. And maybe there'd been a book first, anyway.

Stop it!

'You're fully refreshed? How are the allergies? You slept almost twenty-four hours. I hope the rest helped you.'

Did kidnappers sound calm, rational and solicitous?

Mel drew a breath, said shakily and with an edge of uncertainty she couldn't entirely hide, 'I feel a bit exhausted. The allergies are gone. I guess I slept them off while we travelled between Melbourne and…?'

'Braston.' He spoke the word with a slight dip of his head.

'Right. Yes. Braston.' A small country planted deep in the heart of Europe. Mel had heard of it. She didn't really know anything about it. She certainly shouldn't *be anywhere near it.* 'I'm just not quite sure— You see, I thought I'd be flying from Melbourne to Sydney—'

'We were able to fly very directly.' He leaned towards her and surprised her by taking her hand. 'You don't need to be nervous or concerned. Just stick to what we've agreed and let me do the talking around my father, the king.'

'K-king.' As in, a king who was the father of a prince? As in, this man, Rikardo, *was* a prince? A royal prince of Braston?

Stick with the issue at hand, Mel. Why are you here? That's the question you need answered.

'You are different somehow to what I have remembered.' His words were thoughtful.

'Remembered from our drive to the airport? I don't understand.' Her words should have emerged in a strong tone. Instead they were a nervous croak drowned by the clatter of a baggage trolley being wheeled closer to the plane.

Well, this was *not* the time for Mel to impersonate a scaredy frog waiting to be kissed into reassurance by a handsome prince.

Will you stop with the fairy-tale metaphors already, Melanie!

'You're nervous. I understand. I'll walk you through this process. Just rely on me, and it will be easy for both of us to honour our agreement.'

Mel drew a deep breath. 'Seriously, about this "agreement". There's been—'

'Your Highness, if you and your guest would please come this way.' An attendant waved them forward.

The prince, Rikardo, took Mel's elbow, tucked the wonderful warm wrap more snugly about her shoulders, and escorted her to the steps and down them onto the tarmac.

Icy wind whipped at Mel's hair and stung her face but, inside the wrap, she remained warm. Floodlights lit the small, private airstrip. A retinue of people waited just off the tarmac.

Mel had an overwhelming urge to turn around and climb back onto the plane. She might not be down a rabbit hole, but she was definitely Alice in Crazyland. None of this would have happened if she'd been completely herself when she ordered that ride to the airport and believed it had arrived. Mel would never take someone else's medication again, even if it were just an over-the-counter one that anyone could buy!

'Please. Prince...Your Highness...' As she spoke they moved further along the tarmac. 'There truly has been some kind of mistake.'

What could have happened? As Mel asked the silent question puzzle pieces started to come together.

If he'd called at the right address, then he had expected to collect a woman from there.

Her cousin had been in a strange mood, filled with

secrecy and frenetic energy. At the end of the dinner party, Nicolette had rushed to her room and started rummaging around in there. Had Nicolette been…packing for a trip?

Rik had said he'd arrived earlier than he'd expected to. That would explain Nicolette not being ready. Mel had thought that he'd called her by her first name of Nicole, but it could have easily been 'Nicolette' that he said. She and her cousin looked heaps alike. Horror started to dawn. 'It must have been Nicolette—'

'Allow me to welcome you on to Braston soil, Nicolette.' Rikardo, *Prince Rikardo*, spoke at the same time. He stopped. 'Excuse me?'

Oh. My. God.

He'd mistaken Mel for Nicolette. Mel's *cousin* had made some kind of plan with this man. That meant Rikardo really was a prince. Of this country! As in, royalty who had made an arrangement with Nicolette.

Mel, the girl who'd worked in her aunt and uncle's kitchen for years, was standing here in a foreign country with an heir to the throne, when it was her cousin who should be here for whatever reasons she should be here. How could the prince not realise the mistake? Surely he'd have seen that Mel wasn't Nicolette, even in dawn light and with Mel affected by allergies? Just how well did this prince know Nicolette?

Yes, Mel? And how many times has Nicolette become furious when one of her acquaintances mistook you for her when they called at the house?

'Unless we're in the public eye, please just call me Rik.' He hustled her into the rear of another waiting car and climbed in beside her. A man in a dark suit climbed into the front, spoke a few words to the prince in French, and set the vehicle in motion.

The prince added, ‘Or Rikardo.’

‘You probably have five given names and are heir to a whole lot of different dukedoms or things like that.’ Mel sucked up a breath. ‘I do watch the news and see the royal families coming and going.’ She just hadn’t seen this particular royal. ‘The most famous ones. What I mean is, I’m not an overt royal-watcher, but I’m also not completely uninformed.’

Which made her sound like some kind of overawed hick who wouldn’t have a clue how to behave in such august company. Exactly what Mel was! ‘Please… Prince…Rik…I need to speak to you. It’s urgent!’

‘We have arrived, Your Highness.’ The words, spoken in careful English, came again from the driver.

He’d drawn the car to a whisper-quiet halt and now held the door open for them to alight. Rikardo would get out first, of course, because he was, after all, a prince.

A burst of something a little too close to hysteria rose inside Mel’s breast.

‘Thank you, Artor, and also for speaking in English for the benefit of our guest.’ Rikardo helped Mel from the car. He glanced down into her face. ‘I know you may be nervous but once we get inside I will take you to our suite of rooms and you can relax and not feel so pressured.’

‘S-straight to the rooms? We won’t see anyone?’ Well, of course they would see people. They were seeing people right now. And what did he mean by *their* suite? 'Can we talk when we get there? Please!'

'Yes, we will talk. It shouldn't be necessary at this late stage, but we will discuss whatever is concerning you.' He seemed every inch the royal as he said this, and rather forbidding.

Mel's stomach sank even further. She hadn't meant for this to happen. She hadn't meant to do anything other than take a taxi to the airport. She had to hope it would be relatively easy to fix the mistake that had been made.

Rik whisked her up an awe-inspiring set of steps that led to a pair of equally stunning studded doors. As they approached the doors were thrown open, as though someone had been watching from within.

They would have been, wouldn't they? Mel glanced up, and up again, and still couldn't see the ending of the outside of this enormous palace. Parts of it were lit, other parts melted into the surrounding darkness. It looked as though it had been birthed here at the dawn of time. Mel shivered as the cold began to register, and then Prince Rik's hand was at her back to propel her the final steps forward and inside.

Voices welcomed their prince. Members of the royal retinue of staff stood to attention while others stepped forward to take the prince's coat, and Mel's wrap.

How silly to feel as though the small of her back physically held the imprint of the prince's fingers. Yet if he hadn't been supporting her Mel might have fainted from the combination of anxiety and feeling overwhelmed by the opulence.

The area they entered was large, reaching up three levels with ornate cornicing and inlaid life-sized portraits of royal family members fixed into the walls. A bronze statue stood to one side on a raised dais. Creams and gold and red filled the foyer with warm resplendence. It would be real gold worth more than an entire jewellery store.

'Welcome to the palace.' Rik leaned closer to speak quietly into Mel's ear.

'Thank you. That is…' Mel's breath caught in her throat as she became suddenly very aware of his closeness.

She'd laid her head on his shoulder, had slept the hours of the flight away inhaling the scent of his cologne. On some level of consciousness, Mel knew the pace of his breathing, knew how it felt to have him sleep with his ear tucked against the top of her head. The feel of the cloth of his suit coat against her arm, his body warmth reaching her through the fabric.

For a moment consciousness and subconscious memory, nearness and scent and whatever else it was that had made her aware of him even initially through a fog of medication, filled Mel. She forgot the vital need to explain to him that he'd made a mistake and she had, too. She forgot everything but his nearness, and the uneven beat of her heart.

And then Prince Rikardo of Braston spoke again, softly, for her ears only.

'Thank you for agreeing to help me fulfil my father's demands and yet maintain my freedom…by temporarily marrying me.'

CHAPTER TWO

'THERE's been a terrible mistake.' Rik's bride-to-be paced the sitting room of his personal suite. Tension edged her words. One hand gestured. 'I don't belong here. I'm not the right girl. Look at all this, and I'm—'

'You won't be staying here all that long.' Not for ever. A few months… Rik tried to understand her unease. She'd been fully willing to enter into this arrangement. Why suffer a bout of cold feet about it now? She'd stepped into his suite, taken one glance around and had launched into speech.

'This is an interlude,' he said, 'nothing more.' And one they'd agreed upon, even if she hadn't yet signed the official contract. Rik's aide had the paperwork in a safe place, but it was ready and waiting, and Nicolette had made it clear that she was, too. So what had changed?

She drew a shuddery breath. 'This is gilt and gold and deep red velvet drapes and priceless original artworks and cornices in enormous entryways that take my breath away. This is more than a rabbit hole and a golden pumpkin coach and a few other fables meshed together. This is—' Her brown-eyed gaze locked with his and she said hotly as though it were the basis of evil: *'You're a prince!'*

'My royal status is no surprise to you.' What did surprise Rik was how attractive he found the sparkle in her eyes as indignation warred with guilt and concern on her lovely face. He'd never responded this way to Nicolette. He didn't want to now. This was a business arrangement. His lack of attraction to Nicolette was one of the reasons he'd chosen her. It would be easy to end their marriage and walk away.

So no more thoughts such as those about her, Rik!

'But it is a surprise. I mean, it wouldn't be if I'd already read about you in a magazine or something and I certainly completely believe you.' Shaking fingers tucked her hair behind her ear.

She didn't even sound like the woman he remembered. She sounded more concerned somehow, and almost a little naïve.

A frown started on his brow. He'd put down her openness, the blurting of a secret or two to him when he collected her, to the influence of the allergy medication. But that had worn off now. Suspicion, a sense of something not right, formed deep in his gut. He took a step towards her, studied her face more closely and wished he had taken more notice of Nicolette's features years ago. Those freckles on her nose—? 'Why do you seem different?'

'Because I'm not who you think I am,' she blurted, and drew a sharp breath. Silence reigned for a few seconds as she seemed to gather herself together and then she squared her shoulders. 'My full name is *Nicole Melanie* Watson.'

'Nicole…'

'Yes.' She rushed on. 'I'm known as Melanie and have been since I went to live with my aunt, uncle, and cousin *Nicolette* when I was eight years old. *Nicolette* would fit right in here. I've tried to figure this out since I woke up in your private jet and realised I wasn't at Sydney airport about to get off a plane there and go find a hostel to stay in while I searched for work because I could no longer stay—'

She broke off abruptly.

Sydney airport? Hostel? Search for work? There was something else about her statement, too, but Rik lost the thought as he focused on the most immediate concerns.

'I am not certain I understand you.' His tone as he delivered this statement was formal—his way of throwing up his guard. 'Are you trying to tell me—?'

'I think you meant to collect Nicolette and you got me by mistake. I don't see what else could have happened. When you said my name before, I thought you said Nicole, not Nicolette. I thought I must have given my full name when I ordered the taxi.'

'If what you say is correct…' Rik's eyes narrowed. Could this be true? That he'd collected the wrong woman? 'I haven't seen Nicolette for a number of years, just a photo sent over the Internet. I thought when I collected you that you'd changed and that you looked younger than expected. If you are not Nicolette at all—

Do you look a great deal like your cousin?' He rapped out the words.

'Y-yes, at least a fair amount. And I sound like her. It really annoys her. Acquaintances do it all the time when they come to the house. Mistake us for each other, I mean.' The woman—Melanie—wrung her hands together. 'This is all just a horrible mix-up. I was zonked out on medication, and waiting at the kerb for my ride to the airport to start a whole new life and you took me instead of taking Nicolette, who probably should have been waiting but she's never on time for anything, and you said you were early.'

Horror came over her face. 'Nicolette will be *furious* at me when she finds out what's happened.'

'It is not up to your cousin to take out any negative feelings on you if a mistake has been made.' A thought occurred to him. 'While I thought you were your cousin, you…mistook me for a taxi service?'

'I didn't know then that you were a *prince*!'

Did his lips twitch? She sounded so horrified, and Rik had to admit the idea of being mistaken for a cab driver was rather unique. His amusement faded, however, as the seriousness of the problem returned to the forefront of his thoughts. He didn't notice the way his face eased into gentleness as he briefly touched her arm.

'I'm sure there'll be a solution to this problem.' He bent his thoughts to coming up with that solution. He had planned all this, worked everything out. And after a long flight to get to Australia from Braston…he'd collected a cousin he'd never heard of, who had no idea of his marriage plans, the bargain Rik had struck with his father, King Georgio, or the ways in which Rik intended to adhere to that bargain but very much on his terms.

If he couldn't straighten this all out, his error could cost him the whole plan, and that in turn could cost the people of Braston who truly needed help. Rik held himself substantially responsible for that need.

'It's kind of you not to want to blame me.' She spoke the words in a low, quiet tone and gazed almost with an edge of disbelief at him through a screen of thick dark lashes.

As though she didn't expect to be given a fair hearing, or she expected to be blamed for what had happened whether she was in the wrong or not.

'There's no reason to blame you, Nicol—*Melanie*.' For some reason, Rik couldn't shift his gaze from the surprised and thoughtful expression in her eyes.

She looked as though she didn't quite feel safe here. Or did she always carry that edge of self-protectiveness, that air of not knowing if she was entirely welcomed and if she could let down her guard?

Rik had lived much of his life with his guard firmly in place. As a royal, that was a part of his life. But he knew who he was, where he fitted in the world. This young woman looked as though she should be happy and carefree. She had said she'd been about to start a new life. What had happened to make her come to that decision? To leave her family at dawn with all her suitcases packed?

Had Nicolette contributed to that sudden exit on Melanie's part?

You have other matters to sort out that are of more immediate concern.

Rik did, but he still felt protective of this young woman. She'd suddenly found herself on the other side of the world in a strange place. A little curiosity towards her was to be expected, too. He'd collected a stranger. Naturally he would want to understand just who this stranger was.

He would need her help and co-operation to resolve this problem, and she would need his reassurance. 'This doesn't have to be an insurmountable difficulty. If I can get you back out of the palace, keep you away from my father and create a suitable story to explain that bringing my fiancée home took two trips…'

'It seems such a strange thing to do in the first place, to marry someone for a brief period knowing you're going to end the marriage. Why do it at all if that's the case? How well do you know my cousin?' The words burst out of Mel as she watched Prince Rikardo come to terms with the problem of a girl who shouldn't be here, and one who should be and wasn't.

She felt overwrought and stressed out. What would happen to her plans now? Mel needed to be in Sydney looking for work. Not here suffering from a case of mistaken identity.

And then she realised that she'd just questioned a prince, and perhaps not all that nicely because she *did* feel worried and uneasy and just a little bit threatened and scared about the future. 'I beg your pardon. I didn't mean that to sound disrespectful. I guess I'm just looking for answers.'

'Your cousin is a past acquaintance from my university days in Australia who has kept in touch now and then remotely over the years since.'

So he didn't know Nicolette closely, had potentially never really known her. But he'd said he intended to marry her, albeit briefly. Mel's mind boggled at the potential reasons for that. Nicolette had hugged the secret close. Maybe she'd been told she had to? What was in it for Mel's cousin?

Well, even if it were to be a brief marriage, Nicolette would for ever be able to say she'd been a princess. Mel's cousin would love that. It would open even more doors socially to her. That left what was in it for Prince Rikardo?

'This must all seem quite strange to you, to suddenly find yourself here when you thought you were headed for Sydney, wasn't it?' His voice deepened. 'To start a new life?'

'I did say that, didn't I? When I thought you were a taxi driver and blabbed half my life story at you.' She drew a breath. 'I also meant no insult by thinking that you were a taxi driver.'

'None was taken.' He paused.

Did he notice that she dodged his question about starting a new life? Mel didn't want to go into that.

'Let me get the wheels in motion to start rectifying this situation,' he said. 'Then we'll discuss how this happened.'

For a blink of time as he spoke those words Mel saw pure royalty. Privileged, powerful. He would not only fix this problem, he would also have his answers.

He'd said he didn't blame her, that it wasn't her fault. But Mel couldn't be as self-forgiving. She should have realised something was amiss. There'd been signs. An unmarked car; a driver not in uniform; even the fact that he'd tucked her in the front of the cab beside him rather than expecting her to get in the back. Of course he would demand his answers. Had she really thought she would get off without having to face that side of it?

Would she in turn learn more of why he'd chosen her cousin for this interaction? 'Yes, of course you'll need to set wheels in motion, to contact Nicolette and sort out how to get her here as quickly as possible. I'm more than willing to simply be sent to Sydney. You can put me on any flight, I don't mind. I don't need to see my cousin again.' She didn't *want* to see Nicolette again and be brought to account for all of this, and for choosing to leave the family without a moment's notice, because Mel *wouldn't* go back.

What did Prince Rikardo see in Nicolette?

He didn't have to see anything.

Or maybe he liked what little he knew of Mel's cousin and they could conduct this transaction between them and perhaps even become firm friends afterwards. Nicolette could be charming when it suited her. There'd been times over the years when she'd charmed Mel. Not lately, though.

Mel searched Rikardo's gaze once more. Though his mind must be racing, he didn't appear at all unnerved. How could he portray such an aura of strength? Did it come as part of his training in the royal family? An odd little shiver went down her spine and her breath caught.

What would it be like, to be a prince such as Rikardo Ettonbierre? Or to be…truly in Nicolette's shoes, about to marry him, even if briefly?

Are you sure that his strength is simply a result of his position, his royal status, Melanie?

No. There was something in Rikardo Ettonbierre's make-up that would have demanded those answers regardless, and got them whether he'd ever been trained to his heritage, or not. That would have shown strength, not uncertainty, no matter what.

'We will make all the necessary arrangements. If we do it quickly—' Rikardo strode towards a phone handset on an ornate side table. He lifted the phone and spoke into it. 'Please ask my aide to attend me in my suite as soon as possible. I have some work for him to do. Thank you.' He had just replaced the receiver when a knock sounded on the door.

'That's too soon to be my aide,' he murmured. 'It will be our dinner. You must be hungry.'

The door opened. Members of staff entered bearing covered dishes. Aromas filled the room and made Mel realise just how long it had been since she'd eaten.

'The food smells delicious.' She'd always *cooked* the meals, not had them brought to her on silver salvers. 'I have to confess I *am* quite hungry.'

'That is good to hear.'

Rather than from Rikardo, the words came in a more mature yet equally commanding voice. The owner of that voice stepped into the room, a man in his early sixties with black hair greying at the temples, deep blue eyes and the power, by his presence alone, to strike dumb every staff member in the room.

Mel hadn't even needed that impact to identify him, nor the similarities to the prince. All she'd needed was one look at Rikardo's face, at the way it closed up into a careful mask that covered and protected every thought.

The king had just walked in.

This was the worst thing that could have happened right now. They'd needed to keep her, Melanie, out of sight of this man. Mel's breath froze in her throat and her gaze flew to Rik's. What did they do now? She caught a flash of a trapped look on Rikardo's face before he smoothed it away.

Somehow that glimpse of humanness opened up a wealth of fellow feeling in Mel. She had to help Rik out of this dilemma. She didn't even realise that she'd thought of him as Rik, not Rikardo.

The king's gaze fixed on her, examining, studying. He'd spoken to her. Sort of. Mel didn't know whether or not to respond.

'Indeed, Father, and it is fortuitous that you are here.' Rik stepped forward. He didn't block his father's view of Mel, but he drew the king's attention away from her. 'I would like a word with you regarding the truffle harvest, if you please.'

The older man's eyes narrowed. He frowned in his son's direction and said: 'It *pleases me* to know my future daughter-in-law will eat a meal rather than pretend a lack of appetite to try to maintain a waif-thin figure.'

Waif-thin figure?

Mel worked in a kitchen. She might have been underpaid, but she'd never been hungry. Was it usual for kings to speak their minds like this?

There was another problem, though. Even Mel, with her lack of understanding of royal protocols, could guess that it wasn't appropriate for Rikardo not to introduce her to his father, even if the king had surprised them in Rik's suite.

Should she introduce herself? Why hadn't Rikardo done that?

Because you're not who you should be, Melanie. How is he supposed to introduce you without either telling the truth or lying? Neither option will work just at the moment.

And anyway, why don't you interview all the kings you're on a first-name basis with, and collate the responses to discover a mean average and then you'll know whether they all speak bluntly?

She wasn't thinking hysterically exactly, Mel told herself.

Just don't say anything. Well, not anything bad. Be really, really careful about what you say, or, better still, stay completely silent and hope that Rikardo takes care of this. Didn't he say earlier if you came across his father to let Rik do all the talking?

Yes, but that was before he realised Mel wasn't Nicolette. His father didn't know that, though, and now the king had spotted Melanie. Not only spotted her but spoken to her and had a really good look at her. And if she didn't respond soon, the king might think—

'Your Highness.' Mel sank into what she hoped was an acceptable style of curtsy. She tried not to catch the older man's gaze, and hoped that her voice might pass for Nicolette's next time.

Rikardo had mistaken Melanie for Nicolette. But she'd been puffed up with allergies then. Rikardo strode towards the door of his suite.

At the door, he turned to face Mel. 'If you will excuse us? Please go ahead and eat dinner.' He asked one of the kitchen staff to let his aide know they would speak after Rikardo finished with the king. From outside, Rikardo called in another member of staff. 'Please also show my guest her rooms.'

In about another minute, the king would be out of here. Mel could stop holding her breath and worrying about what she might reveal to the king that could cause problems for when Nicolette arrived.

Mel glanced into Rikardo's eyes and nodded, acknowledging that he intended to leave.

Rikardo swept out of the room and swept his father along with him, even if he was the king.

Melanie thanked the staff for the delivery of the meal. She felt their curious gazes on her, too, and she would have liked to strike up a conversation, to ask what it was like to work in the kitchens of a palace. Instead, she kept her gaze downcast and kept the interaction as brief as she could.

The rooms she would use were lavish. Mel could barely take it all in.

And then finally she was alone.

So she could sit at the royal dining table in Prince Rikardo's suite that had its own guest suite within it, and eat royal food while she waited for the prince to have his discussion with his father about truffle harvesting. She hadn't known the country grew truffles.

But that wouldn't be all of the conversation and it would no doubt be difficult for the prince, but then Rikardo would come back here and tell Melanie his plans, and somehow or other it would all be all right.

Mel turned to the dining table, looked at the array of dishes. She would eat so at least she had some energy inside her to deal with whatever came next.

It *would* be all right. Rikardo was a prince. He would be able to make anything right.

CHAPTER THREE

RIK stood by the window in the sitting area of his suite. Early sunlight filtered across the snowy landscape of mountains and valleys, and over Ettonbierre village below. Soon people would begin to move around, to go about their work—those who *had* enough work.

He had once liked this time best of all, the solitude before the day's commitments took over. Today, his thoughts were already embroiled and his aide already on his way to Rik's suite to discuss yet another matter of urgency. The past two years had been problem after problem. Rik's marriage plans had been part of the solution, or so he had believed. Now…

He had spoken to his father last night. It hadn't been the greatest conversation he'd ever had; it had taken too long, and at the end of it he had known the impossibility of trying to bring Nicolette out here now to pass her off as his fiancée.

Really he'd known that from the moment Melanie had told him he'd collected the wrong girl. Too many people had seen her. Then Rik's *father* had seen her. She had tried not to be too noticeable, too recognisable. But the king *had* noticed. Right down to the three freckles dotted across the bridge of her nose.

Rik had whisked his father out of his suite. He'd bought a little time to come up with a solution before his father formally met his fiancée. But in the end there *was* only one solution.

A soft knock sounded on the outer door of his suite. Rik strode towards it. He didn't believe in the edict that a prince should not do such menial things as open doors to his staff. He and his brothers all worked on behalf of the people of Braston one way or another, so why wouldn't they open a door?

And now you all have a challenge to fulfil. The prize is that your father will come out of his two-year disconnection from the world around him, caused by the queen moving out and refusing to return, and co-operate to enable the economy here to be healed.

'Good morning, Prince Rikardo.' His aide stepped into the room and closed the door behind him. 'My apologies for disturbing you at this hour.'

'And mine for disturbing you late last night.' Rik gave a wry twist of his lips. 'To examine an emailed photograph, no less.'

And the passport of Nicole Melanie, which had been handled by one of his retinue of attendants when they arrived at the airport with his guest deeply asleep.

Nicole, not Nicolette. Only Rik could have spotted that mistake and he'd been otherwise occupied at the time.

'But with a purpose, Your Highness. It is unfortunate that the two women do not look enough alike to ensure we could safely swap them.' Dominico Rhueldt drew a breath. 'I have carried out your wishes and transferred the funds from your personal holdings to the bank account of Nicolette Watson, and ordered the set from the hand-crafted collection of the diamond jeweller, Luchino Montichelli. It will be delivered to Nicolette within two days.'

The man hesitated. 'Your Highness, I am concerned about the amount of money going out of your holdings towards relief to the people. I know they are in need—'

'And while I have the ability I will go on meeting needs, but that doesn't fix the underlying problems.' Rik sighed. It was an old conversation. 'Nicolette. She is happy with this...buy-off?'

A gift of baubles and a cash injection in exchange for her acceptance of the changed circumstances, and her silence.

Though Rik's question referred to the woman he'd organised to briefly marry, he struggled to shift his thoughts from the one he'd carried onto a plane recently.

He glanced at the closed door of his guest suite. Last night when he'd got back, he'd tucked the covers over Melanie. She'd been curled up on the bed in a ball as though not quite sure she had a right to be there. Sleeping Beauty waiting to be woken by a kiss.

The nonsense thoughts had come to him last night. A result of tiredness and the suppression of stress, Rik had concluded. Yet the vision of her curled up there was still with him. The desire to taste softly parted lips, still there. He'd been absorbed in Braston's problems lately.

Perhaps it had been too long since he took care of those other needs.

His aide rubbed a hand across the back of his neck. When he spoke again, his words were in French, not English. 'Nicolette acknowledged the payment and the order of the diamond jewellery as her due as a result of the changed circumstances. She accepts the situation but it is good, I think, that she will be unaware of any other plans you may intend to implement until such time—'

'Yes.' If 'such time' was something Rik could bring about.

'The other matter of urgency,' his aide went on, 'is unfortunately, the truffle crop.'

Rik swung about from where he'd been half gazing out of the windows. One search of Dominico's face and Rik stepped forward. 'Tell me.'

'Winnow is concerned about the soil in one of the grove areas. He feels it looks as it did last year before the blight struck again.'

'He's tested it? What is the result? We were certain we'd prevented any possibility of this happening this year. The crop is almost ready for harvest!' Rik rapped the words out as he strode to his suite. He stepped into the walk-in closet and selected work wear. Khaki trousers, thick shirt and sweater, and well-worn work boots. A very un-princely outfit that his mother would have criticised had she been here to do so. Rik started to shuck clothes so he could don the new ones.

His aide spoke from a few feet away. 'Winnow is doing the testing now.'

'I will examine the soil myself and speak with Winnow.' Rik laced his boots and strode into the sitting room.

'Your guest?' Dominico also glanced towards the closed door of the guest suite. 'Shall I wake her? Inform her of your immediate plans?'

'Allow her to sleep on while she has the chance. She had a long and difficult day before we arrived here. Please ask, though, that Rufusina be prepared to go with me to the groves.'

Melanie heard these words faintly through a closed door. She shifted in the luxurious bed, opened her eyes to a canopied pelmet draped above her head, and remembered curling up for just a moment while she waited for Prince Rikardo to return from speaking with his father. Now she was under the covers. Still in her clothes, but as though someone had covered her up to make sure she'd be comfortable. And that was Rik's voice out there, and it sounded as though he was about to go out.

Who was Rufusina?

'I'm getting up.' The words emerged in a hoarse croak. She cleared her throat, sat up, and quickly climbed out of bed. And called more loudly. 'Prince—Your Highness—I'm awake. I'm sorry I fell asleep before you got back last night. I'll be out in five minutes. I won't keep you waiting.'

Only after she called the words did Mel realise how they might have sounded to members of staff if any were out there with him, and, given he'd just spoken to someone, they probably were.

Heat rushed into her face, and then she felt doubly silly because she hadn't meant the words in that way, and the staff wouldn't care anyway, surely. And Rikardo would send her back to Australia today so none of this would be her problem for much longer.

Mel stopped in her headlong dash to the bathroom and wondered where the burst of disappointment had come from.

From being in a real live palace for a night and having to go home now, she told herself. And perhaps just the tiniest bit because she wouldn't have the chance to get to know Rikardo better.

'That's *Prince* Rikardo to you, Melanie Watson, and why would he want to get to know you? You're a cook. Not even a formally qualified one. You're not even in his realm.' She whispered the words and quickly set about putting herself together so she wouldn't keep the prince waiting.

Well, she *was* in his realm—literally right now. But in terms of having anything in common, she didn't exactly fit here, did she? No doubt he would want to speak to her sooner, rather than later, to tell her how he would get rid of her and how soon Nicolette would arrive to make everything as it was supposed to be.

That would be fine. Mel would co-operate fully. She only wanted to be sent home so she could get on with her life! Preferably avoiding contact with Nicolette in the process.

Outside in the sitting area, Rik's gaze caught with his aide's. 'I cannot be in two places at once right now. It would be rude to abandon Melanie now that she is awake, but breakfast must be offered, and I need to get to the groves.'

'Permit me to suggest a picnic breakfast for you and your guest after you have attended the groves. It would be easily enough arranged.' Dominico, too, glanced at the closed door of the guest suite. 'You might have a nice, quiet place in mind?'

Rik named a favourite place. 'That would be convenient to speak to Melanie there and see if she can find her way clear—'

'I hope I didn't keep you waiting.' The guest in question pushed her suite door open and stepped into Rik's sitting room.

Rik's head turned.

His aide's head turned.

There were appropriate words to be uttered to help her to feel comfortable, to extend grace. Rik wanted to do these things, to offer these things, but for a moment the words stuck to the back of his tongue as he gazed upon the morning face of Melanie Watson.

Soft natural colour tinged her cheeks. She'd tied her hair back in some kind of half-twisted ponytail. Straight falls escaped to frame the sides of her face. She wore a long, layered brown corduroy skirt trimmed in gold, brown ankle boots with a short heel and rubber-soled tread, and a cream cashmere sweater. In her hands she held a wool-lined coat. Her lips bore a soft pink gloss and she'd darkened her lashes with a touch of mascara.

Her clothing was department or chain store, not designer. The hairstyle had not come at the expense of an exclusive salon or stylist but thanks to a single brown hair tie and a twist of her hands. Yet in those five minutes she had produced a result that had knocked Rik out of his comfort zone, an achievement some had striven for and failed to achieve, in various ways, in decades of his life.

'You look lovely.' The inadequate words passed across his lips. A thought quickly followed that startled him into momentary silence. He wanted his brothers to meet her.

Maybe they would, if either of them were around today. And maybe Melanie would be on her way back to Australia before any chance of such a meeting could occur.

He stepped forward, lifted her right hand in his, and softly brushed her fingers with his lips. 'I hope you slept well and feel rested.' He introduced his aide. 'Dominico assists me with all my personal and many of my business dealings.'

In other words, his aide could be trusted utterly and was completely aware of their situation. At the moment, Dominico was more aware than Melanie.

Rik truly did need to speak with her, to set all matters straight as quickly as possible. He hoped that Melanie might co-operate to help him but it was a great deal to ask.

So much for your arrogant belief that you could outwit your father, still get all that you want, and not have to pay any price for it aside from the presence of a fiancée here for a few months.

Rik had collected the wrong woman and created a lot of trouble for himself.

So why did he feel distracted by the feel of soft skin against his lips? Why did he wish that he could get to know Melanie?

He pushed the thoughts aside. There was work to do. A truffle crop to bring to fruition disease-free, and a woman to take to breakfast. 'Will you join me for a walk outdoors? I need to attend to some business and then I thought we might share a picnic breakfast. I know a spot that will be sheltered from wind and will catch the morning sunshine. We can speak privately and I can let you know the outcome of my discussion last night with my father.'

'A—a picnic breakfast would be lovely, but is it all right for people to see me?' Her balance wobbled just enough to make him think she might have been about to curtsy to him. 'I'm sorry I wasn't still awake when you finished speaking with your father last night. It would have been okay to wake me up. I must have crawled under the covers.'

She hadn't. Rik had tucked her in. Had paused to gaze at a face that seemed far too beautiful. He suspected it had occurred to her that he might have tucked her in. The flush in her face had deepened.

Rik realised he still had hold of her hand. He released it and stepped back. 'It will indeed be fine. You are dressed well for the conditions. Shall we?'

Rikardo led Melanie through corridors and along passageways and past vast rooms with domed ceilings. Everywhere, staff worked with silent efficiency, going about their day's tasks.

Without making it seem a big deal, he explained that

she never needed to curtsy to anyone but his father or mother, and to them only in certain formal circumstances.

'Am I likely to meet your mother this morning?' Mel glanced about her and tried not to let an added dose of apprehension rise.

Rikardo shook his head. 'No. The queen is away from the palace.'

'Well, thank goodness for that, anyway,' she blurted, and then grimaced.

But Rikardo merely murmured, 'Indeed,' and they fell silent.

In that silence, Melanie tried not to let her mind boggle at the thought that she was walking through a palace beside a prince, and feeling relieved not to be about to meet a queen, but it all did feel quite surreal. Rikardo nodded to a staff member here or there. He'd said it was fine to be seen out with him by anyone they came across, so Mel would take that at face value. He'd obviously come up with some explanation for her presence.

'The kitchens here would be amazing.' She almost whispered the words, but she could imagine how many staff might work there. The amazing meals they would prepare. Mel felt certain the royal staff wouldn't have cake plates thrown at their heads as her cousin had done to her that final night.

Rikardo turned to glance at her. 'You can see the kitchens later if you wish.'

Before she left for the airport. Mel reminded herself deliberately of this.

'I didn't know that Braston grew truffles. I probably should have known.' She drew a breath. 'I've never cooked with them. My relatives loved throwing dinner parties but they were too—'

She bit the words back. She'd been going to say 'too stingy' to feed their guests truffles.

'Truffles have been referred to as the diamonds of the kitchen. Along with tourism they have represented the main two industries for Braston for some years now.' Rik stepped forward and a man in liveried uniform opened the vast doors of the palace and suddenly they were outside in the morning sun with the most amazing vista unfolding all around.

'Oh!' Melanie's breath caught in her throat. Everywhere she looked there were snow-capped mountains on the horizon. A beautiful gilded landscape dotted with trees, hills and valleys and sprinkled with snow spread before them. 'I didn't see any of this last night. Your country is very beautiful. I'm sure tourists would love to see it, too.'

'It is beautiful, if small.' Pride found its way into Rikardo's voice. 'But much of Europe is, and there are countries with more to offer to travellers. I would like to see an improvement in the tourist industry. If my brother Anrai has his way that will also happen very soon.'

Melanie liked his pride. Somehow that seemed exactly as it should be. And also the warmth in his tone as he referred to a brother. That hadn't been there when he'd spoken about the king or the queen, and, even if she'd only met the king briefly and had tried not to catch his attention too much, Georgio did seem to be a combination of forthrightly spoken and austere that could strike a girl as quite formidable.

You could handle him. If you managed yourself among your aunt and uncle and cousin for that many years and held onto your sense of self worth, you can do anything.

It hadn't hurt that Mel had set up a back-door arrangement and sent lots of cakes and desserts and meals out to a local charity kitchen to be shared among the masses. Her relatives never had caught on to that, and Mel had had the pleasure of giving away her cooking efforts to people who truly appreciated them.

Well, that life was over with now. Over the past year or so the family had forgotten to give her the kind moments that had balanced the rest. They had focused on the negative, and Mel had started saving to leave them. Now she just had to get back to Australia and to Sydney so she could start afresh.

It would be all right. She'd get work and be able to support herself. It didn't matter if she started out with very little. She pushed aside fears that she might not be able to find work before her meagre savings ran out.

Instead, she turned to smile at Rikardo. He looked different out of doors and in profile in these surroundings, more rugged somehow.

Face it, Mel. He looks attractive no matter what light you see him in, and each new light seems to make you feel that he's more attractive than the last one. And that moment of shared consciousness when she first stepped into his sitting room this morning. Had she imagined that?

Of course she'd imagined it. Why would a prince be conscious of…a kitchen hand? *A cook.* Same difference. They were both worlds away from being an heir to a kingdom.

'We commercially grow black truffles here.' Rikardo spoke in a calm tone. 'If you are not aware of it, truffles have a symbiotic relationship with the roots of the trees they grow under.'

'In this case oak trees,' Melanie murmured while she tried to pull her thoughts together. *Was* he calm? If so, his threshold for dealing with problems must be quite high. 'That's what they are, isn't it?'

Her glance shifted below them to the left where grove upon grove of trees stood in carefully tended rows. 'I'd heard that truffles could be grown commercially in that way. I think in Tasmania—'

'That's correct, and, yes, they are indeed oak trees.' He'd taken her arm, and now walked with her towards a grouping of …

Outbuildings? Was that a fine enough word for buildings within the palace grounds? There were garages with cars in them. Sports cars and other cars. Half a dozen at least. They all looked highly polished and valuable. They would go very fast.

Did the sun go in for just a moment? Mel turned her glance away. A man drove past them in one of the vehicles. Rik raised an arm as the driver slowed and tooted the horn before driving on. 'That is Anrai.'

'I thought he resembled you in looks.' Except Rikardo was far more handsome. And having her arm held by him made Mel way too conscious of him.

Small talk, Mel. You're supposed to be indulging in polite, get-to-know-you-but-don't-be-nosy-about-it small talk. 'How many brothers do you have?'

'Just the two, both older than me and busy trying to achieve their own plans—' He broke off.

A worker walked towards them, leading…a pig with a studded red collar around its neck. When the animal saw Rikardo, it snorted and almost pulled the worker over in its enthusiasm to get to the prince.

Rikardo looked down at the animal and then turned to Mel. 'This is Rufusina. She is a truffle hog and will be coming to the groves with us this morning.'

'*This* is Rufusina?' For some reason Melanie had pictured a gorgeous woman in an ankle-length fur-lined coat with long flowing brown hair. Maybe the woman had known Rikardo for ever and had secretly wanted to marry him herself.

Can we say overactive imagination? Well, this was the perfect setting for an imagination to run wild in! Mel tried to refocus her thoughts. 'She's a very interesting-looking truffle hog. She looks very…'

Porcine?

'Very intelligent,' Mel concluded.

'I am sure that is the first thought that comes to all minds.' For the second time since they'd met, Rikardo's lips twitched. Though his words laughed at Mel just a little, they laughed at Rufusina, too, for there was a twinkle in his eye as he watched the hog strain at her leash to get to him, and succeed.

Rikardo then told the hog to 'sit' just as you would say to a dog. The pig planted her haunches and cast an adoring if rather beady gaze up at him. She got a scratch behind each ear for her trouble. Rikardo took the lead.

They were at the groves before Mel had come to terms with her prince having a pet pig, because, whether he'd said so or not, this animal had been raised to his hand.

Mel would guarantee it. She could *tell*. They arrived also before Mel could recover from the beauty of Rikardo's twinkling eyes and that hint of a smile.

And what did Mel mean by '*her* prince' anyway? He certainly wasn't! She might have him for a few more hours, if that, and all of which only by default anyway because she'd been silly enough to think he was a cab driver.

Later, after she'd been returned to Australia, she could write her story and send it in to one of those truth magazines and say she'd spent a few hours with a royal.

She wouldn't, of course. She wouldn't violate Rikardo's privacy in that manner.

Today, in the broad light of Rikardo's…kingdom, Mel couldn't imagine how she'd mistaken him for anything other than what he was, whether she'd been overtired and overwrought and under the influence of an allergy medication or not.

It wasn't until they reached the actual truffle groves that Mel started to register that Rikardo seemed to have somehow withdrawn into himself as they drew closer to his destination. She wasn't sure how to explain the difference. He still had her arm. The pig still trotted obediently at his side on its lead. Rikardo spoke with each person they passed and his words were pleasant, if brief.

But Rikardo's gaze had shifted to those rows of oak trees again and again, and somehow Mel *felt* the tension rising within him as they drew nearer.

'Winnow.' Rik greeted a spindly man in his fifties and shook his hand. 'Allow me to introduce my guest, Miss Watson.'

So that was how Rik planned to get around that one. But would that be enough? Because for all the people that mistook Mel for her cousin, plenty more…didn't.

'Do you have the results of the soil test, Winnow? Are we infected again with the blight?'

This time Mel didn't have to try to hear the concern in Rikardo's tone.

'The test shows nothing, Prince Rik.' The man stopped and glanced at Melanie and then back to the prince. 'I beg your pardon. I mean, Prince Rikardo.'

'It's fine, Winnow. We are all friends here.' Rik dipped his head. 'Please go on.'

Winnow pulled the cap from his head and twisted it in his hands. 'The test shows nothing, but last year and the year before…'

'By the time the tests showed positive, it was too late and we ended up losing the crop.'

'Yes. Exactly.' Winnow's face drew into a grimace. 'I cannot prove anything. Maybe I am worrying unduly but the soil samples that I pulled this morning do not *look right* to me.'

'Then we will treat again now.' Rikardo didn't hesitate. 'Yes, it is expensive and a further treatment we hadn't planned for will add to that expense, but our research and tests show that enough of the treatment will keep the blight at bay. If you have any concern whatever, then I want the treatment repeated.'

The older man blew out a breath. 'I am sorry for the added expense but my bones tell me—'

'And we will listen.' Rikardo clapped the man on the back. 'Order the treatment. I will draw funds for it.'

From there Rikardo examined the soil samples himself, and took Rufusina into one of the groves to sniff about. Mel didn't fully understand the process. The older Winnow kept lapsing into the beautiful local dialect as he spoke with Rikardo.

It was worth not being able to understand, to hear Rikardo respond at times in kind. She felt as though she'd heard him speak to her in the same language but she must have imagined that. In any case it was very lovely, a melodious harmony of tones and textures.

'We will take breakfast up there, if you are agreeable.' Rikardo pointed to a spot partway up a nearby mountainside. He'd handed the truffle hog over to Winnow, who was about to put her to good use in the groves before seeing her returned to her home. And with an admonishment to ensure the pig didn't run off, as she was apparently wont to do on occasion.

But right now…

There was a natural shelving of rock up high where a bench seat and table had been set into it. The view would be amazing. 'Oh. That would be lovely.'

They began the climb. 'The truffles. Will they be okay?'

'I hope so. We've had two years of failed harvests. That has resulted in a devastating financial blow to the country's economy while we searched for a preventative treatment that would work without affecting the quality of the truffles.' He led her to the bench seat and table.

Opposite was a mountain with large sections covered in ice. Mel sat, and her glance went outward and down, over groves of trees and over the village named after the royal family. 'There must be so much rich history here. I'm sorry that there have been difficulties with the truffle industry. From Winnow I gather you play a key role in this truffle work?'

'I run the operations from ground level to the marketing strategies.'

Mel's gaze shifted to the village below. 'You must care about the people of Braston very much.'

'I do, and they are suffering. Not just here and in Ettonbierre village, but right across the country.' He drew a breath. 'I had planned that we should eat while I led up to my request but perhaps it is best to simply state it now and then explain.'

Mel's breath locked in her throat. Rikardo had a request of her? She glanced again at the scene below. Rikardo led a privileged life compared to the very ordinary ones playing out down there. There was a parallel to her life with Nicolette and her cousin's parents. But there was also a difference.

Rikardo seemed willing to go to any lengths to help those who depended on his family for their livelihoods. 'What can I do to help you? To help…them?'

'You are kind, aren't you?' It wasn't a question, and

he seemed as concerned by it as he was possibly admiring of it. 'Even though you don't know what I may want.'

Mel lowered her gaze. 'I try to be. What is it that you need?'

'If it is at all possible, if it's something you can do without it interfering unreasonably with your life or plans and I can convince you that you will be secure and looked after throughout the process and after it, I would like to ask you to take Nicolette's place.' Blue eyes fixed on her face, searched.

'T-take her place?' She stuttered the question slightly.

If Mel had peered in front of her in that moment, she felt quite certain she would have seen a hole. A rabbit hole. The kind that Alice in Crazyland could fall down.

Or leap into voluntarily?

'Just to be clear,' Mel said carefully, 'are you asking *me* to be the one to temporarily marry you?'

CHAPTER FOUR

'I know a marriage proposal must seem quite strange when you expected to be sent back to Australia today.' Rik searched Melanie's face.

He felt an interest and curiosity towards her that he struggled to explain.

And an attraction that can only get in the way of your goals.

He couldn't let that happen. And right now he needed to properly explain his situation to her. That meant swallowing his pride to a degree, something he wasn't used to doing. Yet as he looked at the carefully calm face, the hands clenched together in the folds of her skirt as she braced herself for whatever might come next, it somehow became a little easier.

At worst she would refuse to help him.

That would be a genuine 'worst', Rik. You need her help, otherwise you'll end up locked into a miserable marriage like that of your parents, or unable to help the people of Braston at all because this plan of yours has failed.

'May I be plain, Melanie?'

'I think that would be best.' She drew an uneven breath. 'I feel a little out of my depth right now.'

She would feel more so as he explained his situation to her. He had to hope that she would listen with an open mind.

'The arrangement that I made,' he said carefully, 'was to bring your cousin over here and marry her a month later.'

Melanie responded with equal care. 'You indicated that would be a temporary thing?'

'Yes.' He sought the right words. 'The marriage was to end with a separation after three months and Nicolette would then have been returned to Australia and a quick divorce would have been filed for.'

'I see.' She drew a breath and her lovely brown eyes focused on his blue ones and searched. 'You didn't intend to let your father know those circumstances until after the marriage, I'm guessing? What did you hope to gain from that plan?'

'Aside from my brothers, Nicolette, and my aide, no one was to know of the plan.' He'd intended to outplay his father, to get what he wanted for the people without having to yield up his freedom for it. 'This plan probably sounds cold to you.'

'It does rather reject the concept of marriage and for ever.' Melanie sat forward on the bench seating and turned further to face him. Her knee briefly grazed his leg as she settled herself.

The colour whipped into her cheeks by the cold air around them deepened slightly. That…knowledge of him, that awareness that seemed to zing between her body and his even when both of them had so much else on their minds…

Is something that cannot be allowed to continue, Rik, particularly if she is willing to agree to the business arrangement you're asking for with her.

'In my family, many lifelong marriages have been made to form alliances or for business reasons.' He hesitated, uncertain how to explain his deep aversion to the idea of pursuing such a path. 'That doesn't always result in a pleasant relationship.'

Melanie's gaze searched his. 'It could be quite difficult for children of such a marriage, too.'

'It's not that.' The words came quickly, full of assurance and belief as though he needed to say it in case he *couldn't* fully believe it?

Rik had his reasons for his decision. He was tired of butting heads with his father while the king tried to bully him to get whatever he wanted. His father needed to acknowledge that Rik would make his own decisions. That was all. 'There have been myriad problems in the past couple of years.

'The first year the truffle crop failed it was difficult.' People relied on the truffle industry for their survival. 'Around that same time, my mother, the queen, moved out. That was an unprecedented act from a woman who'd always advocated practical marriages and putting on a good front to the public, no matter what.'

Melanie covered her surprise. 'That must have caused some complications.'

'It did. For once my father found himself on the back foot.'

'And you and your brothers found yourselves without a mother in residence. I'm sorry to hear that. It's never pleasant when you lose someone, even if they choose to leave.' A glimpse of something longstanding, deep and painful flashed through her eyes before she seemed to blink it away. 'I hope that you still get to see her?'

'I see my mother infrequently when there are royal occasions that bring us all together.' Would Mel understand if he explained that his contact with his mother hadn't changed much? That the queen had never spent much time with her sons and what time she had spent had been invested in criticising their clothing, deportment, efforts or choices in life? Better to just leave that alone.

'My parents died years ago.' She offered the confidence softly. 'I went to live with Nicolette and my aunt and uncle after that happened.'

He took one of her hands into his. 'I'm sorry for your loss.'

Dominico had informed him of some of these things this morning after the security check the aide ordered on her came through. The invasion of Melanie's privacy had been necessary, but Rik had refused to read the report, asking only to be told 'anything that might matter'. Though he had to protect himself, somehow it had still felt wrong.

'Thank you.' She gently withdrew her hand, and folded both of them together in her lap.

She went on. 'You've explained about the truffle crops failing, how that's impacted on your people. One year is a problem but two years in a row—'

'Brought financial disaster to many of our truffle workers.' And while Rik pursued every avenue to find a cure for the blight to the truffle crops, his father had denied the depths of the problem because he was absorbed in his anger and frustration over his queen walking out on him.

'On top of these issues, the tourist industry also waned as other parts of Europe became more popular as vacation destinations. Tourism is Anrai's field. He has the chain of hotels and the country certainly still gets a tourist market, but when there is so much more to do and see just over the border…'

'You have to have something either comparable, or totally unique, to pull in a large slice of the tourist market.' Melanie nodded her head.

'Exactly. Our country needs to get back on its feet. My brothers and I have fought to get our father to listen to the depth of the problems.' They'd provided emergency assistance to the people out of their own pockets as best they could but that wasn't a long-term solution. None of them had endless supplies of funds.

In terms of available cash, nor did the royal estate. It had what it had. History, a beautiful palace and the means to maintain it and maintain a lifestyle comparable to it for the royal family. Their father oversaw all of that, and did not divulge the details of what came and went through the royal coffers. It was through careful investment of a shared inheritance that Rik and his brothers had decent funds of their own.

'Despite these difficulties you came up with a plan.' Mel searched Rikardo's face. Her heart had stopped pounding in the aftermath of his remarkable request, though even now she still couldn't fully comprehend it, couldn't really allow herself to consider it as any kind of reality.

It was Alice down that alternative universe hole again, yet it wasn't. He truly wanted her to marry him. For practical purposes, to outwit his father, and just for a few months, but still…he wanted her to marry him.

She started to find it hard to breathe again. 'And somehow your plan involved trading off a brief marriage for sorting out the country's economic troubles.'

'Yes. My father has pushed all three of us to marry. I think we all have expected that Marcelo would have to do that whether he wanted to or not because he is the eldest. It is part of his heritage.'

Mel nodded. 'I thought when I came here, well, I guess I was so overwhelmed by it all that I didn't stop to think that everything might not be rosy just because there's a palace filled with amazing things. Just because you're a prince doesn't mean everything is easy for you. Or for your brothers, either.'

'My brothers and I went to our father in a concerted bid to get him to listen to the seriousness of the problems the people are facing and with our plans for addressing those problems. Leadership reform is also desperately needed, and that is something Marcelo has been working to achieve for some years now.' Rikardo drew a breath. 'Our father finally did listen. We got our concessions from him.'

His tone became even more formal as he went on. 'But that agreement came at a cost. In return for agreeing to requests that will help us protect Braston's people from further financial hardship, his demand was that we each marry within the next six months.'

'To ensure that the family carries on?' Mel asked the question and then wondered if she should have.

Even as a king, did Georgio have the right to push his sons to marry if they didn't feel ready? If they didn't want to? For Rik to go to such lengths to avoid the institution, he must have some deep-seated reasons. Or did he just not want to be bullied? That was reason enough, of course!

Mel might not ever fully understand, and for some reason she felt a little sad right now. Her gaze shifted to the cliff face opposite. Two men were near the top, tourists or locals with rappelling equipment.

Mel had to navigate *this* discussion. And Rik's explanations did help her to start to understand what was at stake, at least for the people of Braston.

Could she decide to just walk away when the futures of so many people hinged on Rik meeting his father's demands? When him bringing her here by mistake could have ruined those plans? If she hadn't been on the street filled with allergy medication…

Whether she'd meant it or not, her actions had contributed to this current problem, and if there was no other way to fix it…

But it's such a big undertaking, Mel. Marriage, even if it is only for a few months! And there'd be publicity and a dress and so much else, and you'd be fooling Rik's father the whole time and then he'd realise he'd been fooled and be very angry.

Yet Mel knew that Rik would protect her; that he would make sure his father didn't bring any of his wrath down on Mel's head. Rik wouldn't *allow* that anger to have its head. 'When it ended you would send me back to Australia, to Sydney. I wouldn't be exposed to the aftermath here.'

'And because we'd give an interview when we dissolved the marriage and let the magazines and tabloids have that, I would hope you wouldn't attract much media interest when you went home.' His gaze searched hers. 'I would direct them towards me and ask you to do the same. At worst there might be some photographs and speculation about you in the newspapers over there for a brief time.'

That was to be expected when such an event had happened, but if all the information were already given, surely the papers wouldn't care much once they realised Mel wasn't going to talk to them, and the split had been amicable? 'That shouldn't be so bad.' The whole thing wouldn't be too scary if she decided to do it. Would it?

She reached for the picnic basket that sat ignored on the table before them, and hoped that Rik couldn't see the tremble in her fingers. 'Would you like coffee? Something to warm your hands around?'

'Thank you.' His gaze, too, shifted to the men on the nearby mountain peak before it returned to Mel. 'I should have unpacked the basket and made it all available to you the moment we got up here.'

The thought of a prince unpacking breakfast for her horrified her but she bit back her words about it and instead, served the food and coffee for both of them.

When she set his plate in front of him, he caught and held her gaze.

'I know what I'm asking isn't easy. I made this plan because I do not feel I can marry, truly...permanently.' He hesitated. 'The demonstration of that institution within my family—'

'Has been about as warm as what I've seen in Nicolette's family.' Mel bit her lip, but that was her truth and there didn't seem to be much point in avoiding saying it now.

They started on their food. There were eggs cooked similarly to a quiche but without the pastry base. Small chunks of bread dipped in fragrant oil and herbs and then baked until they were crisp and golden. Grilled vegetables and fruits and a selection of pastries.

'What you've asked me to do *is* unexpected.' Stunningly so. 'But I ended up here, you can't swap me for Nicolette, and if I don't agree, the game is up with your father and you either have to marry someone for real and stay married to her, or your father won't grant you the "concessions" you asked for.'

'I'm afraid I didn't allow for collecting the wrong woman outside Nicolette's home, but that is not your fault.' He frowned and sipped his coffee. 'It's important you don't make your decision based on guilt. A mistake happened that was out of my control, and yours.'

She did feel at least partially responsible, but Mel kept that thought to herself and instead took a small bite of a tasty grilled vegetable before she went on. 'I'd like to know what the concessions are that your father has agreed to.'

'I am determined that the truffle crop this year will not fail.' Rikardo set down his knife and fork and turned to face her. 'When it flourishes, I'll need a spectacular marketing idea to get buyers back onside to buy our product. Many of them have lost faith because of the blight that struck our crop two years running.'

Mel, too, set down her utensils. 'What is this marketing idea?'

'On the palace grounds there are truffles that grow naturally.' Rik's gaze shifted to where the palace sat in splendour in the distance. 'For centuries those truffles have been eaten only by royals. It probably sounds rather archaic but—' He shrugged and went on.

'These truffles are particularly fine. If buyers are given the chance to obtain small quantities of them in exchange for purchasing commercial quantities of our regular truffles, I believe they will jump at the opportunity.'

'What a clever idea.' Melanie spoke without hesitation. 'People will go nuts for a chance like that. I can also imagine that you might have had a job on your hands to get the king to allow you to use those truffles.'

'Correct. My father tends to adhere to a lot of the old ways and does not want to consider change.' Georgio was strong, stubborn, unbending. Rik preferred to take the strengths he'd inherited from his father, and turn them to better purpose.

As for Melanie, she looked beautiful and innocent and wary and uncertain all rolled into one as she sat beside Rik on the bench. Yet she also seemed well able to think with a business mind, too, and her eyes shone with genuine encouragement for him as she heard his plans for the truffle marketing.

Would she agree to help him out of the corner he'd got himself stuck in? Did he even have the right to ask that of her?

'I don't want to harm you through this agreement, Melanie.' That, too, had to be said. 'I have asked for your help, but if it is not something you can do, you do not have to give it.'

'But you want to help your people.' Her gaze turned to meet his, and held. 'You chose Nicolette because you weren't…romantically attached to her or anything like that, didn't you?'

'I did. That allowed the situation to remain as uncomplicated as possible.'

'It would be easy to end the marriage and get on with what you really wanted to do with your life afterwards.'

He dipped his head. 'Yes.'

'I'm not ready to consider marriage yet. The real thing, I mean.' Even as Melanie spoke the words, a part deep inside her whispered a question. Did she believe she would ever be ready? Did she even feel she had the right—?

What did she mean by that? Of course she had the right, and she would still have the right if she married Rikardo and they then divorced. Melanie pushed the strange question aside.

And she thought about all those people subject to circumstances beyond their control, just trying to get on with their daily lives. People in a lot of ways who would be just like her. Not royal people, but everyday people who simply needed a bit of a hand up.

Mel could do this. She could be of help. She could make it so Rikardo didn't have to lock himself into a long-term marriage he didn't want. Maybe later he would find someone and be able to be happy. The little prick she felt in her chest must have been hope that he would indeed find that happiness.

'I'll do it.' Melanie spoke the words softly, and said them again more forcefully. 'I'll do it. I'll marry you so you can make your plan work. I want to help you.'

'You're quite certain?' Rik leaned towards her as he spoke.

'I am. I'm totally sure.' And in that moment, Mel was. She could help him. She could do this to make up for him not being able to marry her cousin.

'Thank you, Melanie.'

'You're welcome.' Her face softened and the beginnings of a smile came to her lips. Her gaze moved to *his* lips and suddenly she had to swallow because something told her he was going to kiss her as part of that thank you.

She thought it, and her breath caught, and then he did.

Rik's lips brushed hers in a soft press. His hand cupped her shoulder, and even through layers of cloth Mel felt that. Registered that as she received a kiss from a prince.

That was why it felt so remarkable. It had to be the reason—a kiss from a prince to thank her for agreeing to help him out of a tight corner.

Yet Melanie didn't feel as though a prince was kissing her. She was being kissed…by a man, and it felt wonderful in a way no kiss had before.

In that moment her response was completely beyond her control. Her mouth softened against his, gave itself to his ministrations before her thoughts could catch up or stop her. If those thoughts had surfaced, would the kiss have ended there, with a simple brushing of lips against lips? A simple "thank you" expressed in those terms? Because that was indeed what Rik had set out to do.

It had to have been and yet somehow, for Mel at least, it had become something very different.

Mel closed her eyes. For a moment she forgot she was on a mountainside in Europe with a royal prince, seated at a table with a picnic breakfast spread before them and the most amazing scenic vistas on all sides.

She forgot that it was chilly here but that the sun shone and they were sheltered from the wind. A man was simply kissing her and she was kissing him back and that man had a pet truffle hog he'd named and whom he doted on, even though he tried very hard to hide the fact. He cared for his brothers and for the people who lived in his country, and she'd liked him from the moment she'd thought he was a gorgeous cab driver come to take her away to the airport so she could make her way to Sydney.

'Rik.' She'd slept on his shoulder and blabbed at him when she wasn't quite sensible, and, despite all the smart things she should be thinking right now, the kiss felt right.

'Hmm?' He whispered the half-question against her lips.

Mel didn't know whether she said it, or thought it. She simply knew the words.

Kiss me again.

CHAPTER FIVE

I would kiss you for ever and it would not be enough.

Rik thought the words inside his mind, thought them in his native language. Thought them even though they could not possibly be true and he must simply be swept up in gratitude and relief.

Yet deep within himself he knew that now, in this moment, Melanie would welcome the prolonging of this kiss. His instincts told him this. The way she yielded petal-soft lips to him told him this.

It was that thought of her willingness that finally prompted him to stop something that he should not have started in the first place, and that he hadn't expected would make his heart pound. He, who rarely lost his cool over anything, had been taken by surprise by kissing a slip of a girl up high on a mountainside.

'Thank you…' Rik released Melanie and drew back, and for a moment couldn't think what he was thanking her for.

For rescuing him. The prince was being rescued by the same generosity that he'd felt in Melanie's soft lips.

You are on dangerous ground with this thinking,

Rikardo. If she is kind, then she is kind and that is something indeed to be appreciated. But the awareness of each other—that cannot be, and it cannot go on.

He shouldn't have touched her. Arrogantly, he hadn't known that doing so would be such a stunning thing.

The kiss had been startling in its loveliness. It wasn't a manly description. But with Melanie it felt exactly right to describe it in this way.

Melanie was startling in her loveliness, and that came from the generous way she gave of herself.

He'd meant only to touch her lips with his, should perhaps not have considered even that much. Rik would like to say that he'd expected not to feel any attraction to Melanie, that he had expected to feel as indifferent towards her as he had felt towards Nicolette, but he'd known it would be different.

Yet he had kissed her, and had ended up shocked and a little taken aback by just how much he had enjoyed that kiss. Her response to him had felt unrehearsed and open. That, too, had added to her appeal.

Maybe she had simply wanted to kiss a prince.

In many other circumstances, Rik would have accepted the thought and yet Melanie had agreed to help him for no reason other than out of generosity to try to help others. She hadn't asked him what she would get out of the arrangement. She'd wanted to hear the problems and then she'd made a decision based on what she felt she could do to help.

'I guess we just sealed the bargain.' Her words held a tremor. She turned to the picnic basket and started to carefully repack it. 'We should probably get back. Now that we've made this decision, your father will want that official meeting. That's assuming he can fit me into his schedule. I imagine royal families are very busy and I certainly wouldn't presume—'

'It will be all right, Melanie.' She was fully back into 'dealing with a prince and a promise and a royal family' mode and in feeling out of her depth, though she had valiantly jumped into this for his sake.

And for the sake of the people of Braston.

Did that mean she *hadn't* thought of Rik in that light as they kissed? That he had simply been a man kissing a woman, and she a woman kissing a man? Had his impact on her come completely from Rikardo the man, not from him being the third prince in line to the throne of Braston?

It wasn't a question that should even have mattered. Rik had accepted that women were attracted to his title first, sometimes to the man within, second, but always that first was there.

Perhaps some of his questioning came from the relief of knowing he hadn't blown his chance of avoiding being locked into a miserable marriage as part of his bargain with his father.

Melanie's gaze meshed with his. 'Are *you* quite sure you want to do this? I want to help you and help the people of Braston, but in the end what you do has to be really what you want.'

'I'm sure.' He got to his feet and lifted the picnic basket. 'We may not get much done today other than the meeting with my father if he is available, but Dominico will want to get the ball rolling on a few things.'

Melanie agreed. Now that she had committed to marrying Rikardo, she wanted to get things moving.

She didn't want to stop and give herself too much time to think about the next month and the three that would follow it.

That might have been rather easier for her before they shared that kiss. Mel stumbled slightly on the uneven ground. She didn't want to think about the kiss, either! Her heart still beat hard from its impact.

'I have you.' Rik's hand shot out and grasped her arm.

And I have received the most moving kiss I've ever experienced.

Not that Mel *had* a great deal of experience. Her life with the family had kept her busy. Oh, she'd dated here and there with men that she met out in her 'normal' world. At the fresh produce store, or once it was the delivery guy from the local butcher's shop. There hadn't been a lot of time or opportunity.

There is always the time and the opportunity if you want it enough.

Well, now there was a prince.

No, there wasn't. Not like that. She wasn't dating Prince Rik. She *was* going to marry him, but that was for an agreed purpose that had nothing to do with romance. Right. So she was safe from getting any of the wrong kind of ideas about him or anything like that.

Why then, with Rik's hand on her arm, and the memory of a kiss still fresh in her mind and stamped on her lips, did Mel feel anything *but* safe?

From what? Falling for him? That would be insane.

Much more than falling down a rabbit hole or wearing sparkling magic shoes that would take her anywhere.

So focus on getting back to the palace to start this process that will help lift the country's economy. Rather than thinking about kisses, you should think of how you can find out as much as possible about truffle crops so you really can be of help to Rik for the short time you're here.

'Do you have books about truffle cropping in the palace?' She glanced towards the prince.

Yes, *the prince*! That was what Rik was, and Mel mustn't forget it. And since when had she started to think of him as Rik?

He said you could.

And if you have a shred of self preservation left, then you should address him as 'Your Highness' or something equally distancing, in person and in your thoughts.

'I have books at the palace and also at my personal home up in the mountains.' He glanced at her, and then up and beyond her to where those two tourists had found their way to what to Mel looked like a sheer wall of ice.

Rikardo had a second home in the mountains?

Well, duh, Mel. He's got to be about thirty and he's a prince. Did you think he'd still live permanently in a couple of rooms in the palace? Even if those rooms were quite glorious and added up to more like a small house. 'I'd like to look at the books, if that would be okay. I'd like to learn more about the industry.'

She might not be able to do anything to help with the problems they'd had, but if Rik planned to harvest truffles from the royal grounds that, too, would be rather special. Maybe there were records about that, as well.

'The kitchen staff would have special truffle recipes, wouldn't they? Maybe handed down through the centuries? I'd love to see those!' Mel tried hard to walk normally and not lean into him. He still had hold of her arm and her silly response receptors wanted to melt into his side as though they had every right just because he'd kissed her.

He might be marrying Mel, but he was doing that to help him *avoid* a committed relationship.

And Mel was marrying him to help him out, and she didn't need to add the complication of being attracted to him to *that* mix. So it was just as well they'd shared that kiss and put it behind them. They could get on with the business end of things now.

As if it will be that easy, Mel. What about the wedding preparations? The fact that his father will think the two of you want to marry for real?

'I need to have the right things to say to your father!' The words blurted out of her with a panicky edge she didn't anticipate until it was too late to cover it up. 'That is, I don't want to be unable to answer any questions he might ask about how we met, how long we've known each other, that kind of thing.'

'We met through your cousin Nicolette when I was at university in Australia. Six months ago we came across each other on a computer forum and we've been chatting online and on the phone ever since.' He turned his head and deep blue eyes looked into hers. 'I wanted you for my princess. You are calm and pleasant and I felt

I could spend the rest of my life with you. It's not the entire truth, but it's as close as we'll get.'

'Okay. That will work. I know the years that Nicolette was at university, though I didn't attend myself.' There was one other issue, though. 'What's my story? Why did I say yes?'

Before he could answer, she shook her head. 'If your father asks me that question, I'd rather tell him that I will do everything in my power to be as supportive of you as I possibly can in all the time we're together.'

He dipped his head. 'Then stick to that. Commitment to me is implied in such statements. My father should find that more than acceptable.'

'Wh-what will be expected…otherwise?' Mel asked the question tentatively, and she didn't want to be tentative. She needed to know, therefore she was asking. She straightened her spine. 'When we're married, will we be in your suite as we are now, or…?' Despite the straighter spine she couldn't quite bring herself to put it into words.

His gaze met hers. In it was steadiness. 'For the sake of appearances we would be sharing my room and…bed at first. This is something that can be managed with a little creative imagination without needing to cause you undue concern. Just for the look of things, you understand?'

'Just—just part of our overall practical arrangement. Yes. I understand totally. That's very sensible.' Mel tried not to stutter the words, tried to sound mature and au fait with the situation and what it might entail. They might be sleeping together at the start—her mind tried to boggle and she forced it not to—but they wouldn't be *sleeping together.* Not, well, you know. Not like *that.* She drew a breath. 'Right. That's okay, then. We can make that work.'

'We will, Melanie, so do not worry.' His words again held reassurance.

And Mel…relaxed into that reassurance.

They were at a turn in their downward descent where the two mountainsides faced each other when a cry ripped through the air, shattering her composure and bringing Rikardo to an abrupt stop.

'Damn. What's the man doing? He's tangled in his equipment!' Rik dumped the picnic basket and strode towards the source of the cry.

Mel followed, and after a few moments managed to spot what Rik had already seen. A man dangled against that icy outcrop. It was one of the two men she'd seen earlier. The other—Mel couldn't see.

'Stop, you fool!' Rik spoke the words aloud but they were too far away for any hope that the man might hear them.

Even so, Mel echoed the sentiment.

The prince let out a pithy curse. 'If he keeps trying to get loose, he'll drop to the bottom.' He didn't slow his pace, but he turned to glance at her. 'There's no one anywhere near except us. I've rappelled that section many times. I have to see if I can help while we wait for a rescue team to get here.'

He already had a cell phone out, and quickly called for assistance and explained the situation and that he would see what he could do until the rescue team arrived.

Mel could hear someone at the other end insisting the prince must not go anywhere near the dangerous situation, before Rik said, 'Get help here as quickly as possible' and ended the call.

She bit back the inclination to ask him if he *would* be safe enough. 'What can I do, Rik?'

'Keep yourself safe. Do not follow the path I take. Follow the path that's cut into the mountain and you'll reach the same destination. It will take longer, but I'll know you are not at risk. When the rescue team starts up the mountain, point them to where I am.' He strode ahead confidently.

Mel followed at the best pace she could manage. Each moment counted and Rik quickly got ahead of her, and then cut a different path towards the ice-bound cliff. After a few minutes she could hear him shout to the man first in English, and then in French. The conversation continued in French, and Mel could only guess what was being said.

She struggled on, determined to reach Rik and be of help if she could. She was within shouting distance herself when she looked back and saw the rescue team starting up the mountain. Mel waved to them and pointed to Rik's location, and got a wave back from the leader of the team.

Mel kept going, and then there was the man, dangling in mid-air, and Rik saying something sharp and hard to a second man at the top of the cliff before taking that man's unused equipment and kitting up.

The third prince of Braston was over the edge in a breathtakingly short time. Mel didn't go any further, then. She wasn't sure she could have if she tried. Instead she stood frozen in place, completely unable to breathe as all the concern for his safety that she'd pushed back rushed to the surface and threatened to overwhelm her.

She bit back the instinct to call out, 'Be careful.' Considering what he was doing, he would already be at the bottom of the cliff if he weren't taking care.

Nevertheless, what followed made Melanie's blood chill. She'd never watched ice rappelling. It looked risky, and it was obvious from the way he tried to control his slip that Rik didn't have the right boots on his feet for the job.

The stranded man, despite Rik's instructions that even Melanie could tell were to stay still and wait whether they were in French or not, continued to tug and pull at the tangle he was in. Did he *want* to end up at the bottom of the mountain?

'Your Highness, you must wait for us!'

'Please, Prince Rikardo, you must come away from there!'

The words were called as the rescue team came close enough to see what was happening, but it was too late. If Rik didn't do something about this man, he would kill himself. Panic had the man in its grip. The second man showed no apparent interest in proceedings, sitting there with a blank look on his face.

Had Melanie looked like that when she'd taken that medication and faded into sleep?

He's taken some kind of illicit drug, Mel. You've seen

enough of that in Melbourne to recognise it. No doubt Rik recognises it, too.

'You have to make sure that second man doesn't interfere with what Rik's doing or do anything stupid himself.' She spoke the instruction to the head of the rescue team as they drew close. 'He's under the influence of something. It's likely that both of them are, because Rik's struggling to get the stranded one to listen and stop fighting to get free.'

Rik had rappelled out beside the man. He couldn't untangle him, but he was trying to calm him. At his own risk! Even now the man reached for Rik with clawing hands!

'Oh, please, be careful,' she whispered.

She didn't notice that she'd called him Rik as she spoke to the rescue team, or that she'd spoken as though she had every right to that authority. Mel didn't care.

The next ten minutes felt like a lifetime. When the man was hauled up, Rikardo followed. He moved with confidence. Mel had made her way to the top and wanted to grab him once he got up there and…

Shake him? Check that he was unharmed?

Kiss him a second time?

'All is well, though I have asked the team to take both men to the nearest hospital and have them checked over, drug tested and, if need be, charged by the police.' Rik's words were spoken across a very calm surface.

But beneath that calm must be all the anger over the stupidity of those two men.

'Your Highness…' One of the rescue team approached.

'I am well and unharmed but you must excuse me now,' Rikardo said with respect, and firmness.

And then he stripped out of the equipment he'd commandeered, took Mel once again by the arm, and started down the mountain with her.

Mel walked at his side. 'I'm so glad you knew what to do up there. I'd like to see you do that properly one day, with all the right equipment, because I think you would be amazing at it.'

I'd like to see you do that properly one day...

Melanie's words rang in Rik's ears as he put his Italian sports car through its paces on the way to his mountain retreat home.

Her words were a salve to the anger he'd bitten back over the stupidity of those two men. Had they *wanted* to get themselves killed? The other one, when questioned, had said he was waiting for his turn to go out 'alone' and that ice rappelling was 'easy, man'.

The man had been so far gone that he hadn't even comprehended the danger his friend was in. Well, they were both safe now.

Rik let the thoughts go and turned his attention to his driving. He'd held back until he reached the private road that led to his home. This road, he knew better than the back of his hand, every turn, just how much he could give behind the wheel to release the pent-up energy that came from that stressful rappel in someone else's untested equipment. He'd needed this.

He's going too fast. Mel couldn't get the thought out of her head. Her logical mind understood that Rik had control of the car. It was clear he knew this road well. The road itself was wide with plenty of room for dual traffic and yet it was a private road. They hadn't seen any other cars and she guessed they were quite unlikely to do so.

All of this made infinite sense. The paralysing fear inside Mel did not make sense. Her fingers curled into the edges of her seat. Her heart pounded with a mixture of apprehension and the need to get out of this situation at any cost.

'Please stop.' The words whispered through her clenched teeth, whispered so quietly that she didn't know how Rik could have heard them.

All Mel knew was that she wanted out of this car. Now.

'Melanie.' A voice tinged with remorse broke through her fear. The car began immediately to slow and Rik said, 'I'm sorry. I didn't realise you were uncomfortable.'

It's all right. I'm fine. There's no need to slow down or stop.

In her mind, Mel entertained these polite thoughts. But her instincts were in a very different place. She struggled to breathe normally, to not throw her door open and try to get out. The reaction was so intense and so deep that it completely unnerved her. She couldn't speak, couldn't think clearly, didn't know what to say to him, didn't understand why she had ended up feeling like this.

Within moments the car moved much more slowly and fingers wrapped firmly around the hand nearest to him. 'Do you need me to stop the car completely, Melanie? My house is less than a minute away and I'd rather get you there if possible.'

The roaring in her ears started to recede but Mel was still a long way from calm. Her fingers tightened around his. 'I don't know what came over me. I feel stupid for the way I've reacted.'

'You are certainly not stupid.' Rik spoke these words softly as he drew the car to a stop in front of his mountain home. The place was maintained for him, but did not have permanent staff. They would be alone here, and he was glad for that now to give Melanie a chance to recover.

Whatever had happened during the trip had affected her deeply, and he felt she would benefit from space and not having to deal with anyone new just for the moment.

Had the panic come on because of all the pressure he'd put on her? It was a lot to ask a woman to become his temporary princess, to work with him to fool his father into believing the marriage was intended to last a lifetime.

It was a lot for her to find herself here under confused circumstances let alone the pressure Rik had added to that load for her.

You must take care of her. Give her time to calm down.

He got out of the car, opened her door for her and took her hand to help her out. His home was chalet-style, built of log and with a sharply pitched roof. Large windows gave beautiful views from every part of the home and were one-way tinted for privacy. Rik doubted that

Melanie noticed any of it. Her face was sheet-white and the hand he held within his trembled.

'Let me get you a hot drink, Melanie.' He led her inside and to a comfortable leather sofa in the living room.

'Thank you. It is a bit chilly, isn't it?' Melanie sank onto the sofa and didn't argue about who should be preparing the beverages.

Rik didn't waste time, and quickly returned with coffee for both of them. He took his seat beside her. 'This will take the chill away.'

The rooms were centrally heated, but she'd clearly had a shock. It would take time for her body to return to a normal temperature.

Rik had brought that shock about. He had put too much on her. Bringing her to Braston with her waking up from a long sleep to discover she was in the middle of Europe instead of in Sydney. He'd asked her to replace her cousin and briefly marry him. Had piled all the worries about the country onto her, and then had left her to cope with her concern for him while he rappelled onto an icy cliff in dangerous circumstances to deal with a man who didn't want to hear reason, and another who could have added more trouble to the mix.

To cap it off, Rik had come up here to get away from things, and the speed of his driving had frightened her enough that she hadn't been able to even tell him what was wrong.

As Melanie sipped her coffee and colour began to come back into her face Rik set his drink down and turned to her. 'I am sorry that you were afraid during the drive up here.'

'You weren't to know that I would react like that. I didn't know it myself.' She forced her gaze about the room before meeting his eyes. For the first time since leaving the car, she seemed to see her surroundings.

Maybe that, too, helped her, because she said valiantly, 'It was worth the trip. This is a lovely home and the views are amazing. And I feel much better. I'm sure I won't have that kind of problem again.'

'I am pleased that you're starting to feel better. What happened to you? Do car trips always make you uneasy?'

Back in Australia, she'd checked when he collected her from outside Nicolette's home that he felt fresh enough to drive. Rik hadn't thought anything of it.

'That's the first time I've been in a sports car. They go very fast.' As she seemed to consider what had happened she frowned. 'I don't understand this myself. I don't drive, but I'm not usually the type to panic unnecessarily, and with hindsight I *know* that you had control of what you were doing.

'I'm just sorry that I spoiled the drive for you,' she said. 'You obviously needed an outlet after dealing with those two foolish men and keeping your calm so well, both before and after.'

Rik *had* needed that outlet. Sometimes keeping his cool came at a cost to his blood pressure!

'I felt like telling them off myself for being so stupid,' she added hotly, 'and I wasn't the one who had to risk life and limb to go out and stop that first man from falling to his death!'

Maybe if she learned to drive herself, she might feel better informed and more confident to assess the skill of other drivers when they were behind the wheel.

They were side by side on the sofa, and Rik became very conscious of that as they fell silent and gave their attention to their drinks.

After a moment, she spoke with a slight teasing tone in her voice. 'You make very good coffee. Is it allowed, for a prince of the realm to do such tasks as make coffee?'

'And do them well?' He shrugged his shoulders. 'I think in today's world it is, and I would go hungry and thirsty up here if it weren't.'

She was a plucky girl. Resilient. The thoughts came to Rik and lodged. He couldn't help but admire her for that.

'Do you think I could have a tour while we're here?' she asked. 'I'd love to see the rest of your home.'

'Absolutely.' Rik got to his feet and held out his hand to help Melanie rise.

He was getting in the habit of that, of reaching for her hand far too often…

But you will need to do things like that to make the upcoming marriage plans seem realistic to your father.

Even though Georgio would not expect it to be a love match, he would still expect such demonstrations.

'The meeting with my father has not yet been arranged. I think it can wait for a little longer yet.' Rik drew a breath. 'I'd like some time to restore a better mood before I tackle that talk, to be honest.'

'Then I'm glad I asked for the tour.' Mel melted the moment Rik confessed his need to prepare for the talk with his father. And she truly did feel so much better now. 'We can stay here as long as you want. It's a beautiful place.'

Rik was good company and they'd just sort of got engaged, so why shouldn't they stay here for a bit, if they wanted to? She could use the time to ask a few questions about how they would work their way through the next few months, too.

'I'll need a wedding dress.' Visions of past royal marriages scrolled through her mind. 'Something very simple that won't cost the earth.' She turned to Rik. 'How do we pull off a wedding in a month?'

'With a really good wedding planner, and, as you've already realised, with the most simplified plans possible.' He started towards the rear of the house and said firmly, 'Now let me show you the rest of my retreat, and all the views. I think they're worth seeing.'

They were, and Mel looked out of floor-length windows at some very lovely scenery before Rik toured her through the rest of his home. It was surprisingly humble. Well, not humble. It was a delightful four-bedroom chalet-style home but it certainly wasn't, well, a palace.

'I love this place,' she blurted. 'If it was me I'd be up here all the time. Normal-sized rooms, calm atmosphere, no one to tell you what to do.'

'You've just worked out the secrets of my attraction to this home.' He smiled and led her into the final room.

It was an office, with a desk and computer and shelves of books about… 'Oh. Can I look at some of those? Do you have ones that show what the truffles look like when they're harvested? History books? Anything about the *royal* truffles? Cooking? The growth process from beginning to end and the uses of truffle hogs?'

'Yes to all of that. And I trained Rufusina under the tutelage of Winnow. There is a photo album.' Rik brought out the photo album and a selection of books and before Mel knew it she was nose down in some gorgeous pictures, and some very interesting information. He didn't have cookbooks, but he told her that some of the old recipes were still produced at the palace and described some of the dishes.

'Truffled turkey. I'd like to cook that.' Mel thought back through her cooking career. 'The closest I've come to cooking with truffles is using truffle-flavoured oil a few times.'

Rik's brows lifted. 'You had a career as a cook?'

'Yes, working for my aunt and uncle.' Mel glanced at him through her lashes. She'd thought he would have known that already.

They were seated with her on the swivel chair, and him leaning back against the corner of the desk in his office. It wasn't a large room, and as she let herself register the cosiness, his closeness, Mel suddenly became breathless. 'I cooked for them for years. Cakes and desserts were my speciality, but I cooked all the meals, including for dinner parties. They liked to schmooze wealthy—'

She coughed and turned her attention back to the

books. 'These are wonderful resources. It's an intricate industry. You've done well to get the black truffles growing commercially here.'

'Not so well in the past two years.' Rik glanced up and towards the windows.

The frown that came to his face made Mel follow his glance.

She hadn't noticed the change in atmosphere, but now she saw it. 'I didn't know it had started snowing.'

'Yes.' He got up from the desk. 'Why don't you select what books you'd like to bring back to the palace when we return, while I see what's in the kitchen that we can have for our lunch?'

Not that Mel minded either way and it wasn't as though Rik were trying to trap her into spending time with him here. He'd probably enjoy the time away from the palace while he could, but would have been just as content to be up here by himself.

Something in his expression still made her ask. 'How long do you think it will snow?'

CHAPTER SIX

IT SNOWED all that day. When darkness fell, Rik closed the curtains throughout his chalet home and turned to face Mel.

While Rik appeared completely calm Mel couldn't say the same. She stood rather uncertainly in the middle of the living room.

With the prince. Up here in his chalet where he'd just made the decision that they wouldn't be leaving until morning. So they would be here. All alone. Together. For all that time.

'It won't matter too much?' She asked the question in a deliberately businesslike tone that somehow managed to emerge sounding chatty and confiding and breathless all at once. Mel forged on. 'That you can't get back tonight, I mean?'

Even despite the tone, Mel would have said she did well, that the question was at least focused on whether he might have problems because he couldn't attend to duties at the palace tonight.

Yes. That was a good way to put it. 'Your duties—?' Really, she felt quite relaxed about this whole situation.

After all they were just staying in a different location for a night. She'd slept in a bedroom within Rik's suite of rooms last night, which was rather intimate when you thought about it, and that hadn't bothered her.

Not even when you leapt out of bed the next morning because you could hear him speaking just outside your closed door? Because you wanted to get through the shower and look your best for him before he saw you? Because you hadn't been entirely certain whether he'd pulled the covers over you the night before when you might not have looked your best?

'It won't matter at all. I gave Dominico another quick call while I was outside checking the snowfall. He'll take care of anything urgent until I get back tomorrow morning.' His cheek creased as he gave a lopsided and quite devastating smile. *He* didn't seem at all concerned or put out by their circumstances.

Which was great, of course.

That was exactly how Mel would feel in a moment when she finished pushing away these silly thoughts about being up here alone with him and how that might impact on the rest of the evening. It must be because he had kissed her on the mountainside earlier. Or because they'd spent the afternoon poring over truffle books and photo albums that showed many shots of Rufusina being trained by Rik and Rik laughing in some of the shots.

Perhaps it was also because she would be pretending to be engaged and then married to him.

'We'll end up holding hands and kissing…' Somehow the words were attached to the blood vessels in her face.

Heat swept upwards from her neck and rushed into her cheeks.

'Yes,' Rik said in a deep voice. 'At times we…will.'

Rikardo. Prince Rikardo. You'll end up holding hands and kissing Prince Rikardo.

Oh, as though putting it in the correct words made it any better!

Even the reminder didn't hold the weight it should have, and Mel just didn't know what to do about that. Something had happened when he took her hand and got her out of the car and brought her inside and made her a hot drink and set to work to help her get past the ridiculous fear she'd experienced.

He acted just like your dream idea of a very ordinary man, showing a sensitive side while still being very, very strong and being wonderful and appealing and all the things you might want—

But Mel didn't want a man. Well, not for a long time. Not like that in the way of settling down together and falling in love so she ended up vulnerable. She wasn't ready for that! The thought burst through, and was somehow linked to her earlier panic while trapped in the speeding car with Rik.

Maybe she just felt panicky at the moment, full stop.

Maybe she needed to focus on right now because this was enough of a challenge, thanks very much!

Rikardo wasn't an ordinary man anyway. Mel couldn't afford to forget that.

Not while reading truffle books and smiling over Rufusina photos. Not while kissing him on a mountainside because that had been a kiss to seal a bargain.

It might have blown her away, but he'd just kissed her and that had been that. Probably checking to make sure he could make it look believable any time they had to repeat the exercise over the next month and the months after that.

How many times might they…?

Mel's heart tripped.

She contemplated turning into a contortionist so she could kick herself for being so silly. The next months would be businesslike as often as possible. That was what they would be. Now what had they been saying? 'Evening in. Yes. That'll be fine. The only thing that matters is that it doesn't interfere with other plans of yours. The treatment in the truffle groves—has that been done today or do you need to be there to supervise it? That's the one thing I didn't ask about while we studied those books.'

'Winnow has supervised the treatment today. He knows what to do, and Dominico organised payment to cover it.' He brushed this aside as though it were irrelevant.

Not the treatment part, the money part. Was it? Mel hadn't got the impression that the money would come out of some endless royal coffer. If that could happen then Rik wouldn't be stressing over getting the people out of financial trouble to the degree that he was. He'd said that there needed to be reform.

Her eyes narrowed. Had he paid for that treatment himself somehow? Out of money that perhaps shouldn't be invested in that direction because it was for his personal use or he'd earned it himself? She knew so little about him and she wanted to know…everything?

Purely because Mel preferred to understand the people she dealt with!

'We'll treat tonight as an evening off,' he declared. 'If the remainder of this month is very busy, we can remember that we at least had a few hours to—how do you say it? "Veg out and do nothing."'

'Why, yes.' A delighted laugh escaped Mel. She couldn't help it. The sound just flew out. Mel also couldn't drag her gaze from that crease in his cheek, or from the sparkle in his deep blue eyes.

So she gave in and let herself enjoy the moment. It wasn't as though Rik would want to spend the entire night kissing her senseless just because they were alone.

Just because he'd kissed her once already. Just because he was the best kisser she'd ever been kissed by and there would be times in the public eye, at least, when he would kiss her again. Just because he made her want to don sparkly shoes *and* leap into a rabbit hole.

'If we're having a night in,' a night of not kissing each other, 'then I guess we just need to work out how we want to spend our time.'

'Not reading about truffles.' This too was said with a smile.

Oh, she could fall heavily for that smile. She wouldn't, though. Not when she'd reminded herself that she was doing this to help him, and help the people of Braston, and because she'd ended up here by mistake and there weren't a lot of other options for him now, like none at all really, and she could afford the time and effort to help. Did it really make any difference whether she started her new life in Sydney this week or four months from now?

'I think I've taken in as much information about truffles as I can manage for one day, but I'm pleased to know more about the industry. It's obviously really important—to—to people here.' She'd almost said that it was important to Rik, and that was why she'd wanted to understand.

That wouldn't be the key reason, of course. She wanted to be supportive of Rik's efforts. She'd made the commitment to marry him for that reason. But she wasn't obsessing over learning all about his life and work or anything like that.

Are you sure about that, Melanie? Because you seem mightily interested in him, really.

Yes, she was sure! And no she was not ridiculously interested! She was helping to fix a problem that she was partially responsible for creating in the first place. She was no more interested than she should be.

'It's a fascinating industry,' she said in the most dampening tone she could muster. 'The truffle industry. But perhaps we could pass the time this evening some other way?'

Like snuggling on the sofa?

No. Like…well, she didn't know. Cooking? Playing on the Internet?

'How do you feel about television?' Rik indicated the large screen in the corner of the room. 'I have a selection of DVDs I've not yet got around to watching.'

'Watching DVDs would be…' *Smart. Sensible. Safe?*

Better than thinking about kissing the whole night? 'A good idea. I don't mind a good comedy, but I'll watch most things.'

They sat on the floor in front of the DVD cabinet going through choices until she found episodes of an Australian comedy show she hadn't yet watched. 'Oh, you have this series! I've only ever seen a few episodes but it's supposed to be brilliant!'

So they sat side by side on the sofa with popcorn that Rik made in the microwave, and sodas from his fridge, and watched comedy episodes until Mel had giggled so many times that she'd forgotten to feel self-conscious at all in Rik's presence. Instead she had become totally enamoured of the rich, deep rumble that accounted for *his* laughter.

And she forgot to guard against letting herself be aware of him as an attractive appealing man and not a prince who should be held at arm's length because she was only here for a few months and he was marrying her so he could avoid any kind of commitment to a woman, even if Mel didn't know why he seemed to need to do that as much as he needed to. They were almost through the evening, anyway.

So why are you almost holding your breath, Mel, as though waiting for something to happen?

'Goodnight, Mel.' Rik walked Melanie to the opened doorway of her bedroom.

They'd watched their comedy episodes. Mel had paid more attention than he had. Did she feel it the way that he did? This compulsion that ate at him to draw closer, know her, use every avenue and every moment to learn more of her and to let her learn more of him? And a coinciding physical consciousness that seemed to fill the air around them with a charge of electricity just waiting for one small spark to set it ablaze?

Why did this woman make him feel this way more than any other had? Rik didn't want to admit that to himself, but he forced the acknowledgement.

Then admit that you desire her, and that the desire is as much about her personality as it is about her physical appeal.

He'd spent this evening with her and he'd thought about how different their lives were and mad thoughts had come through his mind about bridging the gaps.

Look how well longevity and sticking together had worked for his father and mother. The queen had walked out, had done the one thing Rik and his brothers had never expected. She had turned her back on what she had treated as the core of her duty. And now neither parent would discuss the matter with their sons.

Rik turned his thoughts back to the present.

At times today Mel seemed to have almost forgotten that Rik was a prince. He'd…liked that. But now was not a good time for him to forget the arrangement they'd made. He needed this to work. To be distracted by her beauty and appeal was not the right thing for him to do, to be distracted mentally and in *liking* her so much, even less smart because it spoke of an emotional awareness that couldn't happen. Rik could never trust…

'Good—goodnight, Rik.' She said the words quietly, almost tentatively.

With a question in their depths?

Her small hand came to rest on his forearm and she reached up and briefly kissed his cheek. 'I'll see you in the morning and I'll be ready for whatever needs to be done to help get your temporary marriage plans started, or just to keep out of the way if you need to work in the truffle groves tomorrow.'

Rik searched her face and saw the determination to do the right thing, to dismiss him and her awareness of him at one and the same time. To remain Melanie here and Rikardo there and never the two should cross over their lines.

He saw all that, and he *felt* what was inside her. A very different compulsion that he felt, too, that made him want to lean in and replace that pseudo-kiss with the real thing. To know for himself if the last kiss had been some kind of strange fluke. If her lips would taste as good a second time.

'Sleep well.' He turned and started for his room at the end of the short corridor. 'I will see you in the morning. Thank you for your company this evening. I…really enjoyed it.'

And with that, Prince Rikardo Eduard Ettonbierre of Braston went to his room, stepped inside and shut the door firmly behind him.

Only then did he lift his hand to allow his fingertips to lightly trace where her lips had pressed to his cheek.

It was perfectly fine for him to find Melanie likeable, and to still marry her, end the marriage short months later, and get on with the single life that he wanted, and *needed* to maintain.

He *would not* be marrying for real.

Rik sighed and dropped his hand. For now he needed to prepare for bed.

Tomorrow was a new day and no doubt a new set of challenges.

CHAPTER SEVEN

'I WOULD like to present to you my fiancée, Nicole Melanie Watson.' Rik spoke the words to King Georgio formally, and as though the other impromptu meeting had never occurred. 'My fiancée is known by her middle name of Melanie.'

If the occasion had been less formal, Mel might have smiled at Rik's tweaking of history to suit himself. But this was not that kind of moment. Mel curtsied.

'I am pleased to meet you, Melanie.' Georgio took her hand and air-kissed above the fingers and, while doing so, searched her face. After a moment he gave a slight nod and indicated a setting of leather lounges and chairs to the left.

They were in what Rik referred to as one of the 'great rooms'. It was a large area, and could have felt intimidating if Mel hadn't walked in here determined *not* to be intimidated.

Mel and Rik had made their way down the mountain this morning. He'd driven at a gentler pace and Mel had remained calm until they were almost at the palace.

Nervous anticipation had set in then but Mel felt that was justified.

'Let us get to know one another a little, Melanie,' Georgio said as they all took their seats.

Rik sat on one of the sofas beside Mel. He seemed deeply resolved this morning. Last night, when she'd thought he would kiss her at her door, kiss her *properly,* Melanie had thought he might feel as confused and tempted and aware of her as she did of him. But of course that was quite silly. He might have wanted to kiss her. But that didn't mean his emotions were engaged.

Not that Mel's were!

Concentrate on the king, Mel. This is not the time for anything else.

'Melanie and I first met through a cousin of hers.' Rik added a few details.

When the king nodded, Mel bit back the urge to heave a sigh of relief. But she also had to handle her share of the conversation. 'I admire Rikardo, and the work that he does for the people of Braston. I want to be as supportive of that as I possibly can.'

'That is good.' Georgio's glance shifted from Mel to Rik and back to Mel again. 'And what did you do before you agreed to marry my son?'

'I worked as a cook.' It might not have been a glamorous job. It would probably sound even less glamorous if she admitted she had done that for little money, working for her relatives to earn her right to a sense of belonging.

Note to self, Mel. You never did earn that right and you waited too long to get yourself out of that situation.

A similar set of rites was being played out in this room between Rik and his father.

She turned the highest wattage smile she could muster towards King Georgio. 'My history is humble, I suppose, but there's nothing to be ashamed of in coming from everyday stock.'

'If that "stock" has an appropriate history attached to it.' Georgio's eyes narrowed. 'My son will run a check. I will see this report for myself.'

Like a police-record check or something?

No, Mel, it will be a lot more detailed even than that.

She tried not to bristle at the thought, and at the king's emotionless declaration. As though he did this all the time and would have no hesitation in eliminating her like a blot from Rik's radar screen if she didn't come up to standard.

It didn't actually matter whether Georgio liked her or approved of her or not, provided she could marry Rik so that Rik could carry out his plans.

I still don't like it. My family history is my business. I don't want it exposed to all and sundry.

'Dominico already ran the check.' Rik clipped the words off. 'You may take Melanie at her word, Father. There is nothing in her history to justify the need for you to view the report.'

Mel stiffened inwardly for a second time.

Rik leaned close to her and said softly, 'I'm sorry. It was necessary. Dominico gave me a very light summary of the report.'

Much of Mel's agitation subsided. 'I don't have anything to hide. I just don't like the idea…'

'Of your privacy being invaded.' The twist to his lips was ironic.

Somehow that irony helped Mel to let the matter go.

Georgio straightened slightly in his chair. 'I could order a search of my own.'

A chill formed in the edges of Rik's deep blue irises. 'But I think you will agree there is no need.'

For a moment as father and son locked gazes the room filled with the powerful clash of two strong wills. It occurred to Mel then that there were matters within such families that were very different from 'regular' life. Yes, Rik had ordered a search of her life and history. No, she hadn't liked hearing that. But if Rik hadn't done the search, his father would have ordered it. At least this way Mel wasn't exposed to Georgio reading the entire report.

A moment later Georgio glanced away. Rik had won that round, it was done and the conversation moved on to more general topics.

Rik raised the matter of the truffle harvest. Mel sat quietly listening, but she remained aware of Georgio's examination.

No way would he have accepted a switch between her and her cousin. He was too observant.

So you've done the right thing, Mel, by agreeing to help Rik. And Georgio is a strong-willed man and very set in his attitudes. You're helping Rik to avoid being pushed into a long-term loveless marriage for the wrong reasons, too.

'You have done well this morning, Melanie. I'm proud of you.' Rik spoke the words and then realised it perhaps wasn't his place to feel such an emotion in the rather personal way that he did towards his fiancée right now. She wasn't marrying him for real reasons. She was doing this to help him and she understood that it would all end a few months from now.

Tell her what the buy-off will be in exchange for her assistance.

The thought came, and Rik…pushed it aside once again, for later. He would take care of Melanie, would ensure that she got good assistance to start her on her way with her new life in Sydney when she returned to Australia. When the moment was right to bring the topic up, he would do so. He…felt that she would know inherently that he would…take care of her.

Rik used a key to unlock the door to a small room. 'There will be a number of rings you can choose from for your engagement ring.'

'From the family h-heirlooms?' Mel's footsteps faltered in the doorway.

For a moment Rik thought she might back out of the room, refuse to enter. 'They are not all heirlooms,' he said, 'but yes.'

She drew a deep breath, threw her shoulders back and continued into the room. 'It's probably a good idea to use something from the family's stock of jewellery. The ring can be given back when we're finished, and it won't have cost you anything. We need to find one that fits and doesn't need adjusting, and that you wouldn't choose if you were—'

Doing this for real.

The words echoed unspoken in the room.

The practicality of her determined attitude made Rik want to smile, and yet when they stepped fully into the room and he saw the spread of jewellery that Dominico had laid out for them, a strange feeling swept over him. His gaze shifted from piece to piece until he found a ring that he felt would suit Mel. A ring that he would have chosen for her if their circumstances had been different?

There *were* no different circumstances possible, either now or in his future. Yet to Rik in this moment—

He lifted a ring with a platinum band. The three diamonds were Asscher cut to reflect light off the many facets. The stones were perfectly round, and set with the larger of the three diamonds raised higher than the two to its left and right. Because the ring was simple and the setting not as high as some, the size of the diamonds did not leap out as it might have.

The platinum band would suit Melanie's colouring; the setting would look beautiful on her finger. It was a ring he could enjoy seeing on her for decades.

Well, it would do for the time being. He lifted the ring. 'This was not an engagement ring, but a dress ring of my grandmother that she had fashioned for her later in her life. Her fingers were small and delicate as yours are. I do not know if she ever even wore it. She was rather indulgent when it came to such creations. I…feel the ring may suit you.'

'Oh.' Melanie didn't even glance at the remaining jewellery. And when Rik took her hand gently in his and slipped the ring onto her finger, she caught her breath. Her gaze flew to his. 'It—it fits perfectly. Just as though—'

'Just as though,' he murmured, and there, in the quiet of a small room filled with valuable jewellery that Melanie had been hesitant to go anywhere near, Rik lifted her hand and kissed the finger upon which his engagement ring now rested.

'Just as though we were a real engaged couple, I was going to say.' She whispered the words and glanced down at the ring. 'I didn't expect it to look—'

Right. She hadn't expected it to look right. Rik didn't need her to finish the sentence to know that was what she'd meant to say. He hadn't expected it either. Nor had he expected the sudden sense of well-being and destiny that swept over him when he placed the ring on her finger.

Was he getting in over his head with her somehow despite his determination to treat this as a business transaction? Had he allowed some attitudes and thoughts to slide in wrong directions because, if he hadn't, then how had he ended up with such unexpected feelings in the first place?

Rik should have been sorting out the answers to those questions. Instead he leaned towards her and somehow his arm was around her, drawing her close.

This time when he kissed her it was he who lost himself in a moment that should not have been, lost himself in the taste and texture and the giving of Melanie's lips as he kissed her until he had to break away or—

It would all feel far too real?

You cannot let it become that way, Rikardo. Melanie

is a sweet girl, but she never will be more than a means to an end. You will never marry permanently, not for real and not for love, and not to lock yourself for ever into a loveless marriage.

He would never trust such an emotion as 'love' within that institution. Not when his parents hadn't managed even to love their sons let alone each other.

'I have something else that I wish to show you this morning.' Rik escorted her from the room, Away from a room full of the beauty that should go with emotion and dreams and the love of a lifetime, but had it ever existed within his family? There was that old legend, but …

Rik increased his pace.

'Th-thank you for the beautiful choice of ring, Rik,' Mel said softly as they stepped out of doors and started along an outside pathway that led between vast stretches of snow-covered grounds.

On her finger, the ring felt light and comfortable. It fitted perfectly and maybe that was what disturbed Mel so much. That and the fact that *Rik* had chosen it out of a dazzling array of royal jewellery. Rik had wanted her to wear *this* ring, and then he'd kissed her. It was the second time they'd sealed their agreement with a kiss, and each time became more difficult to treat as just a meeting of lips against lips.

What kind of state would she be in by the time he kissed her on the wedding day?

'I should not have kissed you like that.' His glance meshed momentarily with hers.

Had he read her mind? Considering the messy confused state of the thoughts in there, she hoped not!

Rik went on. 'Our arrangement is not for…that kind of purpose and I should have remembered.'

'Well, it was probably because we'd just been with your father and working so hard to make sure that all went well.' She gave a laugh that sounded just a bit forced. 'We got a little too carried away in our roles but it was only for a moment. It probably barely left an impression, really.'

Her words were just making this worse! She bit her lip. Mel glanced about them and her gaze fell on a small piece of machinery ahead. 'That's an interesting-looking vehicle.'

Rik followed Melanie's gaze.

She was wise to change the topic. He was more than happy to work with her in that respect, though his glance did drop again to her hand where the ring sat as though it belonged there, and then to her soft lips, which had yielded so beautifully beneath his just moments ago. He wanted to kiss her again. Kiss and so much more.

Not happening, Rik.

And yet his instincts told him that the kisses they'd shared had been far more than instantly forgettable to her.

To him, too, if he were honest.

'This is an all-weather buggy.' He explained that Winnow had taken the vehicle out of storage and made sure it was in working order. 'In first gear it doesn't drive any faster than a person can walk. It's easy to handle. All you need to do is steer and make it stop and start. It will drive on snow and it can handle rough terrain but there are plenty of paths here to drive it on. Our appointment with the wedding planner is not for another hour. I thought I might show you how to work this while we wait.'

Her gaze flew to his. 'You want me to drive it?'

'I thought it might be a good way for you to start to be able to get around more while you're here.' In truth there were a dozen ways he could ensure that Melanie could move around the area, and for the most part Rik expected to be with her anyway. Even so…

'I don't drive cars.' She said it quickly, and then tipped her head to the side and looked at the buggy, and back at Rik. 'I've never really had any interest in learning.'

'This is not a car.' He watched her face, and took a gamble. 'But if you don't feel that you can try it—'

Her chin went up. 'Of course I'll try it. That would be like saying I didn't want to try riding a skateboard or making some new dish in the kitchen.'

She was a plucky girl, his Melanie, Rik thought. Before he could pull himself up on the possessive manner of wording that thought, Melanie stepped forward and did an at least passable job of feigning delight at the idea of learning all about the buggy.

'First I will demonstrate.' Rik sat in the driving seat with Melanie beside him and showed her the controls. They were on castle grounds in an area where the worst that could happen was they ended up off the path. He got the buggy moving, explaining as he drove, and then, when he felt Mel was ready, Rik simply got out of the seat and started walking beside her. 'Slide into the driver's seat.'

Mel slid over and gripped the wheel. A moment later she was steering the buggy grimly.

He guided her along, helping her to master steering around corners and stopping and starting. After a few minutes Mel didn't need his help, and even asked if he would get back in with her so she could increase speed to a higher gear.

Finally her hands unclenched and she gave the first hint of a smile before she stopped the buggy and turned to look at him.

'Well done,' he praised. 'I am glad you have been able to do this, Mel.'

'It was fun. It's such a long time since I've completely enjoyed anything that resembled vehicle travel. All the way back to when my parents used to take me every Sunday and we'd go…' Her expression sobered and she frowned as though trying to remember something.

Though she tried to conceal it, sadness touched her face. She climbed out of the buggy. 'I don't remember what we used to do. They…died in a car crash.'

His hand wrapped around her fingers, enclosing her. He wished he could warm her heart from that chill. He wanted to do that for her so much. 'I am sorry—'

'It's all right. It was a long time ago.' Her words relegated her pain to the past. But her fingers wrapped around his…

A member of the palace staff approached to let Rik know that the wedding planner had arrived. The moment ended, but the tenderness Rik felt for Melanie grew inside him.

Duty. He had to attend to his duty.

Rik dipped his head. 'Please tell the planner we will be with her shortly.'

'Yes, Prince Rikardo.' The man walked away.

Melanie turned her gaze towards Rik and drew a deep breath. 'This is the next phase, isn't it? We have to convince this planner that we're doing this for real, even if we do want a simple, quick, trouble-free arrangement.' She seemed to think about what she'd just said, and a thoughtful expression came over her face. 'You must have chosen a great planner, if the woman believes she can achieve that, in a month, for a royal wedding of any description.'

Rik drew a slow breath as his gaze examined her face, flushed with the success of learning to drive the buggy, and her expressive eyes that had clouded when the topic of her parents had come up.

Perhaps he should ask Dominico for a proper look at that report after all. It might tell Rik more about Melanie's background.

Only to help understand her, he justified, and then frowned because, of all reasons he might read the report, wasn't that the most personal and therefore to him, at least, the most unacceptable? 'Dominico seems to believe this planner will be up to the task. Let us go see how she fares with our requests.'

CHAPTER EIGHT

'You have made very rapid plans, Rik.'

'Are you sure you want to marry so quickly? Our father might still have given us what we wanted if we all became engaged and then spoke to him again about the arrangement. That way you could have held off from actually marrying until closer to the six-months mark. Things might have changed by then.'

The words came to Melanie in two different male voices as she went in search of Rik. It was four days later and she'd woken to find her breakfast waiting for her, and Rik already gone to the palace grounds to oversee the harvesting of the first of the special truffles.

'It won't make any difference whether I marry soon, or marry after many months. You know this. Our father will not change his mind or soften his expectations.'

Rik didn't explain the reason for his statement—the brief nature of the intended marriage—and Mel didn't know if he'd told his brothers the truth about it as yet or not. But did his voice sound oddly flat *because* he knew this fact?

She must be imagining it.

You and your over-inflated ego are imagining it together, Mel.

'Good—good morning, Rikardo.' Mel spoke to make her presence known. Not because she minded her impending marriage to Rik being discussed, but because it wasn't right to eavesdrop, even if she hadn't meant to.

'Melanie. I am glad you're awake and have found us.' Rik stepped forward. He touched her hand and gestured to the two men standing to their left. 'These are my brothers, Marcelo and Anrai.'

'Hello. I'm pleased to meet you both.' The words emerged in a calm tone before Mel stopped to remember that she was being introduced to two more princes.

Rabbit hole. Sparkly shoes. Do I look good enough for this occasion, and why didn't I address him as Prince Rikardo or Your Highness?

She drew a breath.

'It is a delight to meet you, Melanie. Our brother has told us about you.' The older man bowed over her hand and managed to make the gesture seem relaxed and European rather than princely and…royal. 'I am Marcelo.'

The first in line to the throne. The brother who would most of all be expected to marry and stay married, whether he wanted to or not. He was dark like Rik, a little taller, and his eyes were such a deep inky blue, they were almost black.

'I am Anrai.' The second brother smiled a killer smile, shook her hand, and stepped back as though content to observe proceedings from this point. His hair was a lighter brown, thick and with a slight wave. It flopped over his forehead and drew attention to sparkling pale blue eyes.

Mel had dismissed him as not as handsome as Rik. She could now see that he would actually be a quite stunning lady-killer, but he still didn't appeal to *her*. She only had eyes for—

'Hello.' Mel tried to smile naturally and not feel overwhelmed by being surrounded by these three very royal men. It wasn't until she glanced at Rik's face that she realised she'd placed herself so close to his side that they were almost touching. Not because she felt intimidated but because…

Well, she couldn't explain it, actually. What she did realise was that she'd been allowing herself to think of Rik more as a man, and less as a prince. At least this meeting had given her that reality check. And it was nice to meet his brothers. 'Have any of the truffles been dug out yet?'

A snort from behind them drew Mel's attention. She turned her head and there was Rufusina. The pig had a quilted coat on and a keen look in her eyes, as though she was sitting in apparent obedience waiting for something.

'Rufusina's obviously champing at the snout,' Mel observed. 'What's the hold-up?'

'There's no hold-up—' Rik started.

'We were just deciding how best to go about the extraction,' Anrai added.

Marcelo's brows formed a vee. 'It is the most stupid thing to wait for a sign from—'

Rufusina lifted her snout, sniffed the air once, and then again.

Rik said under his breath, 'Wait for it.'

Anrai's shoulders stiffened.

The truffle hog sniffed the air a third time and trotted to a group of trees.

'*Now* I will go in there.' Anrai followed Rufusina's rapidly receding form. 'But only because I think she knows where the best truffles are. It has nothing to do with anything else.'

'Marcelo?' Rik turned to his older brother.

'I was not concerned in the first instance.' The oldest brother followed Anrai. 'All the truffles on the palace grounds are exceptional, as has been proved in years past. That is all that matters.'

Rik turned to Mel. 'Would you care to be present while Rufusina does her work and finds us the choicest truffles?'

'I would love to be there.' Mel's curiosity was tweaked. Just what had that "rite of passage" been about? And to be present while such wonderful foods were lifted from their resting places? Imagine *tasting* such a wonderful, rare indulgence!

Rik took her arm and started towards a grove of trees that looked very old. 'It is an exciting moment.'

'Apologies, Melanie, for walking away.' Anrai rubbed the back of his neck with his hand. 'Once the pig sniffs the air three times—'

'It will guide the prince to truffles that are the choicest, and that are possessed of the power to make his deepest hopes come true.' Marcelo said the words with a dismissive twist of his lips. 'You must forgive us, Melanie. We are being foolish this morning, but Rikardo—'

'Asked nicely if you would both like to be present for this event.' Rik jumped in with the words that were almost defensive.

Mel thought about her rabbit hole and the sparkly shoes and how out of place she'd felt when she arrived here, and how different this world was from anything she had ever known. And she looked at three big, brave men who had hovered at the edge of a grove of trees and refused to shift until…

'A magic truffle hog unlocks the key to safe passage, and perhaps to the granting of your wishes?' The words came with the start of a smile that spread until it almost cracked her face in half.

She could have laughed aloud. Mel could have done a lot of things. But then she looked properly at the grove of trees and thought about age and history. Three princes *had* all come to participate in this ritual. Rufusina *had* lifted her nose and sniffed three times and then trotted over here with purpose. Mel sobered. 'How old is the legend? Are there bad aspects attached if you don't do things the right way?'

'Centuries. None of us have ever come near the harvesting of these truffles until now. It's usually left to our staff, but I wanted to oversee it this time.' Rik didn't seem offended by her initial amusement. He did seem a little uncomfortable having to explain the situation. 'The legend is more to do with prosperous lives, and making the right choice of marriages and so on. But I am only concerned with getting good truffles for my overseas buyers.'

'Yes. That is no doubt the priority.' Mel bit back any further smiles. She turned to the others and said to all three of them, 'I'm grateful to have the chance to see this, and I hope to get a good look at the truffles themselves when they're harvested.'

Winnow approached as Mel made this statement.

The three princes were all about business after that. It was strange to stand back and watch these three privileged men go about digging bits of fungus out from beneath beds of rotting leaves. Rufusina did her thing, and Rik praised her for being a good hog, at which the pig sort of…preened, Mel thought fancifully, and checked her own feet to make sure they hadn't sprouted those sparkly shoes while she was daydreaming.

'This one looks good, brother. And smell the pungent odour.' Anrai handed a truffle to Rik.

Rik examined the truffle. 'It is good. Take a look at it, Melanie.'

Before Mel could blink, the truffle had been dumped into her hands. She didn't know much about truffles. Not in this state, but that didn't stop her from wanting to cook with them, to discover if they were indeed as fine as it was claimed, to revere the opportunity to hold this piece of life and privilege and history. 'Will they be enough for your marketing plans, Rik?'

She didn't notice the softness in her tone, didn't see the look exchanged between Rik's brothers as Rik bent his shoulders to protect her from the wind that had sprung up as he answered her question.

‘I hope so, Mel. I very much hope so.’

They gathered the truffles. Some were sent with Winnow to be prepared for travel. Rik placed the others in a basket, thanked his brothers for their presence and saw them on their way, and then turned to Mel. ‘Shall we have that peek at the kitchen that you mentioned?’

‘Y-yes. I’d like that.’ Mel liked it even more that Rik had remembered that small comment of hers from days ago.

They made their way to the kitchens. Rik introduced Mel to the staff and somehow, even though she’d always been on the other side of things in this environment, he made it comfortable and easy. Enough that when he had to excuse himself to attend to other matters, Mel accepted the invitation to remain behind and observe as the staff prepared the midday meals.

‘I’m almost afraid to taste,’ Melanie murmured as Rik removed the cover from the last dish.

They were in his suite. He’d asked for their meal to be sent here, and wasn’t that what people would expect of a newly engaged couple—to want every moment alone? Yet Rik knew that he’d chosen to dine with Melanie here because *he* wanted to keep her to himself more than he perhaps should.

The legend talked of sharing the first meal prepared with the truffles, that the prince must share the tasting process…

He pushed the fanciful thoughts aside. This was a matter of practicality. And perhaps of giving Melanie a moment that she might not otherwise experience. 'Each of the dishes have been enhanced with the addition of the truffles.'

'The kitchen staff said there are different opinions about actually cooking the truffles.' Mel had listened with interest to the discussion about that in the kitchens earlier. She'd learned so much! 'The risotto and the duck dishes both smell divine.'

'Before we start on those, I would like to give you the chance to sample the first truffle in very simple form.' Rik lifted a single truffle from a salver. His fingers shook slightly. He steadied them and lifted his gaze to hers.

It was just a legend. Foolish stuff.

The prince prepares the truffle and offers it to his bride.

Mel drew a shaky breath as though she perhaps, too, felt the air change around them, almost as though it filled with anticipation as she yielded her palate to his ministration…

He shaved transparent slices of truffle onto the pristine white plate. The butter knife slid through creamy butter. Just the right smear on each sliver, a sprinkle of salt crystals.

Rik held the first slice out to her. Soft pink lips closed over it, just touched the tips of his fingers as her eyelids drifted closed and she experience her first taste of…a legend.

'It's almost intoxicating.' Her words whispered through her lips. 'The permeation of the scent, the beautiful texture. I can't even describe how amazing…I feel as though I've tasted something sacred.'

She couldn't have rehearsed those words if she'd tried. Rik took his own slice of truffle, unbelievably pleased in the face of *her* pleasure.

They moved on to eat the other dishes. Melanie experienced each new taste with curiosity and perhaps with a little awe. Rik shared her pleasure and knew that it renewed his own. He couldn't take his gaze from her mouth. He wanted to lean forward and taste the flavour of the truffle, of salt and butter, from the inside of her lips.

It was just a legend.

But Melanie Watson was not a legend. She was a very real woman, and Rik…desired her in this moment, far too much.

They left for France that afternoon. Mel settled into her seat on the family's private plane and observed, with some wonder, Rik's calm face. 'I don't know how you do it.'

'Do what?' He glanced out of the window at the scudding clouds beneath the plane's belly before he turned his gaze to her and gave her all of his attention.

'Remain so calm in the face of being chased all the way to the plane by a wedding planner waving colour swatches and bits of lace and begging for fittings and a decision on the choices for the table settings.'

'We gave her the answers she needed.' A slight smile twitched at the corners of Rik's mouth. 'And perhaps next time she won't wear those kinds of heels for running.'

'I could learn a thing or two.' Melanie had taken to the wedding planner. 'She's doing her best to make things easy for us while we fly all over Europe showing buyers what they'll be missing out on if they don't make an order this year for Braston truffles.'

'In truth we're only going to Paris.' There was a pause while Rik looked into her eyes, and while he registered how committed she had sounded to his country's industry as she spoke those words.

'It's still more exciting than almost anything I've done.' Melanie returned his glance.

How did he do that? Make it seem as though the whole rest of the world suddenly faded away and it were just the two of them? Mel would be hopeless at truly being married to him. There'd be photos through the tabloids all the time of her making goo-goo eyes at him when she didn't realise she was doing it.

Um, where was she?

She would not, anyway. An unguarded thought here or there, or coming to realise that he was a good man and one she could admire, hardly equated to a Rufusina-like devotion to the man.

And you just compared yourself to a truffle hog, Mel. I don't think pigs wear magic slippers. 'Magic trotters, maybe,' Mel muttered, and snapped her teeth together before anything even sillier could come out.

'I hope the marketing trip is successful.' For a moment Rik dropped his guard and let her see the concern beneath the surface. 'There's no room for failure in my plans, but I still…'

Worry?

'All the kitchen staff said the truffles were the best ever. I have nothing to compare to, but I thought they were stunning.' Mel was glad she'd spent the time in the kitchen while Rik finalised plans for their trip.

He'd sprung it on her just as though they were taking a walk around the corner. "Oh, and by the way we're leaving for Paris this afternoon, I'll have the staff pack for you."

She'd let that happen, too, and hadn't even tried to oversee what got put in the suitcases. Melanie Watson, cook, had stayed clear and let the palace staff pack her things for a trip to Paris.

'I'll help you in any way I can, with the marketing efforts.' Mel didn't know if she could do anything. Did being his fiancée count?

Her glance dropped to the ring on her finger. Every time she looked at it, it seemed to belong there more than the last time. It had seemed to be made for her from the moment Rik lifted it from a bed of black velvet and placed it on her finger.

What was happening to her? She was losing the battle to keep her emotional distance from him, that was what. There was no point saying she only cared about the people of Braston, or only admired him because he cared about their futures. Mel did feel all those things, but they were only part of what she felt for him.

Face it, Mel. Somehow you got caught in your own

feelings towards him and, instead of getting them under control or stopping them altogether, they've grown more and more with each passing day.

CHAPTER NINE

'I AM interested, you understand. Braston black truffles have been a high-standard product.' The owner of the group of elite Parisian restaurants spoke the words to Rik with a hint of regret, but as much with the glint of good business in his eyes. 'It is just with your truffles being totally off the market for two years I have found other supply sources.'

This was the fourth restaurant owner they'd seen since they arrived in Paris. The others had come on board, but something told Mel this one might be a harder sell.

They were inside the man's home, seated at a carved wooden dining setting. At the end of the table, a wide glass vase held a bunch of mixed flowers. The moment they walked into the room, Rik's gaze had examined the arrangement.

He'd been checking for gardenias, Mel had realised, and her heart had been ridiculously warmed by the gesture on his part. There were none, but that bunch of flowers looked particularly pretty to her now.

'The blight to our crops was tragic, but we are back

on our feet and, as you can see, the commercial truffles are the same high standard.' Rik lifted one of the truffles he had placed on an oval plate in the centre of the table, took up a stainless-steel shaver and shaved thin slices from the black shape.

As the older man examined the truffle slices, and Mel recalled the almost spiritual moment of trying her first truffle with Rik, he went on.

'I know at this time of year you would be sourcing truffles. I'd like to see Braston truffles back on the menu at your restaurants.'

At his feet was a travel carrier containing more truffles, and from which he had unpacked the plates and shaver as well as a beautiful small kitchen knife with a gold inlaid handle.

'And I'd like to put them there, but—'

'I have an added incentive that may sweeten the deal for you, Carel.' Rik spoke the words quietly.

'And that is?' Carel was the last on their list.

It was almost nine p.m. now and they had been fortunate that the man rarely worked in any of his kitchens these days, preferring to visit as suited him, so he'd been more than happy to meet with Rik at his home.

The incentive of the truffles harvested from royal grounds had worked well with the other restaurant owners. They'd all placed orders for commercial truffles so they could also obtain some of the other truffles. Mel wondered if Carel would be as willing to be convinced. Middle-aged, and ruthlessly business focused, this man was much harder to read than the others.

A surge of protectiveness of Rik rose in Mel's breast.

He shouldn't have to beg for anything. He was, well, he was a prince! And yet that description was not the first one that had come to Mel's mind. Rik was good and fair and hardworking and dedicated and his care for the people of his country ran so deep that she knew it would never leave him. He deserved to be respected because of what was inside him.

Carel tipped his head slightly to the side. 'We have already discussed pricing and you certainly do not plan to give away—'

'Braston's truffle crops at a price that won't help my people get back on their feet?' Rik said it softly. 'No. And deep down I know you would not respect such a gesture if I made it.'

The older man was silent for a moment before he dipped his head. 'You are correct.'

'How would you feel about a complimentary gift of some of the truffles grown on the palace grounds?' Rik watched Carel's face for his reaction. 'To go with your order, of course.'

Mel watched both their faces.

'There are legends surrounding those truffles.' The older man's glance moved to Mel before it returned to Rik and he asked with the hint of a smile, 'Do I need to ask whether you harvested the truffles yourself? I am assuming you have brought them with you to show?'

'You do not need to ask, and I have brought them.' Rik's answer was ironic and guarded all at once.

Before Mel could try to understand that, Rik drew another white rectangular plate out and placed just one truffle on it.

Carel leaned forward to look.

Rik shaved the truffle, allowing the wafer thin slices to fall onto the plate and the pungent aroma to rise.

What exactly did that legend stand for? Mel made a note to find out when they got back to the palace.

'The aroma is muscular with a particular rich spiciness I have never encountered.' Carel lifted one of the slices to examine the texture, and colour.

He looked, he inhaled, and after a long moment he put the truffle slice down. 'I do not know. I'm not convinced that the royal truffles will equate to anything exciting enough on the plate. If I agreed to your offer, I would want to be sure that the truffles were a good enough selling point in terms of taste, not only legend.'

'And yet they *are* the stuff of legends,' Rik said with a hint of the same spark.

This was the business dance, and both men were doing it well.

'Indeed.' The older man dipped his head. 'That is undeniable and an excellent marketing point. But I would be using them at my restaurants for the most expensive dishes only on a very limited basis. They would have to live up to and beyond expectation in all ways.'

'They do. They would!' The words burst out of Mel. She touched the edge of one truffle slice with the tip of her finger and caught and held Carel's gaze. 'These truffles have a flavour and scent you'll never find anywhere else. The texture is beautiful. They provide the most stunning enhancement to the dishes they're used in or when eaten by themselves.'

'This is quite true.' Rik's gaze softened as he glanced

at Melanie's face. She wanted so desperately for this trip to be successful, for him to obtain all the markets for his truffles that he had set out to recapture. 'But I understand Carel's point, too.'

Rik appreciated Mel for that investment in him. It seemed a bland way to describe the warm feeling that spread through his chest as he acknowledged Melanie's fierce support of his efforts. It *was* a bland description, but Rik wasn't at all sure he wanted to allow himself to examine that warmth, or try to know exactly what it might mean.

'For me, I do not have the evidence of this truth.' Carel again smelled and examined the truffle and its slices. 'I am sure my chefs would like to try cooking with these, but they are busy at the restaurants—'

'*I'll* cook them for you!' Melanie got out of her chair. 'Right here and now.'

If Carel had given any indication that he wouldn't allow it, no doubt Melanie would have immediately stopped. But the older man simply watched with a hint of appreciation on his face as Melanie fired up on Rik's behalf. Carel waved a hand as though to say: By all means go ahead.

Rik had to push back a bite of possessive jealousy as he realised the older man was…aware of his fiancée as a woman.

Surely this doesn't surprise you, Rik? Every man would notice her beauty. How could they not?

Melanie stepped into Carel's open-plan kitchen. It was immediately apparent that she was at home in this environment. A chopping board sat on the bench.

She glanced towards the refrigerator. 'May I use anything, *monsieur*?'

Carel smiled. 'Yes. Anything.'

Mel took chicken breast, salad greens and dried raspberries, and then selected a bottle of red wine. Finally she retrieved salt and pepper and cashews and a long thin loaf of bread from Carel's pantry.

Rather than the kitchen knives available to her, Mel walked back to where Rik sat at the table. She took the gold-handled knife from where it rested near Rik's right hand.

As she did so she touched his shoulder briefly with her other hand. 'For luck.'

He didn't know whether she meant the knife, or the touch. Perhaps both.

'Your fiancée has pluck.' The Frenchman spoke the words quietly as he sat back to watch Melanie take control of his kitchen. 'I shall eagerly observe this.'

A half-hour later, Mel drew a deep breath and carried the chicken salad to the table. The meal looked good on the plate, colourful and versatile, full of different textures with the thin slices of truffle heated through and releasing their gorgeous aroma. The wine reduction made a beautiful sauce. The thick slice of bread coated with beaten egg yolk, the lightest combination of chopped herbs and grated sharp cheese and lightly toasted made a perfect accompaniment.

Even so, the proof would be in the taste, not only the visual appeal. Mel placed the dish before her host and brought the other two servings for Rik and herself.

Minutes later, Carel put down fork and knife and

lifted his gaze. He spoke first to Rik. 'The truffles are better than anything I have ever tasted. Cooked in the right way, and served with a little royal legendary on the side, these will be highly sought after at my restaurants this season. I am happy to place my order with you.'

'Thank you.' Rik dipped his head and cast a smile in Mel's direction. 'And thanks to you, Melanie, for this meal. You are a wonder in the kitchen. I did not realise just how skilled you are.'

'I would have you in any of my kitchens, Melanie.' Carel's statement followed Rik's.

And while Mel basked in Rik's surprise and the fact that he'd obviously enjoyed the meal, she had to be judicious about it. 'I have to confess that I watched the truffles being prepared at the palace today and learned all I could from the process.'

She turned to smile at the Frenchman. 'Thank you for your compliment.'

'In truth it is a job offer.' The man's gaze shifted between Mel and Rik. 'Any of my restaurants, any time. Permanent work, good wages and conditions. You would be more than welcome. Not that I suggest you would be available…'

Mel was more "available" than the man realised. She said something that she hoped was appropriately appreciative but non-committal. Carel didn't know that she and Rik wouldn't remain together as a couple, so she couldn't exactly have asked the man to hold that thought for a few months.

Plus there'd be work permits and all sorts of things, and when this was all over Mel would need to be back in Australia. She tried valiantly not to let those thoughts spread a pall over Carel's acceptance. Conversation moved on then. Mel sat back and let Rik lead those topics with their host. And *she* tried to gather her calm, and not think too much about the future. Not tonight. Not here in Paris. Not while she felt…vulnerable in this way.

'I hope you will excuse us if we leave you now,' Rik said twenty minutes later.

They had shared a second glass of wine with Carel but it was getting late. 'It is time for us to return to our hotel.' He thanked the man again for his business, and then he and Melanie were outside.

'I would like to stroll the streets before we go back to our hotel.' He turned to examine her face. 'Are you up to a walk?'

'That would be…I would like that.' Her response was guarded. She hoped he couldn't hear that within her words. Beneath it there was too much delight, and that made her feel vulnerable. 'I'd like to see a little more of P-Paris by night.'

'Then I will get our driver to drop us a few blocks away from our hotel.' Rik did this, and they made their car trip in silence before they got out to walk the rest of the way.

The hotel Dominico had booked for Rik was in a beautiful part of the city. At first Melanie felt a little stilted with Rik, but he linked his arm with hers and told her the history of the area, pointing out buildings. And using the night and this moment to enjoy her closeness?

Dream on, Melanie Watson!

'I never thought I would see places like Paris, and Braston.' Melanie turned her face to look into his. 'It's very beautiful on your side of the world.'

'It is…' His gaze seemed to linger on her eyes, her mouth, before he turned his glance back to the buildings around them. 'We have some time in the morning. Is there something you'd like to do?'

'I would love to see some markets.' Mel tried to keep her enthusiasm at a reasonable level. She did. But the chance to explore Paris, even a small portion of it. How could she not be excited? 'A peek at some local colour?'

'Then we shall find markets tomorrow,' Rik said and tucked her more closely against his side. For a moment he felt, not resistance, but perhaps her effort to maintain what she considered to be an appropriate mental and emotional distance?

He should resist, too, but tonight…he did not want to. And so he walked calmly until he felt her relax against his side, and then he took the pleasure of these moments with her in peace, away from expectations and work commitments and other things that went with being… who he was.

'I am enjoying being anonymous with you right now, Melanie.' His voice deepened on the words, on the confession. He couldn't hold the words back.

'Sometimes I forget that you're a prince.' She almost whispered the words in response, as though they were a guilty secret. 'You make extraordinary things seem everyday and normal. Then I forget who you are and just—' She broke off.

Treated him as a man?

Dangerous territory, Rik. The next step is to believe she likes you purely because of you and not your title, and then there would be a woman seeing the man first.

If Rik allowed himself to form any kind of attachment to that woman it could be difficult to let her go when the time came.

He had to do that, and he had no proof that she liked him in any way particularly. Other than kisses, and could he really say those kisses meant all of these things?

You don't have the faith to look for anything else. You've allowed your upbringing to taint your outlook, to stunt what you will reach out for.

In an attempt to refocus his thoughts, he turned his attention back to their visit to Carel. 'You said you'd been a cook, but I did not know you had such skills as you displayed tonight. You won Carel over to placing that order.'

Rik's compliments warmed Mel. 'I enjoyed cooking with the truffles tonight, and I'm so relieved that Carel liked the dish. I took a risk. I wondered if you might have felt I stepped out of line.'

Mel searched his face. 'I—I could just as easily have *lost* you that deal!'

'I do not think so.' Rik gave a slight shake of his head. 'He was too enamoured of you from the first moment. The job offer he made…'

'Was flattering but it's out of the question, isn't it?' She didn't make a question out of it. Well, it wasn't one! 'I've signed on to help you, not to try to set myself up to cook in a Paris restaurant the day after our m-marriage ends.' Mel crossed her fingers and prayed that Rik hadn't heard that slight stumble when she'd referred to that last bit.

'You are very faithful, Nicole Melanie Watson.' Rik shifted his arm and instead caught her hand in his.

His fingers were strong and warm and familiar, and Mel couldn't stop from curling hers around them.

Rik's eyes softened as he smiled at her. 'That is rare and I admire you for it very much.'

They continued their walk in silence, just strolling side by side as though they had all the time in the world. As though they didn't have a *care* in the world.

But underneath, tensions simmered. If everything were so comfortable and unthreatening, why did Mel's heart beat faster with each step they took? Why did a sense of hope and anticipation mix with her awareness of Rik and make her want their walk never to end, and yet at the same time make her want to return to the hotel because she hoped against hope…

That he would kiss her goodnight again? That this night would never end? That it would end for her in his arms? All such foolish thoughts!

'Here we are.' Perhaps he felt it, too, because he swept her into the hotel without another word.

And it seemed as though time warped then because they were at the door of their suite before she could draw a breath, and yet she remembered the endless silent moments in the lift, just the two of them, wishing she could reach out to him, wishing she had the right…

Face it, Mel. You're starting to care for him. To care

for Prince Rikardo Ettonbierre of Braston. Caring as though you might be...

Caring for a man who was a good man, but also a prince, and that meant he was not any man for her because she was an everyday girl.

Mel didn't know what she was thinking, what she hoped for!

Except for a kiss from…a prince?

No. A kiss from Rikardo. That was what she wanted and needed. He *was* a prince, but he could have been the boy next door and she would have wanted that kiss just as much.

You are in trouble, Mel. Big, big trouble because you can't fall for him!

The scent of brewed coffee met them as they entered the suite. A glass bowl with fruits, a bottle of wine and chocolates sat on the low coffee table near the sofa and chairs, and, in the small kitchenette, a basket held fresh baked croissants. The lights were turned down. The suite looked ready to welcome lovers.

Mel's breath caught in the back of her throat. They weren't, of course. There were two bedrooms. It wasn't as though she and Rik—

'The coffee smells good. Just the ticket after that walk in the night air.' Mel stripped off her coat and followed her nose to the kitchenette. She felt she did really well at acting completely normal and unconcerned.

Except she should have dodged the idea of coffee altogether, said goodnight and headed straight for her room rather than prolonging this. What if Rik thought she'd done that so they could take advantage of this romantic scene? What if he thought she was angling for more of his company for that reason?

'You don't need to have any, of course,' she blurted, and then added, because that could have been taken as rather ungracious, 'but I'll pour you a cup if you like, and if you're hungry I can get you a croissant.'

'Coffee would be welcome.' He briefly glanced at the food items and away again. 'I do not think I will spoil the memory of that meal just now.'

Mel found two cups. She got them out of the cupboard and filled them with steaming liquid, and was proud that her fingers didn't tremble.

There was an enclosed balcony, beautifully warm and secluded with stunning views. They took their drinks out there and stood side by side soaking in the ambiance of the city lights.

They weren't touching and yet Mel felt so close to him, so aware of him. How was she supposed to walk away at the end of this arrangement without…looking back and wishing?

If wishes were horses then beggars would ride. Wasn't that the saying? She wasn't a beggar, but she was also not the princess who lived around the corner from the prince. She and Rik weren't on an even playing field; they never would be. Mel needed to remember that. She had to remember who he was, and who she was.

'I am pleased with this evening's efforts.' Rik set his empty coffee cup down on the ledge, took hers and placed it beside it. 'I've regained four key markets.

There are others to chase but those are smaller and can be done out of Braston over the next couple of weeks.'

'You've taken a big step towards getting the people back on their financial feet.' There was pride in her voice that she couldn't hide. In the soft night light Mel looked into his face and knew that her happiness for him must show. 'You've earned the right to feel some peace.'

'You have played a part in my peace.' He spoke softly, with a hint of discovery and perhaps acceptance in his voice. 'And I should keep my distance from you. I know it, but I do not want to do it.'

Her breath quivered in her throat. 'What is it that you want to do?'

'This.' Rik leaned in and claimed her lips with his.

'Melanie.' Rik breathed her name into her hair. Her face was pressed against his chest. He had kissed her until they were both breathless with it. He wanted to kiss her again, and with his fingertips he gently raised her chin.

Her eyes glowed, filled with softness and passion for him. She'd told him there were times when she had thought of him as a man, not a prince. Rik wanted that acceptance from her now, for her to see him as Rikardo, regardless of what else there might be in his life. For once he simply wanted to be a man to a woman.

He drew her soft curves more securely into his arms and breathed the scent from the side of her neck and let his mouth cover hers once again. Tongues caressed and a low moan sounded. His, and a warning bell began to register in the back of his mind not to do this because there was naivety in the way she yielded to him, as though she was new to this, as though perhaps she wasn't particularly experienced…

'What are we doing?' Melanie spoke in a low tone. She drew back. Shields rose in her eyes, concealing her reaction to him, protecting her. 'This—this isn't the same as before when there was a reason to kiss me. It doesn't matter about Paris, about the romance of being here. I shouldn't have let myself be tempted. I shouldn't have looked for that—'

Her words were disjointed. Discomfort filled her face, and Rik…wished it didn't have to be that way, but hadn't he set them up for exactly this? He'd made his choices. 'I should not have stepped over this line, either. It was not a smart thing to do.'

He wrestled with his own reactions. He'd wanted to take, conquer, claim—to stamp his ownership on her and possess her until she was his and his alone. That urge had bypassed all his usual roadblocks.

'I have never—' He stopped himself from completing the sentence. Instead he tried to turn his attention to tomorrow. 'You must go to bed now, get some sleep ready for our visit to the markets.'

Her eyes still held the glaze of the moments of passion they had shared, but they also held confusion, uncertainty, and unease. She searched his face and Rik saw each emotion register as she found her way back to here and now and…to who they were and to remembrance of the arrangement they shared. *He* should have never forgotten that arrangement, yet when he was near her he couldn't seem to remember even the most basic of principles, of sticking to his word and to their goals.

'Thank you for showing me a little of Paris this evening, and for allowing me to take part in your talks with the restaurateurs.' Her chin tipped up. 'Goodnight, Rikardo. I hope you sleep well.'

CHAPTER TEN

'THANK you for finding these markets for me to see.' Mel let her gaze shift from one market stall to the next as she and Rik walked through them. Somehow that felt much easier than looking the prince in the eyes.

They'd kissed last night and she'd withdrawn. Did he know how far she had stepped over the line within herself by entering into that kiss? Mel was too close to falling dangerously for…a prince. She couldn't do that. She had to be businesslike about her relationship with Rik, even if their surroundings or circumstances felt very romantic or extraordinary.

No matter what, Mel. You have to keep your distance inside yourself no matter what. So treat this outing as an outing. Nothing more and nothing less.

She drew a breath and forced her gaze to his. 'Thank you for making time for us to come here.'

'You are welcome, Melanie.' His tone, too, sounded more formal than usual.

And were his shoulders held a little more rigidly?

Mel tried very hard after that, to focus only on the moment. The markets were a treasure trove of local clothing, some new, brand name and quite expensive but with equally much vintage and pre-loved. It was the latter that appealed to Mel.

'You are sure you don't want to look at the branded items?' When they arrived here Rik had pressed what felt like a very large bundle of currency into Mel's hands, and instructed her that she was not to leave empty-handed.

That, too, had felt awkward. Ironically, not because he had wanted to give her this gift but because they had both let their fingers linger just a little too long, and then quickly withdrawn.

Mel's thoughts started to whirl as they had last night in the long hours of courting sleep that wouldn't come. A part of her wanted to find a way to get him to care for her truly. *That* was the problem.

He didn't, and he wouldn't. Not today, not tomorrow or next week or next month or in any number of months. At the end of their time together he would send her away from him fully. How much more did she need to think about it before she accepted that fact? Accepted that a few kisses in the heat of the moment in a beautiful city didn't mean all that much to a man who could kiss just about anyone, anywhere and any time?

Mel drew a slow breath. She forced air into her lungs, forced calm into her inner turmoil. And she cast her glance once more about the market and kept looking until the blur of colours turned once again into garments piled on tables, and she spotted a pretty skirt and moved closer to look…

'I'd like to buy this one.' It wouldn't break the bank.

In fact, it was ridiculously cheap. But it was exactly what Mel would wear, a long, beautifully warm tan suede that fell in an A-line cut. A memento of Paris. That thought, too, was bittersweet. 'It should fit me, but even if it doesn't I can take it in.'

She held out the rest of the money. 'Thank you for giving me this gift. I'd like to browse a little longer and then I'll be ready to go.' She hoped her words were convincing and didn't sound as strained as she felt.

'You must keep that to spend any time you wish.' Rik pressed the money back into her hands, and waited for her to tuck it away in her purse.

As the days passed after Paris, Melanie showed her strength by being the perfect fiancée to Rik. No one, not his brothers and not his father, could have said that she wasn't fully supportive of him, utterly committed to him.

Not in love with him, perhaps. That kind of acting would be a stretch, but the rest yes. She maintained her role beautifully. She showed no stress. She seemed perfectly content as she forged ahead making plans for their marriage, liaising with all those involved in the preparations as the days slid closer to the first of the three wedding rehearsals. But beneath the surface…

Rik was not content. He couldn't forget holding her in his arms in Paris. He, who had grown up trained to live by his self-control, had felt that night as though he teetered on the brink of losing it. He had longed, *longed deep down inside*, to make love to her but Melanie had broken away.

'You behaved like some smitten, lovelorn—' He bit the words off before he added fiancé. It was already bad enough that he was talking to the walls as he walked along. He *was* Melanie's fiancé. Just not in any normal sense of the word.

Their first rehearsal was tomorrow and he did not feel prepared. Perhaps things were just moving too quickly for his comfort, for him to feel that he possessed that control that he needed to have. All would be safe in Melanie's capable hands. Instinctively he knew this. Provided the actual marriage day went ahead, anything else would not overly matter anyway…

Rik made his way to the kitchen. The palace always had kitchen staff on call. He could have got one out of bed to make him a cup of coffee or a sandwich or to bring him pickings from the refrigerators, but he would rather forage for himself. At least it would pass some time until he managed to nod off, and Mel would be safe and sound asleep in *her* bed while Rik wrestled his demons.

That was part of his insomnia problem, knowing Mel was so close and he couldn't touch her. Mustn't touch her. He strode to the double doors of the palace kitchen and pushed with both hands. Before he even opened them, the scent of fresh baking hit him.

Why would anyone be baking at this time of night? Baking up a storm, he realised as his gaze lit on an array of cakes and cookies spread on the bench.

Something tickled the back of his mind, and was lost as he realised *who* was doing the cooking. 'Mel—'

'Rik! Oh, you startled me.' The cake plate she held

in her hands bobbled before she carefully set it down and placed a lid over it.

'I had permission.' Her words were almost defensive. 'I needed some time in the kitchen. It's what I do when I need—' She cut the words off, waved a hand. 'Well, never mind. I'm almost done here, anyway. All I need to do is leave the kitchen sparkling. It's almost there now.' Mel turned to wipe down a final bench top.

She had dark smudges under her eyes. Was Melanie, too, more disturbed than he'd realised since their trip to Paris despite her valiant efforts to support him? Was she also feeling tortured and struggling with her thoughts?

Leave the cleaning up for the staff.

Rik wanted very much to say the words. He bit them back because it seemed important to her to leave the kitchen as she had found it. Aside from those cakes and cookies.

'The staff told me these could be used tomorrow.' Mel gestured towards the food items. She went on to mention some need for the foods.

Rik only half heard the explanation, because he was looking at those smudges beneath her eyes.

'I don't suppose you're hungry?' She gestured towards a chocolate cake covered in sticky icing. 'It's probably the worst thing to do, but I thought I'd eat a piece and maybe—'

'Relax for a while?' He didn't know what she'd planned to say, but to Rik, standing in the kitchen in the middle of the night unable to sleep, with Melanie obviously also unable to sleep, it made perfect sense to use his insomnia to try to at least help *her* to relax. 'Why don't we take it back with us?'

Mel hadn't expected Rik to walk in on her cooking splurge. He was the reason for it, so maybe it would be good to spend that time with him. Perhaps then she would be able to shake off the feeling of melancholy and impending loss that had become harder and harder to bear as each day passed.

You'd better smile anyway, Mel. He doesn't need to see your face and start wondering what your problem is.

In truth Mel didn't *know* what the problem was. She'd hoped that cooking would shake the answer loose but it hadn't.

'I guess we can make coffee in our suite?' It was only after she said the words that she realised she'd referred to the suite as theirs as though she had every right, as though she had as much ownership of it as Rik did.

'I put a pot on before I left.'

His words made her realise that, while he'd caught her cooking in the middle of the night because she couldn't sleep, he must have had similar problems otherwise he wouldn't have been wandering the corridors and making pots of coffee when normal people would be asleep in their beds.

Mel put pieces of cake onto plates and loaded them onto a tray, which Rik promptly took from her hands. One final glance around the kitchen showed that the staff would have nothing more to deal with than delivering the goodies tomorrow morning, and Mel would try to be available to help with that.

The smell of brewed coffee met them as they stepped into the suite. It reminded Mel of Paris, of being held in his arms and kissed.

'Did the suede skirt fit, or did you have to alter it?' Rik's words made Mel realise that he, too, was remembering.

Her breath hitched for a moment. She forced her thoughts away from the reaction. She'd got through day after day doing the same. Each time any unacceptable thought tried to raise its head, Mel pushed it away. Surely no one would be able to tell just how often she thought about Rik, about those moments? How she longed for them all over again? 'The skirt fits perfectly. I'm planning to wear it tomorrow, actually.'

For the festival being held in the town. Rik hadn't spoken of it, so Mel didn't know what his role of involvement would be, if any. And the kitchen staff had told her that the event itself would be a low budget affair.

That didn't mean it couldn't be fun, though, and it was an unusual theme. Mel at least wanted to take a look. All of which was trivia, really, and yet there were times when trivia felt a little less emotionally threatening than the rest of life!

They sat side by side on the sofa eating cake and sipping coffee. A very ordinary, normal thing to do except for the fact it was after midnight, and this was Rik's suite of rooms, and they were engaged and yet in the truest sense they really weren't.

She blurted out, 'The wedding planner supervised

a fitting of the gown this afternoon. I won't wear it to the first rehearsal tomorrow, of course, but…'

How did she explain what she couldn't understand herself? Just how much that fitting had taken from her emotionally and she couldn't say why because it was just a dress in the end, and the wedding wasn't going to be real, and Mel *knew* all of this.

Mel didn't want to think about why. 'Well, it's a beautiful gown. I'm amazed at how quickly it's being created.' She drew a breath and tried to make light of it as she went on. 'Have you been fitted for your suit?'

'Yesterday.' He glanced towards her. 'I've left you to handle the bulk of the work for this wedding while I attended to other things. I should have supported you better.'

She leaned towards him, shook her head. 'You've been all over the country checking on the truffle harvesting, making sure the orders are going out in perfect condition. That's so important.'

'And that's your generosity shining again.' He lifted his hand to the side of her face. 'You have a tiny dot of cake batter right there.' His fingertip softly brushed the spot.

Mel closed her eyes. Oh, it was the stupidest thing to do but it was what his touch did to her. She melted any time they were close.

'It's there, isn't it?' The feather-light touch of lips replaced his fingertip against her cheek. He kissed the spot where her cooking efforts had made their way onto her face, and then he sighed softly and pressed his cheek to hers. 'All the time that need is there. I do not know why.'

That was as far as he got, because he turned his head to look into her eyes, and Mel turned her head to look into his eyes, and their lips met.

The fire ignited. Immediately and utterly and Rik's arms closed around her and Mel threw hers around his neck and held on. She didn't know if she could have let go if she'd wanted to. This was what had been troubling her. This was what she'd tried to think about and figure out.

Her thoughts formed that far, and then they became action. Her mouth yielded to his, opened to him even as she took from him. She sipped from his lips and ran her tongue across his teeth.

Everything was pleasure, and somehow all of those feelings seemed to have caught themselves in a place deep in her chest where they swirled and twined and warmed her all at once. Rik was the warming power. Everything about him drew her. Mel didn't want to resist being drawn.

'I don't want to leave this, Mel.' His words echoed her thoughts, and he used the diminutive of her name, and Mel loved that.

'I don't want to leave it, either, Rik.'

'Do you understand what will happen?' His words were very deep, emotive and desirous and almost stern all at once.

'I do.' If there was any hesitation in her words it was not because of uncertainty in that decision. 'This—this is new for me.'

Please don't stop because I've admitted that.

'But it's what I want, Rik. I—I have no doubts.'

'I do not want to consider doubts, either.' Rik's words were strong, and yet the touch of his hand was so gentle as he stroked the side of her face, her neck. 'I will cherish you, Melanie. I will cherish you through this experience.'

That made it right for her. It just…did. The tiny bit of fear that had been buried deep down, that she might not know what to do or how to please him, evaporated. He would guide her. Mel could give this gift and share the gift of his intimacy in return. She wanted that. She *needed* it, though she did not understand why that need held such strength.

Rik took her hand and led her to his bedroom. Mel managed to register that the room was similar to her own but with a more manly tone, and then Rik drew her into his arms and kissed his way from the side of her neck to her chin and finally to her lips as their bodies pressed together and Mel didn't notice anything more about the room.

This felt exactly right. That was what Mel thought as her hands pressed against his chest, slid up to his shoulders and she let herself touch his muscular back through the cloth of his shirt. Yet that was not enough. 'I want—'

'What do you want, Melanie? Tell me.' He encouraged her to put her need into words.

And maybe he needed to hear that, too, for her to tell him.

'I need to touch you. I need to feel your skin beneath my fingertips while you're kissing me.' She almost whispered it, but he heard and he guided her hand to the buttons of his shirt.

It was all the permission that Mel needed, and, though she trembled inside, her fingers slipped each button free until his chest was revealed and she could touch his bare skin. 'You're so warm.'

'That is because you are in my arms.' He shrugged out of the shirt and then he gave all of his attention to her and to this exploration that they shared moment-by-moment in giving and receiving and discovering and finding.

When he laid her on the bed, Mel looked into his eyes and though her thoughts and feelings were blurred by passion, impossible to define, every instinct told her. 'This is what I've needed. I know it's right. I want you to make love to me, Rik. Just to share this together, the two of us without thinking about anything else.'

Rik cupped her face in his palm. 'And so it will be.'

Melanie blossomed beneath Rik's ministrations. She was beautiful in every way, and he told her in English and French and told her in the old language of Braston, words that he had never uttered to another woman as he led her forward on this journey.

He hesitated on the brink of claiming her. 'I am sorry that there will be pain. If you want me to stop—'

'No.' Mel let the word be a caress of her lips against his. A sigh inside her. A whisper of need that she gave from her heart, and that was terrifying because Mel couldn't bring her heart to this. That was far too dangerous a thing to do. 'Please don't stop, Rik. I...don't think I could bear it if you did.'

There *was* pain, but she held his gaze and the tenderness in his eyes, the expression that seemed akin to awe as he bent to kiss her lips again, allowed her to release that pain, to let it pass and to trust in him to lead her forward.

He did that, and then there was only pleasure and she crashed suddenly over an incredible wave and he cried out with her, the most amazing experience Mel had ever experienced, and the most powerful, knowing that she, too, had brought *him* to *this*.

Afterwards he held her cuddled against his chest as their breathing slowed. A deep lethargy crept up on Mel. She tried to fight it, to stay alert, to even *begin* to figure out what happened now or what she should say or do. There was so much and she didn't know how to find understanding but she knew she didn't regret this, could never regret it.

But what did it mean to him, Mel? What did it mean to Rik? Is there any possibility now—?

Mel could have been embarrassed, but they had shared this. How could she now feel anything that even resembled such an emotion? There was no room inside her. She was filled with other emotions, inexplicable to her right now, and overwhelming because what they had shared had been overwhelming. She shivered, wishing for his warmth, and then he was there, drawing her close.

He tucked her chin into his chest and she felt tension

drain from him, too, and wondered what his thoughts might be.

'Sleep, Melanie. You need it right now more than you know.' He stroked his fingers through her hair.

Mel slept.

CHAPTER ELEVEN

'If I'd remembered this festival was on today I'd have left the country.' Marcelo's face pulled into a disgruntled twist.

'Oh, I don't know. Is it so horrible having the opportunity to flirt with lots of lovely local women?' Anrai dug his brother in the ribs.

Marcelo didn't crack a smile. 'It is if they then want to marry you!'

Anrai, too, now grimaced. 'I forgot that from last year.'

'And the year before and year before and year before,' Marcelo said beneath his breath. 'You need to stop being such a flirt, Anrai. It will catch up with you one day. Anyway, we had to be here. Rik's first wedding rehearsal is later today.' Marcelo turned to Rik. 'Can you believe the marriage is only a week away?'

'No.' Rik glanced at his brothers, heard the sibling teasing. He might even have wanted to join in, if there'd been any space left in his thoughts or emotions right now for anything other than the woman he'd held in his arms last night.

It was just one week before their marriage.

They had spent just one night in each other's arms.

He should not have let that happen but it had and now he did not know what to do, how to go forward. So many thoughts and emotions swirled, and Rik…did not like to feel out of control, confused, uncertain of his path and yet all he could do was continue because… nothing had changed when in a way…everything had. But nothing at the core of him, nothing of how he was. Of his parents' traits within him.

Nevertheless, Rik needed to find Melanie. The marriage *was* only a week away. They did have a rehearsal this afternoon and…he didn't know if he had irreparably messed things up with Melanie.

And even now you wish you could take her again into your arms.

Rik tried to force the thoughts aside. They were of no use to him, a line crossed that must not be crossed again. He glanced around him. He and his brothers were in Ettonbierre village, and, yes, there was a festival on today.

Rik had forgotten all about it. So had Anrai and Marcelo who'd both only arrived back at the palace late last night and had walked out with him this morning intending to meet a man to discuss tourism plans for the region.

All three brothers had plans and goals. All three relied on the success of each other to allow them to achieve those goals. The prize was recovery for a struggling country, the cost to be their freedom if Anrai and

Marcelo could not also figure out ways to avoid their father's insistence that they lock into lifetime marriages.

Rik tried to dismiss the thoughts. He looked around him. This festival was what Melanie had cooked for in the middle of the night. Just a few hours ago, and then Rik had found her in the kitchen and taken her back to his suite. She'd mentioned the wedding rehearsal. She had probably been worrying about it and that had prompted her cooking spree. And then perhaps other thoughts had pushed those worries aside for a time as they…made love.

And those thoughts had now given her new concerns? Of course they would have. They had given Rik fresh concerns, fresh questions. He had to keep her with him and keep both of them to their agreement. He hoped last night would not have undermined that goal. That was the only *clear* path Rik could define. Surely the only one that mattered, so why did reminding himself bring a sense of loss rather than the sense of eventual freedom it should?

Every thought brought Rik back to the same thing. He and Melanie had made love. That *had* changed things. He'd felt as though his world had shifted alignment and Rik couldn't figure out why he felt that way or what it meant.

He'd woken at dawn with Melanie curled in his arms and a sense of rightness that had quickly changed when the reality of what they had done stabbed him in the chest.

How could that have been a smart decision on his part? Melanie had been innocent and had allowed passion to sway her judgement, but Rik was experienced and should have known not to let this happen.

Not when there was no future for them, no future when their involvement was based on a situation that he had set up to avoid becoming tied down in a relationship. He couldn't bear to perpetuate his family's emotional freeze-out into another generation, to be the one turning the cold shoulder to his partner and receiving the same in return. To have his children asking themselves why they were not fit to be loved.

No. He could not carry that legacy forward.

When he woke this morning and thought of all that, remorse and confusion and a lot of other emotions had set in. Melanie was a giving girl. She would be kind. She would definitely care for her children.

But Rik…could not match those traits. He'd eased away from Melanie and got up. Showered, dressed, told himself he needed to think and that he would wait for her to wake and then they would…

What? Somehow sort themselves out so that last night didn't have the impact on them that it already had done?

She'd been a virgin. She'd given him a beautiful gift. That could never be undone now and even with all his concerns, Rik felt that he *had* been given that beautiful gift, the gift of Melanie in all of who she was, and he didn't begin to know what to do now because he hadn't planned for this and he had nothing to give in return of equal or acceptable value.

A confronting thought for a man who always set out to be in charge of his world, who had been raised into position and privilege and must now acknowledge that in this, he lacked.

'I just want to find Melanie.' He frowned. 'There are a lot of people around. She is the fiancée of a prince now, and shouldn't be unattended without at least two bodyguards with her.'

Rik totally overlooked the fact that he had encouraged Melanie to move about the palace grounds and surrounds using the small buggy vehicle, and had believed she would be perfectly safe where members of the palace staff would never be too far away or the villagers would know she was a guest at the palace.

But the festival would bring tourists and strangers. Anything might happen.

And your protectiveness of her is out of proportion to your ability to let her into the core parts of you that you withhold from the world.

But not from his brothers?

That was different. It was all that he had. Care for his brothers and for the people of Braston. He could not bring normal love and caring feelings to a marriage.

'Hate to point it out to you, brother, but *we* don't have any bodyguards with us.' Anrai raised his brows. 'You're sounding very serious considering the temporary nature of your arrangement with Melanie. Much as I think she's a wonderful girl,' his brother added.

'She is.' Rik didn't notice the tightening of his mouth as he spoke, the flash of warring emotions that quickly crossed his face. Instead his gaze scanned the crowds, searching as he missed the surprised and thoughtful gazes his brothers exchanged before they gave nods of silent decision, told him they needed to find their contact and get on with their meeting, and gave him the space to make his search.

Rik glanced around the crowded village square. There were colourful rides for children to play on, stalls out in the open selling home produce and hand-sewn items. A kissing booth, another to have your romantic future read, another for chemistry tests to find potential matches.

The fair had started out as a proposal day centuries ago as a means for men to woo their potential brides with offers of a fowl or a pig as a dowry. Today it had turned into an opportunity for the folk of Ettonbierre village to let their hair down for a day, for children to play and young men and women to flirt with each other, ask each other out.

He didn't want Melanie anywhere near this.

The jealous, protective thought came from deep within Rik. He had no right to it but still it came. A moment later he spotted her and he strode towards the small group gathered outside the food marquee at the edge of the town square.

'It's very flattering of you to say that to me, and yes I guess it would be fair to say that I am a guest of Prince Rikardo at the palace at the moment.' Mel spoke the words as she tried to edge away from the small crowd that had gathered outside the food tent.

She tried to sound normal, polite and not as deeply confused and overwrought as she felt this morning. Pretending calm until she started to feel it was a method that had worked for her after their trip to Paris. Surely it would work again now?

After Paris you were recovering from a kiss. Last night you made love with Rik. The two aren't exactly on a par. 'I'm really not at liberty to discuss that any further at this time.'

Though Rik had assured her none of the villagers would recognise the ring she wore as her engagement ring, Mel tucked her hand into her skirt pocket just in case, and was proud that she'd managed to think clearly enough to consider that need.

In that same thrust to find some sliver of normalcy in the whirl of her emotions she'd delivered all the cakes she could carry to the fair. She had stepped outside the catering tent intending to take a quick look at the festival before heading back to the palace.

Rik had been out on the grounds somewhere when she had first woken up. She probably could have gone looking for him, but what would she have said? She'd needed a moment to try to clear her head before she faced him.

You wanted more than a moment. After all that you shared with him last night you had no idea how to face him. Why downplay it, Mel, when it's all you can think about and every time you do think about it, you can hardly breathe for the mix of feelings that rushes through you?

She'd fallen asleep in his arms, more drained emotionally and in every way than she had understood. And had woken alone, only to realise she was not alone because doubt had come to rest on her shoulder to whisper in her ear. Doubt about his feelings in all of this. Doubt that she had any right to expect him to *have* any feelings about it. Just above the other shoulder lurked despair. Mel didn't want to acknowledge that, but…

She and Rik had shared something. It had been stunningly special to Mel, but that didn't mean it had been any of that to Rikardo. To the prince. How could it have been?

You managed to forget that little factor last night, didn't you? That he's a prince and you're a cook and his path is carefully set and doesn't include any kind of emotional commitment to you.

'If you change your mind while you are here…' The man in front of her gave an engaging smile and handed her a piece of paper with his phone number on it.

Proposal Day. The festival had a history. Mel had heard it all from the kitchen staff. But nowadays it was a chance for people to get to know each other, date or whatever. Mel wouldn't have been interested before. Now that she'd made love with Rik, she felt she could never be interested in any other man, ever again.

The man turned away. There were two others. Mel managed to quickly send them both on their way. She needed to get out of here, to make her way back to the palace and maybe during that solitary walk she would gather up all the pieces of herself and get them back into some kind of working order. Maybe she could hole up in her room for the entire day to complete that task. Would that be long enough?

It will never be long enough, Mel. You know what's happened.

The thought was so strong, so full of conviction. It forced her hand, and realisation crashed over her, then, whether she was ready for it or not.

She'd fallen in love with Rik. It was the answer to why last night had moved her emotions so deeply that she had wondered if she would ever be the same. The answer was no, she never would.

Because "everyday girl" Melanie Watson had fallen in love with Prince Rikardo Ettonbierre of Braston.

It should have been a moment of wonder, of anticipation and happiness. Instead, devastating loss swept through her because last night had been the total of any chance to show her love to him in that way. A moment that shouldn't have happened.

In return, Rik had made no promises. Not at the start of their marriage agreement, and not last night. He'd given in to desire. That wasn't the same as being bowled over by love so that expressing those feelings was imperative.

Mel was the one who had foolishly given her heart. Well, now she had to get back on her feet somehow. She had to get through marrying him and walking away, to do all that with dignity when all she would want to do was beg him to keep her, to want her, to not reject her or abandon her or punish her for—

What did she mean, punish?

And today there was the first wedding rehearsal. How could she get through that?

'Melanie. What are you doing here? Why were you talking to those men?'

Rik's words shook her out of her reverie, stopped

a train of thought that had started to dig into a place deep down where she had hidden parts of herself. But the interruption did not save her from her sense of uncertainty and panic. That increased.

She glanced at him. Oh, it was hard to look and to know what was in her heart.

Please don't let him see it.

That one glance into his face showed austerity, as though he had stepped behind shields, had taken a fortified position.

In that moment he really resembled his father…

Rik had told her he couldn't buy into a cold relationship. He'd been so against the institution of marriage. He…hadn't believed in love.

Mel had thought that was because he'd been hurt, had seen his parents in a loveless relationship. But looking at him now, seeing that capacity to close himself off when she needed so very much for him to…let her in…

Last night was not the same for Rik, as for you. And whether or not he is like his father, you have to accept what he told you at the start. He won't ever love you, Mel. Not ever.

That attitude must make it much easier for Rik to deal with things like arranging this marriage and knowing he would be able to walk away from it later. It wasn't his fault that he'd asked her to help him. He had the right to try to protect his interests, and he'd wanted to help the people of Braston. His father had put him in an impossible position.

And now you have allowed yourself to end up in one, by falling for him.

All she could do was try to match his strength. She stared at the face she had come to cherish far too much in the short time she had known him, and prayed for that strength.

'Rik. I…' She didn't know what she wanted to say. What she should try to say.

'I was concerned. You may not be safe here, Melanie.'

If his frown showed anything but attention to her presence here at the fair, Mel couldn't discern it.

He went on. 'You are all on your own.'

Oh, she knew that more than well, though she realised that Rik meant it literally in this case.

A thousand moments of trying to escape wouldn't have got her any closer to feeling ready for this. For facing the feelings that had overcome her, and for facing him. She loved him. Deep down in her heart and soul, all those feelings had formed and intertwined and she had no choice about it.

How could Mel combat that? How could she take what had happened last night, and put it in some kind of perspective somehow so that she could contain these feelings, get them under control and then somehow make them stop altogether when it just wasn't like that now?

How could she marry him, live as his…princess but secretly in name only, let herself become more and more familiar with him with the passing of each day and then leave at the end of a few short months and get on with her life as though none of this had happened?

Those pretty, sparkly shoes were nowhere to be found right now.

'I came out to deliver some of the cakes that I baked last night for the festival.' Her words held a tremor and she cleared her throat before she went on. She didn't want that tremor. She couldn't allow it. She just couldn't. He mustn't detect how shaken she felt and perhaps figure out why.

Rik wanted a single life, not to be bound in the very relationship that he'd asked her to help him avoid. The knowledge lanced through her, of how utterly useless it would be to hold out any hope that their circumstances might change.

So press on, Mel. You can do it. One step after another until you get there.

'I wanted a look at the festival.' There. A normal tone, a normal topic of conversation.

A bunch of unspoken words filling the air between them.

She tightened her lips so they wouldn't tremble. 'I thought it might be interesting, and I didn't want the kitchen staff to have to bring all the cakes and cookies themselves.'

'And you had men lined up to ask you out.' His words held no particular inflection.

So why did Mel believe she could hear possession in them?

Because you are engaged to him, but for a purpose, Mel. That's all it is.

They might have been keeping their marriage plans secret from the masses for as long as they could possibly manage, but that wouldn't mean he would be happy to see her out being asked on dates by local men. 'I didn't expect that to happen. I just stepped out of the food tent.'

'I know. I saw.' Rik suppressed a sigh as he searched his fiancée's eyes, her face. She looked overwhelmed and uncertain, shaken to the core.

He blamed himself for that. And into that mix he had brought a burst of jealousy that was completely inappropriate.

'I should have waited for you this morning.' Whether he'd known what to say to her, or not, Rik should have waited. A prince did not avoid facing something just because he did not know how to manage a situation. 'Winnow called early and I went—'

'It's all right.' She touched his arm, and quickly drew her hand away as though the touch had burned her.

Remorse pricked him afresh. Remorse and a confusion of feelings? He pushed the impression aside. There were no warring feelings, just resolve and the need to try to ease them through this so they could go forward. Rik straightened his shoulders.

Melanie gestured in front of them. 'I've probably wasted your time, coming to look for me, too. Let's head back. I'm sure you have a lot of things that you need to do before the—the rehearsal later.'

'There is nothing that cannot wait until then.' But it was good that Melanie would come back with him now. For the first few minutes until they got free of the fair and started on the path back to the palace, Rik let silence reign.

Once they were alone, he slowed his pace. 'We need to talk, Melanie. About last night.'

'Oh, really, I don't think there's any need.' Every defence she could muster was immediately thrown up. She tipped her chin in the air. 'It's just—it was—we have our arrangement! Last night wasn't—it happened, that's all but it doesn't need to make any difference to anything. Nothing needs to change. Really I'd prefer to just forget all about it.'

'But that is not possible.' And even though he knew it should not have happened, Rik did not want…to deny the memory or to let her think— 'I don't want you to imagine that I took what we shared lightly,' he began carefully. 'It was—'

'Lots of people sleep together for lots of different reasons.' She drew a shuddery breath. 'We did because we did. We were…a little bit attracted to each other and maybe we were…curious. Now that curiosity is set to rest it doesn't have to happen again.' Her words emerged in stilted tones but with so much determination.

She was saying all the things that Rik himself believed about their situation. Not dismissing what they had shared, but doing all she could to put it in an appropriate context. This was what he would have tried to do himself, so why did her response make his chest feel tight? Make him want to take her in his arms again and try to mend them through touch when touch had brought them to this in the first place?

They rounded a bend in the road. The palace came into view.

Rik barely looked ahead of them. He could only look at Melanie. Guilt that he had caused her this unease vied with feelings of…disappointment and…loss within him.

How could that be so? He must only feel relief, and… the need to reassure her.

So get your focus back on the goal, Rik. It's as important now as it was at the start.

It was. In her way, Melanie was right. Nothing about any of that had changed. Nothing at the core of him, either. Nothing of what he needed, of what he could give and…what he could not give.

So do what you can to reassure her, Rik, both for now and for later.

'I will look after you for the short term of our marriage, Melanie.' A rustle sounded around a bend in the path and he briefly wondered if Rufusina had got loose again before the thought left him for more important ones. 'You will lack for nothing. I will provide everything you might want, and when you go back to Australia afterwards—'

'I don't need anything extra from you. I still have all the money you gave me while we were in Paris. That's more than enough to see me back to Australia.' Her words were protective, proud. 'I can take care of myself once I've finished being your temporary princess. All that matters is that you've held onto your freedom, and you've got the things you needed—'

'What is this? What is going on here?' King Georgio appeared before them on the path.

Not Rufusina on the loose and foraging.

But Rik's father, becoming angrier by the moment as what he had just heard sank in.

'What trickery have I just heard, Rikardo? I did not say that you could marry temporarily. You must marry permanently!' His gaze shifted to Melanie and further suspicion filled it.

Before the king could speak, Rik took a step forward, half shielding Melanie with his body. 'This situation is of my making, Father. You will not question Melanie or accuse her about any of this.'

'Then you will explain yourself.' Georgio's words were cold. 'And this will not be done standing in the middle of a walkway.'

Security people had gathered in the king's wake.

'You will attend me appropriately, inside the palace. You will not keep me waiting.' Without another word, the older man walked away.

Rik turned to Melanie.

'All your plans, Rik.' Concern and unease filled her face. 'He looked so angry.'

'I must speak to him now, try to get him to understand.' He hesitated. 'You will wait for me?'

'I'll wait in our—in the suite until you can let me know what happened.'

With thoughts churning, Rik took one last look at the woman before him, and turned to follow his father.

CHAPTER TWELVE

I AM stunned.

Rik thought the words silently as he walked towards the grand historic church where he and Melanie were to today rehearse the marriage ceremony. Stunned almost to the point of numbness by what his father had just revealed.

He needed to speak to Melanie now more than before, and when he stepped through the doors of the church, she broke away from the small group of people gathered near the front of the large ancient building, and rushed to his side.

'I couldn't wait for you any longer.' She said the words in a hushed whisper. 'Dominico came to get me and I couldn't tell him anything was wrong. Is—is the wedding off now? What happened? What did your father say?'

Beyond them, Anrai and Marcelo waited, along with the priest and various others expecting to participate in this marriage ceremony next week.

Another brother could be standing there.

'This will shock you, as it did me when my father revealed it, and I would ask that you not tell anyone until I can speak to Anrai and Marcelo.' Rik drew a slow breath. 'The reason that my father pushed so hard for marriages is because there is an older brother, a love child to a woman in England. Two years ago this man discovered his true identity. He's been trying to gain a position in the family through my father since.'

'Is—? That isn't sounding like good news to you?' Melanie's hand half lifted as though she would press it over her mouth before she dropped it away again.

'His existence is the reason my mother left, and he has now gained access to copies of our family law and worked out that he can try to claim ascendancy and, with it, Marcelo's position, rights, and work. If Marcelo is married, his position is safe, but until we are also married, Anrai's and mine…are not.'

'In other words he doesn't really belong within the family.' She said it quietly. 'He's not wanted.'

'He is not royal born.' Rik said it carefully. 'Whether he will find a place within the family, at this stage I do not know. I would like to meet him and discern for myself what manner of man he is and go from there. I would not reject a brother, but I also would not welcome a threat to the security of my country and people.'

'That's fair.' She seemed to relax as she said the words.

Rik went on. 'The old laws—this is part of why Marcelo wants to bring change. This is not merely so we can all maintain our positions. It is to keep the people of the country safe as well.'

'Why would this man push for a position that

shouldn't rightly be his? Surely he must realise that he can't just walk in and take someone's place?'

'My father has no doubt contributed to the man's anger and frustration by refusing to acknowledge him at all when he should have done so many years ago.'

'Well, you can take care of your part in it. You're marrying me. You can say you've been married then. Your position will be safe!'

All but for one vital thing. 'I must *remain married*, Melanie. My plan to marry you and then end the relationship afterwards will not work for this.'

'What—what will you do?' She searched his face and her eyes were so deep and so guarded as she began to realise how this new situation had raised the stakes. 'You'll need to find someone else. You'll need to start looking right away. Someone you can make that kind of commitment with. There must be *someone* you could accept in that way.'

The priest cleared his throat noisily at the front of the church.

Rik's brothers cast glances their way that were becoming more than curious.

Of all settings and times, this had to be about the worst but at least as Rik had informed Melanie of the basics of the issue his thoughts had cleared. He knew exactly what he needed, now, and from whom, but could he yet again convince her?

'You want me to be the one, don't you?' The words came from between lips that had whitened with shock. 'You want me to be married to you permanently?'

'We are already together. I would provide for your

every need. You would live a privileged life, want for nothing.' It would resolve problems, not only for Rik, but also for Melanie. 'You would never again have to fend for yourself, and later if you wanted a child I would…allow it.'

There were other words that tried to bubble up, but Rik needed to protect himself in this—

Her glance searched his face before it shifted to take in the church, the people waiting for the rehearsal to start. 'I can't do it. Not even for the people.' She whispered the words before she added more strongly, 'I've tried hard in my life and I've never rejected people even when they've rejected me, but I won't line up for another lifetime of that.

'I blamed myself for losing my parents in that car crash. I thought after that I didn't deserve happiness, to be alive when they weren't, but that was grief talking. I do deserve happiness. I deserve better from you.'

Melanie turned on her heel and ran from the church.

CHAPTER THIRTEEN

'I'VE made the biggest mistake of my life.' Rik spoke the words to Marcelo as his brother drove them towards the country's small international airport. He felt sick inside, close to overwhelmed and very, very afraid that he might have lost his chance with Melanie for ever by stupidly trying too hard to protect himself and by being too slow to realise…

Rik had lost valuable time searching for Melanie out of doors. He'd thought she must have run to their spot on the mountainside, or perhaps back to Ettonbierre village to lose herself in the crowd there.

As he'd searched, knowing his brothers were also looking, Rik had begun to panic. In her distraught state, what if something happened to Melanie? And all that he had locked down inside him and tried to deny since he and Melanie made love had begun to inexorably make its way to the surface and demand to be known.

'She will not leave the airport.' Marcelo offered the assurance without taking his glance from the road. 'If need be, the flights will all be delayed until we get there. Dominico will take care of it.'

That was a privilege of position that, in this moment, Rik was willing to exploit without compunction. It was Melanie's reaction when he caught up with her that concerned him.

'I have used Melanie without considering how she might feel. Not respected her rights and emotions.' He shook his head. 'I asked her to remain permanently married to me as though she should be grateful for all the privileges she would receive as part of the family.'

'Such as being in a loveless marriage for life?' Marcelo's words were not harsh, neither teasing, but a statement of understanding of things that he and Rik had never discussed about their upbringing.

'I wanted to avoid that at all costs.' Why hadn't Rik understood sooner that his drive to pull Melanie into exactly that long-term relationship had not been fuelled merely by the need to protect his position and that of his brothers, in the knowledge of this unknown brother? It had been driven by need of *Melanie*. And yet he felt no warmth towards this unknown man. 'I cannot find soft emotion in my heart for him, Marcelo. Even now when I realise how I feel about Melanie—'

'One thing at a time,' Marcelo advised. He drew the car to a halt in a no stopping zone in front of the airport. 'We all need to get to know this man. Good luck, brother.'

Rik met Marcelo's gaze as he threw the car door open. 'Thank you.'

Rik drew a deep breath and strode quickly into the airport terminal.

* * *

I'm not going to feel guilty about the money.

Melanie thought this as she twisted her hands together in her lap. She'd packed all her luggage, half dreading that Rik might appear at any moment. Then she'd summoned palace staff to carry it all downstairs and put it in the cab she'd ordered. A real cab this time, with no mix-ups.

She'd bought an airline ticket to get back to Australia. The flight wasn't going directly there. She'd asked for the first one that would get her out of the country and she'd used the money Rik had given her that day in Paris, to pay for it.

It was almost time, just a few more minutes and she would be able to board the plane, and…fly away from Braston, and from Rik, for ever.

Her heart squeezed and she forced her gaze forward. Other people in the boarding lounge talked to each other or relaxed in their chairs, at ease with themselves and their plans. Mel just wanted to…get through this. She felt she was letting down the people, but Rik would find someone else. Prince Rikardo Eduard Ettonbierre of Braston would not struggle to find a woman willing to marry him for life.

Mel couldn't be that woman. Not without love.

'Melanie!'

At first she thought she'd imagined his familiar voice, a figment within her mind because her heart hurt so much. It was going to take time to get past those raw emotions and begin to heal.

Could she heal from falling in love with Rik?

'Mel. Thank goodness you're here.' Rik appeared in

front of her. Ruffled. Surprisingly un-prince-like with his tie askew and his suit coat hanging open. *Real.*

Mel shot to her feet. She wasn't sure what she intended to do when she got upright. Run? Faint? Throw herself at him and hope against hope that he would open his arms and his heart to her?

Get real, Melanie Watson. You're still a cook and he's still a prince and he doesn't love you and that's that.

'I don't have a glass slipper.' His words were low.

And confusing. 'I—I don't understand.'

Words came over the airport speaker system. French and then English. Her flight was being called. Mel had to get on the flight. She glanced towards the gate, to people beginning to go through. Her heart said stay. Her survival instincts said go. Go and don't look back because you've done that "love people and not be loved in return" thing and it just hurts too damned much to do it again. 'I have to go, Rik. I paid all your money to buy the ticket. I can't buy another one.'

'I will buy you another ticket, Mel.' He lifted his hand as though he would take hers, and hesitated as though uncertain of his welcome. 'If you still want to go.'

Oh, Rik.

'Please. I left out something very important when I asked you to marry me.'

'Another bargaining chip?' She hadn't meant to say it. She didn't want to spread hurt, or reveal her heart. Mel just wanted…to go home and yet, where was home now? Could home be anywhere when her heart had already decided where it wanted to be? 'I didn't mean that.'

'You had every right to say it.' Rik gestured to a room to their left. 'There's a private lounge there. Will you give me a few minutes, Mel? Please? You will still be able to make this flight if you want to, or a next one. Anything you want, but please let me try—'

'All right.' She led the way to the room, pushed the door open and stepped inside. Somehow it felt important to take that initiative. To be in charge even if she was agreeing to stall her plans to speak with him.

It was a small room. The lounge suite was quintessential airport "luxury". Deep red velvet with large cushions all immaculately kept. There were matching drapes opened wide and a view of runways with planes in various stages of arrival and departure.

All Mel could see was Rik's blue eyes, fixed on her brown ones, searching as though there was something that he desperately needed to find.

'This isn't a fairy tale, Rik. I know you're a prince but to me you'll always be a man first. You'll be Rik, who I—' Fell in love with. She bit back the words.

'No. There is little of the fairy tale about current circumstances and I confess I was shocked by my father's announcement of a secret brother.' Rik did take her hand now, and led her to a lounge seat.

Somehow they were seated with her hand still held in his and far too much of a feeling of rightness inside Mel's foolish, foolish heart. 'I hope that situation can be worked out so that nobody loses too much.'

'I do not know what is possible. I have not had time

to get all the facts together, let alone think of how to act on any of them.' For this moment Rik brushed the topic aside. 'Melanie, I asked you to marry me permanently—'

'But deep down even though you have to do it, you don't want to be tied in a relationship like that, and I… can't do it when—' She ground to a halt.

'When I offered all those things that don't matter to you, and nothing else? They never have.' One side of Rik's mouth lifted in a wry, self-mocking twist. 'Everything that makes me a prince, that might appeal, doesn't matter to you. I was too slow to think about that, and too slow to understand why I needed so much for you to agree to help me anyway.'

Was it care that she saw in his eyes? Mel didn't want to hope. Not now. Not when she'd made up her mind to go and that was the only solution. 'You'll find someone, Rik. You'll be able to marry and hold onto your job. I'm sorry it will have to be for all your life. I'm sorry for that.'

Each word tightened the ache in her chest. Each glance at him made it harder to keep the tremor out of her voice.

'The thing is, all that has changed for me, Melanie. It has changed because I fell in love with you.' His words were low. Raw.

Real? Mel frowned. Shook her head. There was no allergy medication to blame now. Nothing but a hope and sense of loss so deep that she was afraid she'd heard those words only inside her, afraid to hear them at all, and so she denied. 'No.'

'The moment I took you into my arms and made love to you, I fell in love with you.' This time when he said it, emotion crowded *his* face. 'Please believe me that this is true.'

Mel had never seen that emotion, except…lurking in the backs of his eyes when he held her last night…

Could she believe this? Could Rik truly have fallen in love with her? 'You're a prince.'

'As you said when we first met.' He inclined his head. His eyes didn't twinkle, but memory was there.

'I'm a cook. From Australia.' A commoner with no fixed abode. 'I didn't even know how to curtsy properly.'

Do you really love me, Rik?

Could he really love *her*, Nicole Melanie Watson? 'You said you would never love.'

'I didn't know there would be you, and that you would come to live, not only at the palace, but that you would move into my heart.' He took both her hands into his.

She glanced down. 'The ring! I meant to leave it in the suite.'

'*Our* suite. I am glad you didn't take it off.' He touched the diamonds. 'It is made to be there.' His gaze lifted to hers. 'I know I am asking for another leap of faith, and if you cannot find anything in your heart for me then I will accept it, but I am hoping against all hope that you will agree to give me a chance to show you how deeply I have come to love you.'

'I want to, Rik.' Oh, she wanted to do that with all of *her* heart. 'If you truly love me—'

'I do.' He didn't hesitate. Conviction filled his tone. 'If you can learn to love *me*, I will be the happiest man in the world.'

'That was what you meant about the glass slipper.' She hadn't realised that he wanted to make her his princess truly, in every way. 'I'm a practical girl, Rik. I like cooking and I lost my parents and grew up trying to be loved and my aunt and uncle and Nicolette didn't, and I promised myself I would never be hurt like that again.'

But she'd opened her heart to Rik and he…loved her. 'Are you sure? Because I don't know how you could have overcome all that. You were so firmly fixed that you wouldn't be able to have that kind of relationship.'

'I thought I was incapable of experiencing those feelings. Love, commitment.'

'Your upbringing harmed you.' Mel didn't want to hurt him with the words, but they were part of *his* history, of who he was.

'We have both experienced hurt at the hands of family.' There was regret and acknowledgement, and love shining in his eyes openly for her now. 'But you have set all of my love free.'

Mel believed it then. She let go of the last doubt and took her leap of faith. 'I fell in love with you, too, Rik. I thought I was going to help you to solve a problem and then go back to Australia. Instead I wanted to stay with you for ever, but when you asked me—'

'I stupidly didn't realise what those feelings inside meant.' He drew a breath that wasn't quite steady. 'I thought I'd lost you. I couldn't bear that thought.' Again his fingers touched her ring as he drew her to her feet with him and held both her hands. 'Will you marry me next week, Mel? Give me a chance to show you every day for ever how much you mean to me?'

'Yes.' Melanie said it and stepped into his arms and, oh, it felt right. So, so right, to be in Rik's arms, in the prince's arms, where she belonged. There were no sparkly shoes. She wasn't down a rabbit hole. She had simply…come home to this man of her dreams. 'Yes, I will marry you next week and stay married for ever, and love you every single day while you love me every single day.'

Mel knew there would be hurdles. She was marrying a prince! But she would give all of her heart to him and now she knew that she could trust it into his love and care.

He glanced out of the window and smiled. 'You've missed your flight. Let's go…home and start counting the days until next week.'

'The wedding planner is going to be relieved that she doesn't have to start all over again.' A smile started on Melanie's face and she tucked her arm through Rik's and they left the room and made their way out of the airport to a car parked and waiting for Rik. The keys were in it, just as though it had been brought for him and left specially.

Well, it would have been, wouldn't it? Mel thought. After all, he was a prince.

And Melanie Watson, cook, was marrying him.

For now and for ever.

And that seemed exactly right.

EPILOGUE

'THERE is nothing to be nervous about.' Anrai spoke the words to Melanie as they made their way towards the rear-entry door of the church. 'And thank you for allowing me to be the one to escort you for this occasion.'

Melanie drew a deep breath and glanced at her soon-to-be brother-in-law from beneath the filmy bridal veil. Excitement filled her. This was the moment that she and Rik had worked towards, and that now would be the fulfilment of very new and special dreams for them. 'You know that I love him.'

'Yes. He is lucky. I do not profess to hold similar hope for myself, but I am glad that you have found each other.' Anrai's words were warm, accepting, and then the doors were thrown open and music started and they began the long walk to the front of the church.

Soft gasps filled the air as guests saw the beautiful gown, the train that whispered behind her. A hint of lace. Tiny pearls stitched in layers. A princess neckline for an everyday girl about to become that princess.

Mel's glance shifted to one row of seats in the church. To her uncle, and aunt, and her cousin. Her gaze meshed with Nicolette's for a moment. Nicolette looked attractive in a pale pink chiffon gown. But today the attention was all for Melanie.

For a moment Mel felt a prick of sadness, but she couldn't make her cousin see that love came from within, was a gift so much more important than any material thing.

It was Nicolette who looked away, who couldn't seem to hold her cousin's gaze any longer.

And then there was Rik at the front of the church, waiting faithfully without glancing back until Anrai arrived with Mel on his arm and passed her hand to Rik's arm, placing it there as Mel's father would have done if he'd been here.

Warmth spread through Mel's chest as she looked into her prince's eyes and saw the love and happiness there and somehow she thought her parents might have been watching. She felt their love and warmth, too.

'Dearly beloved…' The priest began the service.

And there before God and his witnesses, Nicole Melanie Watson married Rikardo Eduard Ettonbierre, third prince of Braston.

He *did* have several titles and various bits of land.

His wife-to-be *was* a wonderful cook.

And they were still working on the agreement about who got ownership of any of Rufusina's offspring should the hog ever choose to bless them with a litter.

But Rik and Mel were happy today, and they would remain happy. And Rufusina's offspring were a whole other legend…

* * * * *

THE PRINCE'S OUTBACK BRIDE

MARION LENNOX

Marion Lennox is a country girl, born on an Australian dairy farm. She moved on—mostly because the cows just weren't interested in her stories! Married to a 'very special doctor', Marion writes for the Mills & Boon® Medical Romance™ and Mills & Boon® Cherish™ lines. (She used a different name for each category for a while—readers looking for her past romance titles should search for author Trisha David as well.) She's now had more than seventy-five romance novels accepted for publication.

In her non-writing life Marion cares for kids, cats, dogs, chooks and goldfish. She travels, she fights her rampant garden (she's losing) and her house dust (she's lost). Having spun in circles for the first part of her life, she's now stepped back from her 'other' career, which was teaching statistics at her local university. Finally she's reprioritised her life, figured out what's important and discovered the joys of deep baths, romance and chocolate. Preferably all at the same time!

PROLOGUE

'WE HAVE no choice.' Princess Charlotte de Gautier watched her son in concern from where she rested on her day-bed. Max was pacing the sitting room overlooking the Champs-Elysées. He'd been pacing for hours.

'We must,' Charlotte added bleakly. 'It's our responsibility.'

'It's not our responsibility. The royal family of Alp d'Estella has been rotten to the core for generations. We're well rid of them.'

'They've been corrupt,' Charlotte agreed. 'But now we have the chance to make amends.'

'Amends? Until Crown Prince Bernard's death I thought I had nothing to do with them. Our connection was finished. After all they've done to you…'

'We're not making amends to the royal family. We're making amends to the people of Alp d'Estella.'

'Alp d'Estella's none of our business.'

'That's not true, Max. I'm telling you. It's your birthright.'

'It's not my birthright,' he snapped. 'Regardless of what you say now. It should have been Thiérry's birthright, but their corruption killed Thiérry as it came close to killing you. As far as anyone knows I'm the illegitimate son of the ex-wife of a dead prince. I can walk away. We both can.'

Charlotte flinched. She should have braced herself earlier for this. She'd hoped so much that Crown Prince Bernard would have a son, but now he'd died, leaving…Max.

Since he was fifteen Max had shouldered almost the entire burden of caring for her, and he'd done it brilliantly. But now… She'd tried her hardest to keep her second son out of the royal spotlight—out of the succession—but now it seemed there was no choice but to land at least the regency squarely on Max's shoulders.

Max did a few more turns. Finally he paused and stared down into the bustling Paris street. How could his mother ask this of him—or of herself for that matter? He had no doubt as to what this would mean to their lives. To put Charlotte in the limelight again, as the mother of the Prince Regent…

'I do have a responsibility,' Max said heavily. 'It's to you. To no one else.'

'You know that's not true. You have the fate of a country in your hands.'

'That's not fair.'

'No,' Charlotte whispered. 'Life's not.'

He turned then. 'I'm sorry. Hell, Mama, I didn't mean…'

'I know you didn't. But this has to be faced.'

'But you've given up so much to keep me out of the succession, and to calmly give in now…'

'I'm not giving in. I admit nothing. I'll take the secret of your birth to the grave. I shouldn't have told you, but it seems…so needful that you take on the regency. And it may yet not happen at all. If this child can't become the new Crown Prince…'

'Then what? Will you want to tell the truth then?'

'No,' she said bluntly. 'I will not let you take the Crown.'

'But you'd let an unknown child take it.'

'That's what I mean,' she said, almost eagerly. 'He's an unknown. With no history of hatred weighing him down…maybe it's the only chance for our country.'

'Our country?'

'I still think of it as ours,' she said heavily. 'I might have been a child bride, but I learned early to love it as my own. I love the people. I love the language. I love everything about it. Except its rulers. That's why… That's why I need you to accept the regency. You can help this little prince. I know the politicians. I know the dangers and through you we can protect him. Max, all I know is that we must help him. If you don't take on the regency then the politicians will take over. Things will get worse rather than better, and that's surely saying something.' She hesitated, but it had to be said. 'The way I see it we have two choices. You accept the regency and we do our best to protect this child and protect the people of Alp d'Estella. Or we walk away and let the country self-destruct.'

'And the third alternative?' he asked harshly. 'The truth?'

'No. After all I've been through… You don't want it and I couldn't bear it.'

'No,' he agreed. 'I'm sorry. Of course not.'

'Thank you,' she whispered. 'But what to do now? You tell me this boy's an orphan? That doesn't mean that he's friendless. Who's to say whoever's caring for him will let him take it on?'

'I've made initial enquiries. His registered guardian is a family friend—no relation at all. She's twenty-eight and seems to have been landed with the boy when his parents were killed. This solution provides well for him. She may be delighted to get back to her own life.'

'I guess it's to provide well for him—to let him take on the Crown at such an age. With you beside him…'

'In the background, Mama. From a distance. I can't take anything else on, regardless of what you ask.' Max shoved his hands deep in the pockets of his chinos and, turning, stared once more into the street. Accepting what he'd been thinking for the last hour. 'Maybe he'll be the first decent ruler the country's had for centuries. He can hardly be worse than what's come before. But you're right. We can't let him do it alone. I'll remain caretaker ruler until this child turns twenty-one.'

'You won't live there?'

'No. If there wasn't this family connection stipulation to the regency then I'd never have been approached. But Charles Mevaille's been here this morning—Charles must have been the last non-corrupt politician in the country before the Levouts made it impossible for him to stay. He's shown me what desperately needs to be done to get the country working. The law's convoluted but it seems, no matter who my father was, as half-brother to the last heir I can take on the regency. As Prince Regent I can put those steps into place from here.'

'And the child…'

'We'll employ a great nanny. I'll work hard on that, Mama. He'll be brought up in the castle with everything he could wish for.'

'But…' Charlotte hugged Hannibal—her part poodle, part mongrel, all friend—as if she needed the comfort of Hannibal's soft coat. As indeed she did. 'This is dreadful,' she whispered. 'To put a child in this position…'

'He's an orphan, Mama,' Max said heavily. 'I have no idea what his circumstances are in Australia, but you're right. Once Alp d'Estella's run well then this may well be a glorious opportunity for him.'

'To be wealthy?' Charlotte whispered. 'To be famous? Max, I thought I'd raised you better than that.'

He turned back to face her then, contrite. 'Of course you did. But as far as I can see, this child has no family—only a woman who probably doesn't want to be doing the caring anyway. If she wants to stay with him then we can make it worth her while to come. If she doesn't, then we'll scour the land for the world's best nanny.'

'But you will stay here?'

'I can't stay in Alp d'Estella. Neither of us can.'

'Neither of us have the courage?'

'Mama…'

'You're right,' she said bleakly. 'We don't have the courage, or I surely don't. Let's hope this little one can be what we can't be.'

'We'll care for him,' Max assured her.

'From a distance.'

'It'll be okay.'

'But you will take on the role as Prince Regent?' She sighed. 'I'm so sorry, Max. That's thirteen years of responsibility.'

'As you say, we don't have a choice. And it could have been much, much worse.'

'If I hadn't lied… But I won't go back on it, Max. I won't.'

'No one's asking you to,' he told her, crossing to her day-bed and stooping to kiss her. 'It'll be fine.'

'As long as this woman lets the child come.'

'Why wouldn't she?'

'Maybe she has more sense than I did forty years ago.'

'You were young,' he told her. 'Far too young to marry.'

'So how old is old enough to marry?' she demanded, momentarily distracted.

'Eighty maybe?' He smiled, but the smile didn't reach his eyes. 'Or never. Marriage has never seemed anything but a frightful risk. How the hell would you ever know you weren't being married for your money or your title?' He shrugged. 'Enough. Let's get things moving. We have three short weeks to get things finalised.'

'You'll go to Australia?'

'I can do it from here.'

'You'll go to Australia.' She was suddenly decisive. 'This is a huge thing we're asking.'

'We're relieving this woman of her responsibility.'

'Maybe,' Charlotte whispered. 'But we might just find a woman of integrity. A woman who doesn't think money or a title is an enticement, either for herself or for a child she loves. Now wouldn't that be a problem?'

CHAPTER ONE

A TRUCK had sunk in front of his car.

Wasn't Australia supposed to be a sunburned country? Maxsim de Gautier, Prince Regent of Alp d'Estella, had only been in Australia for six hours, but his overwhelming impression was that the country was fast turning into an inland sea.

But at least he'd found the farm, even though it wasn't what he'd expected. He'd envisaged a wealthy property, but the surrounding land was rough and stony. The farm gate he'd turned into had a faded sign hanging from the top bar reading 'Dreamtime'. In the pouring rain and in such surroundings the name sounded almost defiant.

And now he could drive no further. There was some sort of cattle-grid across the track leading from road to house. The grid had given way and a battered truck was stranded, halfway across.

That meant he'd have to walk the rest of the way. Or swim.

He could sit here until the rain stopped.

It might never stop. The Mercedes he'd hired was luxurious enough but he'd been driving for five hours and flying for twenty-four hours before that, and he didn't intend to sit here any longer.

Was there a back entrance to the farm? There must be if this truck was perpetually blocking the entrance. He rechecked the map supplied by the private investigators he'd employed to locate the child, but the map supplied him with one entrance only.

He'd come too far to let rain come between him and his goal.

He'd have to get wet. Dammit, he shouldn't need to, he thought, his sense of humour reasserting itself. Wasn't royalty supposed to have minions who'd lie prone in puddles to save their prince from wet feet?

Where was a good minion when you needed one?

Nowhere. And he wasn't royalty, at least not royalty from the right side of the blanket.

Meanwhile it was a really dumb place to leave a truck. He pushed open the Mercedes door and was met with a deluge. The hire-car contained an umbrella but it was useless in such a torrent. He was soaked before the door was fully open, and the sleet almost blinded him. Nevertheless he turned purposefully towards the house. It was tricky stumbling over the cattle-grid, but he pushed on, glancing sideways into the truck as he passed.

And stopped. Stunned. It wasn't empty. The truck was a two-by-two seater and the back windows were fogged. The back seat seemed to be filled but he couldn't make out what was there. But he could see the front seat. There were six eyes looking out at him—eyes belonging to a woman and a child and a vast brown dog draped over the woman's knee. He stared in at them and they stared back, seemingly as stunned as he was.

This must be the Phillippa the investigators had talked of. But she was…different? The photograph he'd seen, found in a hunt of university archives, had been taken ten years ago. He'd studied it before he'd come. She was attractive, he'd decided, but not in the classic sense. The photograph had showed a smattering of freckles. Her burnt-red curls had looked as if they refused to be tamed. She was curvy rather than svelte, and her grin was more infectious than it was classically lovely. She and Gianetta had been at a university ball. The dress she'd been wearing had been simple, but it had had class.

But now… He recognised the freckles and the dusky red curls, but the face that looked at him was that of a woman who'd left the girl behind. Her face was gaunt, with huge shadows under her eyes. She looked as if she needed to sleep for a long, long time.

And the boy beside her? He had to be Marc. He was a black-haired, brown-eyed kid, dressed in a too-big red and yellow football guernsey. He looked as if he'd just had a growth spurt, skinny and all arms and legs.

He looked like Thiérry, Max thought, stunned. He looked like a de Gautier.

Max dredged up the memory of the report presented to him by the private investigators he'd hired before he came. 'The boy's guardian is Phillippa Donohue. They live on the farm in South Western Victoria that was owned by the boy's parents before they were killed in a car crash four years ago. We've done a preliminary check on the woman but there's not much to report. She qualified as a nurse but she hasn't practised for four years. Her university records state that her mother died when she was twelve. She went through university on a means-tested scholarship and you don't get one of those in Australia if there's any money. As to her circumstances now… We'd need to visit and find out, but it's a tiny farming community and anyone asking questions is bound to be noticed.'

So he knew little except this woman, as Marc's guardian, stood between him and what the people of Alp d'Estella needed.

He didn't know where to start.

She started. She reached over and wound the window a scant inch down so she could talk to him. Any lower and the rain would blast through and make the occupants of the truck as wet as he was.

'Are you out of your mind?' she demanded. 'You'll drown.'

This was hardly a warm welcome. Maybe she could invite him into the truck, he thought, but only fleetingly for it wasn't an option. Opening the door would mean they'd all be soaked.

'Where are you headed?' she asked. She obviously thought he'd stopped to ask directions. As she would. Visitors wouldn't make it here unless they badly wanted to come, and even then they were likely to miss the place. All he'd seen so far were sodden cows, the cattle-grid in which this truck was stuck, and a battered milkcan that obviously served as a mail box, stuck onto a post beside the gate. Fading lettering painted on the side said 'D & G Kettering'.

D & G Kettering. The G would be Gianetta.

It was four years since Gianetta and her husband had died. He'd have expected the sign to be down by now.

What was this woman doing here? Hell, the agency had given him so little information. 'Frankly we can see no reason why Ms Donohue is there,' they'd said. 'We suspect the farm must be substantial, giving her financial incentive to stay. We assume, however, that eventually the farm will belong to the boy, so there's no security in her position. Given her situation, we suspect any approach by you to take responsibility will be welcome.'

They weren't right about the farm being substantial. This farm looked impoverished.

He needed to tread carefully while he found out what the agency hadn't.

'I was searching for the Kettering farm,' he told her. 'I'm assuming this is it? Are you Phillippa Donohue?'

'I'm Pippa, yes.' Her face clouded. 'Are you from the dairy corporation? You've stopped buying our milk. You've stopped our payments. What else can you stop?'

'I'm not from the dairy corporation.'

She stared. 'Not?'

'I came to see you.'

'No one comes to see me.'

'Well, the child,' he told her. 'I'm Marc's cousin.'

She looked out at him, astonished. He wasn't appearing to advantage, he thought, but then, maybe he didn't need to. He just needed to say what had to be said, organise a plane ticket—or plane tickets if she wanted to come—and leave.

'The children don't have cousins,' she said, breaking into his thoughts with a brusqueness that hinted of distrust. 'Gina and Donald—their parents—were both only children. All the grandparents are dead. There's a couple of remote relations on their father's side, but I know them. There's no one else.'

But he'd been caught by her first two words. The children, he thought, puzzled. Children? There was only Marc. Wasn't there?

'I'm a relation on Marc's mother's side,' he said, buying time.

'Gina was my best friend since childhood. Her mother, Alice, was kind to me and I spent lots of time with them. I've never met any relations.'

She sounded so suspicious that he smiled. 'So you think I'm with the dairy corporation, trying to sneak into your farm with lies about my family background? You think I'd risk drowning to talk to an unknown woman about *cows*?'

She stared some more, and slowly the corners of her mouth curved into an answering smile. Suddenly the resemblance to the old photograph was stronger. He saw for the first time why his initial impression from the photograph had been beauty.

'I guess that would be ridiculous,' she conceded. 'But you're not their cousin.'

Their cousin. There it was again. Plural. He didn't understand, so he ploughed on regardless. 'I am a relation. Gianetta and I shared a grandfather—not that we knew him. I've come from half a world away to see Marc.'

'You're from the royal part of the family?' she said, sounding as if she'd suddenly remembered something she'd been told long since.

He winced. 'Um…maybe. I need to talk to you. I need to see Marc.'

'You're seeing him,' she said unhelpfully.

He looked at Marc. Marc looked back, wary now because he wasn't understanding the conversation. He'd edged slightly in front of Pippa in a gesture of protection.

He was so like the de Gautiers it unnerved Max.

'Hi,' he told Marc. 'I'd like to talk to you.'

'We're not in a situation where visits are possible,' she said, and her arm came around Marc's skinny chest. They were protecting each other. But she sounded intrigued now, and there was even a tinge of regret in her voice. 'Do you need a bed for the night?'

This was hopeful. 'I do.'

'There's a guesthouse in Tanbarook. Come back in the morning after milking. We'll give you a cup of coffee and find the time to talk.'

'Gee, thanks.'

Her smile broadened. 'I'm sorry, but it's the best I can do. We're a bit…stuck at the moment. Now, you need to find Tanbarook. Head back to the end of this road and turn right. That's a sealed road which will get you into town.'

'Thanks,' he said but he didn't go. They were gazing at him, Marc with curiosity and slight defensiveness, Pippa with calm friendliness and the dog with the benign observance of a very old and very placid mutt. Pippa was reaching over to wind up the window. 'Don't,' he told her.

'Don't?'

'Why are you sitting in a truck in the middle of a cattle pit?'

'We're stuck.'

'I can see that. How long do you intend to sit here?'

'Until the rain stops.'

'This rain,' he said cautiously, 'may never stop.' He grimaced as a sudden squall sent a rush of cold water down the back of his neck. More and more he felt like a drowned rat. Heaven knew what Pippa would be thinking of him. Not much, he thought.

That alone wasn't what he was used to. Women normally reacted strongly to Maxsim de Gautier. He was tall and strongly built, with the Mediterranean skin, deep black hair and dark features of his mother's family. The tabloids described him as drop-dead gorgeous and seriously rich.

But Pippa could see little of this and guess less. She obviously didn't have a clue who he was. Maybe she could approximate his age—thirty-five—but it'd be a wild guess. Mostly she'd be seeing water.

'Forty days and forty nights is the rain record,' he told her. 'I think we're heading for that now.'

She smiled. 'So if I were you I'd get back in your car and head for dry land.'

'Why didn't you go back to the house instead of waiting here in the truck?'

Until now Marc had stayed silent, watching him with wariness. But now the little boy decided to join in.

'We're going to get fish and chips,' he informed him. 'But the cattle-grid broke so we're stuck. We have to wait 'til it stops raining. Then we have to find Mr Henges and ask him to pull us out with his tractor. Pippa says we might as well sit here and whinge 'cos it's warmer here than in the house. We've run out of wood.'

'The gentleman doesn't need to know why we're sitting here,' Pippa told him.

'But we've been sitting here for ages and we're hungry.'

'Shh.'

Marc, however, was preparing to be sociable. 'I'm Marc and this is our Pippa and this is our dog, Dolores. And over the back is Sophie and Claire. Sophie has red hair ribbons and Claire's are blue.'

Sophie and Claire. Over the back. He peered through the tiny slot of wound-down window. Yes, there were two more children. He could make out two little faces, with similar colouring to Marc. Cute and pigtailed. Red and blue ribbons. Twins?

Sophie and Claire. He hadn't heard of any Sophie and Claire.

Were they Pippa's? But they looked like Marc. And Pippa had red hair.

No matter. It was only Marc he needed to focus on. 'I'm pleased to meet you all,' he said. This was a crazy place to have a conversation, but he had to start introductions some time. 'I'm Max.'

'Hi,' Pippa said and put her hand on the window winder again. Dismissing him. 'Good luck. We may see you tomorrow.'

'Can't I help you?'

'We're fine.'

'I could tow you.'

'Do you have a tow-bar on your car?'

'Um…no.' It was a hire-car—a luxury saloon. Of course he didn't. 'Can I find Mr Henges and his tractor for you?'

'Bert won't come 'til the rain stops.'

'You're planning on sitting in the truck until then?'

'Or until it's time for milking.'

The thought of milking cows in this weather didn't bear considering. 'You don't think maybe you could run back to the house, peel off your wet things, have a hot shower and…oh, I don't know, play Happy Families until milking?'

'It's warmer here,' Marc said.

'But we want fish and chips,' one of the little girls piped up from the back seat.

'There's bread,' Marc said, in severe, big-brother tones. 'We'll make toast before milking.'

'We want fish and chips,' the other little girl whimpered. 'We're hungry.'

'Shh.' Pippa turned back to Max. 'Can you move away so I can wind up the window? We're getting wet.'

'Sure.' But Max didn't move. He thought of all he'd come to say to this woman and he winced. Back home it had seemed simple—to say what needed to be said and walk away. But now, suddenly, it seemed harder. 'Isn't there anything I can do for you first?'

What was he saying? The easiest thing to do right now would be to walk away from the whole mess, he thought. Someone else could tell these people what they had to know. But then, he'd have to remember that he'd walked away for a long time.

'We don't need anything,' Pippa told him, oblivious to his train of thought, and he dragged his attention back to the matter at hand. Truck stuck. Fish and chips.

'I'm thinking I should talk to Marc about this,' he said, focusing on food. 'This is, after all, men's business. Hunting and gathering. You were heading to the shops when your truck got stuck. Looking for fish and chips.'

'Yes,' said Marc, pleased at his acuity, and Sophie and Claire beamed agreement, anticipating assistance. 'We've run out of food,' Marc told him. 'All we have left is toast. We don't even have any jam.'

Right. He could do this. Jam and fish and chips. But not drowned like this.

'I have a car that's not stuck in a cattle-grid,' he told them. 'But I'm soaking wet. You have a house where I can dry off, and I've come a long way to visit you. Let's combine. You let me use your house to change and I'll go into town and buy fish and chips.'

'We can't impose on you,' Pippa said. But she looked desperate, and he wondered why.

First things first. He had to persuade her to let him help. 'I'm not an axe murderer,' he told her. 'I promise. I really am a relation.'

'But…'

'I'm Maxsim de Gautier. Max.' He watched to see if there was recognition of the name, but she was too preoccupied to think of anything but immediate need—and maybe she'd never heard the name anyway. 'I'd really like to help.'

Desperation faded—just a little. 'I shouldn't let you.'

'Yes, you should. You don't have to like me, but I'm definitely family, so you need to sigh and open the door, the way most families ask rum-soaked Uncle Bertie or similar to Christmas lunch.'

She smiled in return at that, a wobbly sort of smile but it was a welcome change from the desperate. 'Uncle Bertie or similar?'

'I'm not even a soak,' he said encouragingly and her smile wobbled a bit more.

'You have a great accent,' she said inconsequentially. 'It sounds…familiar. Is it Italian or French?'

'Mostly French.'

'You're very wet.'

'The puddle around my ankles is starting to creep to my knees. If you leave this decision much longer I'll need a snorkel.'

She stared out at him and chewed her lip. Then she seemed to make a decision. 'Fine.'

'Fine what?'

'Fine I'll trust you,' she managed. 'The kids and I will trust you, but I'm not sure about Dolores.' She hugged the dog tighter. 'She bites relations who turn out to be axe murderers.'

'She's welcome to try. How will we organise this?'

'My truck's blocking your way to the house.'

'So it is,' he said cordially. 'Why didn't I notice that?'

Her decision meant that she'd relaxed a little. The lines of strain around her eyes had eased. Now she even choked back a bubble of laughter. 'We need to run to the house. We'll all be soaked the minute we get out of the truck.'

'I assume you have dry clothes back at the house?'

'Yes but…'

'I'm bored of sitting in the truck,' Marc said.

'Me too,' said Sophie.

'Me too,' said Claire.

'Right,' Pippa said, coming to a decision. 'On the count of three I want everybody out of the truck and we'll run back to the house as fast as we can. Mr de Gautier, you're welcome to follow.'

'I'll do backstroke,' he told her. 'What's your stroke?'

'Dog-paddle.' She pushed open the driver's side door and dived into the torrent. 'Okay, kids,' she said, hauling open the back door and starting to lift them out.

'Let me,' he told her.

'I'll take the kids. You take Dolores.'

'Dolores?'

'She hates getting her feet wet,' Pippa explained. 'She's had pneumonia twice so she has an excuse. I'll carry her if I must but I have a sore back and as you're here I don't see why you shouldn't be useful. After all, you are family.'

'Um…okay,' he managed, but that was all he could say before a great brown dog of indiscriminate parentage was pushed out of the cab and into his arms.

'Don't drop her,' Pippa ordered. 'And run.'

'Yes, ma'am.'

The house was two hundred yards from the gate, and, even though they ran fast, by the time they reached it they were all sodden. Max's first impression was that it was a rambling weatherboard house, a bit down at heel, but it was unfair to judge when he saw everything through sleeting rain. And over one dog who smelled like…wet dog.

There was a veranda. Marc led the way. Pippa ran up the steps behind him, holding a twin by each hand. Max and Dolores brought up the rear. He'd paused to grab his holdall from his car, so he was balancing dog and holdall. Where were those servile minions? he thought again. Maybe accepting the crown could have its uses.

He wasn't going there, minions or not. He reached the top step, set Dolores down, tossed his holdall into the comparative dry at the back of the veranda, mourned his minions for another fleeting moment, and then turned his attention to the little family before him.

At eight, Marc was just doing the transformation from cute into kid. Maybe he was tall for his age, Max thought, but what did he know about kids? He had the same jet black curls all the members of the Alp d'Estella royal family had, and big brown eyes and a snub nose with a smattering of freckles.

Sophie and Claire were different but similar. They were still not much more than tots, with glossy black curls tied into pigtails and adorned with bright ribbons that now hung limply down their back. They were cute and well rounded and they had a whole lot more freckles than their brother did.

They had to be Marc's sisters, Max thought, cursing his PI firm for their lack of information. But then, what had his brief been? Find Marc and report on where he was living and who was taking care of him. Nothing about sisters.

But surely the powers that be back in Alp d'Estella must know of these two? They'd certainly known of Marc.

Marc was drying himself, towelling his face with vigour. The twins were being towelled by Pippa. All three children were regarding him cautiously from under their towels.

They were bright, inquisitive kids, he thought. Pippa said something to them and they giggled.

Nice kids.

He shouldn't stare.

Pippa was stripping off the girls' outer clothes. She tossed him a towel from a pile by the door. He started to dry his face but was brought up short.

'That's for Dolores.'

'Sorry?' He looked blank and she sighed.

'Dolores. Pneumonia. Prevention of same. Please can you rub?'

'Um…sure.' He knelt as she was kneeling but instead of undressing kids he was towelling dog. Dolores approved. She rubbed herself ecstatically against the towel, and when he turned her to do the front half she showed her appreciation by giving him a huge lick, from his chin to his forehead. She was big and all bone—a cross between a Labrador and something even bigger. A bloodhound? In dog years she looked about a hundred.

'She's kissing you,' four-year-old Sophie said, and giggled. 'That means she likes you.'

'I've had better kisses in my day,' he said darkly.

'Let's not go there, Cousin Max,' Pippa muttered. 'Otherwise I'll think axe again.'

'No kissing,' Max agreed with alacrity and towelled Dolores harder. 'You hear that, Dolores? Keep yourself respectable or the lady with the axe knows what to do.'

Pippa chuckled. It was a great chuckle, he thought. He towelled Dolores for a while longer but he was watching Pippa. She was wearing ancient jeans and a windcheater with a rip up one arm. Her close-cropped, coppery curls were plastered wetly to her head, and droplets of rainwater were running down her forehead. She wore no make-up. She'd been wearing huge black wellingtons and she'd kicked them off at the top of the stairs. Underneath she was wearing what looked like football socks. The toe was missing from one yellow and black sock, and her toe poked pinkly through.

Very sexy, he thought, smiling inwardly, but then he glanced at her again and thought actually he was right. She was sexy but she was a very different sort of sexy from the women he normally associated with.

Where was he going with this? Nowhere, he told himself, startled. He was here to organise the succession; nothing more.

The kids were undressed to their knickers now. 'The quickest way to warm is to shower and we'll do it in relays,' Pippa was saying. She motioned to a door at the end of the veranda. 'That's the bathroom. The kids can shower first. Then me. I'm sorry, Mr de Gautier, but in this instance it needs to be visitors last. Stay here until I call. We'll be as quick as we can.'

'What about Dolores?'

'She can go through to the kitchen if she wants,' Pippa said, holding the door open for the dog. 'Though if you really want I guess she could shower with you.' She smiled again, a lovely, laughing smile that made these bleak surroundings seem suddenly brighter. 'Bathing Dolores usually takes a small army, but thanks for offering. Good luck.'

He didn't shower with the dog. Dolores disappeared as soon as the kids did, leaving Max to wait alone on the veranda. Maybe Dolores had a warm kennel somewhere, Max thought enviously as the wind blasted its way through his wet clothes. Wasn't Australia supposed to be warm?

Luckily the kids and Pippa were faster than he expected. Pippa reappeared within five minutes, dressed in a pink bathrobe with her hair tied up in a tattered green towel. She tossed him a towel that wasn't quite as frayed as the one he'd used for Dolores.

'I assume you have dry clothes in your bag,' she said and he nodded.

'Lucky you,' she said. 'Everything here is wet. It's been raining for days. Shower's through there. Enjoy.'

Everything here was wet? Didn't she have a dryer? He thought about that while standing under the vast rose shower hanging over the claw-foot bath in the ancient bathroom. Everything he'd seen so far spoke of poverty. Surely Marc—and the girls?—were well provided for?

Alice, Gianetta's mother, had cut off all ties to her family back in Europe. 'She married well,' he'd been told. 'Into the Australian squattocracy.' But then, that had been his father speaking, and his father treated the truth with disdain.

Up until now Max hadn't been interested to find the truth for himself, but if these children's maternal grandmother had married into money there was nothing to show for it now.

There were questions everywhere. He showered long enough to warm up; he dried; he foraged in his holdall and dressed in chinos and an oversized sweater that he'd almost not packed because Australia was supposed to be warm. Then he set out to find them.

The bathroom led to what looked like a utility room. A door on the far side of the utility room led somewhere else, and he could hear children's voices close by. He pushed it with caution and found himself in the farmhouse kitchen. Here they were, the children in dressing gowns and slippers and Pippa in jeans and another windcheater. The cuffs of her windcheater looked damp, he thought. What had she said? Everything was wet? Where the hell was a dryer? Or a fire of some sort?

The kitchen was freezing.

Pippa and the kids were seated at the table, with steaming mugs before them. Dolores was under the table, lying on a towel.

'Get yourself warm on the inside as well as the outside before we send you off as hunter gatherer,' Pippa said, and she smiled. It was a great smile, he thought, astonishing himself with the intensity of his reaction. In her ancient windcheater and jeans she looked barely older than the kids. The oversized windcheater made her look flat-chested and insignificant. But still it was a killer of a smile. Something inside him reacted when she smiled.

That was a crazy thing to think right now. He needed to figure things out. Too many kids for a start. And this place… Despite the shower and his thick sweater he felt himself starting to shiver. The temperature was as low as outside. Which was pretty low.

'Hot chocolate?' Pippa offered. She was using a small electric cooker top. Beside the cooker top was a much larger stove. An Aga.

They had an Aga and didn't have it lit?

'We don't have wood,' she said, seeing what he was looking at and guessing what he was thinking.

'I know. Marc mentioned it earlier. Why not?'

'Pippa hurt her back,' Marc volunteered. 'So she can't chop wood. There's a dead tree in the far paddock and Pippa cuts it up when we run out but she can't cut any more until her back gets better.'

'What happened to your back?'

'She fell off the roof,' Marc said, sounding severe for his eight years. 'Trying to nail roofing iron back on. I told her she'd fall off and she did.'

'I didn't have much choice,' Pippa said with a trace of defiance. She was talking to Marc as she'd talk to an adult. 'If I hadn't we'd be in water up to our necks right now.'

'It was scary,' Sophie—was Sophie the red ribbons?—informed Max. 'It was really, really windy. Marc was yelling at her to come down.'

'And then some roof came off and she fell,' Claire added, relishing an exciting story. 'Sophie screamed but I didn't and Pippa grabbed the edge of the roof and hung on. And she cut her hand and it bled and we had to put a bandage onto it.'

'I told her not to do it,' Marc muttered darkly.

What was going on here? Guardian and kids, or four kids?

'I won't do it again,' Pippa told Marc, reaching out to ruffle his dark hair. 'It's fixed.' He looked over to Max. 'How are you related to the kids?'

'I believe Marc's grandmother, Alice, was my aunt.'

'I remember Grandma Alice.' Marc nodded. 'She died just before Mama and Daddy were killed and we were really sad. She said we had royal cousins, but she said they were a bad lot.' He thought about it and drank some of his chocolate. 'I don't know what a bad lot is.'

'I hope I'm not a bad lot.'

'But you're royal. Like a king or something.'

'I'm on the same side of the family as you.'

'Not on the bad lot side?'

'No.'

The girls—and Pippa—were listening to this interchange with various levels of interest. Now Sophie felt the need to interrupt.

'I'm really very hungry,' she said soulfully—martyr about to die a stoic death—and Pippa handed Max his hot chocolate, glanced at Claire who'd gone quiet and made a decision.

'Um…can the family-tree thing wait? If you really are family… Actually we are in a bit of trouble,' she confessed. 'We don't have anything to eat.'

'Nothing?'

'Toast. But no butter. And no jam.'

'You believe in putting off shopping to the last minute.'

'We tried to put it off 'til the rain stopped. But it didn't.'

'I see.' Though he didn't see.

'Could you really go into town and pick up a few supplies?'

'Of course. You could come with me if you like.'

'All of us?' Pippa asked.

He did a quick head count. Maybe…

'Including Dolores.'

He looked down at Dolores—a great brown dog, gently steaming and wafting wet dog smell through the kitchen.

'Maybe I'm fine by myself,' Max said.

She chuckled, a nice chuckle that might have had the capacity to warm the kitchen if it wasn't so appallingly cold. Then she eyed him appraisingly. 'You'll get wet again, walking back to your car. That's not exactly wet-weather gear.'

'Lend him Daddy's milking gear,' Marc piped up. 'He's bigger than Daddy but he might fit.'

'He can wear Daddy's gumboots,' Sophie offered.

'Gumboots?'

'That's Australian for wellingtons,' Pippa said.

'He needs an umbrella,' Claire added. Like all of them she'd been staring at Max with caution, but she'd obviously reached a decision. 'He can use my doggy umbrella.' She fetched it from near the back door, opened it and twirled it for inspection. Pale pink, it had a picture of an appealing puppy on every panel. 'You'll look after it,' she said, as one conferring a huge level of trust.

Great, Max thought. Prince Regents wearing wellingtons and carrying umbrellas with dogs? Thankfully the paparazzi were half a world from here.

There was so much here that he hadn't expected. Actually nothing was what he'd expected. Except Marc. Marc looked just like Max's brother. Which was great. It made things almost perfect.

Except… It made his gut do this lurching kind of thing. A kid who looked like Thiérry…

He glanced at Marc again and Pippa intercepted the look. 'What?'

'Nothing.'

'Why were you looking at Marc?'

'I was wondering why he was dark when you're a redhead.' He knew the relationship but it didn't hurt to check.

'Pippa's not related to us,' Marc told him. 'She's our friend.'

'Pippa's our aunty,' Sophie volunteered, but Marc shook his head.

'No, she's not. She and Mummy were friends and Pippa promised she'll look after us, just like a real aunty. But she's not our real aunty.'

'I wish she was,' Claire whispered.

'I'm just as good as an aunty,' Pippa said stoutly. 'Only bossier. More like a mother hen, really.' She was staring across the table at him as she spoke, her voice…challenging? Max met her look head-on. Had she guessed why he was here?

He had to tell her, but let it come slowly, he thought. It'd be easy to get a blank no, with no room to manoeuvre. Surely the poverty he saw in this place meant he'd at least get a hearing.

Meanwhile… 'Where's this wet-weather gear?'

'I'll show you.' Pippa produced a battered purse and handed over two notes and a couple of coins. 'Our budget for the rest of the week is thirty-two dollars, fifty cents,' she told him. 'Can you buy fish and chips and bread, jam, some dried pasta and a slab of cheap cheese? Spend the change on dog food. The cheapest there is.'

He stared down at the notes and coins in disbelief. 'You're kidding,' he said finally, and she flushed.

'We're momentarily broke,' she admitted. 'Our vats were found to be contaminated. It's only low level—we're still drinking our milk—but it's bad enough to stop sales. We need a week's clear testing before the dairy corporation will buy our milk again.'

'But we can't afford new vats,' Marc interjected. 'Pippa says we're up the creek without a paddle.' He sounded almost cheerful but Max saw Pippa wince and realised there was real distress behind those words.

'That's not Mr de Gautier's problem,' Pippa said, gently reproving. 'But we do have to pull in our belts. Mr de Gautier, I'd appreciate if you could do our buying for us, but that's all we need. We'll be fine.'

'Will you be fine without fruit?' he asked, staring at the list in disapproval. 'What about scurvy?'

'No one gets scurvy if they go without for only a week.'

'No, but…' He searched her face for a long moment, seeing quiet dignity masking a background of desperation. What on earth was she doing here? She seemed to be stuck on an almost derelict farm with three kids who weren't hers and a dog who'd seen better days. The investigators said there was no blood tie. Why hadn't she walked away?

Until now this had seemed easy. He'd expected to be back on a plane by the end of the week. With Marc. Maybe with Pippa as well. It could still happen, but that jutting chin prompted doubts. The little girls prompted more. Plus the way the dog was draped so she was touching everyone's feet.

Enough. He squared his shoulders and accepted an umbrella. Doubts had to wait. He had to go shopping.

CHAPTER TWO

TANBAROOK was tiny. The place consisted of five shops, a pub, two churches and a school. Most of them looked deserted, but there were three cars lined up outside a small supermarket. A Tanbarook crowd, Max thought wryly and went in to join it. He sloshed through the door and four women stared at him as if he'd landed from Mars.

The ladies were at the checkout counter, one behind the register, the others on the customer side. He gave them what he hoped was a pleasant smile. 'Good afternoon.'

'Good afternoon,' four voices chorused.

He grabbed a trolley and turned to the shelves.

'Can I help?' the woman behind the register called.

'I'm fine, thank you. I have a list.'

'Your wife's given you a list?' Heaven knew how long it had been raining, but this group looked as if they'd been propping up the checkout counter for years.

'No,' he said discouragingly, but it didn't work.

'Then who gave you the list?'

'Pippa,' he said, grudgingly.

'Phillippa Donohue?' Four sets of eyes nearly started from four heads. 'The woman on Kettering's farm,' one of them exclaimed. 'I didn't think she had a boyf—'

'He'll be a friend from when she was nursing,' another interrupted, digging her friend in the ribs. 'Maybe he's a doctor.'

Four sets of eyebrows twitched upward and he could almost see the assembling of symptoms. 'Are you a doctor?'

'No.'

Four sets of brows drooped in disappointment, and they turned their backs on him. 'Maybe he's a friend from university,' one said. 'That's where Gina met Donald. He was doing a course on farm bookkeeping. One weekend was all it took for them to fall in love. Wham.'

'Did Phillippa go to university?'

'Of course she did. Nurses have to go to university these days. She went and so did Gina. Not that Gina ever worked as a nurse. She married Donald instead. I remember just after they were married, Phillippa came to visit. Gina was really excited. She said Phillippa was clever. She could have been a doctor, Gina said, but of course there wasn't any money. But she had a really good job. In operating theatres, Gina said. Mind, you wouldn't think she was clever now, holding on to that farm against all odds. Stupid girl.'

The lady giving the information was wearing hair curlers and some sort of shapeless crimplene frock. She had her arms crossed across her ample bosom in the classic stance of 'I know more than you do'. She practically smirked.

'She should go back to nursing,' she told her friends. 'Why she insists on keeping that farm… It's just an impediment, that's what it is.'

'But she likes the farm,' another objected. 'She told me so. That's why she won't sell.'

'Honestly, would anyone like that dump? And she's standing in the way of progress.'

'She says it feels like home.'

'It might be the children's home,' Crimplene conceded. 'But if Phillippa wasn't there they'd be put up for adoption. Which would probably be for the best, and the sooner she admits it, the better. They'll be starving soon.'

'But if she's got a boyfriend…' They turned as one to inspect him again. 'If she's got a boyfriend then maybe she'll have support.' It didn't seem to be an idea they relished.

'You're French,' one of them said, obviously replaying his voice and discovering the accent.

'No.' He might be interested in what they had to say about Pippa, but the last thing he wanted was an inquisition about himself. He redirected his attention to his list. Bread, pasta, dog food. Ha. And the thirty-two dollars and fifty cents had to be a joke. Good coffee was eight dollars a pack. Three packs, he decided, and tossed in another for good measure.

What next? Tea? Surely. And the kids really should have decent hot chocolate—not the watered-down stuff they were drinking now. If Marc was to end up where he hoped, it was time he learned to appreciate quality. He found tubs of chocolate curls with pictures of decadent mugs of creaming hot chocolate on the front. Two tubs landed in his trolley.

He'd turned his back on his audience. They didn't like it.

'Phillippa can't afford that,' the lady behind the checkout snapped. 'Her vats are contaminated.'

'My vats aren't,' he retorted, inspecting the range of chocolate cookies and choosing four packets before moving on to confectionery. What was hot chocolate without marshmallows? Would six packets be enough?

Then there were more decisions. Did they like milk chocolate or dark? Three blocks of each, he decided, but the blocks looked a bit small. Okay, six of each.

On then to essentials. Dry pasta. Surely she wasn't serious about wanting much of this. It looked so…dry. The meat section looked much more appetising. The steaks looked great.

But then, this wasn't just about him, he reminded himself. The steaks looked wonderful, but maybe kids liked sausages. He replaced a couple of steaks, collected sausages, and then thought of Dolores and the great big eyes. He put the steaks back in his trolley.

Then he discovered the wine section. Australian wine. Excellent. And fruit? He wasn't as sure as Pippa about the scurvy thing. That meant fresh produce. Bananas. Oranges. Strawberries?

Of course strawberries. Would they have their own cream or should he buy some?

But there was more to shopping than food.

'I need wood,' he said, and discovered the ladies were staring at his trolley as if they'd never seen such things. 'Where can I find fuel for a woodstove?'

'You can't cut wood in weather like this.'

'That's the problem,' he said patiently. 'And Pippa has a bad back.'

'We know that,' one of the ladies said, starting to sound annoyed. 'She hurt it last week. The doctor told her to be careful. I expect all her fires are out by now.' She sounded smug.

'They are,' Max said shortly. 'No locals thought to help her?'

'She's not a local herself,' another of the ladies said, doubtfully now, maybe considering that they might be considered remiss. 'She only came here when the children's parents died. And she won't sell the farm. We all tell her she should sell the farm. It's a huge problem for the district.'

'Why?'

'We want to put a new road in. There's ten outlying farms—huge concerns—that have three miles or more to get into town. If Phillippa agreed to sell her place we could build a bridge over the creek. It'd be a lot more convenient for everyone.'

'I see,' he said slowly. 'Would that be why her vats have been found to be contaminated?'

'Of course not,' Crimplene snapped, but she flushed. 'But it's nothing more than we expected. She has some stupid idea of keeping the farm for the children. As if she can ever keep it as a going concern until they're adult. It's ridiculous.'

'So she doesn't qualify for help when she's hurt?' He caught himself then. What was the use of being angry—and what business was it of his? Pippa was nothing to do with him. He just needed to do what he had to do and move on.

It was just she looked so…slight. David against Goliath. Or Pippa against Crimplene. He'd prefer to take on Goliath any day, he thought. Crimplene made him feel ill.

'Where can I buy some wood to tide us over?' he said, trying very hard to keep anger out of his voice.

'We have barbecue packs,' the checkout lady said. She also seemed unsure, casting a nervous glance at Crimplene as if she was bucking an agreed plan. 'We sell them to tourists at a big… I mean for premium prices. There's ten logs per bundle at five dollars a bundle.'

Max thought back to the enormous woodstove and he thought of Pippa's fingers, tinged with blue from the cold. He looked at the four women in front of him. They stared straight back and he felt the anger again. Sure, he was a stranger, and it was none of his business, but he remembered the shadows under Pippa's eyes and he couldn't stop being angry.

Anger achieved nothing, he told himself. He was here on a mission. He had to focus.

'How many bundles do you have in stock?' he asked.

'Forty maybe.'

'If I buy them all will you deliver?'

There was a general gasp. 'That's wicked waste,' Crimplene started but the checkout lady was seeing dollars.

'Sure we will,' she said. 'When do you want them?'

'You can't,' Crimplene gasped but the checkout lady was looking at a heady profit.

'Now,' Max told her.

'I'll get hubby from the back,' she said, breathless. 'For that amount Duncan can get his backside off the couch and I don't care if it is against what you want, Doreen. Your precious road can wait. It's uncivilised, what you're doing to that family, and I don't mind who I say it to.' Then as Crimplene's bosom started to swell in indignation she smiled at Max and gazed lovingly at the very expensive produce in his trolley. 'Do you want me to ring these through?'

'Not yet,' Max said, moving further down the aisle, away from the women he wanted suddenly—stupidly—to lash out at. Pippa was to be neglected no longer, he thought. If he bought the entire store out and the population of Tanbarook went hungry because of it, then so much the better. Vengeance by Commerce. He almost managed a smile. 'I've hardly started.'

'Go tell Duncan to start loading wood,' he told the ladies. 'Now do you know where I can buy fish and chips? Oh, and a clothes dryer?'

'He'll probably abscond with my thirty-two dollars and fifty cents.'

Back at the farmhouse, the kids and Dolores were out on the veranda waiting for Max's return and Pippa was starting to think she'd been a dope. What if he never came back? She hadn't even taken the registration number of his car.

Who was he?

Max de Gautier. The royal side of the family.

Pippa smiled at that, remembering Gianetta's pleasure in her royal background. Alice, Gina's mother, had tried to play it down, but Gianetta had been proud of it.

'My great-uncle is the Crown Prince of Alp d'Estella,' she'd tell anyone who'd listen. After the old prince died, she'd had to change her story to: 'I'm related to the Crown Prince of Alp d'Estella.' It didn't sound as impressive, but she'd still enjoyed saying it.

But it meant nothing. When Alice died there'd been no call from royalty claiming kinship. Gina had married her Australian dairy farmer, and, storytelling aside, she'd considered herself a true Australian. Royalty might have sounded fun but it hadn't been real. Her beloved Donald had been real.

Marc came in then, searching for reassurance that Max would indeed return.

'I don't know why he's so long,' Pippa told him, and then hesitated. 'Marc, you remember your mama showed us a family tree of the royal family she said you were related to?'

'Mmm,' Marc said. 'Grandma drew it for us. I couldn't read it then but I can now. It's in my treasure box.'

'Can we look at it?'

So they did. The tree that Alice had drawn was simple, first names only, wives or husbands, drawn in neat handwriting with a little childish script added later.

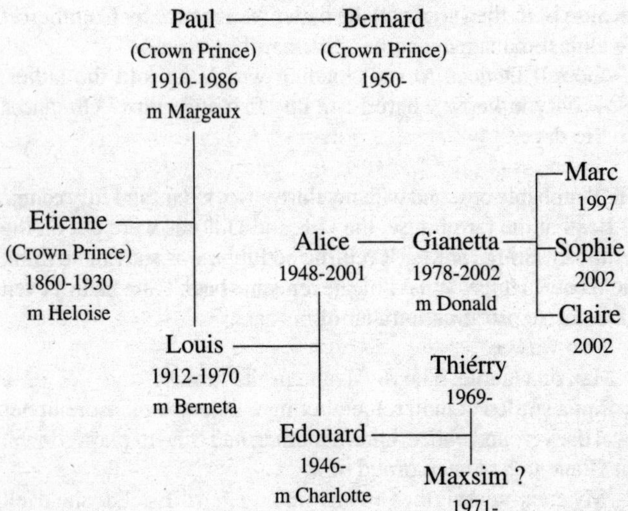

Marc spread it out on the kitchen table and both of them studied it. Marc was an intelligent little boy, made old beyond his years by the death of his parents. Sometimes Pippa thought she shouldn't talk to him as an equal, but then who else could she talk to?

'I wrote the twins and two thousand and two and stuff when I learned to write,' Marc said and Pippa hugged him and kept reading.

'Etienne was your great-great-grandfather,' she told him, following the line back. 'Look, there's Max. His grandpa and your great-grandfather were the same. Louis. I guess Louis must have been a prince.'

'Why aren't I a prince?'

'Because your grandma was a girl?' she said doubtfully. 'I think princes' kids are princes but princesses' kids aren't.' She hesitated and then admitted: 'Actually, Marc, I'm not sure.'

Marc followed the lines himself, frowning in concentration. 'Why is there a question mark beside Max's name?'

'I don't know.'

'Is Max a prince?'

'He didn't say he was a prince.'

'It'd be cool if he was.'

'I hope he's not. I don't have a tiara to wear,' Pippa said and Marc giggled.

Which Pippa liked. He was too serious, she thought, hugging him close. He'd had too many dramas for one small boy. She should treat him more as a child. It was just…she was so lonely.

And thinking about it didn't help.

'Will he come back?' Marc said anxiously and she gave herself a mental shake.

'Of course he will. I'll sweep the floor while we wait.'

'You're always working.'

'Working's fun.'

Or not. But working stopped her thinking, and thinking was the harsher alternative.

Max finally returned, followed by Duncan with a trailer of firewood, followed by Bert Henges with his tractor. It had only taken a promise of cash to get Bert out in the rain. Three men and a tractor made short work of hauling the truck from the pit. They heaved planks over the broken grid and Bert departed—bearing cash—while Duncan and Max drove cautiously across to the house. The kids had been watching from the veranda but as soon as they drove closer they disappeared. Duncan began tossing wood up to Max, who started stacking it next to the back door.

They'd unpacked half a dozen bundles when Pippa emerged. She was holding her broom like a rifle, and the three children were close behind.

She looks cute, Max thought inconsequentially. Defensive—have broom will shoot!—but cute.

'What's going on?' she demanded; then as she saw what they were doing she gasped. 'Where did that come from?'

'My shed,' Duncan said, unaccustomed profits making him cheerful. 'Seems you've got a sugar-daddy, Pippa, love.'

'I do not have a sugar-daddy,' she said, revolted. 'I can't afford this.'

'It's paid for. You've struck a good'un here.' He motioned to Max with a dirty thumb and tossed another bundle.

'Will you cut it out?' She looked poleaxed. 'How did you get the vehicles here?'

'Bert hauled your truck out of the pit.' The wood merchant was obviously relishing enough gossip to keep a dreary country week enlivened until the rain stopped. 'Courtesy of your young man.'

'You didn't get Bert out into the rain?' she demanded of Max, appalled. She stepped into his line of tossing to stop the flow of wood. 'He'll charge a fortune and I can't pay. Of all the stupid… It was just a matter of waiting.'

'You don't need to pay.' Max handed her his bundle of wood. 'I already have. Can you start the fire with this? There are fire-lighters and matches in the grocery sacks. Most of the groceries are in the trunk. I've backed right up so we can unpack without getting wet.'

'Most of the groceries…' She stared at him, speechless, and he placed his hands on her shoulders and put her aside so Duncan could toss him another bundle.

The feel of him…the strength of him… She felt as if she'd been lifted up and transported into another place.

She gasped and tugged away. 'I can't take this,' she managed, staring down into the stuffed-full trunk of his car. There were chocolate cookies spilling out from the sacks. Real coffee!

'Why not? The farmhouse is freezing and it's no part of my plan to have you guys freeze to death.'

'Your plan?'

'My plan,' he said. 'Can you light the fire and we'll talk this through when we're warm?'

She stared blindly at the wood, confusion turning to anger.

'You can't just buy us. I don't understand what you want but you can't have it. We don't want your money.'

'Pippa, I'm family and therefore I have the right to make sure you—or at least the children—are warm and well fed,' he said, gently but firmly. He fielded and stacked another bundle. 'Please. Get the fire lit and then we can talk. Oh, and the fish and chips will be here in fifteen minutes. Home delivery.'

'Home delivery?' she gasped. 'When did they ever…'

'They'd run out of potatoes at the pub,' he said apologetically. 'But Mrs Ryan says Ern can go out and dig some and she'll have fish and chips here by three.'

'I bet he paid her as much as he paid me,' Duncan said cheerfully and he winked at her. 'You're on a winner here, love.'

She stared, open-mouthed, at them both. She couldn't think of a thing to say.

'Light the fire,' Max said—and Pippa stared at him wordlessly for a full minute.

Then she went to light the fire.

It seemed she had no alternative.

She might not like it—well, okay, she liked it but she might not trust it—but he was right; she had no choice but to accept. He was related to the children, which was more than she was.

So she unpacked and as the kids whooped their joy she felt dizzy.

'Sausages,' they shouted, holding each item up for inspection. 'Eggs. We haven't had this many eggs since the fox ate our last chook. Marmalade. Yuck, we don't like marmalade. But there's honey. Honey, honey, honey! And chocolate. More chocolate. Lemonade!'

Distrust it or not, it was the answer to her prayers, and when Max appeared at the kitchen door, dripping wet again, she even managed to smile.

'Wow,' she said. 'I can't believe you've done this.'

'My pleasure. Do you have a laundry? Can Duncan and I have access?'

'To our laundry?' He was dripping wetly onto the linoleum. 'Do you both want to strip off?'

'I don't have any more clothes,' he told her. 'Donald's waterproofs weren't quite as waterproof as I might have liked. But we now have a clothes dryer.'

'A clothes dryer.' What was he talking about?

'I know. I'm brilliant,' he told her, looking smug. 'A little applause wouldn't go astray.'

'Where did you get a dryer?'

'Mrs Aston and Mr Aston paid for their daughter Emma to install central heating just last week,' he said, and his voice changed.

'Those nappies were too much, I said to Ern, I said. They'll be the death of her, with those twins, and young Jason's only just out of nappies and none too reliable. We didn't have any money when we had kiddies but we have now, what with superannuation and all, so the least we can do is pay for central heating. So we did, and now…what does my Em want with a great hulking tumble-dryer when there's a whole new airing cupboard that can take three times as many nappies? You're very welcome to it.'

Max's accent might be French, but he had Mrs Aston's voice down to a T. Pippa stared—and then she giggled.

'You bought us Emma's tumble-dryer.'

'Applause?'

She smiled and even raised her hands to clap—but then her smile died and her hands dropped. 'Max, this is crazy. We really can't accept.'

'My clothes go in first,' he said. 'That's the price I'm demanding. Oh, and I need something to keep me decent while they dry. Can you find me something?'

She gave up. 'I…sure.'

'Two minutes,' he said. 'Me and Dunc are hauling this thing into your laundry and then I want another hot shower. I'll throw my clothes out; you put them in your brand new tumble-dryer and Bob's your uncle.'

'Bob?'

He frowned, intent. 'Bob's your uncle? I don't have that right?'

'It's not a French idiom.'

'I'm not French.'

'You're from Alp d'Estella?'

'Let's leave discussion of nationalities until I'm dry. I only brought one change of clothes and now everything's wet. Can you find me something dry to wear in two minutes?'

It was more than two minutes. Duncan helped Max cart in the dryer, but as Max disappeared towards the shower Duncan headed for the kitchen and a gossip.

'Who is he?' he wanted to know.

'He's a relation of Gina's from overseas,' she told Duncan. 'Gina never heard a word from that side of the family and they surely didn't help when Gina and Donald were killed. If he's being generous now then maybe it's a guilty conscience.'

'You didn't tell Mr Stubbins that Max might be a prince,' Marc whispered as Duncan finally departed with as much information as she was prepared to give.

'Rain or no rain, if I said that we'd have every busybody in the district wanting to visit.' Pippa lifted a packet of crumpets from the table and carried it reverently to the toaster. 'And I'm not feeling like sharing. There's crumpets and there's butter and honey and I'm thinking I'm having first crumpet.'

'Max says there's fish and chips coming.'

'I have crumpets right here,' she said reverently. 'Food now—or food later? There's no choice.'

'Don't you want fish and chips?'

'You think I can't fit both in? Watch.'

'Don't you have to find Max some clothes?' Marc said, starting to sound worried.

'Yes,' Pippa said, popping four crumpets into their oversized toaster. 'But crumpets first.' She handed plates to Sophie, butter to Claire and a knife to Marc. 'Let's get our priorities straight.' She chuckled, but she didn't say out loud her next thought.

Which was that she had a hunk of gorgeous near-to-royalty naked in her bathroom right now—but what she wanted first was a crumpet.

Priorities.

A crumpet dripping with butter and honey and the arrival of fish and chips later, her conscience gave a sharp prod. She did a quick search for something Max could wear, but came up with nothing. She'd kept Donald's waterproofs because the oversized garments were excellent for milking, but the rest of his clothes had gone to welfare long since. She hesitated, then grabbed a pair of her oversized gym pants—and a blanket.

The bathroom door was open a crack.

'Mr de Gautier?'

'It's Max if you have clothes,' a voice growled. 'If not go away.'

'I sort of have clothes.'

'What do you mean sort of?'

'They might be a bit small.'

A hand came out, attached to a brawny arm. It looked a work hand, she thought, distracted. These weren't the soft, smooth fingers of a man unused to manual work. She thought back to the deft way Max had caught and loaded the wood. Royalty? Surely not. She'd seen bricklayers catch and stack like that, with maximum efficiency.

Who was he? What was he?

She stared for a moment too long and his fingers beckoned imperatively. She gasped, put the clothes in his hand and the fingers retreated.

There was a moment's silence. Then…

'These aren't just too small,' he growled. 'These are ridiculous.'

'It's all I have. That's why I brought the blanket.'

'The waterproofs?'

'Belonged to Donald. Donald's dead. We gave the rest of his stuff to charity.'

'I need charity now.'

'We have a tumble-dryer,' she told him. 'Thanks to you. If you hand out your clothes I'll put them in.'

'And I'll sit in here until they dry?'

'If you're worried about your dignity.' He definitely couldn't be royalty, she thought, suppressing a smile. The idea was preposterous.

'You have the fire going?'

'It's already putting out heat. And the fish and chips have just arrived.' She gave a sigh of pure heaven. 'There's two pieces of whiting each, and more chips than we can possibly eat. Would you like me to bring you some?'

'It's cold in here.'

'Then you have my gym pant bottoms and a blanket. Come on out.'

'Avert your eyes.'

'Shall I tell Claire and Sophie and Marc to avert their eyes as well?'

There was a moment's baffled silence. Then: 'Never mind.' There was a moment's pause while he obviously tugged on her gym pants and then the door opened.

Whoa.

Well-brought-up young ladies didn't stare, but there were moments in a woman's life when it was far too hard to be well brought up. Pippa not only stared—she gaped.

He looked like a body builder, she thought. He was tanned and muscled and rippling in all the right places. He was wearing her pants and they were as stretched on him as they were loose on her. Which was pretty much stretched. His chest was bare.

He should look ridiculous.

He looked stunning.

'You can't be a prince,' she said before she could stop herself and the corners of his mouth turned down in an expression of distaste.

'I'm not.' The rebuttal was hard and sharp and it left no room for argument.

'What are you, then?'

He didn't reply. He was carrying his bundle of wet clothes in one hand and the blanket in the other. He was meant to put the blanket round his shoulders, she thought. He wasn't supposed to be bare from the waist up.

He was bare from the waist up and it left her discomforted.

She was so discomforted she could scarcely breathe.

'What do you mean, what am I?' he demanded at last. 'You mean like in, "Are you an encyclopaedia salesman?"?'

'You're not an encyclopaedia salesman.'

'I'm a builder.'

'A builder.' The thought took her aback. 'How can you be a builder?'

He sighed. 'The same way you get to be an encyclopaedia salesman, I imagine. You find someone who's a builder and you say, "Please, sir, can you teach me what you know about building?"'

'That's what you did.'

'Yes.'

'What do you build?'

'Buildings. Did you say the fish and chips have arrived?'

'They're in the kitchen,' she said with another long look at his bare chest.

'Will you stop it?'

'Stop what?'

'Staring at my chest. Men aren't supposed to look at women's chests. I'd appreciate it if you didn't look at mine.'

'It's a very nice chest.'

Whoops.

She'd been out of circulation for too long, she thought in the ensuing silence. Maybe complimenting a man on his chest wasn't something nicely brought-up women did. He was staring at her as if he'd never experienced such a thing. 'Sorry,' she managed at last. 'Don't look at me like I'm a porriwiggle. I shouldn't have said that.'

'It was a very nice compliment,' he said cautiously. 'What's a porriwiggle?'

'A tadpole and it's not a compliment.' She hesitated and then thought maybe it was. But it was also the truth. 'Anyway, it's not what I should be saying. I should be saying thank you for the food.'

'Why are you destitute?' He smiled. 'Tadpoles don't have money?'

She tugged the door open to the rest of the house, trying frantically to pull herself back into line. 'We're not destitute,' she managed. 'Just momentarily tight, and if we don't hurry there'll be no chips left.'

'I can always buy more.'

'Then you'll get wet all over again. That's the very last garment in this house that you might just possibly almost fit into, so let's stop playing in the rain and go eat.'

He sat by the fire in Pippa's gym pants, eating fish and chips, drinking hot chocolate, staying silent while the life of the farm went on around him.

It was almost as if Pippa didn't know where to start with the questions, he thought, and that was okay as he was having trouble with the answers. Any minute now he'd have to tell them why he was here, but for now it just seemed too hard.

Pippa had taken one look at the meat and the pile of vegetables he'd brought and said, 'Pies.' So now a concoction on the stove was already smelling fantastic. Meanwhile she was rolling pastry and Sophie and Claire were helping.

Marc was hanging wet clothes round the kitchen, on the backs of chairs, over something the kids called a clothes horse, over every available surface.

'You can't hang that over me,' Max said as Marc approached him with a damp windcheater and Marc smiled shyly but proceeded to hang it over the arm of his chair.

'The fire's hot. Pippa says the clothes dryer costs money to run.'

'I'll pay,' Max growled and Pippa looked up from her pastry-making and grimaced.

'That's enough. You've been very generous but there are limits. We're very grateful for the dryer and we will use it, but only when we must.'

He stared at her, bemused. She had a streak of flour across her face. The girls were making plaits of pastry to put on the pies.

They were surrounded by a sea of flour and she didn't seem to mind. Had he ever met a woman who worried how much it cost to dry clothes? Had he ever met a woman who looked like she did and was just…unaware?

She was knocking him sideways, he thought, dazed. Which was dumb. He'd had girlfriends in his life—of course he had. He was thirty-five. He'd grown pretty damned selective over the years, and the last woman he'd dated had almost rated a ring. Not quite though. She'd been maybe a bit too interested in the royal connection.

So what was he thinking? He hated the royal connection, so any attraction to Pippa would be disastrous. It was only this weird domesticity that was making him feel like this, he decided. Here were echoes of his childhood at his grandparents' farm. Time out from royalty. Family…

A boy who looked like Thiérry. Cute-as-a-button twins. A snoring old dog.

Pippa.

Pippa had flour on her nose. He had the weirdest desire to kiss…

'Will you stay for dinner?' Marc asked, and he thought no, he needed to say what needed to be said and go. Fast. But he just wanted to…

He bit back his stupid wants. What was he thinking? Launching himself across the kitchen past kids and dog and kissing her? You're losing your mind, boyo.

'I… Pippa, I need to talk to you.'

But she was focused on pies. 'These are ready to put together as soon as I come in from the dairy.' She wiped her hands on her windcheater and smiled ruefully at her floury fingerprints. 'What a mess. No matter. The cows won't mind. But they'll be waiting. I need to start milking.'

'I'll bring the cows in for you,' Marc said, but Pippa shook her head.

'I'll do them myself. Marc, can you look after the girls?' Then she turned to Max, worry behind her eyes. 'I need to go,' she said. 'I assume you'll be leaving as soon as your clothes dry? I… I'll leave Dolores here.'

She was torn, he thought. She needed to milk, but she didn't want to leave the children alone with him. And she couldn't kick him out until his clothes dried. He looked down at Dolores, who was sleeping off one steak and dreaming of another.

'She's a great watchdog.'

Pippa flushed. 'I didn't mean…'

'I know you didn't,' he said gently. 'Do you always milk alone?'

'Marc helps me a bit. We have a place in the shed where the girls can play and I can watch them. But Marc's just got over bronchitis and I don't want him wet again.'

'I can help,' Marc protested, but Pippa shook her head.

'I know you can but I don't want you to. I want you and the girls to stay dry.'

'Are they safe here alone?' Max asked, and then as he saw Marc's look of indignation he thought maybe it was an inappropriate question.

'Marc's more than capable,' Pippa said, hurriedly before Marc could protest. 'He's had to be. But I do have an intercom. I listen in and Marc calls me if there's a problem.'

'There's never a problem,' Marc said stolidly and Max smiled at him. The more he saw of this kid, the more he liked him.

'How long does milking take?'

'About three hours,' Pippa said and Max blinked.

'How many cows?'

'A hundred and twenty.'

'I thought your vats were contaminated.'

'Cows dry out. If you let cows dry off for a week, then there's no more milk until next calving. Which is in six months.'

'So you milk every night and throw the milk away?'

'Twice a day,' Marc corrected him, and turned his big brown eyes straight on Max. 'It's much faster than three hours with two people working,' he said, innocently. 'And these pies will be yummy. We'll have tea much earlier if you help.'

'He's not invited for tea,' Pippa said.

'Yes, he is,' Marc said. 'If he helps you milk.'

'He won't know how to milk.'

'Excuse me,' Max said faintly. 'I can milk.'

They both looked at him as if he'd sprouted wings.

'Cows?' Marc queried and Max grinned.

'Cows.'

'But you're a prince.'

'I'm not a prince. My grandparents had a farm.'

'Hey, Pippa,' breathed Marc. 'He really can milk cows.' He turned back to Max. 'You can stay the night and help Pippa again in the morning. The morning milking's really cold.'

'Hey,' said Pippa.

'He can have Mum and Dad's bedroom. No one else uses it.'

'Who's the adult in this family?' Pippa asked, sounding desperate. 'I haven't invited him to stay.'

'Why can't he stay?' Marc sounded astonished.

Pippa blinked, obviously searching for an answer. 'What if I don't like him?'

'What's not to like?' Marc demanded and Max's chest puffed out a little. 'I know he looks dumb in your pants…' his chest subsided '…but he's bought us all this stuff. I bet he's rich.'

Rich is better than nothing, he guessed.

'I won't stay if Pippa doesn't want me,' he offered.

'She does want you,' Marc said.

'Pippa gets lonely,' Sophie added, distracted momentarily from her pastry. 'Claire and me have got friends at kindergarten and Marc has friends at school. Not now though 'cos school's closed for winter holidays. But no one talks to Pippa.'

'Sophie…' Pippa said helplessly and spread her hands as if she didn't know where to go from here. 'That's not true.'

'It is,' Marc said stolidly. 'No one likes us 'cos you won't sell the farm.'

'I don't want Max to…' She bit her lip and fell silent. Max looked at her for a long minute. She really was battling the odds, he thought. But then she tilted her chin and steadied.

It'd take a lot to get this woman off course.

'I will help with the milking,' he told her gently. 'And if you don't mind, I would like to stay for dinner. I need to talk to you about the children.'

Pippa's face had been wary. Suddenly now though he saw the edges of fear. 'No.'

'No?'

Her chin jutted just a little higher. 'Alice wasn't proud of her royal heritage,' she told him. 'She said she fled all the way to Australia to get away from it and she was never going back. She said it was utterly corrupt, so if that's why you're here we don't want anything to do with it.'

'You don't think you might be jumping to conclusions?'

'Maybe I am. But you haven't come all this way to buy fish and chips. You want something.'

'Maybe I do.'

'Then tell me now.'

'I'd rather do that when we're alone.'

'No. I don't keep things from the kids and they don't keep things from me. I'm their godmother, their guardian and their friend, and I want to keep it that way.'

She met his look, their gaze holding. She didn't look as if she'd budge.

Why not say it? The twins were involved in artwork with leftover pastry. Marc, though, was listening intently. He was only eight years old. Surely decisions should be made for him.

But he glanced at Marc and he saw the same courage and determination that Pippa had. No, he thought. Pippa's right. He wasn't sure what Marc had been through, but his eyes were wiser than his years. Between Marc and Pippa there seemed to be a bond of unbreakable trust.

So he had to say what he'd come to say. To both of them.

'The Crown Prince of Alp d'Estella died last month,' he said. 'Bernard died childless and there's no one left of his line. The succession therefore goes back to Bernard's grandfather and follows the line down. Thus we reach Marc. Marc is heir to the throne. He's the new Crown Prince of Alp d'Estella.'

CHAPTER THREE

EVEN the twins heard that. Or maybe they heard the loaded silence where Pippa stared at Max, appalled, and he tried to figure what she'd say when she finally found her tongue.

In the end it was Marc who spoke first. 'What's a Crown Prince?'

'It's like a king,' Max told him. 'It's a head of a country that's called a principality rather than a kingdom.'

'Is a Crown Prince rich?'

'Very.'

'We're not rich,' Marc said.

'I realise you're not.' Max turned to Pippa. 'But there is money. Bernard was never…scrupulous in his financial dealings, but as Marc is his heir there should have been provisions. There will be now. I expect this may take all sorts of pressures off.'

'What sort of pressures?' Pippa asked

He hesitated again, still unsure. 'Maybe we need to talk away from the children.'

'The girls aren't listening and this is more Marc's business than mine. I need to milk but I guess we need to have this out first.' She perched on the edge of the table and folded her arms. Marc gave her a dubious glance, then did likewise.

Max had come a long way to say this. It had to be said. But first…

'I didn't expect to see the girls,' he said, tentatively. 'Palace sources said that Marc was an only child.'

'He's not. Claire and Sophie were born just before Gina died.

Maybe your palace sources didn't keep up.' Pippa put a hand on Marc's shoulder and gave it a squeeze. 'Will we tell him what happened, Marc?'

'Yes,' Marc whispered. 'Cos he's sort of a cousin.'

'So he is.' Pippa's eyes were carefully expressionless. She sighed, seeming to dredge up energy to tell a dreary story.

'Gina was my best friend,' she said. 'Alice was friend to my mum and she practically adopted me when my mother died. So Gina and I were like sisters. I was bridesmaid at Gina's wedding and godmother to Marc. Gina and Donald were very much in love but they battled to keep this farm going. Alice lived here with them, and I was here a lot, too. Anyway, Alice died just before the twins were conceived. The pregnancy was problematic—Gina was ill and the money was tight. For their wedding anniversary I paid for them to have a weekend in a plush hotel in the city and I came here to milk and to look after Marc. They were killed that weekend.'

'I'm sorry.'

'It was a freak accident,' she said sadly. 'A lorry lost its load and a ton of logs crashed onto them. Donald was killed instantly. Gina lived for six more weeks—long enough for the twins to be born—but she never regained consciousness. She never saw her babies.'

There was a moment's pause. He should say something, he thought. What? 'So you stayed,' he asked at last and she sent him a look that said he was stupid to think she could have done anything else.

'Of course I did. Gina and Donald were my friends. Maybe if it had only been the twins we could have thought of…other options. But I love Marc to bits, and now I love the twins as well.'

'I see.' He hesitated but it had to be said—what needed to be said. 'So you've put your life on hold since Gina's death?'

'I've done no such thing,' she retorted, anger flaring.

'There's no other family?'

'Donald was an only child of elderly parents. They predeceased him by many years. There's no one else.'

'But you were a nurse.'

'And now I'm a dairy farmer. I'm milking cows and sharing my life with Marc and Sophie and Claire and Dolores.'

'My sources say you were a highly skilled nurse.'

'I'm getting pretty renowned in cow circles.'

'This isn't helping,' he said, and she stared at him in astonishment.

'It isn't helping what?'

'Me explaining.'

'You're not explaining. You're making me do the explaining.' She took a deep breath. 'I've talked enough. It's your turn. Go on. Explain.'

'These children are Alp d'Estella's new royal family.'

'These children are eight and four. They're Australian kids.'

'They're that as well, but they have an inheritance in Alp d'Estella.'

She stared. 'What exactly have they inherited?'

'The Crown.'

'A crown's not much use. A dairy farm's a lot more help for paying the bills.'

'I don't see many bills getting paid here.'

'There's no need to get personal. What else do they inherit?'

He paused. This was the crunch, he thought, the factor that had had him thinking all the time that all he had to do was lay the facts before her and he'd have her in the palm of his hand.

But now, suddenly, he wasn't so sure. He glanced at Marc and his words echoed again.

'We're not rich,' Marc had said, but it hadn't been spoken with regret. It was a simple fact.

'The Crown means wealth,' Max said, repeating the words he'd rehearsed when he'd thought he'd known how it would be received. 'Huge wealth.'

'Is Alp d'Estella a wealthy country?'

Max shook his head. He felt weird, he decided. He was bare-chested in Pippa's kitchen, wearing Pippa's gym pants.

Weird.

'The coffers of the Crown have always been separate from the

State,' he said, forging on bravely. 'The royal family of Alp d'Estella has always held onto its wealth.'

'While the peasants starved,' Pippa retorted. 'Alice told us.'

'If he's raised well I believe Marc can go about correcting injustices.'

There was a moment's silence. Pippa's grip on Marc's shoulder tightened. 'So…you'd raise him?' she asked at last.

'No!' It was said with such force that it startled them all. 'No,' he repeated, more mildly this time. 'This has nothing to do with me.'

'Why not?' She frowned. 'Come to think of it… I don't understand. Marc and I read the family tree, or as much as we have of it. If it's male succession, then you seem to be it.'

'No.'

'Or Thiérry…your brother.'

'Thiérry died almost twenty years ago.'

She frowned. 'I guess Alice wouldn't have known that when she wrote the family tree. But…he was in line to inherit after Bernard.'

'Yes.'

'Then why aren't you next?'

'Because the parental names on the birth certificate are different.'

'The names on the birth certificate…' She blinked. He stared right at her, giving her a silent message.

Finally he saw the penny drop.

'Oh,' she said.

'Can we talk about this later?' he asked.

But Pippa seemed too shocked to continue. She blinked a couple more times, then crossed to the back door.

'I have to milk.' She faltered. 'I… If you're here when I get back we'll discuss this then. I'm sorry, but I need to think this through. Look after Max, kids. I just…need time.'

'If there are any questions…'

'Not yet.'

She left. Max was left with Marc and the twins. And Dolores. They were all gazing at him with reproach. Accusing.

'You've made Pippa sad,' Sophie said.

'I haven't,' he said, flummoxed.

'She always goes outside when she's sad,' said Claire. 'She's gone to milk the cows.'

'Yes, but she's sad,' said Marc. 'Maybe she thinks you'll take us away from her.'

'I won't do that.'

'We won't go with you.'

'I don't blame you,' he said, feeling more at sea than he'd ever felt in his life. 'Kids, I promise I'm not here to do anything you don't like. My family and yours were connected a long time ago and now I'm here I'm really upset to find that you're cold and you've been hungry. I want to help, and I won't do anything Pippa doesn't like.'

'Really?' Marc demanded.

'Really.' He met Marc's gaze head-on. Adult to adult.

'I won't be a prince if Pippa doesn't want me to be one,' Marc said.

'I don't blame you.'

He really was a good kid, he thought. Maybe…just maybe this could work. But Marc would have to be protected. And he couldn't be separated from Pippa and the girls. The thought of taking Marc to a distant castle and leaving him with an unknown nanny died the death it deserved. All or nothing.

'I think your Pippa is a really great aunty,' he told them.

'We're lucky.' Marc's expression was still reproving. 'Pippa's ace.' He thought for a minute, his head tilted to the side. 'Is there a castle?'

'In Alp d'Estella, yes.'

'Does it have dragons?' Claire asked.

'No.'

'I don't like dragons,' Sophie said.

'We don't like Pippa being sad,' Marc said, moving the topic back to something he understood. 'She's gone to milk the cows by herself and she's sad.'

'She shouldn't be sad.'

'She gets sad when she thinks about money,' Claire said in a wise voice. 'Did you make her think about money?'

'No. I—'

'Yes, you did,' Marc said. 'So she'll be sad and she's cold and it's raining.' He stared at Max, challenging, and his message was crystal clear.

'You think I should help?' Max said weakly and received three firm nods.

'Yes.'

'I'd better go, then,' he said.

'Don't tell her about dragons,' Sophie said darkly. 'We don't want you to scare her.'

His clothes were still damp. He put them on straight from the tumble-dryer and within minutes they were cold and clammy. He hauled Donald's waterproofs back on—more for the wind factor than anything else as he'd learned by now they made lousy waterproofs.

'Which way's the dairy?' he asked and Marc accompanied him to the edge of the veranda and pointed.

'If you run you won't get too wet,' he said, so Max ran, his oversized gumboots squelching wetly in thick mud.

The dairy was a dilapidated brick structure a couple of hundred yards from the house, with a long line of black and white cows stretching out beside it, sodden and miserable in the rain.

Max walked through a room containing milk vats. The milk wasn't going into the vats, though. It was being rerouted to the drain.

Through the next door was the dairy proper. Pippa was working in a long, narrow pit, with cows lined up on either side.

She had her handkerchief to her eyes as he walked in. She whisked it away the moment she saw him, swiping her sleeve angrily across her eyes and concentrating on washing the next udder.

She'd been crying?

He tried to think of this situation from her point of view. Surely help with the responsibility of raising three kids had to be welcome?

But, he thought with sudden perspicacity, he was related to

the children and she wasn't. She loved these kids. Maybe he'd scared her.

Hell, he hadn't meant to.

'I'm here to help,' he told her, and she finished wiping the udder of the nearest cow and started fitting cups.

'Stay back. Cows don't like strangers.'

'They can handle a bit of unease. Let me put on the cups.' He stepped down into the pit before she could protest. 'You bring them in for me. Once they're in a bail they'll hardly notice I'm not you.'

She looked up then, really looked, blatantly astonished. 'You do know how to milk?'

'I don't tell lies, Pippa,' he said gently. 'I've spent time on a dairy farm, yes. And our farm had an outdated herring-bone dairy just like this one.'

Without a word she backed a little, then watched as he washed the next udder and fitted cups. The cow made no protest. Max was wearing familiar waterproofs and in this sort of weather one waterproofed human was much like another.

Satisfied—but still silent—she headed into the yard to bring the next cow in.

This would essentially halve her time spent in the dairy, Max thought. If Pippa had been forced to bring cows in herself, stepping out of the pit and back down time and time again, it'd take well over three hours, morning and night. Six hours of milking in this weather as well as all the other things that had to be done on a farm, plus looking after the children—and now the vats were contaminated and the milk was running down the drain.

What the hell was she doing here?

But he wasn't the first to ask questions. 'So tell me about this royal thing,' she called as the next cow came calmly into the bail. She had a radio on as background noise, so she had to speak loudly. 'What do you mean different parental names? Is that why Alice put a question mark against your name on the family tree?'

'You've seen the family tree?'

'Alice drew me one for us, a long time ago. It's what she remembered and heard from friends back home, but it's sketchy. You're on there. So's Thiérry. But there's a question mark after you. Why?'

'It's a sordid family story.'

'It can't be any more sordid than mine,' she said flatly. 'If it affects Marc, then I need the truth.'

He shrugged. He'd hated saying it, but then it had achieved what it was meant to achieve. 'My mother was married to Edouard, the Crown Prince Etienne's grandson. Bernard's cousin. She and my father had Thiérry. Then my mother had an affair. She was still married when I was born but my father doesn't appear on the birth certificate.'

There was a moment's silence while she thought that through. Then: 'So you can't inherit?'

'No.'

'But you've had a lot to do with royalty?'

'No. My mother had nothing to do with Bernard or his father. We've been in France since I was a baby.'

'You speak great English.'

'My Grandma on my mother's side is English. She drummed English into me from the time I was a tot, refusing to let me grow into what she called a little French Ruffian. She'd be delighted you noticed!'

'Right.' She nodded, more to herself than to him. She hauled her handkerchief from her pocket and gave her nose a surreptitious blow. Then she put her shoulders back, as if she was giving herself courage. She ushered another cow forward, and then, astonishingly, she started to sing.

An old pop song was playing on the radio. Max recognised it from years ago. Many years ago. His grandmother had liked this song. 'Tell Laura I Love Her' was corn at its corniest, but Pippa was suddenly singing as loud as she could, at full pathos, relishing every inch of tragedy.

The cows didn't blink.

He did. He straightened and stared. Pippa was a wet, muddy, bedraggled figure in a sea of mud and cows. Five minutes ago she'd been crying. He was sure she'd been crying.

She was singing as if the world were at her feet.

He went back to cleaning, putting on cups, taking cups off. Listening.

'Tell Laura' was replaced by 'The Last Waltz' and she didn't do a bad rendition of that either. Then there was Olivia Newton-John's 'I Am Woman' and she almost brought the house down. He found himself grinning and humming—but a lot more quietly than Pippa.

'You don't sing?' she demanded as she sang the last note and gave her next cow an affectionate thump on the rump.

'Um…no.'

'Not even in the shower?'

'I'm admitting nothing.'

She chuckled. 'That means you do. Why don't you sing along?'

'I'm enjoying listening to you.'

'So sing with me next time.' But the next song was one neither of them knew, which was clearly unsatisfactory.

'I'll write to their marketing manager,' she said darkly. 'Putting on newfangled songs I don't know the words of is bad box office.'

'So what do you have to sing about?' he asked into the lull.

'I can't find anything to sing about with this song.'

He glanced at the source of the music—a battered radio sitting at the end of the bales. 'You want me to change the channel?'

'There speaks a channel surfer,' she said. 'Men! They spend their lives looking for something better and miss out on the good stuff.'

'Good stuff like "I Am Woman"?'

'Exactly.'

'So what's put you off men…exactly?'

'Life,' she said theatrically and gave an even more theatrical sigh. 'Plus the fact that no one finds my fashion sense sexy.'

Fashion? He could hardly see her. She was a diminutive figure in waterproofs that were far too big for her. Her boots were caked in mud and there was a fair bit of dung attached as well. She was a shapeless, soggy mass, but she was patting the cow before her with real affection, waiting for the next song to start before launching herself into her own personal theatrical performance.

Was she sexy? Maybe not but here it was again, a stirring of something that was definitely not unsexy interest.

Which was crazy, he told himself again, even more severely than the last time he'd told himself. He'd come here for one reason and one reason only. He expected to put Marc on the plane to Alp d'Estella—with or without attachments—and then get the hell out of this mess. He'd thought this through. He could fit the requirements of the regency in with his current work. He'd install Charles Mevaille as administrator. Charles was more competent than he'd ever be. Sure there'd be times when he needed to intervene personally, but for the most part he could get himself back to the life that he loved.

Did he love his life?

Whoa. What was he thinking? He surely loved his life better than a life of being in the royal goldfish bowl—and he liked his life better than the one this woman was leading.

But she sang. She sang straight after she cried.

So she was better at putting on a cheerful face than he was. The singing must be a part of that, he realised. It was a tool to force herself away from depression.

Why was she here?

He washed the udder of a gently steaming cow, and attached the cups with skills he'd learned as a kid. Despite her singing, Pippa hadn't relaxed completely. She was watching him, he knew, uncertain yet that she could trust him with cows that were her livelihood.

What had she been facing if he hadn't turned up this afternoon? What would they have eaten? Maybe Pippa would have figured some way to feed them. She looked like a figuring type of woman.

But the house had been freezing, and she hadn't figured out a way to stop that. Surely this farm wasn't a long-term proposition?

It couldn't be, and that must make a proposition of another life welcome. But he wasn't sure. She'd obviously been told enough of Alp d'Estella's royal family to react with disgust.

That wasn't surprising. Alice—Gianetta's mother—had fled to Australia for much the same reasons as his own mother had fled to France. Alice had done it much more successfully though, living her life in relative obscurity.

'Excuse me, but Peculiar's cups need taking off,' Pippa called, hauling him back to the here and now. He'd been wiping teats and putting on cups without paying attention to the end of the queue. But…

'Peculiar?'

'The lady with the white nose and the empty teats at the end of the line. She was first in and now she's ready to leave.'

'You call a cow Peculiar?'

'You want to know why?'

'Yes.' He removed Peculiar's cups and released her from her bail.

She didn't go.

'See,' Pippa said.

'If I had the choice I wouldn't want to head out into the dark and stormy night either.'

'She never wants to go outside. And when she's out she doesn't want to come in. The other cows look at her sideways.'

'So you gave her a nice reassuring name like Peculiar.'

'I could have called her Psycho but I didn't.'

He gave the cow a slap on the rump. 'Out.'

Peculiar retaliated by kicking straight back at him. But Max had spent years of his life in a dairy and he was fast. He side-stepped smartly, just out of range of the slashing hooves.

'Neatly done,' Pippa said. 'But see? Psycho. I always milk her first and get her out of the way.'

'You could have called her Psycho then.' Peculiar was ambling out now, content that there was no more opportunity to wreak havoc. 'Peculiar gives warm connotations of a mildly eccentric aunt.'

'I'm a nice person. I'm giving her leeway to reform.'

He stared out at her through the rain. Pippa was nice? She definitely was, he thought. Nice, and very, very different.

'What the hell are you doing on a dairy farm?' he demanded.

'Same as you. Milking cows.'

'But you're a nurse.'

'That was my first job. I have better things to do with my life now.'

'Since Gina and Donald were killed.'

'What do you think? Should I say, Ooh, my career in nursing is far more important than taking care of my best friend's orphaned children? Don't stop now, Mr de Gautier. Big-bum's waiting for her cups.'

'Big-bum.'

'The next cow,' she retorted. 'Do what I do for a bit, Mr de Gautier. Do what comes next and don't look further.'

She turned her back on him, ostensibly to bring in the next cow, but he suspected it was more than that—a ruse to bring the conversation to an abrupt end.

Which suited him. He had enough information to assimilate for the time being.

Marc's voice came back to him. 'This is our Pippa.' It had been a declaration of family.

Would Our Pippa agree to accompany the kids?

Do what comes next and don't look further. He attended to Big-bum. She was indeed…Big-bum?

He shook his head, trying to clear emotions that were strange and unwelcome. He was here to give a message and go. He was not here to learn by heart a hundred and twenty cows' names.

Pippa looked about fourteen, Max thought. And then he thought: She looks frightened.

She ushered in half a dozen more cows and he milked in silence. There were a couple of soppy songs on the radio but she'd stopped singing.

'You're here to take the children to Alp d'Estella,' she said into the stillness and he raised his head and met her challenging look head-on. Not for long though. Her eyes were bright with anger and he was starting to feel…ashamed? Which was crazy. This was a fantastic opportunity he was handing these children. He had no reason to feel ashamed.

'And you,' he admitted. 'If you want to go.'

'When did you arrive in Australia?'

'About nine hours ago.'

'From France?'

'Yes.'

'Then you'll have jet lag,' she whispered, so softly he barely heard. 'You'll not be making sense. We'll leave this discussion for later. Meanwhile turn the radio up, would you? It's not loud enough.'

'You don't want to talk any more?'

'Not now and maybe not ever,' she snapped. 'Our life is here. Meanwhile let's get these ladies milked.'

'You need to think about—'

'I don't need to think about anything,' she snapped. 'I need to sing. Turn the radio up and let me get on with it.'

'Yes, ma'am.' There was nothing left for him to say.

It took them just under two hours. Pippa saw the last cow amble back down to the paddocks with relief. She closed the gate and turned to fetch the hose but Max swung out of the milking pit and reached the hose before her.

'I'll sluice the dairy,' he told her. 'You go in and get warm.'

'I need to clean the vats.'

'Why? We haven't used them.'

'I have to figure what caused the contamination.'

'Old tubing?'

'Maybe, but I can't afford new so all I can do is scrub.'

If the tubing was corroded no amount of scrubbing would help and from the despair etched behind her eyes he thought she knew it. 'Pippa, don't worry about it tonight,' he said gently. 'You look exhausted.'

'You're the one with jet lag.'

'You're the one who looks like you have jet lag.'

She flushed. 'There's nothing wrong with me that another hot shower won't cure.'

He smiled at that, thinking of how many hot showers had been enjoyed today. 'Lucky you have a decent hot water service.'

'If we ran out of hot water I might be tempted to walk away,' she told him. 'But don't worry. I won't. Regardless of your plans for our family.'

'Pippa…'

'I'm going,' she said and cast him a darkling look. 'I don't have a clue what's going on, so I'll take a shower and leave you to my dairy.'

She left him to it. By the time she reached the door he was already working methodically with the hose, sluicing from highest level to lowest. He knew what he was doing.

Which was more than she did.

She knew so little of this royal bit—only what Alice had told Gina. But: 'We're best out of it,' she'd said. 'Gina needs have nothing to do with them, and neither do I. They're corrupt and they're evil. It's a wonder the country hasn't overthrown them with force. Anyway I refuse to look back. I'll only look forward.'

Alice had died too young, Pippa thought sadly—a lovely, gracious lady who'd made Pippa's life so much happier since Gina had brought home her 'best friend from school'.

Pippa owed them everything. She and Gina had been so close they were almost sisters. They were both only children of single mothers, but Gina's mother had cared, whereas Pippa's…

'Gina and Alice were my family,' Pippa told herself as she squelched through the mud on her way back to the house. 'And Gina's kids are now my kids. If Max What's-His-Name thinks he can step in and take over…'

She shook herself, literally, and a shower of water sprayed out around her. Dratted men. Men meant trouble and Maxsim de Gautier meant more trouble than most. She knew it.

But right now he was back in the dairy and she'd reached home.

She poked her nose through the back door and warmth met her and the smell of the makings of her pie simmering on the stove and the sound of Sophie and Claire giggling. They were sitting in front of the fireguard playing with their dolls. Dolores had nosed the fireguard aside and was acting as a buffer between twins and fire, soaking up all the heat in the process.

She was a great watchdog, Pippa thought fondly, and then she thought: Max has done this.

But if he thinks he can seduce me…

Wrong word, she thought, suddenly confused. It was a dopey word. It should have been if he thinks he can influence me with money…

The seduce word stayed in her mind, though, refusing to be banished.

Marc had been setting the table—with their best crockery, she noted with astonishment. When he saw Pippa alone in the doorway his face drooped in disappointment.

'He's gone.'

'He's coming after me. He's sluicing the dairy.'

The droop turned into a grin. He laid cutlery at the head of the table—a position they never used. 'Have a shower and put something pretty on,' he told her.

'I don't have something pretty.'

'Yes, you do. The stuff you wear to church.'

'The pink cardigan,' Sophie volunteered.

'It's a bit old,' Claire added. 'But it's still pretty.'

But he's dangerous, she thought.

But she didn't say it. She couldn't. She was being ridiculous.

She was the children's legal guardian. Max had no rights at all where they were concerned.

And he had no right to make her feel that he was…dangerous…where she was concerned.

She showered, and in deference to the kids' decree she donned her church clothes—a neat black skirt and a pretty pink twin-set. It was a bit priggish, she thought, staring into the mirror, but it was the best she had, and she wasn't out to impress Max.

But she did shampoo her hair and blow-dry her curls, brushing until they shone. She did apply just a little powder and lipstick. But that was all.

She turned from her reflection with a rueful grimace. Once upon a time she and Gina had spent hour upon giggly hour getting ready for special evenings. Now Gina was dead and the only cosmetics Pippa possessed were a compact for a shiny nose and a worn lipstick. And the only good outfit she had was her church gear.

Enough. She stuck her tongue out at her reflection. She headed back to the kitchen, but paused before she entered. There was the sound of kids giggling and Max's deep voice talking to them.

On impulse she deviated to the office.

The office was a bit of a misnomer. It was a tiny space enclosed at the end of the veranda. Pippa stored the farm paperwork here, and she had an ancient computer with dial-up internet connection—as long as the phone lines weren't down. They weren't. She typed in Alp d'Estella and found out what it had to say.

> Of the group of four alpine nations—Alp Quattro—in southern Europe, Alp d'Estella is the largest. The four countries depend heavily on tourists; and indeed each country has stunning scenery. Alp d'Estella is known throughout the world for its magnificent shoe trade. Alp d'Estella's skilled tradesmen supply exquisitely made handmade shoes to the catwalks of London, Paris, New York and Rome.
>
> Politically, however, there is trouble in paradise. Each of the Alp Quattro countries is a Principality and their constitutions leave absolute power in the hands of the Crown Prince. Alp d'Azuri, a neighbouring country, has with the help of the current Crown Prince, moved to revoke these powers and is now seen as politically stable. Alp d'Estella, however, is a country in crisis.
>
> The death of the Crown Prince a month ago with no clear successor has left the country more corrupt than when the Prince was alive. Prince Bernard led a puppet government which, if no one claims the throne, will become the de-facto government. Poverty is widespread, as is corruption. The nation's only industries are being taxed to the hilt

and are now threatened with bankruptcy. The succession must be sorted, and sorted quickly, in order to restore order.

This was why Max was here. To organise the succession. To an eight-year-old.

What did Marc know about running a country?

Nothing. It was ridiculous. But there was no time to discover more.

She took a deep breath, disconnected and went to tell Max how ridiculous it was.

CHAPTER FOUR

PIPPA couldn't tell Max anything for a while, for the children had decreed tonight a party.

Pippa could hardly believe the transformation. They'd all just recovered from world's worst cold virus, with Marc sickest of all. The last few weeks had been dank and miserable. Cold seemed to have seeped into their bones, but now she couldn't hear so much as a residual cough. With the warmth and with the wonderful food—and maybe with the excitement of Max's visit?—they'd found a new lease of life. The twins had put on their best dresses. They'd tied a huge red bow around Dolores' neck—she looked very festive fast asleep by the stove. And, from a sad, coughing little boy, Marc was transformed into master of ceremonies, bossing everyone.

'Give Mr de Gautier red lemonade,' he ordered Pippa when they sat down to eat, and when Pippa didn't move fast enough he sighed and started pouring himself.

'He's bought wine,' Pippa said mildly, but the children stared at her as if she had to be joking—wine when there was red lemonade?—and Max accepted his red lemonade with every semblance of pleasure and raised a glass in crimson toast.

'You see what it's like?' Pippa demanded, smiling and raising her glass in turn. 'I try to be in charge…'

'Pippa's no good at being bossy,' Marc told Max, and Max grinned.

'She was pretty non-bossy in the dairy. I'm thinking she's more an opera singer than a dairy maid.'

The operatic singer blushed crimson. 'There's no need…'

'Now, don't defend yourself,' he said, ladling pie onto the twins' plates. 'There's no need. It was truly marvellous singing. It's a wonder the milk didn't turn to curds and whey all by itself.'

'You…'

'What?'

She stared at him. He kept right on smiling and she kept right on staring. The table stilled around them.

'Would you like some pie?' he asked gently and she gasped and reached for the pie dish with her bare hands. Which was dumb. There was a dish cloth lying ready but she hadn't used it. The pie dish was very hot. She yelped.

He was up in a flash, tugging her chair back. Propelling her to the sink.

'I'm fine,' she managed, but he had her hands under the tap and it was already running cold.

'I hardly touched it.'

'You yelped.' His hands were holding hers under the water, brooking no opposition.

'I did not yelp.'

'You did so,' Marc volunteered from behind them. 'Are you burned?'

'Do you need a bandage?' Claire demanded, then slipped off her chair and headed for the bathroom without waiting for a response. 'You always need a bandage,' she said wisely.

'I hardly touched it,' she said again, and Max lifted her fingers from the water and inspected them one by one. There was a faint red line on one hand, following the curve of her fingers.

'Ouch?' he said gently and he smiled.

There was that smile. Only it changed every time he used it, she thought. He was like a chameleon, fitting to her moods. Using his smile to make her insides do strange things. She looked up at him, helpless, and Sophie sighed dramatically in the face of adult stupidity and handed her the dishcloth.

'Dry your hands,' she said and edged Max away. 'We don't

need bandages,' she called to her twin. 'There's no blood. You'll be all right, won't you?' she told Pippa. 'There's chocolate ice cream for dessert.'

'You guys are amazing,' Max said. 'You take it in turns to play boss.'

'It works for us.' Pippa tugged her hands away—which took some doing—and returned to her place at the table with what she hoped was a semblance of dignity. 'Everything's fine.'

But everything wasn't fine. Everything was…odd. Max was still smiling as he ladled her pie without being asked.

Her insides felt funny.

It was hunger, she told herself.

She knew it was no such thing.

The rest of dinner passed uneventfully, which was just as well for Pippa's state of mind. She ate in silence. The children chattered to Max, excited by the food, the festive occasion and the fact that this big stranger seemed interested in everything they said. He seemed really nice, she thought, but she tried to keep her attention solidly on food.

'I need to put the kids to bed,' she said when the last of the chocolate ice cream had been demolished. 'Don't wash up until I get back.'

'I'm helping Max wash up,' Marc said and Pippa practically gaped.

'You're offering?'

'If Max can do dishes then I can.'

She gazed at him, doubtfully—this little boy who was growing to be a man.

She knew nothing of raising boys, she thought. She knew nothing of…men. She had nothing to do with them. There was not a single inch of room in her life for anything approaching romance.

Romance? Where had that thought come from?

From right here, she told herself as she ordered the twins to bed. For some dumb reason she was really attracted to Max.

Well, any woman would be, she told herself. It's not such a

stupid idea. He's connected to royalty, he has a yummy accent and he's drop-dead gorgeous.

So you're not dumb thinking he's attractive. You're just dumb thinking anything could come of it.

Dumb or not, she read the twins a really long book and tucked them in with extra cuddles. She called Marc and did the same for him. When she finally finished, Max was in the living room, ensconced in an armchair by the fire, with Dolores draped over his feet.

Pippa had hardly been in this room since summer. It was cold and unwelcoming and slightly damp. Now however the fire had been roaring in the firestove for hours. Max was cooking crumpets on a toasting fork. He'd loaded a side-table with plates and butter and three types of jam. The whole scene was so domestic it made Pippa blink.

'Haven't we just had dinner?'

'Yes, but I saw the toasting fork and I need to try it. And now I'm feeling like crumpets, too.'

The fire was blazing. 'How much wood are you using?' she said before she thought about it and Max cast her a look of soulful reproach.

'There's more where it came from and the least you can do is make a guest feel warm.'

'You're no guest.' She was feeling desperate and desperate times called for desperate measures. Or bluntness at least. 'You're here to take Marc.'

'Don't dramatise. You know I can't do that. You're Marc's guardian. Well done?'

She blinked. 'Sorry?'

'How do you like your crumpet?' he asked patiently. 'I'm getting good at this. The first crumpets ended up in the fire—this toasting fork has no holding power. But the last one I made was excellent. You can have this one. Do you like it slightly singed or charcoal-black?'

'We'll be out of wood again by the end of the week, and I'm not letting you buy more.'

'I'm hoping you'll be in Alp d'Estella by the end of the week.'

Pippa took a deep breath. Things were happening way too fast.

'We're not going to Alp d'Estella. You can't have Marc.'

'He has a birthright,' Max said, flipping his crumpet.

'Maybe he has, but it's here.' She closed her eyes. The effort she'd been making since Max had arrived slipped a little. Her vocals in the dairy had been a last-ditch attempt to find control and it hadn't worked.

She felt so tired she wanted to sleep for a month.

'Pippa, this is impossible,' Max said, laying his crumpet down, rising and pushing her into the chair he'd just vacated. 'Tell me why you're doing this?'

'Doing…what?'

'Trying to keep this farm going against impossible odds.'

'It's all the children have,' she whispered. 'It's all I have.'

'I don't understand.' He shifted the sleeping Dolores sideways. Dolores didn't so much as open an eye. He hauled another chair up beside her and sat down. 'I need background.'

'It's none—'

'It is my business,' he said gently. 'It seems to me that I'm the only relation these kids have. Now that doesn't give me any rights,' he said hurriedly as he saw alarm flit across her face. 'But it does make me concerned, succession to the throne or not. Tell me about you. About this whole family.'

She hesitated. She shouldn't tell him. What good would it do? But he was looking at her with eyes that said he was trying to understand, that he might even want to help. The sensation was so novel that she was suddenly close to tears.

She fought them back. No way was she crying in front of him.

'Why is the farm so poor?' he asked.

'I told you,' she said, rattled. 'The vats are contaminated.'

'You were poor before that.'

'It's not a wealthy farm.'

'And?'

'And Gina and Donald didn't have insurance. They couldn't afford it. Then the medical costs for Gina and the twins were exorbitant, as was paying someone to keep this place going until I could cope. I'm paying that off still.'

'Is the farm freehold?'

'There are still debts.'

'But a sizeable chunk is paid for?'

'Yes.'

'According to the ladies in the Tanbarook supermarket you could sell it tomorrow.'

'I could,' she said and bit her lip. 'Actually I have two buyers. The developers who want to use it as a road, or the Land for Wildlife Foundation. There's a project going to make a wilderness corridor from the coast to the mountains north of here, and this place would be an important link.' She managed a smile. 'They'd pay less but if it was up to me I'd sell the land to them.' Her smile faded. 'But of course it's not up to me.'

'Why not?' He frowned. 'You could sell, to whoever you choose to sell to, and you could take another nursing job.' Then as she started to protest he placed his finger on her lips. It was a weird gesture of intimacy that felt strangely right for here. For now. 'Hush,' he told her. 'I'm not stupid. I accept you won't leave the children. But I'd assume you could get a reasonable income from nursing, and the farm would bring in something. That must mean you could have a life where you'd at least be warm and well fed.'

'The kids' inheritance is the farm. That's all they have.'

'I disagree. They have you. An inheritance isn't worth starving for.'

'You don't think it's important?'

'Not that much.'

'Then why are you going to this trouble to make sure Marc inherits this principality?'

He hesitated. Then he spread his hands, as if deciding to tell all. 'There are lives at stake.'

She stared. 'That sounds ridiculous.'

'It's true.'

'Really?'

'Really.'

'Why?'

'If there's no Crown Prince then the country reverts to political rule, which at the moment would practically be a dictatorship. That's why you haven't heard of Marc's inheritance before this. The politicians want nothing more than for the royal succession to die and for them to be in sole charge. The local farmers are being bled dry with taxes as it is. If it gets worse…well, I'm not overstating it when I say there will be starvation.'

'But that's…that's crazy. Marc can't have anything to do with that.'

'He doesn't need to. He simply needs to be allowed to take on the title. The rest can be managed around him.' He hesitated, and then forged on. 'Because my mother was still married to Edouard when I was born and because I was half-brother to Thiérry, I can accept the role of Prince Regent. That means until Marc is twenty-one, I can make decisions for him. We can get the country back on track.'

'But…' she shook her head '…this is nonsense. How can I possibly expose Marc to something so weird?'

'It's not so weird,' he said and smiled. 'It's lovely. You could come for a holiday and see. When did you last have a holiday?'

She stared at him blankly.

His smile faded. 'When, Pippa?'

'I…when I was nursing I'd come here sometimes and help.'

'Have you ever taken the children on a holiday?'

'No, but—'

'Alp d'Estella's in the middle of summer right now,' he said persuasively. 'The castle's great.'

'Claire says it'll have dragons.'

'Dragons?'

'All castles have dragons,' she said, distracted. 'Or at least something scary.' She shook her head as if trying to clear fog. 'You want Marc to be Crown Prince? He's far too young to be anything of the kind.'

'It's Crown Prince in name only. Until he's of age the responsibility is mine.' He hesitated. 'Pippa, I know Alice didn't trust the royal family, but the old line is dead. Marc represents the new line. A new hope for the future.'

She took a deep breath. 'It sounds nonsensical,' she whispered. 'How can I possibly trust you?'

'You don't need to trust me,' Max said, steadily, as if he wasn't offended and had in fact anticipated her qualms. 'I've set my credentials before your Minister of International Affairs and he'll vouch for my integrity. My mother also knows your countrywoman, Jessica, who married my neighbour, Raoul, Crown Prince of Alp d'Azuri. I believe your women's magazines have written her up, so maybe you've heard of her? Jessie's pregnant and blissfully happy, but she's not so tied up in her own contentment that she doesn't interest herself in the affairs of her neighbours. Both she and her husband have sent their personal assurance that Marc will be safe. They guarantee that if you don't think it's satisfactory then you're free to take Marc and leave. At any time.'

She blinked. She had indeed heard of Jessica, the Australian fashion designer who by all reports was living happily ever after in her fairy-tale palace with her handsome prince. The Princess Jessica had written her an assurance? The whole thing was unbelievable.

There were so many questions. She could only manage a little one. An important one. 'It's warm?'

He smiled. 'It's warm,' he said softly. 'Not only that, we have three swimming pools—a lap pool, an outdoor recreational pool and one indoors and heated for inclement weather. Not that it'll be inclement at this time of the year. It'll be beautiful.'

He was seducing her with sunshine. She had to keep her head.

'You would be able to leave,' he added, gently but definitely, and his big hands came out and covered hers. 'I promise, Pippa. I'm asking that you come for a month. One month. Then you'll know the facts. You'll know what's on offer. You can make up your mind from a position of knowledge.'

'But the cost,' Pippa said weakly. She should pull her hands away but she couldn't make herself do it.

'It's taken care of already.' Then as she looked startled the pressure on her hands intensified. There was no way it should make her feel secure and safe, but stupidly it did. 'Pippa, I know I'm pushing you,' he said. 'But I'm in a hurry. The succession has to be worked out fast. Yes, you have some thinking to do but you can't think without having seen what's on offer. A sensible woman would come.'

'Sometimes I'm not sensible,' she said and she glowered and his smile changed a little, genuine amusement behind his eyes.

'I can see that. But maybe your sensible side will out?'

She stared at him, nonplussed. The lurking twinkle was dangerous, she thought. Really dangerous.

Concentrate on practicalities. 'But there's passports and things…'

'I have friends in high places. I can have passports in twenty-four hours.'

'Twenty-four hours? Are you some kind of magician?'

'Just a man who's determined to have you see what you need to see.'

She was dumbfounded. 'But…the cows,' she whispered at last, and Max grinned as if that was the last quibble out of the way.

'I talked to Bert. He'll be more than happy to take over the milking for now. I gather he did it before? He'll use his dairy and his vats are clean, so he can be paid for the milk. No obligation, he said, and why would there be? He'll even milk Peculiar.'

'You know Bert wants to buy us out. This is making it easier for him.'

'Maybe it is but we're making no promises,' Max said evenly. 'You're just taking time to think. It won't increase the pressure. Regardless of what you decide, these children are eligible for lifetime support from the royal coffers. You'll never be hungry again. I promise.' The grip on her hand strengthened, a warm, strong link that made her feel…wonderful. 'I swear.'

She blinked and blinked again. She would not cry.

This was a fairy tale. She shouldn't let herself be conned. But in truth… In truth she'd fallen from the roof last week and it had scared her witless. Not for herself so much as for the children. She was all they had. If anything happened to her…

She had to think about it.

And warmth…

'Who else will be at the castle?' she managed, trying desperately to focus on practicalities.

'Servants.'

'How many servants?'

'Thirty or more. I'm not sure.'

Her eyes widened. She should pull her hands away, she thought desperately, but she sort of…couldn't.

'Your family?' she whispered. 'Your mother?' She hesitated but she knew absolutely nothing of this man and there was one question that was pretty major waiting to be asked. 'Your wife?'

'My mother's in Paris,' he said evenly. 'And I'm not married. But that's of no importance as I won't be at Alp d'Estella myself. I'll escort you there and then leave.'

She blinked. He'd leave? 'Why?'

'I have no place in Alp d'Estella. It's Marc who inherits. Not me.'

Her hand was withdrawn at that, hauled away before he could react and tucked firmly in the folds of her skirt, as if she was afraid he might try to reclaim it. He couldn't. The fairy tale was dissipating. 'Now, hang on a minute,' she said. 'You're expecting to dump us and run?'

'I wouldn't put it quite like that.' The twinkle faded.

'How would you put it? You've given us all these assurances but if you're not there how can I know they'll be held good?' She frowned. 'Anyway, what does Prince Regent mean?'

'It's a caretaker role. I get to do the paperwork, and make decisions on behalf of the heir to the Crown until he's of age. I can do that from Paris, mostly.'

'But if you're illegitimate—how can you be Regent?'

'There's no one else.'

'I don't understand.'

'I've only just had it explained to me myself,' he said ruefully. 'But it seems the Alp d'Estella constitution—or whatever they call it when it's to do with royal succession—has a stipulation that the regency can be held by someone with blood ties to an heir to the throne. Parent, sibling or half-sibling. I guess it was drawn up in the days when death in childbirth was common, and so was death in battle. An older half-sister may well be all there was to care for the rights of a young prince.'

'But…if your real father isn't royal…'

'That's why I'm here four weeks after Bernard died and not before. I thought I had nothing to do with it. However there are people in Alp d'Estella desperate to see the current regime displaced. They realised the vague constitutional wording—blood ties to *an* heir rather than *the* heir—meant that I could take the regency on. If I don't take it on, the politicians will, and there's no way you could let Marc walk into that.'

'So what do you get out of it?'

'Nothing. But the country is desperate for decent rule.' He hesitated. 'Do you know anything about the Alp countries?'

'Not much.'

'They're four principalities,' he said, sighing, as if this was a tale he'd wearied of telling. 'And they've been degenerate for generations. The princes running them come from a long line of families where indulgence is everything. We now have corrupt politicians who know the only way to advance is to please royalty. The Crown Prince of our nearest neighbour, Alp d'Azuri, has set about changing that. Raoul—your Jessica's husband—has used his sovereign powers to instil a democracy. The change is wonderful. That's where the idea came from that change is possible, but it can't be done unless Marc accepts the Crown.'

'But Marc's too young to decide.'

'It doesn't matter. Once he's installed as Crown Prince, no matter how old he is, measures can be put in place to get the country on an even keel. He can forfeit the Crown later if he wants, but I do need time to get a proper parliament in place.'

'You can do that?'

'From the background, it seems that, yes, I can.'

Pippa sat back in her chair and stared at him. Awed. 'You mean what I agree on, right now, right here, while I'm still thawing from milking, will affect the lives of…'

'Millions. Yes, it will. But don't let me pressure you.'

'You're mad.'

'Yes, but I bought you steak and firewood and I helped you milk. I can't be all bad.'

She shook her head, trying to clear her jumbled thoughts. 'Don't think you can inveigle me into doing stuff. I didn't ask for help.'

'I don't want to inveigle you to do anything.'

'Bully for you.' Pippa was feeling so lost she didn't know where she was. She picked up the toasting fork and absently held the half-cooked crumpet to the flames again. Then she put it down. She couldn't concentrate.

'All I know of this country is from you,' she whispered.

'That's right. But I can give you assurances, and not just from me.'

'But, you see, I'm all the children have,' she said apologetically. 'How can I put them at risk?'

'You won't be putting them at risk.'

'But you won't be there.' She took a deep breath. 'We could come,' she admitted. 'I might even be prepared to take a chance. But only if you were there.'

'I can't.'

'Why not?'

'I have a life. My building—'

'I had a life too once,' she snapped. 'My nursing. I've put my life on hold for these kids. So how important is forming a parliament? You'd put your life on hold for how long for this kingdom of yours?'

'It's a principality.'

'Kingdom—principality—it makes no difference,' she snapped. 'But I won't do this alone. It scares me stupid. I won't let you guilt me into it because the country might starve, and then watch you walk away and leave me to do it alone. You're a de

Gautier. Illegitimate or not, you know the reputation of your family. Alice ran for a reason and I'm not as stupid as I look.'

'I never said—'

'You don't have to say,' Pippa said. 'Stupid is as stupid does. You hold this place out to me like a carrot on the end of a stick. Warmth. Castles. Swimming pools. And you…a Prince Regent who looks like you stepped out of a romance movie, telling me I have to agree or the peasants will starve…'

'You don't think you're being just a touch melodramatic?'

'Of course I'm being melodramatic,' she yelled, so loudly that Dolores was forced to raise her head in faint reproach.

'There's no need to yell,' Max said, starting to sound exasperated, but she'd gone too far to draw back now.

'There is. I have no guarantee that you care one bit about this little boy you barely know. Or his sisters. I won't be bludgeoned into taking them to a country I don't know, unless I have some cast-iron guarantees.' She held up each finger in turn. 'One, you agree that we're staying for a month and only a month. We can all leave freely any time after that, and if the children are unhappy then we can leave earlier. Two, you organise that this farm will be cared for while we're away. You seem to have enough money. Three, you agree that Marc is not to be made aware that anyone's welfare depends on him. Four, you stay for the entire month. You leave whatever you do in Paris as you're asking me to leave whatever I do here.'

'That's not f—'

'Fair?' she queried, and turned and shook the loaded toasting fork at him. 'Who's talking fair?'

She was gorgeous, he thought suddenly. She was just…gorgeous. She looked like an avenging angel, in faded serviceable clothes and wielding a toasting fork like a sword. Her cheeks were two bright spots of colour. Her eyes were flashing demons.

He thought…he thought…

He thought he wanted to kiss her.

Dumb move, he told himself desperately. Really, really dumb.

He really, really wanted to kiss her.

'Well?' she demanded and he tried to think what he should be thinking.

'The castle is pure luxury,' he said weakly. 'There's no need for me to stay.'

'I don't want you to stay,' she said, surprising him, 'but as guarantee of the children's safety you must.'

He gazed at her, and she gazed back, meeting his look head-on and not flinching.

He still just wanted to kiss…

'I do what I have to do,' she said. 'Do you?'

'Yes, but—'

'Then it's settled. You'll stay?'

'I need—'

'You'll stay?'

'Yes,' he said, driven against the ropes and acknowledging he had no choice. 'I'll stay in Alp d'Estella, yes.'

'Excellent,' Pippa said and glowered. 'Not that I want you near us, mind. You unsettle me.'

'Do I?' He started to smile, but she raised her toasting fork again.

'I have no idea why you unsettle me and I don't like it,' she told him. 'So stop smiling. It just unsettles me more. And there's only one more stipulation that has to be met.'

'Another!'

'It's the most important.'

'What is it?'

She stared down at her feet. Dolores had rolled over onto her back, exposing her vast stomach to the radiant heat.

'As long as we can figure out the quarantine issues, Dolores comes too. All or none. Take us or leave us.'

He stared down at the ancient mutt—a great brown dog looking like nothing so much as a Hound of the Baskervilles. A sleeping hound of the Baskervilles. 'She'd be happier here.'

'In the middle of winter? Kennelled without us?'

'Most dogs—'

'She's not most dogs. Alice gave me Dolores as a puppy when

my mother died. She's been with me ever since—my one true love. Who needs men when I have Dolores?' She retrieved the half-baked crumpet, looked at it with regret and started another. 'Wicked waste.'

'Taking a dog to Alp d'Estella?'

'Interrupting the toasting process. It really messes with the texture. Let's get back to important stuff.'

'Which is?'

'Crumpets.'

'Sure.'

But he still really, really wanted to kiss her.

He didn't. She didn't even guess that he wanted to. Forty-eight hours later Pippa found herself in a first class airline seat somewhere over Siberia, heading for…Alp d'Estella?

There'd been so much to do before she'd left that she'd fallen into an exhausted sleep almost as soon as the plane took off. Now she woke to find the internal lights were off and the light from outside was the dim glow of a northern twilight. Across the aisle Sophie, Claire and Marc were solidly asleep. They'd enjoyed having a seat each at first, but then the twins had bundled in together and Marc had lifted his arm rest so he could join them.

They looked like a litter of well-fed puppies. Down in the hold, Dolores was hopefully sleeping as well, in a padded, warmed crate she'd inspected with caution but deemed fit for travel-snoozing. Kids and dog. Pippa's responsibilities.

Was she putting them at risk? she wondered for about the hundredth time. Surely not. She'd rung the people Max had given as referees and they'd confirmed his story. Max was honourable, they'd said. She'd be safe.

But the kids would be safer at home.

Maybe, but they'd be cold and hungry. With the state of her bank balance she'd been close to needing welfare. And if anything happened to her…

She hadn't succeeded with the farm, she thought miserably, and where was life sending her now? The enormity of what she'd promised eight years ago washed over her, as it had time and time again since Gina's death.

What cost a promise?

'Have you ever thought of walking away from them?' Max asked from right beside her and she jumped about a foot.

She could barely see him. His seat was at a slight incline and hers was out flat. She struggled with some buttons and her seat rose to upright.

She passed him on the way up.

There was a moment's silence while she sat bolt upright and felt stupid. Then he leaned over her and touched her seat control again. Her seat sank smoothly to the same incline as his.

She smelled the masculine smell of him as he leaned over.

Their faces were now six inches apart.

She backed up a little, fast, and she felt his smile rather than saw it. 'Worry not,' he told her. 'I'm no ogre, Pippa, hauling you off to my dark and gloomy castle, to have my wicked way with you.'

'You can hardly have your wicked way when I'm chaperoned by three kids and a dog,' she managed and she tried to relax. But he was still smiling and she was feeling very…very…

Very she didn't know what. If only he weren't so damned good-looking. If only he weren't so…disconcerting.

He was very disconcerting. And mentioning wicked ways hadn't helped a bit. He was so…

Sexy.

There were things stirring inside her that had been repressed for years. She swallowed and told herself that these ideas had to go straight back to being repressed again.

They refused to cooperate.

'Have you left the farm since Gina's death?' he asked and she shook her head.

'You've never wanted to?'

'No. When Alice died, Gina worried there was no extended family. I told her I'd always be there for her kids. It seemed dumb at the time, but I guess that's what most parents do. They worry about protecting their kids for ever.'

'And now you'll look after these kids for ever? That's some promise.'

'Gina and Alice were my family. The kids are my family now.'

'Tell me how that happened? Why were you so close to Gina and her mother?'

She hesitated. There was something about the half-light, the warmth of the pillows and blankets of her bed-cum-seat, and Max's face being six inches from hers, that meant she either had to accept this closeness or withdraw completely.

She'd hardly spoken of her past. But now…

'When she was a kid my mother…drank too much,' she whispered. 'So did Alice.'

'Alice drank?' He frowned. 'Gina's mother? My aunt?'

'Alice used to say it ran in her family,' she whispered. 'The royal side. She had a huge fight with her parents and ended up in Australia. She was wild for a long time. With alcohol. Drugs maybe? I don't know. Anyway she got pregnant and that's when she met my mother. They were both on their own and pregnant and trying to stay clean. They were friends for a bit. After I was born my mother reverted, but Alice never touched a drop from the time she got pregnant. Whenever my mother was so ill she couldn't take care of me, Alice was there. In the end it was like Alice had three children. Gina, me and my mother. Only Gina and I grew up. My mother died when I was twelve.'

'I'm glad Alice was there for you,' Max said, his voice carefully neutral. 'It must have been really tough.'

'It was. But Alice made it less so. She had no support yet she managed to help Gina and I both through nursing. And when Gina met Donald…that was the wedding to end all weddings. It was our happy ever after.'

'But happy ever after is for fairy tales.'

'It is,' she murmured. 'But Alice died after Marc was born—she had an aneurism—thinking we were all happily settled. So she did have her happy ever after.'

'She was broke, though?'

'There was never any money.'

Max frowned. 'Our side of the family always thought she'd married well.'

'I suspect she told her parents that. She just wanted to be shot of them. She hated what the royal family stood for.'

'That makes two of us,' he said bleakly. 'Three counting my mother.' But then he shook his head, as if chastising himself for going down a road he didn't want to pursue.

'But you?' he said gently. 'How can you be happy?'

'I'm happy.'

'Have you ever had a boyfriend?'

Hang on a minute… What had that come from? 'Mind your own business.'

'I'd like to know.'

'You tell me yours, then,' she said astringently. 'And I'll tell you mine.'

'Okay,' he said surprisingly. 'I've had girlfriends.'

She shouldn't ask. But suddenly she was intrigued. 'Not serious?'

'They find out I have money and all of a sudden I'm desirable. It's a great turn-off.'

'That's tough,' she said, but her voice was loaded with irony. 'You know, I was actually engaged to be married when Gina and Donald were killed. Tom thought Dolores was bad enough, but when he found I intended to take the kids he couldn't run fast enough.'

'As you say—tough.'

'No,' she said evenly. 'These kids are my family, as much as if I'd borne them myself. If Tom didn't want them, then it was his problem.' She shrugged and smiled. 'And maybe I don't blame him. Three kids and dogs is a huge ask.'

'It's a huge ask of you.'

Her smile faded. 'Not so much. I love them to bits. And you… If you threaten their happiness—their security—you'll answer to me, Max de Gautier.'

'I'd never do that.'

They fell silent then, but it was a better silence. She felt strangely more at peace than she'd been in a long time. Which was dumb, she told herself. She was heading somewhere she'd never heard of and she had to stay on her guard.

But she wasn't totally responsible. She glanced across at the sleeping children and she thought in a few minutes the stewardess would bring them something to eat and she didn't need to work out how to pay for it.

And she was sitting beside Maxsim de Gautier. Any woman would feel okay sitting beside this man, she thought. There wasn't any chance he might be interested in her—what man would look twice at a woman loaded with three kids, a king-sized debt and a dog?—but she was woman enough to enjoy it while she had it.

'Why does saving Alp d'Estella matter so much to you?' she asked, suddenly curious.

'It just does.'

'No, but why?' she prodded. 'You've been brought up in France. Why do you still care about a little country your father or your grandfather walked away from?'

'I just…do.'

He wasn't telling the truth, she thought. Why? She stared at him, baffled.

'Tell me how you learned to milk cows?' she demanded, moving sideways, and the tension eased a little.

'That's easy. My mother was born on a dairy farm south of Paris. My maternal grandparents still live there. It's run by my uncle now, but it's great. I spent the greater part of my childhood there.'

'Your father's dead.'

The pleasure faded from his voice. 'I didn't have any contact with…either of the men my mother was involved with.'

'And your mother? Where's she?'

'In Paris.'

'When did—Thiérry's father—die?'

'When I was fifteen. I've always referred to him as my father too.'

'When did your brother die?'

'At the same time.'

'They were killed together?'

'In a car crash. Yes.'

'Oh, Max.'

She paused. There were things here she wanted to find out, but she didn't know the right questions. 'Do you build in Paris?' she said at last and he nodded.

'Yes.'

'What sort of buildings?'

'Big ones.'

'Skyscrapers?'

'Yes.'

She blinked. She'd never met anyone who built skyscrapers.

'Do you work for someone?'

'How do you mean?'

'Do you have a boss?'

'I…no. I had a fantastic boss. I became his off-sider but he died three years ago. I took over the firm.'

'So you're the head of a building firm that builds skyscrapers.'

'You could say that.'

'You're very rich?'

'You disapprove?'

'No.' She hesitated. 'Well, maybe I do, but I guess it's handy.'

'It certainly is,' he said, and he smiled.

He needed to cut that out, she thought crossly. She'd just started to focus and, wham, he smiled, and her thoughts scattered to the four winds.

She bit her lip and bulldozed on. 'So this boss… You said you went to a builder and asked him to teach you how to build.'

'I did.'

'But you had money from the royal family?'

'No. My father gambled using the royal name as collateral,' he said. 'It's taken years to get my mother free of debt. Yes, there was an offer to help from the old prince, but my mother would have died rather than accept it.'

'Tell me about the car crash?' she asked, tentatively now, unsure whether she was intruding, but needing to know.

He didn't take offence. It seemed he'd decided to answer as honestly as he could. 'My father was drunk,' he said bluntly. 'The royal curse. But unlike Alice, he didn't fight his addiction. The Alp d'Estella royal family is not a pedigree to be proud of.'

She thought about that for a moment and didn't like what she thought.

'Yet you're propelling Marc into the middle of it?'

'I suspect you'll be strong enough to keep him level-headed.'

'You didn't think that before you knew me,' she reasoned. 'Yet still you wanted Marc to come.'

'I did.' He was silent for a moment, deep in his own thoughts. 'Maybe I hadn't thought things through then, either,' he admitted. 'I knew Marc stood to inherit. I thought he was a child. It couldn't change his life so much, and there's so much at stake. But, yes, I've had qualms since and I've seen that you have the strength to ignore…what the palace can offer.'

She hesitated. 'You can't possibly know that's true.'

'And yet I do.'

'But you?' she said, pushing it further. 'How do I know you don't just want to be Prince Regent for money and power?'

'For the same reason I know you won't be seduced by money and power,' he said evenly, and lifted her fingers in the dark and held them against the side of his face. 'You know me and I know you.'

She felt…breathless. 'That's just plain dumb.'

'But it's true.'

'It's smooth talking,' she said crossly. She was out of her league and she knew it. 'I'm a nobody and you're Prince Regent.'

'Nobody's a nobody. Don't insult yourself.' And he didn't let go of her hand.

He was a restful man, she thought. He didn't feel the need to fill the silence. He let the silence do the talking for him.

But his hold on her hand was growing more…personal, and she wasn't quite sure the silent bit was all that wise. He was too close.

He was too male.

'So how did you get to own a construction company?' She finally managed to pull her hand away. He let his eyes fall to her fingers, then raised his eyes and smiled with a gentle mockery. He understood what she was doing.

'I told you. I went to—'

'A builder and got a job. How old were you?'

'Fifteen. The farm couldn't support us.'

'Your mother wasn't working?'

'My mother was in the same car crash that killed my father and Thiérry. She's paralysed from the waist down. The farm's not big enough to pay off my father's debts or my mother's medical bills.' He shrugged. 'The builder who employed me was an old friend of my grandparents, so, yes, I did have family connections, but I believe I've more than earned the position I'm in now.'

'So who's paying for these plane tickets?' she asked, frowning. 'You or the Alp d'Estella government?'

'I'll be reimbursed.'

'If this works out.'

'As you say.' His gaze met hers, steady and forthright. But there were things he wasn't telling her, she decided. There were things she had to figure out for herself.

'You need to wash,' he told her, cutting in on her thoughts. 'They'll be bringing breakfast.'

'At four in the afternoon?'

'You're in a whole new world. Welcome to breakfast.'

'I feel dizzy.'

'Just take one step at a time,' he said and touched her face in a gesture of reassurance that shouldn't be enough to send warmth right through her entire body. It shouldn't be enough but it definitely was. Her hand came up instinctively and met his. Once more he grasped her fingers in his and held.

This was a gesture of reassurance, she told herself frantically. No more.

'It'll be okay,' he said.

'Will it?'

'Yes.'

'I don't see how I can fit in. But I won't leave the children.'

'Of course you won't.'

'But to stay in this place…'

The hold on her hand was suddenly compelling. 'Pippa, I won't increase your burden. I promise you that. Let's just take every day as it comes and we'll see what happens.'

'But—'

'It's okay, Pippa.' He stared down at her in the half light, and his grip firmed, strong and sure.

The silence stretched out.

She gazed up at him, waiting…

'Would you mind if I kiss you?' he asked.

Her heart missed a beat. Would she mind?

'No,' she whispered, for some dumb, crazy reason that for ever after she couldn't fathom. But say it she did. For some things were inevitable.

Like the touch of Max's mouth on her lips.

She shouldn't have been expecting it—but she was. She'd been expecting it since that night by the fireside. She'd been…wanting it. And here it was.

The feel of him… The taste of him… The glorious sensation of melting into him in the dim light.

It was a culmination of circumstance, she told herself hazily. It was the warmth of these wonderful seats, after being cold for every waking moment. It was the hazy feeling of having just woken from sleep to find him beside her. It was the softness and luxury of alpaca blankets and goose-down pillows.

More. It was the strength of the man beside her, and the way his smile lit his eyes. It was the strength of his voice as it reassured her. It was the sense of being protected as she'd never been protected.

It was just… Max.

The moment was so seductive that she'd have had to be inhuman not to respond, and of course she responded. Her need was overwhelming. Her face lifted as if compelled, and her lips met his. Her hands rose to hold his face, getting the angle right, deepening the kiss, taking as well as giving…

Losing herself in the wonderment of him.

The kiss went on and on. Endless. It was a drifting, sensuous pleasure that lifted her out of her cloud of indecision and uncertainty and worry, and left nothing but pleasure.

He'd said it was okay. For now she'd believe him. Unwise or not, it was all she could do.

She surrendered herself to the kiss absolutely and in those few magic moments, before reality reasserted itself…well, those few moments were a gift to treasure.

They might be part of an unwise fantasy, but they were magic, all the same.

She was heading for a fairy tale, she thought mistily.

Anything could happen.

Breakfast happened.

'We didn't mean it,' she said breathlessly as the lights went up.

'I meant it,' he said and he smiled.

'Well, I didn't,' she muttered as she took herself off to the bathroom. 'This is just…ridiculous.'

CHAPTER FIVE

THEY got busy after that, which was just as well, and then the plane landed. From the moment the wheels touched the runway, the sensation of being in a fairy tale intensified until Pippa was pinching herself to believe she was awake. Had Max just kissed her? Had she just been transformed, from frog to princess?

Weird.

Normal passengers got to descend the steps from the plane and immerse themselves in the muddle of luggage location and ongoing transport. Not so Pippa and her little family.

For a start as the plane came to a halt there was an announcement. 'Could passengers remain in their seats to allow the Alp d'Estella royal family to leave the plane.'

It took a few disoriented seconds before Pippa realised the royal family was them. That the airline staff were standing in what seemed a guard of honour to welcome them.

The children had been fast asleep as they'd landed and they were still half asleep when they left the plane. Max carried Claire and Sophie, and Pippa led a dazed Marc.

'I don't want Pippa carrying anything,' Max growled to the nearest steward as Pippa went to lift her holdall. 'She's hurt her back. And our very elderly dog is in the hold. Could you locate her as soon as possible, please?'

They were two tiny instances of Max caring, Pippa thought. Her back was better. She'd forgotten it, but Max hadn't.

Pippa, who'd hardly been cared for in her life, felt a sting of tears as she reached the red carpet to find Dolores already being invited to leave her doggy crate. She stooped and hugged her dog, then turned and watched Max juggle a sleepy twin in each arm, and tease Marc a little as they gave her time to reacquaint herself with Dolores.

Tears were dumb. She should be soaking up every single thing. The ladies of Tanbarook would never believe her, she thought, and that made her tears change to a smile. Photographers were everywhere. What would be the reaction if Pippa's face was plastered over the news-stand back in Tanbarook?

'What's funny?' Max asked.

A limousine was waiting at the edge of red carpet, its uniformed chauffeur saluting. Even Dolores looked stunned. Her nose was sniffing the warm air. Sun!

'It's warm,' Marc breathed and stooped to inform Dolores. 'It's warm, Dolores. We're going to a castle and it's warm.'

'I want Tanbarook to see us now,' Pippa whispered and Max chuckled.

'You want a family shot for the tabloids? Marc, hold Pippa's hand and lean against me. Leave Dolores there—we'll arrange ourselves around her.' Max edged close to Pippa, and before she knew it he'd organised them into a tight shot.

'Smile,' he told Pippa.

'Why?' She was astounded.

'We're the closest thing this country has to a royal family. Tanbarook *is* going to see you. Smile.'

She managed a weakish sort of smile but she was so confused her head was threatening to spin off. 'I'm not family,' she muttered, staring down at Dolores, who was licking Max's boots. 'Isn't Dolores supposed to go into quarantine until she's vet-checked?'

'We had a vet check her before she left. She's a royal dog now. And you're as royal as I am. We're royal by association. The royal family.'

He was smiling at her as photographers snapped around her and she felt her color rising by the minute. 'I should be like the governess, standing ten steps back.'

'Same with me. But you won't let me leave, and if you leave the kids and Dolores will howl.'

'I wouldn't,' Marc said, affronted. 'But Dolores might,' he conceded.

'There you go. Smile,' he ordered again. 'Pippa, there's only one thing worse than publicity, and that's publicity when you're glowering. It makes you look like you're constipated.'

She choked. 'Gee, thanks.'

'I just thought I'd mention it. So smile.'

'I'm smiling,' she said through gritted teeth. 'And neither the kids or Dolores are scared of you. They think you're the next best thing to Father Christmas.'

'Little they know.'

'There's the ogre side of you as well?'

'I'm not exactly a family man.'

'Why not?' It was out before she thought about it—a direct response to something she needed to know. To something that had to be sorted before she took one step further.

And Max's smile faded.

Why not? he wondered, as the cameras clicked around them and he tried to resurrect his smile. Why had he never taken that last step? From lover to husband…

Marriages were fraught. His mother's marriage had led to irretrievable disaster. 'Don't ever marry,' she'd said to him over and over. 'You can't ever know how someone will turn out. Oh, Max, take lovers, do what you need to be happy, but be so careful…'

He'd hardly decided not to marry because of his mother's experiences, but then, it had made him so careful that such a decision had almost been made for him.

'You're not gay, are you?' Pippa asked thoughtfully and his thoughts hit a brick wall. He turned and stared at her. Stunned.

'What did you say?'

'Smile,' she reminded him. The photographers were clicking from every angle. 'I was asking whether you're gay.'

'Didn't I just kiss you?'

'That's proof you're not gay?'

'Yes,' he said, revolted. 'It wasn't a platonic kiss.'

'No,' she said thoughtfully, 'but then I didn't really inspect it for platonic. Maybe I wouldn't recognise it if I saw it. I lead a very sheltered life.'

She was teasing him, he thought. She was trying to get him to react, here and now, in front of the country's press.

'Shut up,' he said, carefully pasting on his smile and carefully no longer looking at her. 'One more word, Phillippa Donohue, and I'll set the twins down and teach you what a platonic kiss isn't.'

'In front of everyone? You wouldn't dare.'

'No,' he said, sounding regretful. 'You're right. I wouldn't. But only because it'd make our lives even more complicated than they already are. Which is very complicated indeed.'

Okay, so that little interlude made her flustered. The stilted welcome speech made by an official made her more flustered still. And the ride from airport to castle, in the back of the limousine with Max in the seat opposite, the children snoozing beside them and Dolores draped over their feet, made her even more flustered.

'That was a dumb thing to do,' she managed about ten minutes after they'd left the airport, which was the time it had taken to figure anything at all to say.

'What was?'

'You kissing me.'

'I didn't kiss you in front of the photographers,' he said virtuously. 'I wanted to but I had my arms full of twins.'

'You kissed me on the plane.'

'That was necessary. Because I suspected that you suspected I was gay. And I was right. Not that my kiss seemed to reassure you.'

'It reassured me,' she said hastily and went back to staring out the car window.

The scenery was amazing.

She'd read about these four tiny countries. There'd been a fuss in the Australian press when Pippa's countrywoman had married the Crown Prince of Alp d'Azuri. There'd also been a write-up and potted history of how these countries had come to be, and she'd found time to reread it on the internet before she'd come.

A king in a large neighbouring country, way back in the sixteenth century, had had five sons. The boys had grown up warring and the old king had foreseen ruin as the sons had vied for the Crown.

So he'd pre-empted trouble. He'd carved four separate countries from his southern border, and told his younger sons that the cost of their own principality was lifelong allegiance to their oldest brother.

His plan hadn't worked, the article had told her. Granting whole counties to men with a lust for war was hardly a guarantee of wise rule. The four princes and their descendants had brought four wonderful countries to the brink of ruin.

Ruin? Pippa stared out of the car window and saw lush river valleys, towering mountains, quaint cottages, herds of cream and white cows, the odd goat, tiny settlements that might almost have come from a photograph from a hundred years before. It didn't look…ruined.

'It's beautiful,' she breathed.

'If you like postcards,' Max said shortly. 'But the reality's less than beautiful. You were cold and hungry this winter. These people are cold and hungry every winter.'

She glowered again, suspecting pressure. 'Don't you dare show me starving peasants. I won't be responsible.'

'I couldn't anyway,' he conceded. 'It's summer and the harvest this year will be a good one. Things are okay at the moment.'

'But not for long?'

'Yes, for long. If we can pull this off.' He looked down at the sleeping Marc and his mouth quirked.

'I won't—'

'No. You agree to nothing. Let's just see how it goes. Meanwhile if you look to your right you'll see the castle…now.'

'Oh.'

As an exclamation it was totally inadequate, but it was all she could think of. Built into the side of one of the towering alps, the castle was a mass of gleaming white stone, set against the purple of the mountains behind. She stared out, stunned, as the castle grew larger against its magnificent backdrop. It was all turrets, battlements and towers, like something straight out of a fairy story.

She nudged Marc, but he'd settled back into sleep. They were now in the middle of the children's night and the future Crown Prince of Alp d'Estella had drifted back where he belonged.

Frustrated, she bent over to wake the twins, but Max caught her hand.

'Leave them. They'll see enough of it in the future.'

There was something in his voice that caught her. She stared across at him, and then turned and looked again at the castle. The battlements seemed to be looming above them, towering over the tiny town nestled underneath.

'You don't like it,' she said.

'I don't like what it represents.'

'What does it represent?'

'Too much power. Too much money by too few people.'

'You're rich yourself.'

'I earned my money through hard work,' he said shortly. 'The princes in this place got their money by taxing their people until they bled. You'd think I'd have anything to do with that?'

She thought about it, wondering. Thinking back to the family tree.

'Your grandfather left the palace and went to France?'

'Yes. But he's not really my grandfather.'

'So you've had no contact with the palace?'

'I…no.'

'Does that mean maybe?'

'My…my father did,' Max said shortly. 'More fool him.'

'You blame the palace for what happened to your father? And to Thiérry?'

'My mother does and she should know.'

'Right,' Pippa said and cast an uneasy glance down at Marc. This was getting tricky. 'So if Marc takes on the Crown you'll hold Thiérry's death against him?'

'That's ridiculous.'

'As ridiculous as staring out at that great hunk of stone and saying that's what killed your brother?'

'I didn't say—'

'No, but you meant,' she said. 'I look at that castle and think fairy tale. But you look and see a dead brother. A psychologist could have a field-day with that.'

'A field-day!'

'Yes, you know—a day when everything's on show. Like your emotions now.'

'They're not on show.'

'No?'

'No.'

She grinned. She had the great Maxsim de Gautier flummoxed. Excellent.

'This is serious,' he told her.

'Nonsense,' she said soundly, beginning to relax. 'This is fun.'

It might have fun potential but it was so grand it took her breath away.

The limousine swept inside the castle grounds and pulled to a halt in a vast forecourt ringed by fountains. The chauffeur moved swiftly, opening the door for them, even saluting.

Ignoring Max's protest—her back really was better—she gathered the nearest twin—Claire—into her arms and climbed out. At the sight of what lay ahead she gasped. She stared around her for a couple of awed moments while her stomach sank at the enormity of where she'd found herself.

There were thirty or more servants forming a guard of honour to the grand front entrance—vast marble steps set between marble columns flanking doors wide enough to accommodate a Sherman tank. The servants were dressed as the type of domestic servants Pippa had seen on television. The women were in severe black with frilled white aprons and white caps. The men were in total black, or, even more amazingly, red and black livery.

'You're kidding?' Pippa breathed to Max. 'This is something out of a movie.'

'These people take royalty seriously,' Max said severely, and Pippa gulped and nodded, stifling an inappropriate desire to giggle.

'I can see that they do.'

A middle-aged man was standing apart from the servants, dressed in what looked like a military uniform, heavily decorated. He was big and heavy set, with a handle-bar moustache that made Pippa want to giggle again.

'Welcome home, Your Highness,' he told Max in careful English and Max winced.

'I'm not Your Highness until I'm sworn in as Regent, and this is not my home.' He gestured to Marc who was stirring into wakefulness in his arms. He set Marc onto his feet and reached back into the car to collect Sophie. 'This is the new Crown Prince of Alp d'Estella and his sisters. I'd like to take them straight to the nursery. It's been prepared?'

'Of course.' The man looked at Marc for a long moment, an enigmatic expression on his face. Then he shrugged and turned his attention to Pippa. 'This would be the children's nanny?'

'I'm their guardian,' Pippa said, more firmly than she felt, and she clutched Claire so hard that the little girl muttered a protest.

'I see,' the man said, assessing her from her toes up. She was wearing faded jeans and a comfortable windcheater. Max should have warned her, she thought, starting to feel vaguely hysterical. She needed a tiara or six. 'We'll prepare a bedroom for you in the Queen's wing,' the man said and she forgot about tiaras.

'Where are the children sleeping?'

'In the nursery.'

'Is that in the Queen's wing?'

'No, but—'

'I sleep where the children sleep,' she said. 'Isn't that right, Max?'

'Of course it is,' Max said. 'Pippa, this is Carver Levout. Carver is Chief of Staff here. Carver, this is Miss Phillippa Donohue, the children's guardian. Whatever Pippa says regarding the children's welfare goes.'

'Yes, sir,' the man said woodenly, but the glance he gave

Pippa wasn't wooden. It was appraising. It made Pippa stop feeling like giggling. She shivered.

'You'll be fine here,' Max said bracingly. 'Carver will introduce you to the staff and they'll look after you. I guess you'll all need to sleep. I'll carry the kids up to their bed before I leave.'

She froze. 'Before you go where?'

'To a hotel down in the village. I'll check with you tomorrow that you have everything you need.'

He was the picture of innocence, she thought. His nerve was breathtaking. 'Excuse me, but you're staying here,' she managed.

'As I agreed to,' he said smoothly. 'In the hotel in the village.'

'You're staying at the castle.'

'I never said—'

'You did,' she said, more bluntly than was polite but she wasn't feeling polite. She was damned if she was going to be left alone with…Carver? What sort of name was that? He even waxed his moustache, she thought. Urk.

They were all waiting for Max to reply. Pippa and thirty servants and Carver. 'Pippa, I'm hardly going far,' Max said reasonably. 'I'm five minutes' drive away. I said I'd stay in Alp d'Estella. I didn't say I'd stay at the castle.'

He was talking to her as if she were dumb. Right, she thought. She was fine with dumb. But it was going to be dumb and stubborn. Without a word she climbed back into the car with Claire, settled the twin on the seat beside her before holding her hands out for Sophie. 'Marc, pop back in the car, love. We're all staying where Mr de Gautier is staying.'

Max looked taken aback. They all looked taken aback. Except Dolores who hadn't shifted out of the car yet. 'Pardon?' Max demanded.

'You heard. Where you stay, we stay.'

'Why?'

'Not because you kissed me,' she muttered, lowering her voice so the assembled reception committee couldn't hear. 'But because this place gives me the heebie-jeebies. I'm not royal. I'm not staying here.'

'That's ridiculous. You don't need to be royal to stay.'

'Neither do you have to be a commoner to go. But if you're going, then I'm going. You got me here under false pretences.'

'I didn't.'

'You did.' She glanced again at the rows of servants and she quailed. There wasn't much that spooked Pippa Donohue, but she was spooked now. She hugged Sophie too hard, and the child muttered a sleepy protest. 'Max, I mean what I say,' she said, trying not to sound belligerent. Trying to sound matter-of-fact. 'Hush, Sophie, we're nearly home. Max says it's just five minutes' drive away.'

Max stared down at her, baffled. 'You have to stay here.'

'You're going to make me, how?'

'It's ridiculous.'

'It is, isn't it?' she agreed. 'You said you'd stay.'

'I didn't.'

'If you didn't then it's semantics and you tricked me. I don't like being tricked.'

'Pippa, I can't stay here.'

'Then neither can we.' She looked behind him. 'You know, everyone's listening to this. It's pretty undignified, don't you think? If I were you I'd come to a decision, and there's only one decision to reach.'

'I don't want to stay in this place,' he told her. He'd tried to make his voice matter-of-fact, but it didn't work. She heard a tinge of desperation behind it, and it almost moved her. But then Pippa glanced down at the child in her arms, at Marc who was looking confused, at Claire on the seat beside her and at Dolores at her feet.

Then she looked at Moustache. She didn't know why but Carver Levout made her nervous and she had nothing to go on here but her instincts. She was responsible for this little family. She couldn't afford to be swayed by Max's desperation.

'If there are reasons you can't stay here, then they hold true for us all,' she whispered. 'If I'd known you were afraid to stay then I'd never have agreed to come.'

'I'm not afraid.'

'Then what are you?'

'I just…hate it.'

'That's just as bad.'

'Pippa—'

'It's only stone and wood and thirty or so servants. Oh, and I hear tell it has three swimming pools. So if it's not scary, it might be fun.'

'But Thiérry…' He stopped short. His brother's name was an involuntary exclamation, Pippa thought, and she wondered why.

'Where does Thiérry come into this?'

'He doesn't.' He pressed his lips closed as though that was the end of the matter. She stared up at him for a moment and then thought maybe that was a plan. She pressed her own lips together and looked straight ahead.

Standoff.

She hadn't counted on Sophie. She'd stirred into wakefulness in Pippa's arms, wriggled until she could see and she'd looked beyond Max to the castle. 'We're here,' she said sleepily. 'It's just like my picture books. But bigger. Why aren't we getting out of the car? Claire, Claire, wake up.'

Right on cue Claire woke. 'We're here?' she demanded. 'We're at the castle?'

'Yes, but Pippa won't let us stay,' Marc said, trying to figure it out. ''Cos Max won't stay and she's scared of all these people.'

'She's not scared,' Max said shortly. 'She's just pigheaded.'

'There's two of us being pigheaded,' she told him. 'And I'm not backing down.'

'Hell, Pippa—'

'You stay or we go.'

'You could all go.' It was Carver, standing behind them, listening intently.

'We're all staying,' Max snapped.

She stared at him. She'd won, she thought, but it didn't feel like winning. What was it that he was afraid of?

But Carver was waiting. He had to have an answer, and she wasn't going to let him see she was rattled. 'Then that's settled,' she said smoothly. 'Okay, we all need to be introduced. Sophie, you take one of Max's hands and, Claire, you take the other. Marc, you walk in front. You guys go along the row of people here and find out who everyone is.'

'You need to be introduced too,' said Marc.

'I'm not royal,' Pippa said. 'I'll come up behind and bow and scrape to anyone above second footman.'

'This isn't a joke,' Max snapped.

'It's not,' she agreed, but she smiled. Only she knew the effort it cost her. 'But neither is it Greek tragedy. Let's make this fun, Max. Let's go.'

Max had no intention of making it fun. He was stiffly formal, right up until they were shown the nursery and left alone.

'You rest,' he said. 'I'll see you at dinner.'

'If you leave the palace, then we're out of here, even if we have to walk,' Pippa warned him, still trying to sound pigheaded but suspecting she just sounded intimidated. Liveried footmen had deposited their sad-looking luggage in a dressing room big enough to hold clothes for a small army. A couple of maids were unpacking. At the thought of the scant possessions they were unpacking Pippa felt like sinking.

She shouldn't be clutching at Max, she thought, but she had no choice. He was her lifeline to her other life.

'You've made that clear,' Max said stiffly. 'But the children need rest and so do I. I'll see you at dinner.'

'Um, don't leave me,' she muttered but he was already turning away.

She was alone. With three kids and two maids and a dog.

There was too much to think of here. All she wanted to think of was Max. She wanted to run after him. She'd hurt him by insisting he stayed here, she thought, but what was she to do?

The casual friendliness was gone, replaced by a stiff formality she couldn't understand.

Where was the man who had kissed her?

She couldn't run after him, and she had to forget the kiss. That was just a dopey thing to do in the dark on the plane, she told herself, but there was a part of her that was saying it was no such thing. It wasn't just a kiss.

Yes, it was.

Whatever, she told herself harshly. There was no time for wondering about Max now.

They were in a vast school-room-cum-sitting room, with desks at one end and huge settees around a fire at the other end. It was hardly cold enough to warrant a fire, but Dolores headed straight to it and Pippa looked at the logs piled high at the side with longing. If she could transport those to Tanbarook…

What else? There were doors leading off the main room, and the kids were opening them. They led to individual bedrooms, each with a massive four-poster bed.

'Wow,' said Marc. He approached the first bed with caution. It was six feet or more across and almost three feet high, hung with crimson velvet and gold brocade. Marc clambered up and tugged the twins up to join him.

The three kids wriggled into the pile of pillows mounded against the bed head, like puppies exploring a new basket. 'It's really soft,' Sophie called wonderingly, giving a tentative bounce. 'Pippa, will you sleep here with us?'

'Sure,' she said.

'Excuse me, miss,' one of the maids—the oldest one?—said, in tentative English.

'I speak your language,' Pippa said, trying out her language skills. To her delight it seemed to work. The woman's face relaxed a little and she reverted. 'Well, then… Mr Levout said we were to show you to the bedroom at the end of this wing.'

'I'm not sure why Mr Levout thinks it's important, but I'm sleeping here.'

There was a touch of hand-wringing at that. It seemed an effort to say it, but the woman finally succeeded. 'Mr Levout won't like it.' It sounded like a threat.

'Then the kids can sleep in the bedroom Mr Levout chose for me. We'll all sleep there.'

There were three gasps of dismay from under the mound of pillows, and two gasps of dismay from the maids. 'Mr Levout will think it's inappropriate.'

'I'll explain it to Mr Levout.'

'You can't.' They looked afraid, Pippa thought incredulously. Why?

'I'll explain it's nothing to do with you. I'll tell him it's just me being pigheaded.'

'Miss, we'll get into trouble if we don't do what Mr Levout wishes.'

Trouble? These two were well past retirement age, Pippa thought. What could Levout do? Sack them? Surely they'd be looking forward to retirement anyway.

She took a deep breath. She was probably only here for a month, she thought, so there was no need to make trouble when it could be avoided. But if, she thought, *if* Marc did end up as Crown Prince, then the ground rules had to be set now. Even if these two were about to retire.

'I gather Marc…' She caught herself. 'I gather His Highness, Prince Marc, is to be the new Crown Prince of Alp d'Estella. I'm his legal guardian. Any decision regarding the children will thus be made by me. Not by Mr Levout. Not by anyone else. Do I make myself clear?'

Two jaws sagged.

'Well?'

'Oh, my dear,' the oldest woman said, and she beamed. 'Oh, yes, miss.'

'You ought to stand up to him,' the other woman breathed. 'No one else does.' She looked to where the kids were enthusiastically bouncing on their four-poster. 'He'd have a heart attack if he saw that.'

Pippa turned and looked at the kids. They'd tugged off their shoes before bouncing. As guardian, could she demand anything more? 'They're allowed to bounce,' she said.

'Oh, yes, miss,' the oldest maid breathed and she chuckled. 'I have a grandson who loves bouncing.'

'You have a grandson?'

'I have three.'

'Excuse me, but why are you still working as a maid?'

There was blank incomprehension. 'We need to,' the woman said at last. 'Jobs are scarce.'

'You don't have pensions?'

'Pensions?'

'Well,' Pippa said and set her shoulders. 'Maybe it's just as well we came after all.'

What was she saying?

The maids left soon after and they were left alone.

The children bounced. They explored every inch of the nursery. Then the four of them—Dolores excused herself as she'd found a fire—took themselves further, checking school rooms, bedroom upon bedroom, living rooms, libraries, great halls, ballrooms… They knocked at each door and when there was no response they peered inside.

They grew more and more awed.

They found the inside swimming pool. It was huge, with a special lap lane designed with wave blockers so the water stayed calm all the time.

'I want a swim,' Marc breathed.

'Tomorrow.' Pippa gazed round with awe. 'Let's go outside and see if we can find the other two pools.'

'Where is everyone?' Marc asked. 'All those people.'

'Below stairs, I guess,' Pippa said, giving a nervous giggle. 'That's what they say on telly about where the servants live. But take no notice of me. I'm guessing.'

'Should we go downstairs and say hello?'

'I guess we said hello when we arrived,' Pippa said cautiously. 'I'm not too sure anyone wants to say hello after that. Let's go outside. It seems…safer.'

CHAPTER SIX

MAX spent two hours with Levout, which were two hours more than he wanted to spend with the man, but there were practicalities to work out. If he was stuck here then he might as well sort them out now. He emerged from the castle offices feeling vaguely tainted. He hated being related to this family. So many wrongs…

But at least now they could be sorted. He'd watched Levout trying to hide dismay as he'd gone through the initial changes he wanted instigated, and he thought, You don't know the half of it. These were just palace changes. Tomorrow he'd start looking wider.

But now he was starting to be nervous about Pippa's whereabouts. She'd threatened she'd leave if he didn't stick around and he knew her well enough to realise she'd carry through with a threat. If she thought he was no longer in the castle…

He'd check. She'd probably be resting, he decided, and he headed for the nursery, climbing the vast staircase three stairs at a time.

The nursery was empty.

He rang the bell and an elderly housemaid appeared, looking apprehensive.

'Where are the children?' he asked.

'They're with Pippa. I mean…Miss Phillippa.'

'Did she ask you to call her Pippa?'

'Oh, yes,' the woman said, and her nervousness disappeared

in a smile. 'I said to call me Beatrice but she said I was old enough to be her mother and she'd only call me Beatrice if I called her Pippa. She said that goes for all the staff, but we talked about it and thought maybe we wouldn't call her that in front of Mr Levout.'

'Very wise.' What was the gossip below stairs? he wondered. They probably knew more than he did. 'Is she in her room?' he asked.

'She says she's sleeping here in the nursery.'

He stared at the enormous nursery. It was more like a gallery than a nursery, he thought. If he'd been stuck in here as a kid, alone, he'd have had nightmares. Maybe Pippa was right. But…

'Are there enough beds?'

'There are five bedrooms. But Pippa says they only need one.'

'That's ridiculous.'

'Yes, sir.'

He looked at Beatrice, who looked back at him, expressionless.

'You don't agree?'

'I have grandchildren,' she said gently. 'If one of them was the new Crown Prince, maybe I'd be sleeping with him, too. And maybe the dog as well.'

She met his gaze, without a hint of a smile.

'You're saying it's unsafe.'

'No, sir. At least… ' She hesitated. 'Sir, I'm only a maid. But if it was my child who was Crown Prince, I'd hold him close.'

'Because…'

'I couldn't say, sir,' she said softly, turning back to her unpacking, leaving him vaguely worried. What was she telling him?

He'd promised Pippa they'd be safe. Was he sure? He thought back to Levout's concerns. A lot of petty officialdom stood to lose substantial income if what Max planned came to pass.

Yeah, but they'd had a prince on the throne for four hundred years. Surely they couldn't object—or do anything about it if they did object?

All the same, suddenly he thought that Pippa and Dolores sleeping with Marc wasn't such a bad idea.

That worried him as well.

Dammit, these weren't Pippa's children. Here he was, asking her to be responsible again.

Where was she?

'They were on the south lawn a little time ago,' Beatrice offered. 'They were playing in the fountain.'

The fountain? The huge marble monstrosity with dragons and warriors fighting it out on the front lawn?

He crossed to the French windows and stared down at the fountain-cum-sculpture in the middle of the immaculately manicured lawn.

There was no Pippa and no children but beside the fountain was a muddle of discarded clothes, and a patch of pristine lawn had been muddied.

Beatrice walked over to the window and peered where he was peering.

'Our head gardener treats every blade of grass as a treasure. To let the children muddy it…'

'You think he'll be angry?' Max stared at the mud in bemusement. 'Whipping at dawn? You've met Pippa.'

'I've met Pippa,' the woman said and she ventured a cautious smile. 'Maybe you're right. Maybe he won't be angry. It's so wonderful to have children in the palace again. Maybe she has enough joy in her to charm even the gardening staff.'

She did. By the time Max reached the offending puddle the head gardener, a man in his seventies, was on his knees, carefully washing mud from the lawn. Before Max could reach him, another man appeared with half a dozen planks.

'What's going on?' he asked, expecting complaints, but none was forthcoming.

'Miss Pippa and the children enjoyed the fountain,' the gardener said mildly. 'So we thought we'd build a small deck so they could get in and out without muddying the lawn.'

A deck. For a fountain where there were swimming pool alternatives.

'Did you tell them about the swimming pools?'

'Oh, yes,' the gardener said and he chuckled. 'The lady asked would I prefer to paddle in a normal pool or duck in and out of dragons. I'd never thought of it like that. But, yes, I could see her point.'

This was amazing. After only two hours in the castle Pippa was already instigating changes. And making friends. Max glanced cautiously around, thinking of Carver Levout. Chief of this whole administration. 'Has Mr Levout given the okay?' he asked.

'No, sir, he hasn't,' the man told him, hauling his cap from his head in a gesture of deference. 'But Miss Pippa said we could refer this to you. She said as Prince Regent you're in charge now. Miss Pippa says she's sure you'll agree. Do you not, sir? Do you want us to stop?'

He didn't want anything. He surely didn't want to be so enmeshed in the workings of this place that he had to think about things like decking.

He had no intention of being hands-on in this place. There might be issues with how Carver ran the palace but he was competent, and Max intended to save his energy for the big battles.

'Where is she now?' he asked, and if his voice was a bit grim he couldn't help it.

'Miss Pippa saw the cows coming in to be milked,' the gardener said. 'I believe they've gone to the dairy to help. Sir, do you wish us to stop building the decking?'

What the heck? 'You've started now. You might as well continue.'

The man smiled. 'Yes, sir,' he said.

Pippa and the children were indeed in the dairy, perched on a top rail overlooking the cows going into the bails. The twins and Marc were dressed in knickers and nothing else. Pippa was in jeans and a T-shirt. Her jeans were rolled up to the knees and her T-shirt was knotted under her breasts, leaving her midriff bare. They were all dripping wet.

They saw him and they waved him to come closer. No sound, though. They knew their cows.

'Hi,' Pippa whispered. 'I thought this'd be really foreign but it's just like home. Without Peculiar.'

Peculiar. He thought back to the cow who'd be even now causing trouble in Bert's yard. 'I bet there's another Peculiar here,' he said darkly. 'There always is.'

'There isn't,' she said. 'I've been talking to the guys here and they're saying these girls are really placid. I'm thinking we might take a few test-tubes home.'

'Test-tubes?'

'For cross-cultural fertilization,' she said patiently. 'Don't you think that'd be ace?'

'We might get some calves just like these,' Marc said. The kids were glowing, high on warmth and good food and fun and excitement. They'd been good-looking kids back in Australia, Max thought, but now he looked at their beaming faces and he felt a twinge of…pride? They hadn't complained once, he thought. He'd seen them tired and hungry and right out of their comfort zone but still they giggled and looked out on life as an adventure. Marc would make a great prince.

Pippa had done a wonderful job of raising them.

Would she agree that they stay?

'Nothing's decided,' Pippa said before he could open his mouth.

'How the hell do you know what I'm thinking?'

'I can see it. I look in your eyes and I see this plus this plus this equals…ooh, let's see…sixty-seven? And then you open your mouth and out it comes. Sixty-seven. Easy.'

He didn't like that it was easy. He was feeling more and more confused.

'Well, how do you understand what these guys are saying?' he asked. 'And the gardener. How did you talk him into building decking?'

'He's building decking?'

'To protect his grass.'

'What a sweetie.'

'You talk French? I didn't know you spoke French?'

'I talk a type of French,' she said. 'I've always been told it's a hybrid, some sort of rural dialect. Now I've discovered where it comes from.' She beamed. 'Here. Well, of course it makes sense, but how lucky's that?'

'I don't understand.'

'Alice,' she said simply. Then, as he looked even more confused, she explained. 'Alice left her family when she was little more than a kid. She got into trouble, she ended up having Gina and being stuck with me, and she made the best of our life together. But there must have been a part of her that was homesick, for every night she'd read to the two of us in her own language. It became fun—it was Gina's and my secret language when we were at school. After Gina got married we had to stop—Donald kept thinking we were talking about him—but it's still a part of me. Finding there's a whole country that speaks it is a joy.'

'It's fun,' Marc said in the same language, and Max stared.

'The kids too?'

'Gina started it with Marc, maybe to make Alice happy. I kept it up. It's always seemed comforting. Some sort of a link. And now we know who we're linked to.'

Wow. He'd brought back family who spoke the language. The enormity of this almost took his breath away.

His task was suddenly a thousand per cent easier.

'Why didn't you tell me?'

'You didn't speak it to us. I honestly didn't know what it was until I heard it here.'

'I do speak it,' he said, switching effortlessly. 'My mother… well, there was an insistence that Thiérry learned it and it was easier for us to practise together.'

She frowned and tugged the two little bodies on either side of her closer so they couldn't topple off the rail. 'So we speak the language—sort of. Why does that make you relieved? I can understand pleased, but not relieved.'

'I was just pleasantly surprised.'

'And relieved.'

'You can't read my feelings.'

'Yes, I can.'

'Then don't,' he snapped, and the cow nearest him swerved his head and gave him a reproachful look.

'Shh,' Sophie whispered. 'We have to be quiet until the cows get to know us.'

'I wonder if I can help milk,' Pippa said.

'You surely don't want to.'

'No.' She peeped a smile. 'But it might make Mr Levout happier. He obviously thinks I'm one of the workers.'

'He's got another think coming. Speaking of which…he's having dinner with us tonight.'

'Really?'

'Really.'

'Eggs and toast in the nursery?'

'Don't push your luck. Do you have anything to wear to a formal dinner?'

She stared. She looked down at her dripping jeans and her bare feet.

She giggled.

'Sure,' she said. 'As formal as you like. I'll wear my dry jeans.'

'Pippa…'

'Don't fret,' she said. The rail they were perched on was four feet high. He was standing right beside her, so she was just above his head height. She reached out and ran her fingers through his hair, an affectionate ruffle such as one she might have given Marc. Or Sophie or Claire. So there was no need for him to react…as he did. 'I won't disgrace you,' she said.

'I know that,' he said stiffly and moved away.

'I won't do anything else either,' she told him, quite kindly. 'There's no need to back off like a frightened horse.'

'I did not!'

'Yes, you did,' Marc said. 'Don't you like it when Pippa rubs your head?'

'No. Yes. I…'

'He doesn't like getting his feathers ruffled, kids,' she told them, turning her attention back to the cows. 'Leave him be to settle. What time's dinner, Mr de Gautier?'

'Seven. The kids will be fed at six. And before you say you and the kids are sticking together, Beatrice, the older of the two maids in the children's wing, will sit with the children. If they give the slightest sign of needing you she'll fetch you. But by the amount of excitement they've had today I suspect they'll be well asleep.'

'So might I be.'

'You slept for fifteen hours on the plane. I've got a crink on my shoulder to prove it.'

'On your shoulder?'

'Where your head landed. You fell sideways.'

'I did not.'

'No, you didn't,' he agreed cordially and she glowered.

'How can I fall sideways in a first class seat?' she demanded.

'You wriggle in your sleep.'

'Well, you snore.'

'I don't!'

'Oh, yes, you do. We need an independent arbitrator. Failing that I refuse to accept responsibility for your crink.'

'I accept your lack of responsibility,' he said and grinned. 'But about dinner. You think you might stay awake until seven?'

'I'm pretty hungry,' she told him. 'But I guess I can always pinch a toast finger from the kids to keep me going.'

She was gorgeous.

Max left them and walked slowly back to the castle entrance, past the gardeners busily erecting their decking, past the pile of kids' clothing…

The castle had subtly changed already.

She was gorgeous.

They were all great, he told himself hastily. The kids and Pippa would breathe new life into this place. He just had to persuade them to stay and things would be fine. The kids could have a glorious time. The load of responsibility would be lifted from Pippa's shoulders and he could leave and get on with his life.

For the first time since he'd been approached after Bernard's death, the awful feeling of being trapped was lessening.

Okay, he still needed to be Regent. He'd accepted that. But back in Paris his construction company was waiting, and in four short weeks he could be back there. He could keep on with the work he loved. He could cope with the legalities of the regency from a distance. He could stay low-key. Okay, he'd accept a bit of publicity now as he persuaded Pippa to keep the children here, but after that he could disappear into the background.

His mother need never be brought into it. It was a solution that suited them all. It felt great.

Or it should feel great. There was one little niggle.

The children's safety?

That was crazy. The maid hadn't said outright she was worried. He was reading too much into it.

Pippa would keep things safe.

And there was another niggle.

Pippa was gorgeous.

So what?

So he wanted to kiss her. He'd already kissed her and it had felt excellent. He wanted, quite desperately, to kiss her again.

Which was dumb. Even one kiss was dumb. Even though for him it had been a light-hearted bit of fun—it must have been—she might not have thought of it as that.

Of course she had. She'd giggled. She'd ruffled his hair then as she'd ruffle one of the kids' hair. She was beginning to hold him in some sort of affection, he thought. She was starting to think of him as family.

Which was good.

Except…did he want her to see him as family? Even that was too close. She'd bulldozed him into staying here for a month and that was a month too long.

He should telephone his mother and let her know what was happening.

Not yet, he thought. He needed to get things sorted first.

What sorted?

It was his thoughts that needed sorting, he decided. His normally razor-sharp intellect was fogged with one sprite of a red-headed woman in soggy jeans and with a bare midriff.

A red-headed woman…

'Excuse me, sir.' He'd been walking up the vast steps to the castle entrance, but as soon as he walked through the doors he found a deputation waiting. Two footmen, carrying boxes. One ancient retainer in topcoat and tails. 'Can you spare a moment?'

He stopped and frowned. 'You are?'

'I'm Blake, sir,' the man said, in the country's mix of French and Italian but with a heavy English accent. 'I was valet to the last prince, and to his father before him.'

'The devil you are.' Max's eyebrows rose. 'They really had valets?'

'Yes, Your Highness. I knew your mother,' he added gently. 'And your father.'

'Right.' Max had his measure now and he'd recalled information he'd read just that afternoon. The castle was full of people like Blake. Blake had been on the castle payroll for sixty years, but the death of the last prince had left no provision for retirement. Long-serving staff had been paid peanuts for years. Unless they stayed working here they'd be destitute.

He'd get reparation under way tomorrow, he thought, watching the old man take one of the parcels from the footman. His hands were shaking as if he had early Parkinson's.

'This is your dress regalia,' the old man said, handling the box with reverence. 'When you flew in before going to Australia you left some clothes behind and we took the liberty of taking measurements and having this made. It would mean a lot to the staff if you were to wear it tonight, the first night of the new order in this Court. Your Highness.'

He lifted the lid with reverence and held it out.

Max stared at Blake. Then he stared down at the box as if he'd just been handed a box of scorpions.

'Dress regalia.'

'As befits the Prince…Regent. You know, we were concerned

that the monarchy would disintegrate,' Blake explained. 'But today there's been children's laughter on the lawn and it's not just the staff who are deeply thankful. It's all of the country. But this little prince is only eight years old. We're not so foolish that we think he can possibly rule. You've agreed to be Prince Regent and that means for the next thirteen years you're the country's ruler.' He hesitated. 'As you should be,' he added softly. 'Starting tonight.'

'No, I—'

'Levout says you'll be a puppet ruler,' the old man said, more softly this time, so softly that the two footmen behind him couldn't hear. 'We desperately don't want that to happen.'

'I'll stay in control from a distance.'

'From France?'

'Yes.'

The man's rheumy old eyes misted. 'Sir, that won't work.'

'Of course it will work.'

'This country needs you. For measures to be put in place…well, the people in charge here have been in charge for a very long time.'

'I'll be in close contact.'

'Your Highness…' The man fell silent. There was laughter from outside. Max looked out to where Pippa and the kids were collecting their clothes in readiness to come inside. The children were playing some sort of keepings-off game, and clothes were going everywhere. Pippa was dodging about on the grass, barefooted, laughing, grabbing Marc and hauling him up to whiz him round and round until he shrieked with delight, then setting him down and chasing a chortling twin.

They'd been here for less than a day. They'd changed the castle.

Could he walk away?

'She'll love it,' he said softly and the old man followed his gaze.

'She has enough responsibility in looking after the children.' It was almost reproof.

'There are people here who'll help her.'

'Are you saying you want her to take over the administration?'

'There's not that much administration.'

'If you please, Your Highness—'

'Don't call me Your Highness. And he'll gain a crown.' Max was watching Marc duck away from Pippa with a shriek of laughter. 'It's not as if he's getting nothing.'

'No, sir. Marc will gain a crown. The little girls will be princesses. What will your position be? And what will Miss Pippa get?'

Max's gaze swivelled to stare at him. He'd never met this man until tonight. 'You know nothing of this,' he snapped.

'No, sir,' the man agreed. 'I'm only…your valet. And an old friend to your mother. But you do need to make a statement tonight to the castle and to the press. We're suggesting a photo opportunity in the great hall after dinner.'

'A photo opportunity?'

'Mr Levout said we need no such thing,' he said. 'But we need…the country needs a statement that things are changing.' He motioned to the magnificent clothes. 'We need an official prince.'

'You really want me to dress up?'

'Do you have a choice, sir?'

'Of course I—'

'Do you want the press agreeing with Levout that nothing will change?'

'Dammit… We can't have a photo session without warning Pippa.'

'Shall we make it tomorrow?'

'Three or four days,' he snapped. 'Maybe Thursday.'

'Very well, Your Highness,' the old man said, smiling. 'I'll let the appropriate people know that there'll be an official photograph session on Thursday. But meanwhile I hope you'll wear this uniform tonight, to give Levout the appropriate message.'

'I—'

'He'll be in ceremonial dress,' Blake said smoothly. 'I imagine he'll want to put you on the back step.'

'Dammit…'

'I'll be in your room in an hour to help you dress,' Blake said gently. 'It will be an honour. Your Highness.'

* * *

This wasn't right.

She stared at the vast dressing room mirror. Her reflection came back at her from six directions.

Freckles. Coppery curls but short. Snub nose and freckles. Black skirt to her knees. Pink twin-set that had seen better days. Sensible shoes.

Yuk.

She dusted her freckles until they disappeared, stared at herself some more, wiped off too much face powder and saw her freckles emerge again. She grimaced and went into the bedroom.

Beatrice was there. The oldest housemaid. House-matron, Pippa thought. Calling her a housemaid was ridiculous.

She was sitting on the edge of the bed. The kids were curled up under sumptuous covers, waiting to be told a story.

'I should stay,' she said. 'The kids are still awake.'

'We're good,' Sophie said cheerfully. 'Dolores is asleep under the bed and Beattie's going to tell us a story.'

'Just like our grandma did,' Marc added shyly.

'I know a lot of stories,' Beatrice said and smiled at her. 'Go on with you. We know where you are if we need you.'

'In the dining room.'

'The state dining room,' Beatrice corrected her. 'There are six dining rooms.'

'And the state dining room…'

'Is the biggest?'

Pippa took a deep breath. 'Why the biggest? Why tonight?'

'We're all wanting to make a statement to Mr Levout,' she said simply. 'That there's a new royal family in this palace.' She checked Pippa's dress out and her nose wrinkled. 'My dear, have you nothing more…formal?'

'No,' Pippa said bluntly. 'But I'm not actually family. It doesn't matter.'

'No,' Beatrice said doubtfully. 'But the Prince Maxsim—'

'Won't be dressed up,' Pippa said. 'He knows the limitations of my wardrobe. He wouldn't dare.'

* * *

She was just a little bit…wrong?

Pippa came down the vast stone staircase, her exploration with the kids holding her in good stead. An ancient butler—the average age of these retainers must be about ninety!—was waiting for her. He swept open the huge double doors into the state dining room. She trod over the threshold and she stopped dead.

Tassles. Sword. Medallions.

Max.

She forgot to breathe.

She'd never seen anything more gorgeous. His Royal Highness, Maxsim de Gautier, Prince Regent of Alp d'Estella.

His suit was jet-black, and it fitted him like a glove. There was a touch of white at his throat and at his wrists, accentuating his tan, the darkness of his eyes and his deep black hair. A vast array of medals and insignia was arranged across his breast. A purple sash slashed across his chest. There were gold tassels on his shoulder—epaulets? There was a braided gold cord on the opposite shoulder to his sash, and another tassel at his hip.

He was wearing a sword.

She had to breathe. She told herself that. Okay, breathe. You can do this.

He took a step towards her and smiled and she forgot to breathe all over again.

'Phillippa…'

It was a couple of moments before she figured out how her voice worked. He was waiting for her to respond. He'd called her Phillippa.

He'd set this up. This formal situation, this amazing dress…

For a girl in a pink twin-set.

'You rat,' she managed at last. 'You bottom-feeding pond scum.'

He blinked. 'Pardon?'

'I'm wearing my church clothes,' she wailed. 'My Sunday best for Tanbarook. What do you think you're doing?'

'Phillippa, here's Mr Levout.'

They weren't alone. For the first time she realised there was another man present—Carver Levout. Like Max, Levout was also in ceremonial regalia. He looked a lot less impressive than Max, but a million times more impressive than Pippa.

One of the buttons had fallen off her cardigan during transit. Pippa had decided since she couldn't find it she'd leave her cardigan open and hope no one would notice. Levout noticed. He stared pointedly at the gap where the button should be, and it was all Pippa could do not to run.

'She's a real provincial,' the man said in his own language to Max, crossing the room to take her hand in his. 'What a drab mouse. Shouldn't we be feeding her in the servants' quarters? She'd be much more comfortable.' He smiled and raised her hand to his lips. 'Charming,' he said in English and then reverted to his own language to add, 'How the hell are we going to cope with her in the public eye? She'll have to be seen as the nanny.'

There was a deathly hush. Levout looked suddenly uncomfortable. Maybe he guessed…

Forget guessing. It was time he knew. 'Then we're four provincials together,' she said, sweetly in his language. 'Marc and Sophie and Claire and me. Plus our dog. Provincials all.'

Levout stared. Then he flushed. It was no wonder he'd assumed she wouldn't speak this language. How many people did? 'Mademoiselle, I'm devastated,' he started.

'You're also excessively rude. Both of you.'

Max said nothing. He stood in front of the mantel, quietly watchful.

She ignored him. Or she pretended to ignore him. She'd never seen a man in a dress sword…

Concentrate on something else, she told herself fiercely. Like the table. The mahogany table was twelve feet long and it was so highly polished she could see her face in the wood. There was a place laid at the head. There were two places set on either side, halfway down. The cutlery was ornate silverware, each piece a work of art in its own right. There were, she counted, six crystal glasses by each plate. An epergne was set in the middle of the table, silver and gold, all crouching tigers and jungle foliage.

'Goodness,' Pippa said faintly. 'This is amazing. I'm amazed.'

But then she shrugged. She still carefully didn't look at Max but addressed herself instead to his companion. 'I'm not welcome here,' she said. 'You've made that clear. You guys can play fancy dress by yourselves. I'm going to the kitchen to see if I can find myself a vegemite sandwich.'

'Pippa…' Max said.

'Yeah, I'm Pippa,' she said. 'If you wanted Phillippa you should have given me warning, but what you see is what you get. See you later.' She turned and swept out of the room with as much dignity as a girl in a twin-set with a missing button could muster.

Max caught her before she'd taken half a dozen steps across the hall. He seized her by her shoulders and turned her to face him.

She was furious. It didn't take a clairvoyant to see that. Her eyes were bright and wide, and there was a spot of burning crimson on each cheek.

She turned but she didn't react. She had her arms tightly folded across her breasts.

'Let me go,' she muttered and she took a step backwards, tugging away.

He released her. 'Pip, I'm sorry.'

'What the hell were you thinking?'

'I don't—'

'There's no need to try and show me up,' she snapped. 'I've never denied I'm a provincial.' She took a deep breath and tilted her chin. 'I'm even proud of it.'

'You're not a provincial.'

'Oh, sure. Max, I'm a child of a single mother. I've scraped a living as best I could. For the last four years I've worked as a navvy on a farm.' She held out her hands, showing work-worn fingers with nails that were cracked and stained. 'I'm illegitimate poor trash and I bet he knows it. I bet you've told him.'

'I haven't. And there's no need to be melodramatic.'

'Says the prince with a dress sword,' she said scornfully. 'I've never seen such a melodramatic outfit in my life.'

'It is, rather,' he said ruefully and stared down at his costume. 'Do you know these pants have fifteen buttons?'

'Fifteen…' Momentarily distracted, she stared at the line of buttons leading from groin to hip. 'Wow.'

'It took me three minutes to do them up,' he said. 'Honest to God.'

She shook her head, dragging her gaze away with difficulty. He was all too good at distracting her. The man was too distracting altogether. 'So you've achieved what?' she demanded, a trifle breathlessly. 'By doing up fifteen buttons?'

'Believe it or not, I've made an old man happy.'

'Levout?'

'There's no way I'll make him happy. He's nervous as hell. What he's just heard has made him even more nervous and what I set in motion in the next few days will give him a palsy stroke. But my valet—'

'Your valet!'

'Ridiculous or not, I have a valet. He's eighty-four. He and the rest of the servants organised this outfit specially and they'd have been desperately hurt if I hadn't worn it tonight. As would the team of people who worked their butts off to get it ready for me. It's amazing.'

'Amazing,' she agreed and tried to turn away again.

He caught her and twisted her back to face him. 'Pippa, you must see how desperate these people are for reassurance. All these people. The royal household and the outside community. This place is a microcosm of the country. We're important.'

'You're important,' she snapped. 'Not me. I'm a provincial.'

'Will you leave it?'

'Not the least bit of warning?' she demanded, still fixated on her missing button. 'No, Pippa, you might want to think about what you're wearing tonight 'cos I'm coming in fancy dress?'

'I thought if I told you what I was wearing you wouldn't come at all. And I didn't know what I was wearing last time I saw you. I'd have had to send a message to the nursery.'

'Or come yourself. It wouldn't be so impossible.'

'I won't come to the nursery.'

'Why not?'

'I don't intend to spend any more time with you than I must.'

Um…maybe that wasn't the wisest thing to say, he thought. He reran the words in his head. Nope, that hadn't sounded good. It had been a really dumb thing to say.

Just because it was true…

The color had drained from Pippa's face. 'What do you mean?' she said at last and he spread his hands.

Okay, maybe it had to be faced. 'Hell, Pippa, you know what I mean. This thing between us…'

'What thing?'

'I shouldn't have kissed you on the plane.'

'No.' She shook her head. 'At least we agree on that.'

'I don't want to give you any ideas.'

Her jaw dropped. 'Of…of all the conceit,' she stammered. 'And so unnecessary. Provincials don't have any ideas. You of all people should know that. After all, you've been mixing with me for days. Of all the arrogant, mean-minded, conceited, over-dressed popinjays—'

'Popinjays?'

'I read it somewhere,' she snapped. 'It's what you are.'

'Levout will be listening to every word.'

'Really?' She raised her voice.

'Look, it was your idea that I stay here. Not mine.'

'Don't you dare do this to me.'

'Dare do what?'

'Take my concern for the children as some sort of interest in you. I don't want you here. Your presence, however, guarantees security for Marc and Sophie and Claire. You go, then we go. But you're right. We needn't spend any more time together than we must. Not because I just might jump you, Maxsim de Gautier, but because I might slap your handsome, arrogant face.'

'You wouldn't,' he said.

And once again he knew he'd said the wrong thing.

She'd never hit anyone in her life. She'd never dreamed of doing it. But now, as they stood in this gilded hallway full of ancient, over-the-top artwork, chandeliers, servants in the doorways, Levout standing open-mouthed behind them, the emotions of the last few days found irresistible expression.

As a slap it was a beauty. It was straight across his cheek. The sound of the slap was louder than the voice she was using.

She backed off and stared at him. What little vestige of color she'd had before was completely gone now.

'Pippa…' he said, uncertainly, and she raised her hands to her face as if her head needed support. As if it were she who'd been slapped.

'I-I'm so sorry,' she stammered, aghast.

'You don't—'

'I'd never slap. I never would. It's just…'

'We've hauled you right out of your comfort zone.'

'I don't have a comfort zone,' she whispered. 'The farm? Taking care of the kids by myself? That's not comfort. What I use as a comfort zone is independence. I don't need anyone. I don't need you. And for you to assume that just because you kissed me I'd see you as some kind of love interest…'

'I never assumed that.'

'Yes, you did,' she said steadying a little. 'And maybe you're right. Maybe I have been a bit too attracted to you. But now…' She shrugged. 'Well, I've been told and I'm not stupid, regardless of what you think. We're here for a month while I figure out whether the kids could have a future here. You're my…bond, if you like. My surety. I'm demanding that you stay here too. But only until I figure out whether we're safe. If that's tomorrow then you can take yourself back to Paris.'

He hesitated. He should finish this. But there were imperatives. 'Pippa, the press…'

'What about the press?'

'They want to see you again.'

'Not me.'

'They want to see the children. They need a photo opportunity.'

'Then we'll set one up. Let Beatrice know and I'll make sure they have clean faces.'

'They want to meet you. Tonight if possible.'

'No deal.' She backed again so she was at the foot of the stairs. 'Now is there anything else?'

'Then Thursday. For an official portrait? We have to let the press see us.'

'Thursday,' she snapped. 'Fine. I'll sew on my button for the occasion. Make sure it's at night 'cos twin-set and skirt looks dumb in this heat.'

'Dinner is served,' the butler intoned from behind them and Max winced.

'Can we delay it for a little?'

'No,' Pippa said and squared her shoulders. 'We're all hungry but we're not eating together.' She walked over to the tray the butler was carrying—three bowls of soup. She lifted one and smelled. 'Yum. Asparagus. My favourite. I'll take mine out on the terrace.'

'You can't,' Max said blankly.

'Watch me. Or don't watch me. In fact I forbid you to watch me. You and Mr Levout go back to your dress-ups. This provincial's going to eat her meal outside. That way I can burp and slurp just the way I like.'

'That's ridiculous.'

'I'm not ridiculous,' she snapped. 'You're the one with the sword.'

CHAPTER SEVEN

PIPPA might be in a fairy tale, but three days later she was starting to be just a bit…bored? When they were on holidays on the farm the kids played happily independently. Here she stuck with them like glue, but after three days she was wondering if it was more to protect herself than to protect the kids.

Carver still gave her the creeps, but it was Max she was avoiding. Max and his wonderful uniform. How dared a man look so sexy?

All the staff were treating him as if it were Max who was the Crown Prince.

They weren't treating him as if he was an illegitimate outsider.

She was uneasy, puzzled, and increasingly she was restless.

'The last two princes spent very little time at the castle,' Beatrice told her. 'The casinos at Monte Carlo were more their style, and our rulers encouraged them.'

'Your rulers?'

'We have a President and a Council. Mr Levout is on the Council. They run this country.'

'Why haven't we met this President?'

'I suspect he's desperately trying to work out how these children can be blocked from the throne. If he can, there's no one else in direct succession and the Principality will disappear. That would leave the Levout family in control.'

'Max doesn't want that.'

'And thank God for Max,' Beatrice told her. 'He is a wonderful prince, and he seems to be a good man.'

There it was again, the blank acceptance of an outsider as a prince.

'Yeah, but not necessarily a nice one,' she managed, and Beatrice regarded her with the beginning of a tiny smile.

'I don't know about that,' she said. 'Maybe we'll wait and see.'

So she waited. But by the fourth day she was openly admitting she was climbing walls.

How could she be bored in a place like this? she wondered. There was as much wonderful food as she and the children needed. There was no need to milk a hundred and twenty cows twice a day. In fact, the dairyman had refused her offer to help. 'It wouldn't be proper,' he told her and he refused to budge. There were swimming pools and wonderful gardens. There were gentle people waiting on her every whim, even eager for her to have whims.

For Pippa, who'd worked hard every day of her adult life, it felt wrong. Max wasn't used to this either, she thought, and she wondered how he was taking it. She wasn't asking him, though. Whenever she saw him she'd head for the nearest child.

She was being a coward, she knew, but he seriously unsettled her, and life was strange enough without being…unsettled.

'Let's leave this relationship businesslike,' she told him when he confronted her. 'If there's something you need then of course we'll talk, but the castle staff got the wrong idea when I slapped you and there's no way we want to encourage that.'

'The wrong idea? That I've brought back with me a termagant?'

'I don't know what a termagant is,' she said huffily. 'And I've got far too many good manners to ask.'

She waited for him to respond. He didn't, though. He stood and gazed at her for a long moment and then turned away.

Good.

But increasingly their disassociation seemed ever so slightly silly. And she had to admit that she missed him. She looked up termagant in the dictionary and huffed in indignation—but it was a bit lonely to huff by yourself.

'You've been by yourself for years,' she scolded herself, but it didn't work.

She'd sort of got used to Max.

But the avoidance seemed to be working both ways, and a girl had some pride.

On the fourth day she finished breakfast, looked at the day stretching out in front of her and decided on a walk. 'Right round the castle grounds,' she told the kids and they groaned.

'But Beattie's grandkids are coming,' Marc said. 'Beattie says Sally's the same age as me and Rodrick's the same age as Sophie and Claire. Aimee's bigger than everyone but Beatrice said she knows skipping games.'

'They'll be fine with me,' Beatrice told her. She'd been making their bed—Pippa wasn't even permitted to do that. 'I promise I'll keep them with me all the time. Why don't you go for a walk by yourself?'

Because I'm scared of meeting Max, she thought, but that was a dumb reason. She couldn't voice it. She looked helplessly across at Beatrice and Beatrice smiled.

'He's not an ogre, dear,' she said gently. 'Blake says he's a sweetheart. He says he takes after his lovely mother. Bless him.'

Oh, great. Yeah, he's a sweetheart and that's the whole problem, she thought, but she couldn't say that either.

Right. A walk. She gave herself a firm talking-to, which consisted of standing in front of her six-dimensional mirror and talking severely to all six of her. Then she waved goodbye to her various images and went to find Dolores.

But Dolores wasn't interested either. Sixteen was really old for such a big dog, and she'd suffered badly this winter. Here she moved from fire to sunbeam and back again, soaking up the warmth with the same intensity she'd once reserved for rabbits. She was stretched out now on the patio, soaking in sun, and as Pippa bent to pat her she barely raised the energy to wag her tail. As Pippa stroked her she gave a long, slow shudder of pure, unadulterated bliss.

'At least I've done the right thing by you, girl,' Pippa whispered, blinking hard. She knew Dolores didn't have long. To give her another summer…

She'd done something right.

But she missed her dog by her side. She now had no kids, no work, no dog. The sensation as she took herself off for a walk was strangely empty.

'Other people have holidays,' she told herself. 'Get over it.'

But she couldn't. What she saw stretching out before her was strange—a life here as the children's guardian. A life that wasn't her life.

A life even without Dolores?

'Oh, forget it with the maudlin,' she told herself. 'Walk.'

She walked. It was a long way around the castle grounds—too far to walk in a morning. She walked for an hour, around a vast lake, through woods where she startled deer, into the hills behind the castle, but she still wasn't halfway round. Finally she gave up on the perimeter and veered cross country.

The woods here were so dense they were almost scary, but there was hammering and shouting and sounds of construction in the distance. Where there was construction there was civilisation, so she pushed her way through overgrown paths to find it.

It *was* a construction site. It was a small cottage, with what looked like an extension being built at the back.

Max was up on the roof. He was wearing faded jeans and a heavy cotton workman's shirt, open at the throat and with sleeves rolled up to the elbows. He was fitting roofing slates. The sun was glinting on his dark hair. He was laughing at something someone below had just said.

He looked…

Whoa.

She would have backed away—fast—but he saw her. His hands stilled. The slate in his hand was set down with care.

'Pippa,' he said and the pleasure in his voice gave her a completely inappropriate wash of warmth. Maybe he'd found the last four days as long as she had.

He didn't look bored, she thought with a pang of jealousy. He looked…

Whoa again.

'Hi,' she managed, trying to keep her voice in order. 'I've been walking.'

'Hiking, more like. You're miles from home. Did you bring a packed lunch?'

'No, I—'

'You're bored?'

'No,' she lied, looking about her. There were three other men on the site, elderly men—of course—working on a pile of bricks.

'They don't need help at the dairy?' Max asked.

'They say it's not seemly.' She glowered. 'How come it's seemly for you to fix roofs but not for me to milk cows?'

He grinned. 'Desperate times lead to desperate measures. Sleeping by the pool is great for an hour but I get itchy fingers. You want to clean some bricks? Is your back up to it?'

'My back's fine. Why are you cleaning bricks?'

'This house is for Blake and Beatrice.' He motioned to one of the elderly men who raised his cap in a deferential greeting. 'You've met Blake? He and Beatrice lived here for over forty years. But five years ago there was a storm and the back section collapsed. See that pile of bricks over there?' She looked to where he was pointing. 'That's the remains of the fireplace. Anyway Blake and Beatrice moved into the servant's quarters in the palace but the servant's quarters needs a bomb. It'll take time and patience to get it brought up to scratch. Meanwhile I thought we could rebuild.'

We. She looked cautiously around her, recognising the butler, the valet, and one of the footmen. Average again about ninety.

'Right,' she said.

'The boys are chipping old mortar off the bricks. Want to help?' And he smiled.

Damn him, why did he do that? He just had to let those dark eyes twinkle and she was lost.

She should go.

But this was a real job. She ached for a job. Of the three geriatrics, one was holding the ladder in case Max ever came down. The other two were chipping gamely at old mortar.

She watched them work for a minute. At this rate they'd be lucky if they had the bricks cleaned by the end of the millennium.

But why was Max here? 'I thought you said there were lots of administration things that needed doing.'

'Not until the succession's in place. The lawyers are working on it.' He picked up his slate with purpose. 'Meanwhile are you going to help or are you going to stand there distracting me?'

'I'm not distracting you.'

'Little you know,' Max growled. 'Give the lady a pair of gloves, Blake, and let's get this moving.'

He sat on the roof replacing tile after tile, his hands moving methodically but his mind all on the lady beneath him.

She was amazing. She was cleaning at a rate more than double that of the old men, but she chattered to the men as she worked, distracting them just as much as she was distracting him, but for a purpose. As she cleaned she slipped her finished bricks into one of three piles, so the piles in front of her companions were growing at the same rate as hers. Giving them back their pride.

The men were enjoying her. They worked together, they paused and laughed and wiped their brows and they stopped for a drink, but she methodically worked on. Jean, the footman who'd been holding the ladder, decided it didn't really need holding and went over to help.

Well, why wouldn't he? She was…magnetic.

And she was surely used to hard work. The bricks were hard to clean but they were flying through her hands. At the thought of what she'd been facing for the last four years his gut clenched.

So he'd solved that problem. He'd brought her here.

But she'd never be seen on the same pegging as the children, he thought. Levout was making that perfectly clear. She was a provincial, no blood relative of the heir to the throne, and with no delineated role as his was.

Maybe she'd leave.

No. She'd never leave the children.

But what would her position be?

They stopped for half an hour at lunch time and Max used his cell-phone to check the children.

'Our visitors are staying for lunch,' Beatrice said happily. 'And then they'll all need a nap. Tell Pippa to come home if she wants to, but there's no need.'

Max relayed the message and saw confusion wash across her face.

'They still need you,' he said gently.

'Of course.'

'Have a sandwich.'

'Thank you,' she said, and took a huge cheese sandwich from the pile, biting into it like a man.

He grinned.

'What?' she demanded.

'Nothing.'

'Yeah, and I wipe my mouth on my sleeve too,' she said darkly. 'Butt out, Your Highness.'

'Of course.'

The men had brought beer. 'We'll send to the house to get something more suitable,' Blake told him. He seemed distressed that Max and Pippa were sharing their plain luncheon. Pippa shook her head and lifted a bottle.

'Hey, we're not proper royalty,' she said. 'We're just hangers on. This is wet and it's cold and if anyone tries taking this from me I'll spray them with it.'

'You are royalty,' Blake said, eyeing Max with reproof, but Max ignored him. Finally the men chuckled and relaxed. Gentle banter continued as they sat under a huge oak and surveyed their hard work.

Max hardly participated in the banter. He leaned back and listened to Pippa laughing with the men, joking with them, teasing with them.

Her jeans and her T-shirt were coated in brick-dust. There was dust in her curls and a streak down her cheek where dust had mixed with sweat. She'd scraped her arm and there was a trickle of dried blood to her wrist. She was laughing at something one of the men was saying, and she was drinking beer straight from the bottle.

She was the loveliest thing he'd ever seen.

Yeah, right, and where was that going to get him? Into disaster?

He couldn't go there even if he wanted to, he thought. How the hell would his mother react? I've fallen in love with the guardian of the new Crown Prince. I have to stay in Alp d'Estella.

She'd break her heart. After all that had been done to her… After all she'd done to herself… How could he ask it of her?

He looked up and saw Pippa watching him.

'It looks grim,' she said.

'What?'

'What you're thinking.'

'I was thinking about slates.'

'Really?' she said and hiked her eyebrows.

Their telepathy wasn't a one-way thing, he thought, and he turned away, ostensibly to pack up the lunch gear but in reality so she couldn't see his face any more. He had to get this under control.

It was bad enough that he was here now, and his mother knew he was here. After the official photo shoot she'd see him in every glossy magazine in Europe.

He grabbed a handful of slates and carted them up onto the roof. No one saw him go—even Jean, his ladder holder, was chuckling over something Pippa had just said, hanging onto every word. Good, he thought. It was good that they were falling in love with her. It was great for the people. It was great for the country.

But what would her position be?

It had to be made formal, he thought, or she'd be shunted into the background for ever. Which meant that he had to drag her into this photo shoot, whether she liked it or not.

'Pippa, we're giving a press conference this evening,' he called from the safety of his roof, and she stared up at him.

'How did you get up there?'

'I climbed.'

'No one held your ladder. Those slates are heavy.'

'I'm fine. Jean has better things to do than hold my ladder. But about this shoot.'

'Shoot?'

'Photo shoot. Introduction to your new royal family.'

'I'll dress the kids up.'

'Beatrice is sorting something for them,' he called. 'There's actually traditional costume for royal children.'

'It's very splendid,' Jean, the footman, told her gravely. 'And colourful. The girls' dresses have fourteen petticoats.'

'And the boy's costume is just as colourful,' Blake added. 'It had petticoats too, but the last prince put his foot down aged all of four so we converted it to trousers. It has what looks like a small apron over the front but it's unexceptional and most children are envious when they see it. Beatrice measured the children the first night you were here and the costumes are ready.'

'Well, that's sorted,' Pippa said, and went back to brick-cleaning. She looked perturbed, though, Max thought. Worrying that things were being taken from her control. As indeed they could be if she wasn't included.

'We'd like you to dress up too,' he called, and Pippa paused mid-brick.

'Me.'

'Yes.'

'I'm not royal.' She made a recovery and waved a brick in his direction. 'Do I look royal?'

'Yes, miss,' Blake said severely, answering before Max could get a word in. 'We believe you look extremely royal. Don't we, Jean? Don't we, Pascal-Marie? Almost as royal as His Highness, Prince Maxsim.'

'Yes,' his companions agreed gravely.

'Then I'll come to the shoot wearing what I've got on,' she said and grinned and started chipping again.

'You can't,' Max called. 'This is important, Pippa. These photographs will be in every major glossy worldwide.'

She paused, mid-chop. 'Even in Tanbarook?'

'I'm guessing even in Tanbarook. Aussie girl becomes a European princess…'

'I'm guardian of a prince. That doesn't make me a princess.'

No. It didn't. That was the problem, he thought. There was only one way she could become a princess—and there was no way he was going down that route.

But she had to have a formal role. She was the children's guardian. She had to be in the shoot if she was to retain any sort of authority when he left.

'Miss, the castle can't be left with just three royal children,' Blake told her, echoing Max's thoughts.

'Levout will take charge again,' Pascal-Marie—the butler—added. 'Levout's like a bear with a sore head now that Prince Maxsim is here. But Prince Maxsim intends to leave at the end of one month.'

'We might too,' Pippa said and the old men's faces fell.

'No.'

'Possibly not,' she whispered.

'Then you need to have a role here,' Max called. 'My deputy or something similar. The people have to know you. You need to be part of the press conference.'

'In my twin-set? I still haven't found the button.'

'Beatrice could organise you something,' Blake said, but he sounded doubtful. 'Maybe her ideas are a little old-fashioned…'

'No,' Max said, shoving a slate into place and concentrating on the next one. 'There's a reasonable shopping centre in the village. I'll finish here in an hour and take you.'

'I've no money for clothes.'

'You're the guardian of the heir to the throne of Alp d'Estella. You should have been getting a suitable allowance long since. You are now. Get used to it.'

She didn't want to go to town with him.

Pippa chipped on, seemingly concentrating only on her bricks but in reality twisting the forthcoming journey into all sorts of threatening contortions.

It was only shopping, she thought, but she'd be alone with Max and she didn't want to be alone with Max.

She could take the children.

Right, and they'd be so good while she chose a frock. Ha. Shopping with them was a nightmare at the best of times.

Who else could she take?

No one without saying straight out that she didn't trust Max, and it wasn't actually that she didn't trust Max. She didn't trust herself.

She worked steadily on, trying to get her head together, trying to stay calm.

An hour later Max came up behind her, took the brick from her fingers and she jumped about a foot.

'Enough.'

'I haven't done enough,' she said, suddenly breathless, and the men around her laughed.

'You've put the rest of us to shame, miss,' Blake said. 'You deserve a rest. Have fun.'

'Let's go,' Max said and lifted her chisel from her hand. 'Work's over for the day.'

'I won't be able to leave the kids. I've been away from them all day.'

'Let's check, shall we?' he said. 'Make no assumptions, scary or otherwise.'

'Why would they be scary?'

'We both know the answer to that,' he said softly. 'Though neither of us know what to do with it.'

Was he saying he was as attracted to her as she was to him? Pippa sat in the passenger seat of a neat little sports car and tried to concentrate on the scenery, but it was impossible to concentrate on something other than the man beside her.

Was he saying the avoidance of the last four days had been part of his plan as well as hers?

Good, she thought. Great. If they both thought this relationship was impossible then they could do something about it. Or do nothing, which would be a much more suitable plan.

She was sitting as far apart as she could, which was a start—though you couldn't get very far apart in a tiny sports car.

'Does this car belong to the palace?'

'It's mine. Do you like it?'

'I do,' she said politely. The little car practically purred as they negotiated the scenic curves around the mountains. 'Actually it's smashing,' she admitted. 'The kids would love it.'

'Just lucky they were too busy to come, then.'

They had been too busy. When Pippa had gone to find them they had been in the vegetable garden, sorting worms from loamy compost. Dolores had been nearby, sleeping in the sun and keeping a benign eye on her charges.

'We're making a carrot bed,' the twins told Pippa. 'We need worms. M. Renagae says there can never be enough worms in a carrot bed.'

They were fitting into this life to the manor born, Pippa thought. It was only Pippa who felt…foreign. She'd asked—uselessly—whether they'd like to go into town to shop and they'd regarded her as if she were a sandwich short of a picnic.

So now she was alone with Max, and he was staring ahead as if he was as determined as she was not to cross the line.

'What sort of dress do I need?' she asked.

'Several. A long gown for the formal photo and a couple more for dinners.'

'I eat with the children.'

'I hope after I leave that you'll stand in my stead on State occasions.'

'You're assuming I'm staying.'

'I'm assuming you're thinking about it. This place has to be better than where I found you.'

'It might be,' she said, still cautious. 'Max, what are you afraid of?'

'I'm not afraid.'

'Then what? What aren't you telling me?'

'Nothing.'

'Don't lie to me,' she snapped. 'I know there's something. It's just intuition but I know there's…something.' She hesitated, but it had to be said—what she'd been thinking these last four days. 'It's not just the castle. It's royalty itself, so much so that you're scared of even being with me.'

'I'm shopping with you now, aren't I?'

'Only because you're trying to persuade me to take the next step—whatever that is. For the last four days you've been avoiding me as much as I've been avoiding you. Why? Because you're scared you might get attached to me and to the kids? Or is it that you're scared you might be called into account for what you've done?'

'Your imagination's acting overtime,' he said grimly.

'I know it is. But all I have is my imagination as I don't have facts.'

'You don't need—'

'Don't you dare tell me what I need or don't need,' she flashed, swivelling in the car to face him. 'You've talked me into coming here with your promise of warmth and luxury and relief from responsibility, but the responsibility's followed me and I'm damned if I'm letting your charm and good looks and…your princeliness deflect me from figuring out what I have to figure. Just because you wear a stupid dress sword—'

'Princeliness?'

'Don't laugh at me.'

'I wouldn't.'

'You would if you thought it would help. But I still get the feeling you're afraid. If not of me—and that's crazy—if not of emotion, then what?'

'Nothing.'

'Stop the car.'

'I can't. There's only two hours before the shops close.'

'Then talk fast,' she snapped, suddenly sure of herself. There was something. If not fear, then what? She was responsible for Marc. She had to find out. 'Please stop the car,' she repeated. 'I'm taking not one minute's more part in this charade before I know what I need to know.'

* * *

He stopped in a pullover catering for tourists who wanted to gaze down the valley at the winding river and the spectacular mountains beyond. The scenery was awesome, but Max gazed straight ahead and saw nothing. 'What do you want to know?' he said blankly.

'About your family, for a start,' she said. She wasn't sure where she was going with this. She wasn't even sure that she wasn't a bit crazy. She stared down at her hands, which were suddenly the most interesting things she could find to look at—apart from Max and there was no way she was looking at him any more. 'I want to know about Thiérry. Tell me about the car crash.'

'Thiérry died in a car crash when he was seventeen.' He said it as if goaded.

She flashed a look at him then, just for a moment, and then looked back at her hands. 'With your father. Who was drunk?'

'Of course with my father,' he exploded. 'Of course he was drunk. He's a de Gautier. The blood's cursed.'

'Ooh, who's being melodramatic?' she whispered and he stared at her in astonishment.

'You're accusing me of melodrama?'

'If you're talking about cursed blood, then, yes, I am,' she said with asperity. 'Tell it like it is, Max. Don't try and make my blood curdle. I'm a nurse, remember? It takes a whole lot more than curses to curdle my blood.'

'I guess it would.'

She looked at him for a long moment, gave a tiny smile and a decisive nod.

'That's better. Now start again. Your…father was responsible for Thiérry's death? How did it happen?'

He sighed. 'Okay. The whole story. Not that it helps anything.'

'I'm listening.'

'My father…' He sighed again. 'Apparently there's been contention and hatred in the royal family for generations. My father was raised thinking he was owed a birthright, that he had a claim on the throne, or at least part of its wealth, but the way the succession's written he got nothing. He spent much of his time here, freeloading on the old prince. He married my mother which was the only sane thing he did in his life, but the marriage didn't last. She was seventeen and besotted with royalty, and he met and married her on a whim. By the time she had Thiérry she knew it was a disaster.'

'And she couldn't…leave?'

'Are you kidding? My father was seeing Thiérry as a potential heir to the throne. The old Crown Prince Paul was an invalid. There was only Bernard, and Bernard was…effete. There's clauses written into most royal marriages, and ours is no exception. If the marriage ends then any children stay under the sole care of the sovereign.'

He paused, his eyes bleak and cold and distant. Pippa didn't say anything. She couldn't think of anything to say.

'So my mother had an affair,' he said at last. 'Desperation? Who can blame her? She became pregnant with me, and the old prince kicked her out of the castle. He was so angry that he kicked them all out—my father and Thiérry included.'

'So then…'

'My father was furious, of course, and humiliated, but he was back to living on his wits, and he didn't want a baby. So he turned his back on all of us. Mama was permitted to return to her parents' farm, taking Thiérry with her. We saw no more of the royal family. Only then the old prince died. Bernard became Crown Prince but still hadn't married, so Thiérry was his heir and my father appeared on the scene again. Thiérry was seventeen—a rebellious teenager hating the poverty we were living in—and my father was demanding to show him his heritage.'

'But not you,' she whispered. 'Where do you fit in?'

'I don't. I was the product of an affair. I was worthless.'

She swallowed. But then she thought of the things that weren't making sense. Blake's insistence on Max's royalty. The servants' insistence. They'd all been in the castle then…

They'd have known. There was something in the way they deferred to Max, as if he were the Crown Prince.

'You were really his son,' she whispered, knowing suddenly that it had to be true, and he didn't deny it.

'Yes,' he said at last. 'But I've only known myself for a few weeks. I was approached to take on the regency. I refused and finally my mother told me who I really was. She'd never spoken of it. I know it now, and, for some reason I can't figure, Blake knows it. But as far as I know, no one else. She lied because she couldn't bear to live here, and by lying about my parentage at least she'd still have me.'

'Oh, Max…'

'So there you have it,' he said bleakly. 'The makings of tragedy, from which I, as a supposed bastard, was excluded. My father, in his expensive car, in his amazing royal regalia, must have seemed like something out of a fairy story to seventeen-year-old Thiérry. But my mother was appalled. I still remember the shouting. The tears. Finally Mama agreed that Thiérry could visit the castle, but she insisted on accompanying him.'

'Of course.'

'You know, my mother would love you,' he said dryly. 'You sound just like her—a mother hen ready to take on all comers.' He smiled but she didn't smile back

'So what happened?'

'Boring really. Predictably horrible. He loaded them into his too-fast car, he drove erratically—probably shouting at my mother all the time—and they all came off one of the cliffs somewhere close to here. My father and Thiérry were killed instantly. My mother's now a paraplegic.'

Pippa had stopped looking at her hands. Instead she was staring down at the river, looping lazily round the base of the cliffs below.

'Oh, Max,' she said at last. 'Oh, poor lady.'

'Mama knows as I do that someone has to accept the Crown if the people aren't to face ruin. But she won't go back on what she's said. That I was the result of an affair. That I have no connection to the palace. The fact that I look like a damned de Gautier…'

'There's DNA testing.'

'So there is. If I wanted to prove it.'

'But you don't?'

'I won't do it to her. For why? To take a throne I don't want? If I can organise things without it…if I can set up the regency…' He sighed. 'You do what you have to do.'

'Of course.' She linked her fingers again, but her gaze was still on the river. The trap was closing in on her, she thought dully, as it had closed on Max. It might be a gilded cage, but it was a cage for all that. 'You know what I'd really like?' she whispered.

'What?'

'To go back to nursing.'

'Nursing!'

'Don't say it like it's a bad smell,' she snapped, and suddenly she was furious. Here she was again, in the middle of a mess, expected to pick up the pieces with no complaint. Well, she might, but, dammit, he was going to understand that she was giving up something too. 'If you knew how hard I worked to get my nursing qualifications… Every summer I've worked my fingers to the bone to get enough money to keep me at school. That started from the time I was ten, working illegally peeling potatoes for our local fish and chip shop. But somehow I did it. I finally qualified as a nurse and I loved it. Independence! You can't imagine. I kept right on studying. I wanted to be the best nurse in the world, but you know what? Life just got in the way.'

'Life as in Marc and Claire and Sophie.'

'And you,' she said bitterly. She glared at him. 'Oh, there's no use complaining. But don't you dare look at me now and say there's a really luxurious castle and you'll be waited on hand and foot so what else can you possibly want from life? I bet that's what your father told your mother. So here I am. I don't even have a definite role. I'm not royal. I can't help in the running of this country. I'm going to have to put up with people like Levout patronising me until Marc is twenty-one and I can get on with my own life. Whatever that is. I don't think I have one,' she said. 'You sure as hell don't think I do.'

'Pippa…'

'Start the car,' she said wearily. 'Yes, you're in a bind, but I am too. I need to think. Meanwhile there's no need to be nice to me any more. I know what you want now and I need to decide on my own terms. Let's find this dress.'

'I'm sorry.'

'No, you're not. You're on track to get out of here. Start the car.'

'If I could—'

'Yeah, and if I could,' she retorted. 'But we can't. We're stuck in this royal groove and you have three and a half weeks of it left and I'm looking at thirteen years. Let's go.'

'I don't feel I can.'

She sighed. 'Of course you can,' she said. 'Like me, you have no choice. I agree, your mother's given you no choice. I bet if I met her I'd agree with your decision entirely. I'm sorry I flung that at you. It served no purpose.'

'Except to make me see what I should have seen last week.'

'There's no point.' She took a deep breath. 'Max, it was dumb for me to say that. It was just…anger, and anger achieves nothing. I don't usually let fly. It won't happen again.'

'I hate this.'

'That makes two of us.'

He stared at her for a long minute, and then raised his hand to her face and cupped the curve of her cheek. She let his hand rest there for a moment, allowing herself the luxury of taking warmth and strength that she so desperately needed. But she couldn't depend on it.

She was alone. She knew it. She'd been alone in Tanbarook and she was alone here. The future stretched out before her, bleak and endless.

Bleak? Hey, she was going to live in a castle. 'Don't *you* start being melodramatic,' she said out loud and Max frowned.

'Pardon?'

'I was talking to me.' She lifted his hand away, but she didn't quite release it.

'You're a wonderful woman.'

'I am, aren't I?' she said and she summoned a smile. 'But I need a dress.'

'Sure you do.' But he was gazing at her with such a look…

'Don't you dare kiss me,' she muttered and hauled her hand away.

'Why not?'

'You know very well why not. You and me? No and no and no. We're in enough of a dilemma. A casual affair would mess things between us for ever.'

'I'm not talking about a casual—'

'You're not talking about anything. Take me shopping, Max.' She twisted so she was staring straight ahead and her fingers started knotting again. 'What are we waiting for?'

'I don't have a clue,' Max said slowly. He stared at her for a long moment, but she didn't look at him. Conversation ended.

Finally he turned the key in the ignition and steered his car out of the pullover and around the cliffs into town.

CHAPTER EIGHT

THE village might be tiny, but it catered for money.

'Monaco's within easy driving distance and we have amazing summers,' Max said. He was playing tourist guide, his smooth, informative chat proving the safest of conversations. 'So we have Europe's wealthy summering here, driving between here and the casinos.' He pulled into a parking lot in front of a dozen quaint shops. 'Daniella's your best choice. The dress shop on the corner.'

'You'd know that, how?'

'Beatrice told me,' he said, looking wounded.

Pippa even managed a laugh. 'Okay. Daniella's it is. How much do I have to spend?'

'As much as you like.' He climbed out of the car and came round to open her door. 'The royal fortune is entailed. That means it's been kept safe and there's more than enough to pay for you to wear what you like. Diamond-studded knickers if that's what takes your fancy.'

She choked. 'It doesn't.'

'How did I know you'd say that?' He grinned. 'Let's go.'

'You're not shopping with me.' She was too close to him, she thought. Damn him for his good manners. She wanted him back on the other side of the car.

'Of course I'm coming.'

'Of course nothing. I'm having no man saying, "Nope, that's not suitable," or "That color makes you look consumptive," or, "Gee, I like that one, it gives you great bazookers."'

'Bazookers?'

'See, you don't even know the language. How do I pay?'

He hesitated, but her chin was tilting in a gesture he was starting to know.

'Fine,' he said, conceding defeat. Maybe she was right. They needed to keep their distance. He produced an embossed card. 'You need a couple of dinner dresses, one over-the-top evening dress and anything else that catches your eye. I'll be drinking coffee in Vlados, over the road.'

'Fine,' she repeated, and looked at the card. 'You sure this'll work?'

'I'm sure. Daniella will recognise it. She'll probably have heard about you. She'll certainly have heard about the children. Pippa…'

'Yes?'

She was standing in the late-afternoon sunshine, chin tilted, dredging up courage. David against Goliath.

It was important to maintain distance.

He couldn't. It was too much for any man. It was too much for him.

'Good luck in your hunting,' he said softly. His fingers caught her under the chin and tilted her chin just a tiny bit more. He kissed her. Softly, fleetingly, withdrawing before she had time to react.

'Go to it, my David,' he told her and he smiled and turned away to find his coffee shop.

Max bought a newspaper. He settled in at Vlados and ordered a coffee. He drank half a cup; there was a commotion in the entrance and there was Pippa.

She was in the midst of a group of uniformed men. Subdued. In her simple jeans and her T-shirt and sandals, she looked absurdly defenseless. David defeated?

He was on his feet and moving towards her before she saw him.

'Pippa?'

She turned, relief washing over her face. She broke away from the men and met him halfway across the restaurant. She was not only defeated, he thought. She was furious. Her eyes were sparking daggers and spots of high colour suffused each cheek.

She tossed down the card on the nearest table. With force. 'Great idea, Your Highness.'

'What?'

'I don't look royal.'

'You look pretty good to me,' he said and smiled, and then he stopped smiling as she looked around as if she was searching for something to brain him with. 'Hey, I'm not the bad guy here. At least,' he said cautiously, 'I don't think I am.'

'You're not,' she said, glaring at the group of men she'd just left. 'But you gave me the stupid card.'

'The card was a problem?'

'The whole idea was a problem.'

'Are you going to t—'

It seemed she was going to tell. 'I'd barely set foot over the threshold,' she told him. 'Before Daniella herself—all coiffure and glitter—came snaking out from behind the counter and wondered if I was in the right shop. I said I needed three formal dresses and if she had formal dresses then I was in the right shop.'

He was baffled. She looked really close to tears, he thought. He badly wanted to hold her but if he did…she'd back off, he thought, and he made a huge effort to make his voice noncommittal. 'So?'

'So she became very formal. She showed me a dress which looked okay, even if it did look like it was at the bottom of the range she carried. I said could I try it and she said, for security, could she see some form of identification as well as my credit card. I was getting pretty peeved, but I need a damned dress so I gave her my passport and your dumb royal card.'

'I see,' he said, really cautiously. He didn't see.

'So instead of helping me change into the dress she showed me into a cubicle. Then while I was wrangling zips she rang Levout. Who said I had no authority to charge anything to the castle and I must have stolen the card and he'd send the police straight away.'

'You are kidding,' he said slowly, but he knew already that she wasn't. Uh-oh.

'So I came out of the change room looking the ants pants in a little black number that would have knocked your socks off and I was met by six policemen. Six! And they wanted to haul me away in all my finery. Only then Daniella set up a screech about her dress, which she said costs a fortune, which, by the way, I was never going to buy because it was scratchy, and she made me take it off. Then and there. She made me change without going into the cubicle. She told the men to face the street but she wouldn't let me go back into the change room. She watched every step of the way in case I hurt her precious frock. I was humiliated to my socks and she watched me change like I was a criminal and even though I was wearing the most respectable knickers in the world all the time I was getting so…so…'

Hell. His hands were clenched into his palms so hard they hurt.

'Anyway, I got back in my own gear,' she muttered, as if she was trying hard to move on. 'Then the police said I was under arrest, and I saw red. I said I hadn't stolen your stupid card and that you were here and you'd sent me to buy a dress and you're in charge of their stupid police force and you'll sack the lot of them and if they didn't check with you first you'll have their necks on the guillotine first thing in the morning.'

'Hey,' he said, almost startled out of anger. 'Guillotine?'

'Well, maybe I didn't say quite that,' she muttered, glowering. 'But it's what I meant. Daniella's horrible coiffure would look great in a bucket, and I'd knit and watch like anything. Anyway, then they thought they'd check with you. So they frog-marched me over here—well, why wouldn't they when Levout assured them I was nothing to do with you? Now they've seen you and they're really nervous. But they're waiting on your command right now, to take me out and shoot me at dawn.'

There were six burly police officers in the doorway, muttering fiercely among themselves. Looking uncomfortable. As well they might.

'They seem to know you,' she said, anger becoming calmer now. 'Not me, though. I'm a provincial.'

'I'll go talk to them.'

'Good. I'll go steal a beer from the bar.'

'Maybe a coffee would be better. Vlados will fetch one for you.'

'Why not live up to my reputation?'

'Pippa?'

'Yes.'

'Have a coffee.'

By the time he reached them, the policemen were pretty sure they were in the wrong. Pippa's anger must have been obvious, as was the conciliatory hand Max put on her shoulder as he left her.

'Did she have rights to use the card?' the officer with the most stripes asked before he said a word.

'Yes,' Max said, dangerously calm. 'You saw our photographs taken the day we arrived? Did you recognise her?'

'Yes, but she isn't royal. We're sorry if we've made a mistake, though. We were acting on Levout's orders.'

'You have made a mistake. And what possible authority does Levout have over you?'

'He assured us the card was stolen.'

'You haven't answered my question. Was it his suggestion that made you force Miss Donohue to strip in the centre of the shop?'

'I…no. That was Miss Daniella's idea. She was concerned about her clothing.'

'And you agreed? You stood by while someone was forced to strip in public?'

'I…'

'There'll be changes,' Max said wearily. 'Starting from the top.'

'If you mean dismissal…' the man said unhappily.

'I'm not talking about dismissal. And, much as my friend over there would like an even more gory fate to befall you, I'm not interested in that either. I want names and ranks, written here.' He motioned to the waiter. 'This man will do it for me. There'll be repercussions, but meanwhile all I have to say is that Levout has no authority to act on my behalf in any capacity whatsoever. Is that clear?'

'That's clear,' he was told unhappily, and he left them writing their names while he returned to Pippa.

'This is a symptom of the mess we need to deal with,' he told her grimly. 'People with friends in high places can order the police force at whim. If you agree that Marc can stay here then I can fix this.'

'Oh, great,' she muttered. 'More blackmail.'

'I'm not blackmailing.'

'Just holding a gun to my head.'

'There are guns to both our heads. You tell me what to do. Brand my mother a liar in public? And surely you don't want to go back to the farm?'

'No, I—'

'And you wouldn't leave the kids here without you.'

She hesitated. Just for a moment she hesitated. 'No,' she said finally. 'Of course I wouldn't. And you know that. Toe-rag.'

'You're calling me a toe-rag?'

'Yes,' she said bluntly. 'I am. You're saying you'll fix this but from a distance? From back in Paris while you build your buildings? I can't take on a proxy role and neither can Marc. If this country is such a mess—'

'I'm doing all I can. Hell, Pippa, until five weeks ago I was a carpenter.'

'And I was a dairy maid,' she said, trying for a smile but not succeeding. Her shoulders sagged. He wanted to…he wanted…

He couldn't. At least he couldn't without speaking to his mother. Hell.

The police were filing out. 'Did you threaten something really messy?' she asked, without much hope.

'No.'

'Just as well,' she said, and tried again to smile. 'I'm not worth it.'

'You are worth it. Pippa, I'm so sorry. You're being sent from humiliation to humiliation. At Tanbarook, and now here.'

'I'm fine.'

'If you stay we have to figure out a role.' Even if he sorted things with his mother—even if he accepted what was starting to seem inevitable—she had to have a place here.

But she was shaking her head. 'Kids' guardian is the only role I want. Me and Dolores can sit in the sun for the rest of our lives. Where's the problem in that?'

'I—'

'Look, let's just organise this damned photo,' she said. 'If it really has to be taken. But I'd rather walk on nails than go back to Daniella's.'

'She's the only decent dress shop in the village.'

'What's that over there?'

She gestured towards the window. People were wandering into what looked like a dilapidated village hall. 'It looks like some sort of repertory company,' she said. 'There are billboards all over the front, and ladies have been going in with dresses.'

'So?'

'So if it's anything like any repertory company I've ever been involved with—'

'You're involved with repertory?'

'I've been Katisha in a Gilbert and Sullivan hospital Christmas pageant.'

The dragon lady in The Mikado? 'I don't believe it,' he said faintly.

'Want to hear an excerpt?'

'No!' Dammit, he wanted to hug her. He hated the bruised look behind her eyes. He wanted…

He couldn't. Hell, he needed to talk to his mother.

She was moving on.

'If this is a repertory company like any I've been involved with they'll have a room full of used costumes out the back. If you get to wear a dress sword, surely I can find something suitable to match.'

The repertory players were fascinated. 'Go right ahead,' they said, laughing among themselves at the thought of the props of their pageantry being used for such an occasion. 'We have costumes here a hundred years old.'

'Excellent,' Pippa said, notably brightening. 'A can-can dancer? Maybe not.'

'We don't usually lend them,' the wardrobe mistress told them. 'We use them over and over again. But for an occasion like this and if it saves you from paying money to that Daniella…'

'She's not popular?' Max queried.

'She's the only business in this town to make money,' the woman said darkly. 'The rest of us live hand to mouth but Daniella is a friend to the palace.'

That was said with such disdain that both Pippa and Max paused in their search and stared.

'I didn't mean you,' the woman said, flushing a little. 'We have such hopes, Your Highness,' she told Max. 'With you and your family settled in the palace…'

'Just family,' Pippa said. 'Not him.'

'Pippa, leave it,' Max said shortly. 'We came to find you a dress.'

'So we did. Or I did. But I don't need you to help me choose.'

'I'd like to help.'

'Yes, but I don't want you to,' she said, brightness fading. 'I need to get used to working this thing out on my own. Go watch a play rehearsal.'

She emerged a half hour later carrying a really big parcel. She looked pleased, but as she emerged and saw Max waiting for her in the late-afternoon sunshine her smile died.

Why did she stop smiling when she saw him? He didn't like it. 'What did you find?'

'Wait and see.'

Okay. He deserved this. He unfolded his long frame from the stone wall where he'd been sitting. They walked half a block to their car—and Daniella herself came bustling out of her shop to intercept them.

'Your Highness,' she called, and Max paused.

'Get in the car, Pippa.'

'Are you kidding?' She summoned a smile. 'I want to punch her lights out.'

'You're not allowed to punch anyone's lights out.'

'Really?' she said, quasi hopeful.

'Just because you walloped me doesn't mean you can get used to it.'

'No?' She bit her lip, her entrancing twinkle back. 'But I'm really sorry I walloped you.'

'That's fine. It was an entirely justifiable wallop.'

'And walloping Daniella isn't?'

'Not if we don't want a law suit.'

She signed theatrically, but she pinned on a smile as she turned to face the approaching Daniella.

Daniella was in her mid fifties, pencil slim, platinum blonde, dressed in sleek, expensive black. She was clicking hurriedly toward them on six-inch heels.

'I need to apologise,' she said, breathless and passionate, but she spoke only to Max. 'If I'd realised she really had authority—'

'She?'

Daniella motioned to Pippa. 'This woman. You need to get an identification system for authorised servants, Your Highness. The old prince let us know clearly who could buy things on his behalf.'

'Pippa is the guardian of the Crown Prince. She has the royal card.'

'Yes, but she has no money on her own behalf,' the woman said. 'And the little prince is too small to have her in charge. I didn't know what her credit limit was. Let me know and I'll accommodate her.'

'Hello? I'm right here,' Pippa said, but she was ignored.

'Pippa has authority to spend as much as she pleases,' Max snapped.

'The old prince never gave carte blanche to any of his servants.'

'Pippa is not a servant,' he roared, in a voice that startled them all. A toddler, being pushed in a stroller nearby, started to cry.

'What is she, then?' Daniella asked, looking at Pippa as if she were pond scum. Well, she had seen her in her bargain-basement knickers, Pippa conceded. She just knew Daniella wore kinky lace. But she couldn't get a word in edgeways.

'She's Pippa,' Max said through gritted teeth. 'She's part of the new order of things, so you'd better get used to it.'

They were building an audience. The players from the hall emerged as well. They'd obviously watched them leave and the sound of Max's roar had been just too enticing. They were crowding onto the pavement to watch.

'Pippa needs a tiara if she's going to be part of the royal family,' the wardrobe mistress called. 'Come back and I'll find you one.'

'No, thanks,' Pippa called. 'It wouldn't be seemly.'

'Why wouldn't it be seemly?' Max demanded. 'Why can't you have a tiara?'

Pippa blinked, thrown off stride. 'I'd look ridiculous.'

'I'll buy you a tiara.'

'You do that,' the wardrobe mistress called. 'She should have a real tiara. Everyone says she loves the new little prince to bits.'

'But she's not part of the royal family,' Daniella snapped.

'Your part of the royal family is dead and gone,' one of the players called. 'The Levouts' time is finished.' Then, as Max and Pippa looked confused, he explained. 'She's Carver Levout's mistress. She thinks she's royal herself.'

Suddenly the atmosphere was nasty.

'Can we get out of here?' Pippa asked and Max nodded and held the car door open.

'We need to go,' he called. 'Thanks for your help with the dress.'

'Who helped with the dress?' Daniella demanded, white-faced. Maybe she was realising she was missing out on a commission she just might need in the future.

'We did,' the wardrobe mistress called. 'Ooh, it's lovely. She's going to look really royal.'

'Especially beside him,' one of the players added. 'What a hunk.'

'They make a lovely couple,' the wardrobe mistress said mistily. 'A real royal couple.'

'We're leaving,' Max said, revolted, and slipped into the driver's seat beside her. He gunned his little car into life, but they were surrounded by players, smiling and laughing and edging Daniella out of the picture.

'We're so glad you're here,' was the general message, though it came in many shapes and forms.

Max nosed the car forward.

'A real family,' the wardrobe mistress sighed.

'Levout's day is over,' someone else called. 'As of next Friday,' they yelled. 'We're aching to see Levout's face when those documents are finally signed.'

They drove in silence. Pippa stared straight ahead, her face expressionless.

Max was feeling ill.

What was happening here? Why was it such a mess?

He had to get back to Paris.

It had taken him twenty hard years to get where he was now, he thought dully. Some said he'd been lucky, and that was true. His former boss had been a fantastic craftsman and his skills, combined with Max's business acumen, had been a winning combination. But Max had earned his luck. He worked seven days a week, always obliging, always learning, desperate to achieve a fortune in his own right. A fortune that wasn't tainted by royalty.

He'd achieved his aim. He and his former boss had created one of the biggest construction firms in Europe. His mother had one of the finest apartments in Paris and the best of medical care.

None of it was paid for by royal money.

To abandon his career and come back here because of guilt.

No and no and no.

Marc would make a fine prince, he told himself. He and the twins would be happy here.

Only because Pippa would stay with them. Because he was forcing Pippa to stay. He was giving her no choice.

And he had a choice. He'd rejected becoming Crown Prince, but if it would take that look off Pippa's face…

But would she go back to the farm? Would her sense of honour let her stay here?

'What's happening next Friday?' Pippa asked, cutting across his thoughts. 'What documents are being signed?'

He grimaced. He'd meant Pippa to be happily settled in the castle, determined never to revert to poverty, before he set this before her. Why was it suddenly so complicated?

He loved her?

The thought was so incredible that he took his foot off the accelerator for fear of doing something dumb.

Love?

Impossible. He didn't do love.

'Tell me about Friday,' she demanded in a small, cold voice and he forced himself to focus.

Friday.

'The succession has to be decided by next Friday.' Somehow he made his voice free of inflexion. 'The incumbent to the throne has to accept that position within sixty days of Bernard's death.'

'The incumbent. You mean Marc.'

'I guess so. Though you'll have to sign in his stead.'

'Because you won't?'

'I can't sign for him.'

'I mean you won't be Crown Prince.' She brushed her arm across her eyes in a gesture of weariness. 'No. Of course you can't.'

'Pippa, this will be a wonderful life for you.'

'It will,' she said dully. 'I can see that.'

He swore and shoved his foot on the brake. The car stopped dead, right in the middle of the road.

'I hate doing this to you.'

'Sure.'

'No, really.'

'Just leave it, Max.'

'I can't,' he said miserably. 'Hell, Pippa, to drag my mother through such a mess…'

'I can't see that's necessary.'

'I mean figuratively.'

'Oh,' she said flatly. 'Figuratively. I see.'

'You don't see,' he said and he reached out and took her shoulders, turning her so she was forced to meet his gaze. 'My mother was a teenage bride—seduced by my father's looks and money. He got her pregnant. The only reason he married her was that he was in the midst of a row with his own father at the time. Louis wanted him to marry an heiress and he married my mother out of spite.'

'You don't need to tell me this.'

'I need you to understand.'

'I do understand.'

'Pippa, you're gorgeous.'

'Oh, right,' she said and tried to pull away. 'Cut it out.'

'I mean it. Hell, Pippa, all I'm thinking about is you. I'm trying to sort out the succession, the politics, the way the country needs to be structured and all I can think about is you.'

'Then stop thinking about me,' she said angrily. 'You're making me miserable, and I can't be miserable. I'm going back to the palace to be chirpy like I always am. I'm going back to singing.'

'Like you were in the dairy. To block things out.'

'You're blocking the road.'

'Pippa—'

'You're blocking the road.'

'Dammit, I'm the Prince Regent of Alp d'Estella,' he growled. 'I'm at least the Prince Regent. If I want to block a road then I damn well can.' He glared at her for all of a minute, daring her to gainsay him.

She didn't gainsay him.

'You just sit there looking at me…' he growled.

'What am I supposed to do?'

He knew what he was supposed to do. His path was suddenly crystal-clear.

He kissed her.

He kissed her, and suddenly confusion fell away. Whatever else was wrong in this crazy world, this was right.

She tasted…like Pippa.

Nothing more. Nothing less. He wanted nothing else.

Pippa.

His hands grasped her shoulders so he could pinion her lips

right where he wanted them. His mouth claimed hers. For a fraction of a moment she held herself rigid, as if she might pull away—as if she might react with horror, slap him once more?—but it was the sensation of a moment. Nothing more. He felt her resistance slump out of her. He felt her lips open under his.

Pippa.

She was perfection. His hands lowered to her waist and he gathered her close. Dammit, the gear stick was in the way. Why the hell did he have such a tiny car? He was hauling her close, closer and still the damned gear stick was between.

He'd break the thing if he could.

He couldn't. There was no room on her side of the car for him, or his side for her. Outside there was bare bitumen.

He had to make do with what he had. Which was Pippa, kissing him as he was kissing her. Opening her lips and letting him taste her as deeply as he wanted. Letting his hands hold the curves of her, slip under her T-shirt to feel the silken smooth curve of her bare skin.

He wanted her. He wanted her as he'd never wanted a woman. He wanted her in his bed, and more.

Her hands were in his hair, making him crazy. Of all the erotic sensations… She was deepening the kiss all by herself. Wonderful woman, he thought, amazed by the cleverness of her gesture. Wonderful, wonderful sprite. A red-headed minx who had the knowledge that if she pulled him tighter the kiss couldn't be broken…

He was nuts. He was granting her intellect for one simple gesture. The idea made him smile from within, a great, warming, inward sigh of pure wonder.

Any woman might have done the same, he thought, but there was only one Pippa.

The kiss was endless. Neither of them was willing to break the moment. Maybe if this had been another time, another place, with just a fraction more privacy, without the awful impediment of a gear stick, then they would have taken this further, tumbling into glorious passion.

But they couldn't. They were in the middle of a one-way cliffside road.

Someone was watching.

Max had closed his eyes, savouring the moment. Suddenly some extra sense made him open one eye.

Cautiously.

There were three men and a woman right beside their open sports car. Their audience was watching with every evidence of enjoyment.

'Don't mind us, M'sier,' one of the men said, and he recognised one of the players from the village. 'Our director tells us to study real life. Romain thought we should sound the horn so you could move your vehicle, but, no, I said, one is only young once and maybe we have forgotten. It does no harm to remind ourselves.' He gave a rueful smile. 'The play we are performing, you see,' he said, apologetic but still smiling. 'I play a young man with a young man's passion. Like yourself. But I'm fifty-three years old and I should not be cast as a young man. No matter. All our young have left to try and find work in Italy or France so we are left to do what we can. But it does the heart good to see such reminders.'

Max's eyes were wide open now. As were Pippa's. She was still in his arms but she'd burrowed her head into his shoulder. She choked.

'You laugh and I'll have to kill you,' he whispered.

'Or kiss me again?' she whispered back and he fought to maintain a straight face. Kiss her again? Mmm.

But his audience was waiting for a response. 'I was just comforting Miss—'

'Oh, yes,' the only woman in the group said, understandingly. 'It's very nice that our Prince Regent comforts the guardian of our new Crown Prince. It's a very satisfactory thing to happen. You and this lady? Yes and yes and yes.'

'Levout said at the end of one month you intend to go back to Paris,' the first player told him, settling in for a mid-road chat. 'We asked how is that possible—when the country needs a ruler as much as we do? But of course it's nonsense. Miss will never leave the children. And you…the rumour is that the lady, your mother, was not exactly truthful with your father. All the servants are whispering. Before when we don't see you we accept that she play—how you say—fast and loose. But you…you are a de Gauiter. Yes and yes and yes. So now… This is good.' He grinned. 'This miss will need much comfort. And not in Paris.'

'Hey, I do not need much comfort,' Pippa squeaked, tugging herself away. As much as she could. Which wasn't very far, as Max's arms still held her.

'Miss, if you need to deal with the likes of Levout and his compatriots you will need help,' the woman said. 'He is like an octopus. His tentacles are everywhere. His people will wish you nothing but evil.'

'That's nonsense,' Max said, but he felt suddenly uneasy. Or more uneasy. These people were verbalising what he already suspected.

And her words were heard and understood by Pippa. 'Let's go home,' she said, no longer laughing. 'Marc—'

'He's fine.'

'Yes, but I want to go home. Please, Max.'

'Sure,' he said and he let her go.

'You keep them all safe,' the woman said.

'This is a wonderful family,' another added. 'We wish you joy.'

'We wish us all joy,' the woman added. 'And maybe it comes true. Maybe it comes true for all of us.'

They drove for the next few minutes in silence. Max stared straight ahead, his mind whirling.

What they'd said was right. He couldn't leave her.

But his mother… His construction company… How could he let them go? And how could he stay here? He'd stay here for what? To keep Pippa safe? And spend the rest of his life in the goldfish bowl as well?

He wanted to pick them all up and take them back to Paris. Be done with the whole sordid mess.

Hell.

'If you grip the steering wheel any harder you'll break it,' Pippa said conversationally, and he eased his grip. A little. With enormous difficulty.

'It's not a great choice, is it?' she said softly.

'No.'

'By Friday next week, you say?'

'Yes.'

'There's a lot of thinking for both of us,' she whispered. 'Meanwhile… Max, please don't kiss me any more. It clouds the issues and we badly don't need clouds.'

The vague sense of unease they'd felt at the player's mention of evil was unfounded. They arrived back as the last of the day's sun played tangerine light on the massive stone walls and turrets, turning the place into more of a fairy-tale setting than it already was. Pascal-Marie, the butler, met them sedately, and Beatrice was close behind. All was well.

'The children have gone to sleep,' Beatrice told them. 'They were too excited to have an afternoon nap. Because the formal photograph session is set for eight tonight, we fed them early and put them to bed. I thought we could wake them at seven.'

'I'll check them,' Pippa said, crossing to the stairway.

'Pippa?' Max called after her and she paused, three stairs up.

'Yes?'

Pippa.

He couldn't think of a thing to say.

'Oh, there is a problem with your dog,' Beatrice added and Pippa stilled. Maybe all wasn't well.

'With Dolores?'

'She's asleep by the fire in the front sitting room,' Beatrice said. 'She romped with the children in the fountain this afternoon. Like a great puppy. We dried her off, and she went to sleep in the sun. It's probably laziness but when the children went up to bed they couldn't persuade her to join them.'

She was through to the sitting room in an instant. Max followed.

The old dog was still sleeping. This room faced south west, with windows all round. Dolores would have had direct sunlight, with the fire adding a little top-up warmth if necessary. The rugs here were inches thick. Why would an old dog move? Max thought appreciatively.

'Dolores,' Pippa whispered and dropped to her knees. The dog opened her eyes, gave her tail a feeble wag and closed her eyes again.

Pippa lifted the old head and cradled it on her lap, running her hand over her flank, letting her fingers lie on her chest. 'Dolores?'

'Is she okay?' Max asked, feeling he was intruding on something personal.

'She's okay,' Pippa whispered, laying her cheek on the old dog's head. 'She's just really, really old, and it'll have been exciting with the children today. The vet told us that this would be her last winter.' She looked up at Max and her eyes glimmered with unshed tears. 'But thanks to you she's had a summer instead of a winter. She has sunbeams and log fires.'

But still that sheen of tears. 'Hey…'

'Could you carry her upstairs for me?'

'To the children's bedroom?'

'I might stay in a room by myself tonight,' she murmured, stroking the dog's soft ears. 'The beds are big but not so big to hold three kids, me *and* Dolores. The kids are feeling safe and happy now, so Dolores and me will sleep next door with the door open.'

Dolores and me. She was sleeping with a dog. Dolores nuzzled against her cheek and he found it within himself to be jealous of a disreputable, ancient Labrador-something.

'Fine,' he managed, neutrally, and he stooped to lift her.

Pippa rose with him, her hands still on the big dog's head.

Dolores' eyes stayed closed.

'She trusts you,' Pippa whispered. 'She knows people, does Dolores. She's never been wrong yet.'

She was too close. The hint of tears in her eyes was damn near his undoing.

Dolores gave a gentle snore, breaking the moment.

'You're sure you want to sleep with her?'

'What's a little snoring between friends?'

What indeed?

He was gazing at Pippa. She was stroking Dolores' ears.

'Let's go,' she said, and he thought, Right, let's go.

He so badly wanted to gather her into his arms. How could he do that with an armful of dog?

It was just as well he couldn't, he thought. What he wanted wasn't…sensible.

So he carried her dog upstairs. Pippa hurried up before him, and by the time he reached the bedroom beside the children's she was spreading a feather-down quilt she'd tugged out of the blanket box.

'That's probably an heirloom,' he said and she put her hands on her hips.

'Well?'

'Nothing,' he said meekly, and set Dolores down.

Dolores opened one eye and her tail gave an infinitesimal wag.

'I'll light the fire,' he said. It was already set in the grate. The room hardly needed heating yet he knew she'd want the dog warm. Besides, it gave him a reason to stay an extra few moments.

'We'll be right,' Pippa said, and walked to the door and held it wide, waiting for him to go. 'Thank you, Max.'

He was being dismissed. She needed a rest, he thought. Or she needed to be alone with her dog.

'Photographs at eight?'

'I'll be there.'

'What about dinner?'

'I'll ask Beatrice to bring something up. I need a nap if I'm going to be beautiful for photos.'

He didn't want to go. She looked so alone. But she was waiting for him to go, glancing sideways at her dog, holding the door wide.

'If there's anything I can do…' he said uselessly and she nodded.

'Thank you. But there isn't. Please, Max, just go.'

Max returned to his bedroom. He paced.

Then he went down to the sitting room Dolores had just

vacated. The fire was still burning in the grate. The room was in darkness but he didn't turn the light on.

He paced some more.

'Will you be dressing for dinner, sir?' Blake sounded apologetic, as if he knew he was interrupting serious thought.

'No.' He dragged himself back to the here and now. Blake was standing in the doorway looking worried. 'I'll skip dinner.'

'Cook has prepared roast duck,' he said reproachfully. 'Miss Pippa has said she's not hungry. I believe Cook will be hurt if no one eats her duck.'

Max closed his eyes. Obligations everywhere. Pippa's obligations. His obligations. An obligation to duck.

This one at least he could fulfil.

'Fine. I'll dress and then I'll eat Cook's duck.'

CHAPTER NINE

MAX felt ridiculous.

He'd thought the uniform he'd worn the night they arrived was stunning. This one though was even more so. Deep blue and brilliant crimson, it was so startling that when he saw himself in the mirror he started to laugh.

'Sir, it's wonderful,' Blake said with reproach. 'You look so much more handsome than the old prince.'

'I'm only Regent,' he said, staring at the rows of honours on his chest. 'This is crazy.'

'You're our sovereign,' Blake said reproachfully. 'At least until the little prince comes of age.'

Damn the man. He'd had it with the reproach.

'Well, as long as Pippa has something to match,' he growled, thinking of Pippa as he'd last seen her, a waif with tear-filled eyes and an ancient dog. She was as far away from this as it was possible to be.

'Beatrice tells me Pippa's dress is just the solution,' Blake said reassuringly. 'She says it will make us all smile.'

As she'd said, Pippa didn't appear for dinner. He ate in solitary splendour in the grand dining room. Levout was absent as well—which made Max nervous, but he'd rather eat without him than with him. The duck was magnificent. He said all the right things, even though he was having trouble tasting.

He kept thinking of Pippa.

And Dolores. Dammit, he was worrying about a dog.

'Ask Miss Pippa if she'd like us to call a veterinarian,' he told Blake, and Blake looked at him with even more reproach.

'Sir, we asked her that ourselves. She says no, there's nothing wrong with the dog but old age.' He gave a rueful smile. 'There's nothing a veterinarian can do about that.'

'I guess not.' He half rose.

'Chocolate meringues, sir,' the butler said reproachfully. 'And then coffee and liqueur.'

Reproach, reproach, reproach.

So there was no time to return to Pippa's room before the shoot. He made his way to the ballroom as requested at eight.

Beatrice was there, with the three children all rigged out as royal children had been rigged throughout the ages.

'Wow,' he said, astonished. 'You look like something out of Hans Christian Andersen.'

'We look beeyootiful,' Claire said, pirouetting to prove it.

'You've got a sword,' Marc said with deep envy. 'How old do I have to be to have a sword?'

'Twenty-one.'

'But aren't I a Crown Prince?'

'Yes, but I get to carry the sword.'

''Cos Max is the boss of us,' Sophie said, pirouetting with her sister. 'Max fights the baddies.'

'There aren't any baddies,' Beatrice said. 'Let me fix your hair ribbon, Claire.'

'Where's Pippa?' he asked. This was to be the official royal portrait. The photographer—a woman in her seventies—and her two spritely—only sixty if a day—assistants were set up and ready. One of the assistants was approaching him with a palette and brushes.

'What's this?'

'Make-up,' she said. 'So you don't shine.'

'No,' he growled. 'I like shine. Where the hell is Pippa?'

The door swung open.

Pippa.

What the hell…?

This was a transformed Pippa. She was a sugar-plum confection in pink and white and silver. She was a gorgeous apparition that made him blink in disbelief.

Her dress was a floor-length ballgown, with hoops underneath to make it spread wide. Her scalloped neckline was scooped to show a hint of her beautiful breasts. The pink and silver brocade curved in and clung to her waistline, as if the dress had been made for her.

She smiled at them all and twirled in much the same manner as the twins.

She had gossamer wings attached to her shoulder blades.

She was carrying a silver wand.

'Who needs a wish?' she said, and she giggled.

'You're a fairy godmother,' Sophie said, awed, and Pippa chuckled.

'You have it in one. I spent today trying to figure what my role tonight could be. I was feeling a little like Cinderella but then I thought, no, my role is already decided. I'm your godmother. I agreed to bring you guys here—with or without pumpkins—so that's obviously who I am. We have two Prince Charmings and two Sleeping Beauties—' she grinned at the twins '—only you're not asleep any more. So here we are.'

'We could bring Dolores in and she could be the horse,' Marc said, entranced, and a touch of a shadow flitted across Pippa's face. It was so fleeting that Max almost missed it. But he was sure.

'How's—?'

'Dolores really is Sleeping Beauty,' she said, cutting across Max's question. 'You wake her and you'll be the Wicked Witch of the West. Okay, you guys, let's get ourselves photographed.' She twirled again. 'Don't you think this is just the right outfit?'

'No,' Max said, frowning. He was out of his depth here, he thought. But surely Pippa shouldn't be the godmother. What the hell should she be?

Not Cinderella, that was for sure. No maid in tatters, this.

'You look really, really pretty,' Marc said stoutly, casting Max a look of…reproach. *Et tu, Brute?* He dived forward to grab her hand. 'We have to stand right here, Pippa.'

'You look wonderful,' the photographer said, smiling with real appreciation. 'The tabloids will love you to bits.'

'You'll win hearts,' Beatrice said.

Everyone was smiling. Except him.

It felt wrong. Gossamer or not, she didn't feel like a fairy godmother.

She felt… She felt…

She felt like Pippa.

The shoot lasted over an hour. By then the children were drooping again. Pippa looked exhausted too, Max thought, but she wasn't letting on.

'Enough,' he decreed at last, and the photographer sighed and straightened from her tripod.

'Yes, sir,' she said. 'You're all so photogenic I could keep on for hours. But this will keep the press happy. I'll let the media have whatever they want.'

'Great.' That was why they'd done it. To keep the pressure off. Now they were free of pressure until Friday week.

Then, if Pippa agreed, he'd be free of media pressure for ever.

It should feel good. But now he looked at Pippa's strained face and he thought she'd found this harder than he had. She'd worked at making it cheerful—she was still bouncing, swiping kids with her wand and threatening them with fairy dust if they didn't head straight to bed—but there was something akin to desolation behind the façade.

He'd hauled her out of poverty, he thought, but she knew that riches and glitter weren't enough.

He knew that, too. Could he walk away from this mess? Pick her up and carry her to Paris?

With three kids and a dog?

His mother would adore them.

'Can I help put the kids to bed?' he asked.

'Not tonight.' She carefully didn't look at him. 'And, Beatrice, we don't need you either. We'll be fine. We'll see you in the morning.' She prodded the closest princess with her wand. The princess gave a sleepy giggle and headed bravely to the stairs, fairy godmother in pursuit.

'Goodnight, sir,' Beatrice said, with all the deference in the world. And then she paused.

'You know, Pippa loves you,' she whispered. 'That has to count for a lot.'

Max stared at her.

How did Beatrice know?

But maybe…maybe…

He wanted to sleep himself, but first he had to front Levout. The official had disappeared for days. He appeared now, standing in the entrance hall, waiting for him, smiling urbanely.

'I believe there was some problem in the village earlier in the evening.'

Max nodded curtly. 'Your friend Daniella.'

'And the players in the town hall.'

'There was no problem with the players.'

'Oh, yes,' Levout said smoothly and he smiled. His smile made Max uneasy. 'There's always been conflict between the people and the palace. I just came to let you know it's sorted.'

'What's sorted?'

'Daniella came to see me, and we've looked into it straight away. We don't like those type of people intimidating our tradesmen and women. These gatherings are clearly inappropriate for our village. So… The hall they've been using is dilapidated. All those tatty costumes in the back are home for vermin. It's surely a safety risk. We've boarded it closed, and in the morning we'll send in bulldozers.'

Max stilled. 'You have no right.'

'We have every right,' he said urbanely. His smile was surface only—behind his eyes was pure venom. 'You might, as Prince Regent, be able to institute changes at parliamentary level, but according to the constitution only a ruling Crown Prince can interfere with daily minutiae. As there will be no ruling Crown Prince for thirteen years we have no problem.'

'A prince has no right to interfere…'

'Exactly.' Levout's oily smile broadened, but underneath there was something akin to hate. 'Which is what I dropped by to tell you. We—the current mayor and our associates—will keep on running the day-to-day affairs of this country as we see fit, regardless of what you do at a higher level. You can return to Paris as you plan and leave it safely to us. Oh, and we don't despair of the future, either. The young prince is already eight years old. By the age of twelve we may be able to persuade him to let things run as generations of monarchs have done before him.' His smile became a sneer. 'What you do, he can be persuaded to undo.'

'Pippa will never allow him—'

'Teenagers revolt,' Levout said softly and smiled. 'Especially if they're encouraged to do so. And Miss Donohue has no authority at all.'

Was Levout right? The lawyers he'd talked to before going to Australia had talked about changing the constitution from an overriding sovereignty to a democracy. They hadn't gone into minutiae.

If Levout was right, it was a mess. For Pippa to cope with it… He couldn't ask it of her. But to walk away…

He had to talk to the lawyers again, he thought. He had to figure out just what Levout and his cronies could really do.

But by next Friday? By the time decisions had to be irretrievably made?

He couldn't leave Pippa.

That was the crux of the matter. The more he thought, the more his mind came back to Pippa. Pippa tonight in her crazy fairy godmother dress, acting as if she hadn't a care in the world, making everyone here smile. Tomorrow she'd make the whole country smile as they woke to their morning newspapers.

His mind stilled, retaining that indelible image of Pippa smiling for the camera.

And the players tonight…

All our young have left to try and find work in Italy or France so we are left to do what we can.

Enough.

He didn't need to contact lawyers.

He went inside to telephone his mother.

It was two in the morning. He should be asleep, but he'd lain in the moonlight and stared at the ceiling and thought he'd go nuts. Pippa would be asleep. It was crazy to go to her now. She needed to sleep and so did he.

He couldn't.

At three he gave it up for a bad job. He rose and paced to the window. And paused.

There were people on the lawn in front of the castle. The scene was lit by the moonlight. Three figures. One was one long and lean and stooped. One was smaller. Digging? Another figure was a little apart, moving about in the rose bed.

Pippa. And Blake. And Beatrice.

He reached for his clothes and in less than a minute he was out there.

What the hell…?

No one reacted as he came catapulting out the entrance. They kept doing what they were doing. He strode across the lawn, past the fountain and the new decking. Yes, it was Beatrice, snipping roses in the moonlight. Pippa and Blake were digging by the side of the rose garden, just out from the windows of the sitting room.

By the time he reached them he had it figured, and he felt sick.

'Pippa,' he said as he reached them, but she kept right on digging. Blake, however, paused for a breather, resting gratefully on his spade. The ground was dry and hard, Max thought. Blake was too old to be digging.

'Beatrice and I wanted to wake you,' Blake said, sounding relieved. 'But Pippa wouldn't let us.'

'Dolores?' he asked, and Blake nodded.

'She died earlier this evening. Before the photo shoot.'

'Before the photo shoot?' He stared at Pippa, and then muttered an expletive. 'Before the shoot! What the hell do you think you're doing?'

'What does it look like we're doing?' Her voice was laced with tears. 'We have to bury her.'

'Tonight?'

'I don't want the children to see…' She gulped, and wiped her face fiercely with her sleeve. 'They said goodbye to her. When they woke to get dressed for the photographer she was still sleeping, almost normally. But I could feel her heart… It was missing. It was so weak. She could no longer stand, and she was barely conscious. Back home the vet said he'd expected this to happen. Maybe if I'd let you call the vet she could have had a little more time. But she spent today with the children. Beatrice said the children were all over her, exactly as she loves. Then tonight she went to sleep in a sunbeam, by the fire, and you carried her up to my bed. When her breathing got weaker I thought… I thought, for her this day has been perfect. I'm not going to ask her to go on.'

'But you didn't tell the children?'

'The children knew she only had a limited time,' she whispered. 'When they woke for the photo shoot I told them to pop in and say goodnight to her. They all did. I packed her with hot water bottles and tucked her under the duvet. Then, just as I was thinking I couldn't leave her to go to the photo shoot, she just…died.'

'Beatrice knew,' Blake said heavily. 'But Pippa wouldn't let us tell anyone.'

'I didn't want the children to see her dead,' she said fiercely. 'They don't need to. If I thought it would help then, yes, but Marc's had enough death and talk of death. He's old for his years as it is. Tomorrow I want to tell them Dolores died in the night and we buried her here, under her beloved sunbeams. We'll decorate her grave. It'll be sad, but it won't be…'

'It won't be gut-wrenching like burying her is.' Max thought back to Thiérry's funeral. 'No, Pippa,' he said gently. 'You're right. But for you there's no choice but to do the gut-wrenching. How you managed to do the photo shoot…'

'It was the bravest thing we've ever seen,' Blake said, and sniffed. 'She wouldn't let Beatrice tell you…'

'She's my dog,' Pippa said, almost fiercely. 'It's my grief.'

'It's a shared grief,' Max said, and enough, enough. He took the spade from fingers that were suddenly lifeless, and he let it fall as he took her in his arms. He held her close, hard against him, kissing the top of her hair but just holding her. Just holding…

And at last, here they came. The searing sobs that had been so long coming.

Had she cried when her mother died? he wondered. Or Alice? Or Gina and Donald? Somehow he doubted it. All that time she'd been alone, or supporting others.

She'd never be alone again. He made himself that promise, then and there. Never.

There was an ancient stone seat nearby. When the worst of the sobs subsided he lifted her and set her down, beckoning Beatrice and Blake to sit beside her.

'Hold her,' he said to the elderly servants. 'Just sit there, Pippa, and wait. I'm starting what I should have started five weeks ago.'

'Five weeks ago, Your Highness?' Blake queried.

'That's when my mother told me.'

'I wondered,' Blake said softly.

'But you knew?'

'Yes, sir,' Blake said simply. 'The old prince depended on me absolutely. He wouldn't sack me, so I was the only one who was safe. So I was the one she said was your father.' He smiled, misty-eyed in the moonlight. 'May I say, Your Highness, that it would have been an honour. For Beatrice and I, it still is an honour.'

* * *

He thought about it while he dug the grave, swiftly and cleanly, using the muscles he'd gained in another life. Then he put such thoughts aside. While Blake and Beatrice cut more roses, he went with Pippa to bring her dog down for burial. He held her hand as they walked upstairs, and she clung as if she needed him.

The big dog lay where she'd died. She looked at peace, Max thought, an old dog at the end of a life well lived, but even so he found himself swallowing hard.

'I don't know what to wrap her in,' Pippa said helplessly, but Max knew.

'Your sweater,' he told her. 'Maybe two of your sweaters, or anything else of yours that you can spare. That's what she'd want to be buried in.' He cupped Pippa's tear-stained face and smiled tenderly into her eyes. 'But she's not a chihuahua. Maybe we'd better add in one of mine for good measure. Dolores was never a one-sweater dog.'

So Dolores was buried, at four in the morning, with all the dignity and reverence they could muster. There were four of them there to say goodbye. Pippa, Max, Blake and Beatrice. Blake and Beatrice took the burial as seriously as Pippa did.

As did Max. It was right. It was a strange little funeral, but lovely for all that. The night was serene and beautiful. The scent of the roses was rich and sweet, and there was an owl calling from the woods nearby.

It was as good a goodbye as was possible, Max thought, and even though Pippa didn't speak he knew she felt the same.

'Come back to bed, sweetheart,' he told her as they finished laying roses over the tumbled earth. 'We'll decorate it properly in the morning.'

'I…' She shook her head, as if trying to shake a dream. 'I don't know…'

'Well, I do,' he said softly and he swept her into his arms and held her tight. 'You're spent, my love. Don't object. Just do what you're told.' And Beatrice and Blake smiled mistily as he carried her inside, up the sweeping staircase, back to her bed.

When they reached the bed the bedclothes were still tousled from Dolores and the fire was still crackling in the grate. He lay her gently on the pillows but her arms were around his neck and she drew him down with her.

'Don't leave,' she whispered.

Leave was the last thing he intended to do. She was cradled against him, soft and warm and lovely. She smelled of the roses she'd held. She tasted of tears. He felt his heart shift within him as he'd never known it could, and, as he stroked her hair, as he kissed her sweet mouth, as he held her close against him, her breasts moulding to his chest, her body curved and suppliant in his arms, he knew that he could never leave.

'Pippa,' he whispered and she held his face in her hands, kissing him, passive grief slowly fading as passion stirred to take its place.

He kissed her back, the kisses becoming hot and demanding as he felt her response. She wanted him.

Beatrice's words came back to him. 'You know, Pippa loves you.'

Could that be true? Could such a miracle have happened?

Maybe. Maybe.

She was possessive now, her lips claiming his mouth as fiercely as his claimed hers. Her hands were holding his body against hers. Her fingers were feeling the contours of his back, his hips, his thighs.

His fingers slipped under the soft fabric of her T-shirt. She had no bra. Like Max, she'd shed her finery with speed this night, and she'd felt no need to dress in more than a cursory manner.

Her breasts were moulded to his hands. Her nipples were taut under his fingers. He breathed out, a soft sigh of sensory pleasure, of acceptance that this miracle could somehow be happening, that this woman could possibly be his.

Maybe she did love him, he thought exultantly. She loves me before I've promised her a thing. She loves me despite what I've been trying to make her do.

And somehow it made the world right. His world, which had been torn apart when Thiérry was killed, or even earlier, when his mother had lied, when his parents' marriage had fractured, was somehow settling back on its rightful axis. Love conquered all. It does, he thought exultantly. Damn the critics, the cynical. He had his Pippa. He'd found love.

'Pippa.'

The word was an echo of his thoughts. For a moment he didn't react, thinking it was just a part of this night.

But he felt Pippa still in his arms. She put her hands up to his hair and let her fingers run through, as if somehow imparting a message that this had to be interrupted. Her name wasn't part of the night. She was being called.

The outside world was slipping in.

Reluctantly he loosened his hold and she twisted in his arms. He could barely see her in the firelight, but the night-light was on in the sitting room and the slight figure in the doorway was unmistakable. It was a little boy in too-big pyjamas, his voice wavering toward panic. 'Pippa?'

'Marc.' Pippa was out from his arms, rolling off the bed, crossing to fold the little boy into her arms. 'Marc, what is it?'

'Who…who's there?'

'I'm here,' Max said gruffly, trying to make his voice sound normal. 'I was just…'

'Max was giving me a cuddle,' Pippa said. 'Did you hear us? Did we scare you?'

'No.' He faltered, looking towards the bed. Max flicked on the bedside lamp, thanking his lucky stars that Marc hadn't waited for another five minutes. For if he had…

'Where's Dolores?' Marc whispered and the night stilled. 'I woke up and you weren't with us. And I thought about Dolores. Where's Dolores? I was just…scared.'

'She's dead, Marc,' Pippa said, hugging him close. She was stooped to his level, hugging him against her, and the sight was enough to make Max feel…feel… Hell, he didn't know what he felt. He'd spent his whole life avoiding relationships and now here he was, in the midst of so many relationships he didn't know where to start.

But Pippa seemed too choked up to talk. The responsibility was suddenly his. 'Dolores died peacefully in her sleep,' he told Marc, and Marc looked over Pippa's shoulder and met his gaze head-on. 'That's why I'm here hugging Pippa.'

'Really?'

'Really.'

'Where is she?' He gazed fearfully around the room, and Max thought, yes, Pippa had been right to speed the burial. Sometimes children needed to be involved in all things, but not this time. Not when Marc's grief for his parents was still raw.

'Pippa and I buried her,' Max said.

'Where?'

'Just below these windows. Near the rose garden.'

'In the moonlight,' Pippa whispered. 'And where the sun shines all day.'

Marc swallowed. 'I should… I should have helped,' he said and damn, Max was as close to crying as he'd been for years. This waif of a child was squaring his shoulders like a man. He was under no illusion that Marc would have used the spade if he'd had to.

'You know, you can't see the grave from here,' he said, crossing to the windows and looking out. 'It's too dark. Would you like to come down and see what we've done?'

Marc considered. 'Yes,' he said at last. 'Please.'

'You should be asleep,' Pippa said ruefully, but Max shook his head.

'No. He needs to see the grave. Will you come with me?' He held out his hand to Marc.

'Yes.'

'I'll come, too,' Pippa said, but Max caught her shoulders and forced her to turn to him.

'No,' he said softly and he kissed her, softly, tenderly, as she needed to be kissed. 'You're dead tired, my love. You've cared for Dolores. You've cared for all of us. Now it's time for the men of the family to take care of you. Marc, Dolores was Pippa's dog for a long time, much longer than you or I have known her. She's feeling very sad. And she's tired. Will you tuck Pippa into bed while I fill hot water bottles?'

'Okay,' Marc said, cautious but game. 'Pippa, you have to get into bed.'

'But I—'

'Don't argue with us,' Max said firmly. 'We're in charge. You know, Marc and I have some serious talking to do, too, and it's a good time for us to do it now, when all the womenfolk are asleep. So, Pippa. Bed.'

'Bed,' said Marc.

She stared at them for a long moment. Prince Regent. Crown Prince. Her men, giving orders.

She smiled wearily at them both and she went to bed.

She didn't sleep, but, safe under the covers, warmed by the fire and by the hot-water bottles Max had filled, she felt as at peace as she'd ever felt in her life.

Dolores' death was a grief but not an overwhelming one. She'd known this was coming, and for it to happen in this way was a blessing. She knew it. And now… She'd thought she'd be bereft, but she wasn't.

For things had changed. Max was no longer looking at her as if she was some sort of trap.

She was no longer alone.

She wasn't sure of the whys or wherefores, but she let her thoughts drift where they willed, content to let tomorrow take care of itself. Somewhere downstairs Max was having a heart-to-heart talk with Marc. What about? Maybe she should be in on the conversation, but she trusted Max.

She trusted him with her life.

She rolled over and one of her hot-water bottles slid out on the floor. No matter. She didn't need it.

But Max had given it to her. For some dumb reason it seemed important to retrieve.

She slid out from under the covers and groped in the darkness ntil she found it. She went to climb back into bed, but, almost s an afterthought, she crossed to the window.

And saw…

Max and Marc were on the seat she'd so recently vacated. 'hey were talking steadily. Max's arm was around Marc's shoul-ers. She blinked.

And then she looked at the grave.

For she could see the grave now. No longer a darkened mound ı a darkened garden, it was an oasis of light.

The boys—the men, she corrected herself—had brought out andles. They'd found tea-light candles, many candles.

There was a perimeter of candles around the grave. And then, mong the roses, the candles spelled out letters.

DOLORES.

Where had they found so many candles?

No matter. She could see the colours of the roses, illuminated y the candles. She could almost imagine she could smell them. 'he grave looked wonderful

Beside the grave, Max and Marc spoke earnestly on.

She blinked and blinked again but she didn't cry. The time for rying was over.

She hugged her hot-water bottle to her. Max wouldn't come ack to her this night, she knew. She didn't need him to.

Tomorrow was just…tomorrow.

CHAPTER TEN

PIPPA woke and sun was streaming in the window. Her door wa wide open, and the children were filing in.

They were dressed and washed and sparkling, the twins pigtails plaited, neat as pins, and full of importance.

Sophie was bearing a glass of orange juice.

Claire was carrying a plate of fruit.

Marc was balancing a tray holding toast, pots of jam and tub of butter curls.

Max was bringing up the rear, carrying coffee.

'Good morning,' he said, and her heart felt as if it did somersault. 'Or almost good afternoon.'

She stared at the clock. Eleven!

'We let you sleep in,' Sophie said. ''Cos you were up in th night looking after Dolores.'

'Oh, Sophie…'

'I told them Dolores died,' Marc said, matter-of-factly. 'We'v put more flowers on her grave. Sophie put pansies on and Clair chose pretty white flowers with yellow middles. They'll di pretty soon but Max says we'll all go for a drive later to a garde place. We'll each choose what we want to plant on Dolores grave. And Max said we can light the candles every night for a long as we want.'

'That's…that's lovely.'

'But you need to get up,' Claire said importantly. ''Cos w have a visitor.'

'Who?'

'Sort of a grandma,' Sophie said and she giggled.

'She says we can call her Grandma, anyway.' Marc sounded a bit uncertain. 'But she says only if you think it's okay.'

'Who is it?' Pippa asked, intrigued.

'My mother,' Max said.

She blinked.

'And she's waiting for you to wheel her round the garden,' he told the kids. 'Use the ramp at the side door and don't take her anywhere the wheelchair can get stuck.'

'We won't,' Sophie said and dumped her orange juice and ran. Closely followed by Claire.

'And I'm not going to be Crown Prince any more,' Marc added, setting down his toast with care. 'Max and me talked about it last night and we have a plan. It's really good. But can I go and help wheeling? They might crash the wheelchair if I don't.'

'Go right ahead,' Max said, placing his hand on the boy's thin shoulder and giving him a squeeze of affection. 'You're a kid in a million.'

Marc gave a self-conscious grin, smiled shyly up at his hero—and bolted.

Pippa was left with Max. She should feel shy too, she thought. She didn't. She just felt…right.

'How soon is soon enough to ask you to marry me?' Max said, and her world stilled.

'What did you say?'

'You heard.' He set down the coffee pot on the floor. 'I was intending to wait until you'd eaten your toast, but you're far too beautiful to leave hanging around for long. Someone else might snatch you.'

'I have three kids,' she said, trying hard to keep breathing. Her heart was doing really funny lurching things. 'No one else wants to snatch me.'

'More fool them,' he said and sat on the bed and pulled her into his arms. 'They don't know what they're missing. I have the most wonderful woman in the world in my arms right now. How fantastic is that? I can't believe my luck and I'm waiting not a minute longer. You need to say you'll marry me, my lovely Pippa. You must. Please?'

Her heart was singing, but somehow she found the strength to pull away. He released her with seeming reluctance, but he did let her go.

She pulled far enough back until she could see his face. 'Max, why?'

'I love you.' He smiled, that lovely, lurking smile that had her heart doing hand springs. 'As simple as that. As easy as that. All the conniving I've done—the figuring, the way I've tried to structure our lives—and in the end it comes down to this. I love you, Pippa, and I love you with all my heart. I want to be beside you for as long as we both shall live. Everything else has to come in after that. We'll organise our lives. We'll organise the Crown and the country. But we'll organise these things around the most important thing in my life. Which is being with you.'

She didn't answer. She couldn't. She'd surely forgotten how to breathe.

'Say you'll marry me,' he said, urgently. 'Pippa, I'm not asking you to step away from the children. I know you love them to bits, and, believe it or not, I do too. I thought last night how could I walk away from Marc? There's been so many things to think about. For the last few weeks it's been crazy. First it was how I could accept that I was truly a de Gautier. Then could I walk away from this country? After that how could I walk away from you? And now there's the kids, worming their way into my heart. I love them too, Pippa, I love this whole damned catastrophe. I want to marry the lot of you.'

'And take us to Paris?' It had to be said. She was torn between disbelief and a magic, wondrous hope.

'No, here's the thing,' he said ruefully. 'Because I can't do that either. I listened to those elderly players yesterday saying their kids were having to leave the country. I thought about fractured families. I thought about this wonderful little country that can be so much if it's well managed. And I thought about the buildings I've been proud constructing. Yes, I can be proud of my buildings but here… Pippa, here we can build a whole country.'

'But how…?'

'There's so much we can do,' he said, exultant. 'The people who talked to me initially in Paris—disaffected citizens who are aching to be allowed to set decent government in motion—are desperate to help, and they will. If I stay on as Crown Prince…'

'You'd take that on?'

'Yes,' he said firmly. 'It's not fair to ask that of Marc. It never was, but it's taken the love of a wonderful woman to make me see it.' He grinned. 'And also to see that it might not be so much a burden as a privilege. I've talked to Mama. She's agreed—with sadness but I'll make her see it need not be a grief. We'll set the DNA testing in place to prove things. But you know what? I've been thinking and thinking. I thought it'd be great if Marc stands to inherit. I talked to him about it last night and he agrees. So… We can formally adopt. The kids will be our kids, along with whoever else comes along. That way it's Marc who stands to inherit. How perfect is that?'

'But…' It was too much to take in. 'You love them that much?'

'I love them so much I can't do anything else,' he said, and he tugged her into his arms and held her tight. 'Pippa, last night I rang my mother in Paris. Like me, her life has been desolate since Thiérry died. We've put things on hold. But last night I talked to her about what we can do—what we all can do—if we have the courage to take this on.'

'You've really asked her to…'

'Yes,' he said, stroking her hair, kissing the top of her head. 'Yes, I did. I told her that once upon a time I remembered her talking of a vision she had of how this country could be. She married as a green girl, marrying the fairy tale. I told her we could live the real fairy tale. We could make this country great. And we could be a family.'

'Your mother…' She was finding it hard to get her mouth to form words.

'You'll love her,' he said, urgently, putting her away from him a little so he could make her see. 'She's a wonderful, wonderful woman and she'll love you to bits. You'll love her to bits. She's nervous now, but she's brave enough to want to try, and she's already falling for the children. She'll help us, Pippa. There's no way one person can be sovereign in this country. We need a family.' He hesitated. 'But there is one problem.'

'Only one?'

'She has a dog,' he said, rueful. 'A weird-looking mutt called Hannibal she saved from the street several years ago. She has him here.'

'She brought her dog?'

'I rang her last night and talked this all through with her,' Max confessed. 'Before I'd finished talking, she was organising plane tickets. She and Hannibal flew into Monaco at dawn and she hired a car to bring her here. She's ready to be part of this, and so is her disreputable mutt. But, Pippa, it's asking a lot of you. You'll have three kids, a husband, a mother-in-law, a castle full of devoted retainers and a maniac dog whose sole desire in life is to destroy every shoe he ever sets eyes on. Beatrice says as far as she knows there's never been a dog in this palace, and now it's looking like Dolores might have been the start of a dynasty.'

His grip on her hands grew urgent. 'I've thought it all through. All night… There's been so much to think of. We could donate the kids' farm to be the wildlife corridor you were so enthusiastic about. Maybe we could keep the house so we could visit every now and then—but not in midwinter. It'd almost be worth the plane fare to tell the Tanbarook supermarket ladies ourselves.'

He hesitated, waiting for her to smile. Waiting for her to say something. Nothing came.

'But is it too much, do you think?' He held her shoulders, desperately anxious. 'Do you think you can take it on?'

'I…'

'And your nursing,' he added, figuring he had to set all the facts before her before she refused or accepted. 'There's a hospital in the village. There's been no young nurses in the place for years and it's really run-down. I thought maybe you could take t on as your special project. There are more hospitals through he country. So much to do. And me… As soon as we've finished Blake's house we'll move on to rebuilding the village hall. I've had to move fast to stop demolition this morning and that's only he beginning. There's so much. We'll make this country the greatest of the Alp Quartet. Raoul thinks he's done well in Alp d'Azuri. He doesn't know the half of what great can be.'

'Hush,' Pippa said, half laughing, half crying. 'Max, do you know what you're saying?'

'I surely do.' He paused, his smile fading as their gazes locked. The plans fell away. There was only this moment. This man, and his woman.

'Pippa, will you take us on?' he whispered. 'I know you haven't been born into it. I know you can walk away. But we need you so much. Will you wave your wand, my wondrous fairy godmother? Will you marry me?'

She smiled at him, her eyes misting with unshed tears. Her Maxsim, Crown Prince of Alp d'Estella. Her own true love.

Would she marry him? How could she not?

And it was a first.

'I never heard it said that any fairy godmother got to marry Prince Charming herself,' she whispered, drawing him into her and holding him close. 'But there's always a first, my love. Move over, Cinderella. Yes, my lovely prince. My Max. My love. Yes, will.'